Emma Hannigan

The Heart
of Winter
x

HACHETTE
BOOKS
IRELAND

First published in Ireland in 2014
by Hachette Books Ireland

First published in paperback in Ireland in 2015
by Hachette Books Ireland

Cataloguing in Publication Data is available from the British Library

ISBN 978 1 444 797138

Typeset in Bembo Std by Palimpsest Book Production Limited,
Falkirk, Stirlingshire

Printed and bound in Great Britain by
Clays Ltd, St Ives plc

Hachette Books Ireland's policy is to use papers that are natural, renewable and
recyclable products and made from wood grown in well-managed forests and other
controlled sources. The logging and manufacturing processes are expected to
conform to the environmental regulations of the country of origin.

Hachette Books Ireland
8 Castlecourt Centre
Castleknock
Dublin 15

An Hachette UK Company
Carmelite House
50 Victoria Embankment
London EC4Y 0DZ

www.hachette.ie
www.hachette.co.uk

For Cian, Sacha and Kim with love.

Wicklow County Council

Attention: Mr Joey Craig
Huntersbrook House
Wicklow
Ireland

Dear Mr Craig

We are delighted to inform you of our decision to grant your commercial licence as requested. From this date forward Huntersbrook House has permission to operate as a commercial venue. Please note our terms.

* Licence to serve alcohol must be gained by applying to the address at the foot of this notice.
* The owners may host events on the grounds. Insurance for such events may now be applied for using this document.
* Huntersbrook House may host paying guests in an overnight capacity.

We will forward all relevant documents to enable full registration of your home as a business.

Kind regards

M. Brennan

Wicklow County Council

Huntersbrook House

PIPPA SHOT THROUGH THE MAIN GATE OF HER childhood home, Huntersbrook. Almost instantly she passed the gate lodge to her right. The two-bed bungalow with its painted wooden-framed windows and immaculate hanging baskets reminded her of the cottage from *Hansel and Gretel*, minus the cauldron witch and cruelty, of course. It blended in so well, she found it hard to remember it hadn't always been there. Grandma had built it a few years ago as her own oasis, away from the hustle and bustle of the main house. Sadly, she'd passed away before she could really make it her own. Still, Pippa mused, as it had transpired it was a good thing. Her parents Holly and Paddy had taken up residence there a couple of years ago and seemed to have found it quite easy to mould it into their permanent home.

It was still weird to Pippa that none of them actually lived in Huntersbrook House any longer. The stunning Georgian residence had been in the Craig family for generations. But the downturn in the economy had forced them to rethink things. Rather than letting it go, they'd come together as a family to save it.

As she zoomed up the drive she remembered her mother's finger-wagging the last time she'd come home. 'Do you absolutely *have* to drive that fast, Pippa? What difference will it make to your journey from the gate to the front door? Seconds? You need to slow down, my girl. Just look at the wonderful scenery that's on offer if you choose to glide down the driveway toward the house.'

Pippa grinned triumphantly as she glanced back at the dust cloud she'd created. She knew she was being a bit of a brat, but she'd always had a problem with doing as she was told. Her mother was right about one thing though, Huntersbrook and the surrounding land was pretty spectacular. After the muggy, traffic-jammed chaos of Dublin city, this really was like a slice of heaven on Earth. Not many houses boasted such an expanse of unspoilt land, bereft of freshly constructed housing estates or even purpose-built shopping centres. The rolling fields as far as the eye could see were a joy.

Grinding to a halt at the back of the main house, Pippa jumped out of her car and stood onto the side, leaning on the door. Craning her neck, she tried to squint across to the right and into next door. Her sister, Lainey, had married Matt from next door and was now living in the farmhouse with her baby son, Ely, and father-in-law, Jacob. Their houses were very much separate, but close enough for Lainey to feel as if she hadn't really left home. That was one of the many differences between the sisters. Pippa would get on a plane train or jet-ski at the drop of a hat if she thought it would lead to an adventure of any kind. While Lainey had always been a home-bird and was perfectly content living a stone's throw from Huntersbrook.

As she walked in the side door to the kitchen Pippa was greeting by a happy screech from Ely.

'Hello baby nephew!' she said scooping him into her arms. 'Hi Lainey,' she said rushing to kiss her sister on the cheek. 'I thought you might still be across the path in your lair.'

'Joey said to be here for ten,' she said. 'It's almost ten fifteen now. I've made scones and the coffee and tea are waiting for boiling water.'

'Organised to within an inch of your life as usual,' Pippa teased. 'Where are Mum and Dad? I didn't notice any sign of life at the gate lodge just now.'

'Might that have been because you careered by at a thousand miles an hour?' Lainey asked.

'Who, me? Drive too fast? Nah,' she said. 'Have you seen them this morning?'

'Last I spotted, Mum was wrestling with an apple tree she bought. Dad is pottering in a shed, I'm guessing. Do you know what Joey's up to?'

'Not a breeze,' Pippa said picking a tasty sugary bit from a scone.

'Hey, get away,' Lainey said slapping her hand. 'I'm putting them in a basket and we'll all sit and have them nicely once Joey arrives. I can't bear the way you pick like that.'

'I get it from Mum,' Pippa said shrugging her shoulders. She put a wriggling Ely down so he could continue playing with his wooden bricks on the kitchen floor.

'That's not a good thing,' Lainey said crossly. 'It's so rude to pick food like that. Besides, remember the saying Grandma used to recite? "Little pickers wear big knickers",' said Lainey smugly.

'Well my knickers haven't changed size since I was sixteen,' Pippa said slapping her own backside.

'Don't I know it,' Lainey sighed. She looked down at her own figure. Instead of losing the post-baby weight after Ely's birth last year, she'd kind of filled in around her saggy tummy. Even though her mother and Pippa shared that annoying picking habit, neither of them ever put on weight. She, on the other hand, seemed to put on half a stone by even being in the same room as a calorie.

'I wish I had your metabolism,' Lainey said wistfully. 'I try so hard. I'm good for a week and then I seem to lose the run of myself and eat my way back to square one.'

'Don't be too hard on yourself,' Pippa said. 'You grew a person inside you. That has to have a totally nasty effect on your body, right?'

Lainey stopped short and stared at her sister. With her dark sleek ponytail trailing down her slender back and her stick thin legs in her painted-on-tight jeggings, she could easily pass as a model.

'We can't all look like you,' Lainey snapped.

Pippa threw her head back and whistled before bursting out laughing. 'Touchy touchy! Jaysus, someone got out the wrong side of the bed this morning. How about I go into the pantry and pull a black sack over my head and sit in the corner rustling?'

In spite of herself, Lainey's scowl turned into a grin. 'Shut up, Pip,' she said swatting her arm playfully. 'I suppose I'm a bit over-sensitive. Mum didn't help by telling me yesterday that I look "good and solid".'

Sadie, who'd been their housekeeper for over forty years, came through to the kitchen from the hallway.

'Ah now Lainey,' she said gently. 'I couldn't help overhearing you just now. Your Mum didn't mean any harm with that remark. I was there. She was trying to say that you're toning up with all that walking you've been doing.'

Lainey sighed. It was typical that everyone would take Holly's side. Nobody seemed to recognise that she treated *her* differently from the others. She'd never dare make a remark like that about Pippa. Even if she did, Pippa would probably drop-kick her, Lainey mused. Maybe that was what she needed. To be more forceful with her mother. Maybe then she'd treat her with a little more respect and little less disregard.

'Your mother loves the bones of you three,' Sadie continued. 'Even though you girls and Joey are grown-ups now, she still sees you as her babies.'

'Huh,' Lainey said unable to let the comment slide. 'When I was a baby she handed me over to Grandma. She was too delicate to cope with me and yet now she expects me to be unfathomably capable in everything I do.'

'Your mother would walk over hot coals for each one of you,' Sadie said firmly. 'I remember the time you had chicken pox, Lainey. You weren't more than four or five. You had the worst dose I've ever seen. You scratched and cried and your mother stayed awake for four nights on the trot bathing you in bread soda baths.'

Lainey busied herself with setting the table. Not for the first time, she felt Sadie had a rose-tinted image of what had gone on during her childhood. Lainey and Holly had been like sandpaper rubbing off one another from as far back as she could remember. No matter what Sadie or anyone else recalled, Lainey knew the truth. Holly had been there physically while Lainey was small, but mentally she'd been in a dark and clouded place where nobody, least of all her daughter, could reach her.

The sound of a car pulling up on the gravel outside made Lainey sigh with relief. She was uncomfortable with this conversation and didn't want to get into anything negative with darling Sadie.

'Here's Joey,' Pippa confirmed. 'This better be good. I don't appreciate being hauled out of bed at the crack of dawn at the weekend.'

'It's half ten, Pippa!' Sadie said with a giggle. 'Although knowing you it was dawn before that pretty little head of yours hit the pillow.'

Joey arrived in looking very smug.

'What's happening?' Pippa asked, attempting to grab the A4 envelope he was carrying.

'Ah-ah, all in good time,' he said slapping her hand away. 'Mum and Dad are on the way. They're having a healthy discussion about an apple tree,' he said. 'They're getting battier by the minute, you know?'

'We know,' Pippa said. 'They were never exactly "normal" but the passing of time is certainly taking them to a whole new level of insanity,' she grinned.

'I'm getting out of here before I swat one of you with a tea towel,' Sadie said. 'Anyone would think this place is flanked by dotty geriatrics. I'd challenge any of you to a game of Scrabble and beat you. My mind is as sharp as a razor and your parents are babies in comparison to me. So be careful who you're labelling as past it.'

Sadie disappeared, tutting and muttering about the youth of today.

Lainey laughed. 'That'll tell you, Pippa. Jeez, I have to hand it to Sadie, there are no flies on her!'

'Quick one before the folks arrive,' Joey interjected, glancing back to make sure there was no sign of them. 'I need a bit of girly advice here.'

'Ooh excellent,' Pippa said leaning in.

'Turns out I'm ninety-nine per cent sure I'm about to be promoted at work.'

'Hey that's amazing, Joey,' Lainey said rubbing his arm. 'Good for you.'

'Yeah, thanks. I'm stoked. But it's kind of a bit awkward. It's going to mean a fair bit of social stuff. Skye isn't really wired for sound when it comes to fancy-schmancy outings. Would you two be a little bit mindful of her over the next while?'

'In what way?' Lainey asked.

'Well, help her out with stuff to wear and all that kind of malarkey.'

'I'll do that,' Pippa said instantly. 'Oh I'd love to give her a makeover. I tried a few times when we shared the flat, but she never seemed that interested.'

'Hold up a second,' Lainey said looking concerned. 'Skye is beautiful just the way she is. She's admittedly quite bohemian in style, but that's part of who she is. I'm not sure she'd be too happy with either of us barging in and telling her what to look like.'

'No and I don't expect you to do that,' Joey said attempting to back track. 'It's just that our social calendar is going to fill up quite a bit and these corporate do's are a different kettle of fish from what she might be used to. Just keep an eye, that's all I ask.'

'Sure,' Pippa said looking as if it was a perfectly reasonable request. Lainey wasn't so sure. She was probably overthinking things as usual, but she couldn't help feeling slightly protective of Skye.

'Joey,' she ventured. 'Mum and Dad are about to walk in, but being the elder lemon here, don't forget the reason you feel in love with Skye to start with. You love her because she's different. Am I right?'

'Yeah. Sure,' he said. 'Forget I said anything. It was literally just a thought and I only suggested it so she wouldn't feel ill at ease. Maybe I'm on the wrong page. I'm only a man after all,' he said bumping her shoulder and smiling.

Holly and Paddy arrived in amidst hugs and kisses. By the time they were all seated at the table with a cuppa and a fresh warm scone, they were all begging Joey to put them out of their misery and tell them why he had called them all to a family meeting.

'It's really good news,' he announced. 'We've been granted a commercial licence! We're good to go as far as the authorities are concerned. Huntersbrook House, the venue, can officially open!'

Joey raised his coffee cup high in the air. 'A toast to Huntersbrook House and her bright future.'

'To Huntersbrook,' they all chimed, grinning widely at each other.

Lainey smiled as she clinked cups with each of her family members. None of the gripes and cribs really mattered once they could all pull together when necessary. She glanced over at Pippa and Holly. Her mother had her arm around her sister and was kissing the side of her head affectionately as she smiled in delight. Lainey adored Pippa, but she couldn't help noticing that her mother had never been that affectionate with her. As if to bridge that painful gap, she scooped Ely from his high chair and spun him around in the air, making him giggle loudly.

'Wee,' she said. 'Huntersbrook is going to be a destination to be reckoned with, baby boy!'

They all clapped as Ely joined in, bashing his chubby hands together, lapping up the good humour.

Pippa

PIPPA WAS RELIEVED TO GET OUT OF HER OFFICE
for a bit. Her head was wrecked from all the pressure at the
moment. She'd spent the weekend in Wicklow going through list
after list of jobs that needed to be done at Huntersbrook. She'd
come to work this morning for more of the same.

A text from Joey's girlfriend, Skye, asking her to meet for a
quick coffee was a Godsend.

'Hey,' Skye said as she came up behind her in the café. 'How
are things?'

'Skye!' Pippa spun around to kiss her. 'You're looking summery!'
She looked Skye up and down and took in her powder blue
cheese-cloth maxi dress. While she wouldn't be caught dead in
flat Jesus-style sandals, Pippa felt Skye could carry them off. 'You're
the only adult I know who looks good with a daisy chain in her
hair,' Pippa said. 'Tea?'

'Please,' Skye said. 'Just a herbal one, please.'

'And some sort of grease stroke fat to eat?'

'Why not! I'll have a Danish pastry. I'm famished.'

'I'll get it, you grab a table before they're all gone,' Pippa said.
She ordered a large black coffee and the other things for Skye.

'So how are tricks?' she asked as she placed the tray on the
sticky table. 'Ugh! I can't bear sitting in other people's juice.'

Skye laughed and tucked into her Danish.

'I went onto your website to do a bit of updating for you,'

Skye said through a mouthful. 'You haven't added any new stock since I last worked on it. What's the story with it?'

'Ugh, I've so much going on at the moment. The website is so far down the list of priorities right now, if I'm honest. I'm struggling with work and this darn Huntersbrook stuff, without the added annoyance of the website.'

'Oh,' Skye's voice dropped. 'I thought you were keen on building your site and making your own business out of it. You were doing so well, Pippa. It seems a bit of a shame.'

'Yeah, whatever,' she waved her hand. 'I'll get to it at some point. Besides I'm loving the young, free and single girl about town thing. Summer in Dublin is always amazing. So much happening and too little time to fit it all in, you know?'

'Are you feeling better about going out now?'

'Totally, why?'

'Well, you know . . . after being attacked. I know it shook you to the core.'

'Oh that,' Pippa sipped her coffee. 'Nah, it was a freaky random thing. I've put it well behind me.' Pippa took another drink of her coffee, even though it was like ingesting molten lava. She didn't want to think or talk about the attack. She'd had a close shave and it still woke her at night.

'Well if you're sure you're OK . . .' Skye looked unconvinced.

Pippa waited a few minutes before broaching the subject Joey had asked her about.

'So Joey was telling me there are a few work type events on the horizon.'

'Oh right.' Skye didn't seem bothered either way.

'Yeah,' Pippa pushed. 'I know some of those can be real toffee-nosed things. Women dripping in diamonds with the latest labels on show, yadda, yadda.'

'Ha!' Skye said. 'Well none of that crap concerns me. You know me well enough at this stage, Pippa. I've never been what one would call a slave to fashion. Those ladies who lunch are hardly on my radar. I never was and never will be interested in that kind of stuff.'

'Yeah totally. But it might be . . . Uh how do I put it . . . *expected* of you . . .'

'What do you mean?' Skye said with a look of total puzzlement.

'It's just that I sell a lot of clobber to bosses' wives from the big corporations. They're a forceful bunch at times. I'd hate you to feel like a fish out of water, that's all. If you want to borrow some bits, I have quite a wardrobe at this point. Or you could totally get stuff via my personal shopping website,' Pippa said nonchalantly.

'Are you serious?' Skye laughed easily. 'Thanks Pip, but for a start your stuff wouldn't go over my ankles, let alone any other body part. You're about a quarter of my size. And secondly, I have loads of dresses for those arsy events. Joey knows I have my own style and that I don't kow-tow to peer-group nonsense. Especially those women who have nothing else to do but stare at their reflections morning, noon and night. I can just hear them now, spouting some crap that behind every good man is a good woman!'

'Totally! You're so right,' Pippa said nodding fervently. 'I'd better get back to work. No doubt Brianna has a nest of vacant mirror-gazers looking for me to sell them over-priced gear!'

Skye giggled and linked her arm as they walked out. When a text message came through on both of their phones almost simultaneously, Pippa guessed it was from one of the Craigs.

They both read it and sure enough it was Paddy, issuing an invitation for the coming weekend.

'Yay!' Skye said, 'the thought of a lovely weekend at

Huntersbrook with your lot will get me through the week. Nothing like a bit of Craig family time!'

They kissed goodbye and Pippa stood for a moment and watched Skye meandering down Grafton Street before heading back to work herself. She certainly wasn't of the same mind as Skye. In truth, Pippa was sick to the back teeth of 'Project Huntersbrook'. When her family had come up with the idea of turning the place into an events venue for weddings and parties, she'd been on board instantly. She'd envisaged fabulously glam events with cool rich people walking the grounds in wax jackets during the afternoon, before throwing wild and lavish all-night parties. The reality was endless meetings and lists of mind-numbingly boring chores. Still, they had the green light from the council now, so maybe the fun would start soon.

As she walked, she tapped out a text to Paddy: 'sounds like a blast Dad, hope I can get there, but not sure yet.'

She felt mildly guilty for lying, but not concerned enough to fess up and turn up.

Skye had made her feel guilty when she mentioned the website just now. Pippa knew she'd let that slide lately. When she first came up with the idea of an online shopping site and Skye had set it up, she'd been stoked about it. But now, as she juggled the store job and the website, Pippa's patience had all but run out. It was too much work for too little money. None of the labels she pushed on her site were forthcoming with freebies either. The profits were meagre and she knew unless she injected more time and energy into the whole thing, it was never going to set the world on fire. But was that where she wanted her time and energy to go?

She had reached the department store where she worked. Bill, the doorman, winked at her and held open the door with a great show of chivalry that made Pippa giggle.

'Bill, when are you going to leave that damn wife of yours and run away with me?' she teased.

He grinned widely. 'Still a bold strap, I see,' he said, wagging his finger at her.

Bill was the about the only thing she still liked about this place. Before she began working here eighteen months ago, Pippa had adored the place. She would become giddy as she walked through the cosmetic halls, up onto the designer clothing floors and as for the shoes . . . After her first week as a *bona fide* employee she had gushed to Lainey, 'I feel like Aladdin walking into the cave of jewels every time I go to work.'

Somehow that had all changed, and the last six months had really dragged. The buzz of the store was well and truly quashed. The fragrance hall gave her a sickly headache and the rails of clothes made her feel both envious and claustrophobic. The staff discount was negligible. She'd thought she'd have all the latest designer gear at high-street prices. But that was a farce. The samples at the make-up counters had all been stopped, too. The management treated the staff like slaves. It was all about clocking in and out, customer satisfaction and reaching targets. There was very little room for fun and zero scope for anything free.

Of course, Lainey and Joey had no sympathy for her whatsoever. Joey loved to tell her that life wasn't a party, it was all about hard work. What kind of a life philosophy was that? She was twenty-five, for crying out loud! She was single, with no dependants. Why shouldn't she believe the whole world was waiting to entertain her? What was the problem with that? The way Pippa saw it, if she moseyed around being mediocre, exciting things weren't going to land in her lap. But if she opened her eyes and broadened her horizons, who knew what could happen?

She often wondered if she'd been born into the wrong family.

Maybe her parents were given the wrong baby at the hospital? Lainey and Joey were so damned sensible and strait-laced. Lainey was all loved up with her husband, Matt, and their baby, Ely, which was super cool. They were happy. She was glad for them. Joey and Skye were vomit-inducingly in love. It was all fabulous and Pippa was honestly stoked for them, but she couldn't bear the thought of existing like them. And suddenly it wasn't just her family opting for a boring life – it felt like everyone was abandoning the ship of good fun. All her friends had become so bloody dreary all of a sudden. Her oldest mate, Lucy, used to be great fun, but since she'd spent every cent she owned on getting onto the property ladder, she was such a drag. Every suggestion was met with, 'Sorry Pip, I can't afford to do that any more. I'm a mortgage-holder now.'

Sod that, thought Pippa crossly. Who gave a toss if she rented or owned her apartment? What did it matter? There were years ahead for all that sensible stuff, whereas being young and free wouldn't last forever. What was it that Oscar Wilde said about youth being wasted on the young? She wasn't about to do that. She'd looked fear in they eye the night she was attacked, and she was damned if she was going to live a little, narrow life – she was determined, more than ever, to grab every opportunity and live, live, live.

❄

The week dragged. It felt like a year since she'd seen Skye and a decade since she'd had a decent night out. With all the meetings at Huntersbrook last weekend Pippa felt enslaved in a life that was far too grown up and sensible for her longing-to-party mind. She put the finishing touches to the artwork for the new French shoe label her boss had taken on, then stretched out her back. She'd been bent over her desk without moving for the past couple of hours, and her shoulders felt locked into position. She was in charge of all in-store signage, along with most of the artwork for their printed advertising campaigns. It was a dream job, but slowly it was becoming a bit of a nightmare – thanks in no small part to a play-by-the-rules boss who was driving her crazy lately.

It was now three o'clock on Friday afternoon. Pippa could see the lucky shoppers strolling happily by outside, as they enjoyed the low-lying lemony light of an October afternoon. Pippa loved autumn, it was such a pretty season with the changing light and the colours of the leaves. As she stared out, she decided there and then that it was far too nice to be stuck in work for a second longer. She logged off her computer, grabbed the finished artwork and strode into her boss's office.

'I'm feeling totally nauseous, Brianna,' she said. 'I'm going to shoot off home, if that's OK with you? Time of the month and all that,' Pippa said pulling a face.

Brianna looked at her watch.

'I see,' she said frostily. 'Don't make a habit of this, Pippa. Might I remind you that you've missed two Mondays this month already. If I didn't know you better, I'd swear you're putting all your energy into partying rather than working of late.'

'Ah seriously, Brianna,' Pippa said making her best stricken-face. 'I would never pull a sicky. I love my job. I'm living the dream! Why on earth would I jeopardise it?'

Brianna's face softened. 'Sorry, Pippa. I'm jumping to conclusions. I apologise. You go and take it easy. See you bright and breezy Monday morning. I'll need you refreshed and raring to go for the Paris trip next week. Missy from evening wear is coming too, as it happens.'

'Really?' Pippa said, raising an eyebrow. Everyone in the store knew that Melissa Hassett, AKA Missy, was only working there because her father owned most of the shares in the place. Dubbed by the other staff as Missy *Hilton*, this girl was someone Pippa had been meaning to get to know for the past month.

'She seems to be doing very well in evening wear by all accounts,' Pippa said.

'Yes,' said Brianna dryly. 'If you count helping yourself to one of each style as lucrative.'

'Can she, like . . . take what she wants?' Pippa asked in astonishment.

'God, no!' Brianna scoffed. 'She pays, but it's all a bit of a joke in reality.'

'Why?'

'Well her credit card is "connected to Daddy's",' Brianna said in a sneering voice. 'So she's in the happy position of playing a game of one for me, one for the rail. If only we all had a doting father with a bottomless pit of cash, then we'd . . . Eh . . . Right, so that's that.'

Pippa was furious when Brianna seemed to realise she was speaking out of turn and forced a smile. 'Anything else, Pippa?'

'Just this – I finished the Beau Chausseur artwork. Here.'

Brianna took it and squinted closely at it. 'Fantastic work, Pippa,' she said smiling warmly. 'I love it. It's just right.'

Pippa smiled. Work might be a drag right now, but it still felt good to get the recognition she deserved.

'OK, so feel better and I'll see you on Monday.'

'Sorry?' Pippa asked, forgetting she was supposed to be feeling ill. 'Oh right, yeah. Thanks. I think I'll just go home to the country and be with my folks and go for some lovely walks. Fresh air and some quiet family time. A hot water bottle and our golden retriever at my feet and I'll be right as rain.'

'OK Pippa, see you.' Brianna's eyes had already reverted to her work as Pippa pulled the door shut and waltzed onto the escalator.

Sighing happily, she congratulated herself on the added touch of the retriever just now. Brianna would never know that Jess was a Jack Russell and Millie a mongrel. As far as Pippa was aware, Brianna thought she came from a Downton Abbey-type place. Pippa liked to think she presented herself as being arty yet rather refined.

'Hiya!'

Pippa looked around to find Suzie, one of the nail technicians, waving a perfectly shellacked hand from the step above her.

'Hi Suzie,' she said. 'How's it going?'

'Good. I'm finished for the weekend, TG. Zach and Luke and some of the girls from home furnishings are going to the beer garden, you coming?'

'Won't it be freezing?' she asked with a giggle.

'Ah they have outdoor heaters. But you know me, even the sight of the sun is enough to bring on a session. At least it's not snowing!'

'Now that sounds like a plan,' she said. 'I need to be careful though, I've just escaped early by telling Briann-ta-saurus I've got period pains.'

'Nice one,' Suzie smiled. 'See you there in five?'

'Cool,' said Pippa.

By the time she grabbed her jacket from her locker in the staffroom and touched up her make-up, Pippa could almost taste the gin and tonic she was going to order.

Careful to avoid walking below Brianna's office in the wrong direction and possibly being scuppered, Pippa went the long way to the beer garden. Ten minutes later, she was pouring the tonic into her gin as she positioned herself directly under an outdoor heater.

'That heat is divine,' she said pulling her shades down off the top of her head. 'Amazing how a few shards of sunlight mixed with a gas heater and a gin and tonic can make me feel like I'm in a tropical country!'

'Beats shuffling around listening to the piped muzak in the men's department,' said Zach. He managed to look positively Italian, even though he was from Glasnevin. 'If one more uppity git looked down his nose at me today, I swear I would've swung my fist at him.'

'Like hell you would,' Pippa scoffed. 'And risk bruising one of your precious paws? I can just imagine you having a fight, it'd be a cross between the doggy paddle and Riverdance!'

Zach pretended to be offended as he tossed his head to the side.

'I'll have you know I was vicious in school,' he said dramatically. 'I had to be, growing up gay in an inner city all boys' school. I'd swear there are more pleasant borstals than the place I went.'

'Really?' Pippa asked, giggling. 'Sorry, I shouldn't laugh, but I can't imagine you as a playground hooligan.'

'I wasn't quite as refined as I am now,' he said with a sniff. 'I wasn't able to express my true self. I had to play the hard man and do what the other lads were doing. They'd have savaged me otherwise.'

As the beer garden gradually filled up with staff members, Pippa began to relax.

'God I'm so glad I'm not down for late night opening this evening,' she sighed. 'On a Friday, it'd be rude to stay in work.'

She had so much fun with her colleagues, but she was so sick of the actual *working*. The hours were so limiting too. She'd never intended having a boring nine to five job. As far as she was concerned, that was for losers.

In her dreams, Pippa was rich and famous with a lavish lifestyle that involved shopping, partying and sleeping, in that order. She'd even settle for being a kept woman if the right guy came along.

But so far it hadn't happened that way. She'd honestly thought she was on to a good thing with her website. In the beginning she'd made really good money from it. But that had all evened off now and she'd kind of lost interest in it.

'I need a new challenge,' she said now to Zach. The gin was relaxing her and her thoughts were starting to bubble up of their own accord.

'But you have the website,' Zach said. 'That must be great fun to do.'

'Nah, I'm bored of it now. I'm thinking of selling it, in fact. It's making great waves, but I'm worked to the bone with Brianna. It's all too much for me. I need more spare time. Before I know it, I'll be old and cruddy with nothing but a wardrobe of ball-busting suits and a stray cat to show for myself.'

'How much are you selling it for?' Zach asked immediately. 'I'd love to own something like that. I'd expand it to include men's wear too. I've had enough of dealing with the public face-to-face. I've been thinking of moving on for a while now. I think your site could be just the thing.'

Pippa sat up a little straighter. She'd only said she wanted to sell as a throw-away comment. She was actually thinking of shutting it down fullstop.

'I'd have to get an evaluation done and work out the potential profits going forward,' she said feeling like she was on Dragon's Den all of a sudden.

'How long do you reckon it would take to get that information?' Zach asked eagerly.

'Eh . . . I could ask my brother Joey to do some number-crunching for me. Or my brother-in-law Matt is an accountant, too . . . Tell you what, Zach, leave it with me and I'll try and get you a ballpark figure by Monday, yeah?'

'Deadly,' said Zach. 'I have a few quid stashed away and I'd love to have my own business. I was thinking of my own boutique, but I don't have the funds for anything that big and as I said, I'm just about done with Jo Public.'

'The website is amazing actually because I don't buy any stock, I just put stuff together from regular stores. I have some pretty decent deals with some labels now. Especially the ones I sell a lot of. The discounts mean I make a healthy profit on some lines.'

'Wow, I feel shivers down my spine,' said Zach dramatically. 'I'd love it.'

Pippa thoroughly enjoyed the rest of the evening. As soon as the sun went down and the darkness engulfed them, she began to feel chilly. She would have gone home but as it turned out, Zach was so eager to stay on the right side of her that he plied her with drinks before dragging her to a club, where he introduced her to his friends.

'This is Pippa, AKA the queen of fashion.'

Pippa adored being adored. Whether the men were gay or straight, after enough gin, she wasn't choosy. Attention made her purr and once she was the centre of everything, she was happy.

As Zach appeared with a tray of Martinis complete with sparklers, Pippa snatched her phone.

'Photo op!' she shouted, holding up her mobile. 'Scootch in beside me, Zach! Selfie time!'

Pippa smiled drunkenly as she posted the picture on Facebook with the caption: *Friday night tipples – shaken and stirred!!!*

Lainey

LAINEY KNEW SHE WOULD NEVER TAKE THIS VIEW for granted. Even though she'd grown up right next-door at Huntersbrook House, a ten-year stint of city living had made her realise just how special her childhood surroundings really were. From her bedroom window in the old farmhouse, she could see the starboard side of Huntersbrook in all its glory as the low early morning sunshine warmed the glittering granite walls. Her childhood bedroom was literally a stone's throw (if she were an Olympic discus specialist) from her marital one.

'Ready to go?' Matt asked as he walked into their bedroom with baby Ely in his arms.

'Nearly,' she said, 'I need to grab Ely's change bag.'

'I'm sure everything he needs is already next-door. We won't be too long and besides, Sadie can pop over here if she's stuck for anything.'

'I know, but I'd prefer to make babysitting as easy as possible for her. She's not young and a quick trip across the field is easy for us, but Sadie's arthritis has been acting up lately. I know we think of her as invincible, Matt, but she is in her eighties.'

Matt grinned as he jiggled baby Ely, tickling him. 'I think you're underestimating Sadie. You know she'd wring your neck if she heard you insinuating she's past it.'

'I am not,' Lainey protested as they shut the door of the farmhouse and headed across the well-worn path to Huntersbrook. 'I wouldn't dare!'

'I'm sure Holly would be delighted to look after him if we're stuck again,' Matt ventured.

'Mum has enough on without us dumping Ely on her,' Lainey said quickly. 'Besides, we're only going for a short while. Getting supplies for the fencing won't take long. No point in asking Mum to trek all the way down the drive when Sadie will be there already. She's been off blackberry picking and is making her world famous jam for the larder.'

Ely waved his arms in delight as they approached the side door of Huntersbrook, which led to the main kitchen.

'Can you believe he's fourteen months old already?' Lainey said.

'Time flies when you're having fun eh?' Matt grinned.

'I know we've been doing plenty of practising,' Lainey said with a smile, 'but I have a good feeling that we're going to get pregnant this month.'

'There's no hurry, love,' Matt said. 'Ely's only a baby still.'

'True, but I want at least three, if not four babies. I don't want to be an older mother. I'm thirty-two, so the clock is ticking.'

'Better have a set of twins by lunchtime in that case,' he said dryly. She swatted his arm and pushed the door open to greet Sadie.

Ely threw his arms out to Sadie, and she motioned for them to go quickly. Lainey and Matt seized the opportunity to bundle straight back out the door.

'It's getting really exciting now,' Matt said as they walked quickly to the car. 'We've so much to look forward to and it's going to breathe new life into this place.'

Lainey smiled. She was just as excited as Matt. Huntersbrook had teetered on the edge for a while. Three years ago things had come to a head and her parents had sat them all down and broken the news that they couldn't afford to run it any longer, now that Paddy was retired and they were living on their pensions. For a while it looked like it would have to be sold, but then they had held a sumptuous wedding ceremony there for Lainey and Matt just two years ago. The day had prompted so many compliments from the guests that they'd come to the conclusion the house should be used for lots more weddings parties and functions. The idea of Huntersbrook, the venue, was born and they'd been throwing money and energy at it ever since.

It was exciting, but Lainey couldn't help gazing at the flip side, too.

'What if we pour all our combined savings into this project, and it all flops?' she suddenly said to Matt.

'That's the chance we've got to take,' he said easily as he turned the car and headed down the laneway to the main road. 'There are no guarantees in business, love, but I'd be astonished if it doesn't take off. Besides, having Joey and me number-crunching means there isn't a euro being wasted.'

'True,' she grinned. 'Most businesses use one accountant, we have two perfectionists at the helm.'

As Matt drove towards Wicklow town, Lainey's mind wandered to her mother. They'd had yet another spat the day before. Lainey had gone to pains to match up the paint colours and accessories for each of the bedrooms. Holly had shown little or no interest, until there was something she didn't approve of.

'Why would you put three pictures the same on a wall?'

'It's sold that way,' Lainey said. 'It's supposed to be like that.'

'I think it's ridiculous. Why would a person want to look at the same badly painted flower three times in a row?'

'It's a simple image that picks up the colours in the curtains and bedspread without being too in-your-face,' Lainey reasoned, curling her fingers into the palm of her hand to keep her cool.

'No, sorry, I don't get it,' Holly said, shaking her head. 'I'd prefer one decent picture to three dreadful ones. I hate that mass-produced tat as well. Get Ely to draw something with brightly coloured crayons and frame that. At least it'd be original.'

Lainey felt her composure slipping. 'Mum, the only thing Ely does with crayons is eat them. The whole point of my efforts here is to make over the house to appeal to a wide market. It has to be fresh and coordinated, and you're being really rude about it.'

'Do whatever you think is right,' Holly conceded. 'I was only voicing my opinion, Lainey. Please don't go off in a huff.'

'I'm not in a huff,' she snarled through her teeth.

'That's a matter of opinion . . .'

Lainey was going to retort, but she stopped herself. What was the point? She and Holly had been here so many times: Lainey trying to do something right; Holly telling her it was all wrong. With Joey and Pippa, their mother was encouraging and warm. Lainey seemed to get all her negative traits directed at her. She was the eldest, and it had always been like this. She'd be given out to, ridiculed, told she was doing it all wrong, then she'd have to stand by and watch as her brother and sister were coddled and fussed over. Her mother just treated her differently, that was all there was to it. And now she felt tired fighting to be treated the same as the others. Her mother made her feel too weary for words.

As Matt pulled up in Wicklow town, Lainey forced all cross thoughts from her mind. She wasn't going to allow her mother to spoil this new venture. From here on in, she resolved to make a concerted effort to avoid conflict with Holly. Besides, she had too much good stuff going on to bother with negativity.

As they walked toward the DIY store Lainey linked arms with Matt.

'Ooh they have a fabulous double buggy in the window of the baby shop,' she said. 'Let's have a quick look. I want to price it.' She steered him through the shop's door.

'Why?' Matt looked alarmed. 'Is there something you need to tell me?'

'Not yet,' she smirked. 'But soon I hope.' She spotted the buggy and dragged him over to it.

'It's eight hundred euros,' Matt said in shock. 'Does it come with a motor and a full-time nanny?'

'That's what decent double buggies cost,' Lainey said knowingly. 'There's no point in buying a cheap one, either. It'd only break and then we'd be shelling out twice.'

'I'd rather not shell out at all. Let's just keep practising and not have another child until Ely can walk. What do you say?'

Lainey giggled and followed him out of the shop. She knew Matt didn't share her overwhelming desire to have another baby. But he idolised little Ely and she knew he'd be the same way with the next one . . . Or two . . . Or three . . .

Joey

ON SATURDAY MORNING, AT THE UNGODLY HOUR
of five am, Joey stooped to kiss Skye, but she was dead to the
world. They were meant to travel down together today, but he'd
see her later at Huntersbrook. First, he had to sort everything
with his boss, Clive, who needed a brainstorm with him regarding
a potentially lucrative new client, then he'd be free to join his
family. He was eager to help his father and Matt. There was a
host of jobs they could do themselves and make necessary savings.
Once the house was running as a venue and they had some kind
of income, he'd relax. So far the house was absorbing money like
a sponge, with nothing to show in return.

Grinning, he cleared a woolly strand of curls from Skye's face
and gazed at her for a moment. Desire raced through him as he
touched her. She was all woman and best of all, she was happy
in her own skin. After almost two miserable years with domi-
neering Sophia, he was finding his time with Skye blissful. He
was finished with women who were obsessed with how they
looked. Trophy girlfriends were a thing of the past for Joey. Sure,
they looked good at business events, draped across your arm, but
he couldn't get enough of Skye's realness and kindness and her
unselfconscious way of moving and dancing and being, real. He'd
made the right decision, leaving Sophia and following his heart
into Skye's arms. Reluctantly, he grabbed his keys and headed for
the office.

Clive was already elbow-deep in paperwork when Joey arrived almost an hour before the agreed time.

'Did you actually go home last night?' he joked to Clive.

'Yeah, just about,' he said. 'Although I'd probably have been wiser to stay here. Janet is like a woman possessed. She's taken on the role of coordinator for the black-tie ball at the end of the month and she's living and breathing it at the moment.'

'I thought you had a PR firm handling the weekend?'

'Yeah, we did. But Janet blew a gasket and said all their ideas were passé and boring. I stupidly told her if she didn't like what they were doing, she could do it herself . . .'

'. . . and she took the baton and ran with it?'

'Precisely,' Clive said rubbing his face vigorously. 'She's using it as a way of saying "told you so". I'm fine with that, but Christ, she's a perfectionist. Every detail is being micro-managed. Did you know there are fifteen shades of pink napkin? And we're not having pink after all, just for the record.'

Joey laughed. 'I thought my mother was bad. She's got this obsession with Christmas and believe me, once Hallowe'en is over, it's all hands on deck in our house, whether you like it or not.'

The men settled down to work. The others arrived for the session and they made great headway over the next three hours. Clive motioned to Joey to stay behind once the others began to make a move for the door.

'It won't take long,' he said.

Joey glanced at his watch. It was lunchtime already. He really needed to get to Huntersbrook. He didn't want the others thinking he wasn't pulling his weight. It was enough to have one silent partner in Pippa. But then, nobody expected much else from her.

Once the office had emptied, Clive asked Joey to sit next to him.

'You've had a fantastic financial year, Joey,' Clive began. 'I've had several long sessions with the other partners and we all agree that it's time we drafted in some young blood.'

Joey's heart was racing. This was what he'd been praying for. There'd been whispers around the office that he was in line for a promotion but as far as he was concerned nothing was solid until he signed on the dotted line.

'So, we would like you to consider becoming an official partner.' Clive held his hand up to prevent Joey answering immediately. 'I do have to warn you, though. It's going to involve even longer hours than you currently serve. It'll mean many more meetings with other employees and quite a bit of evening and weekend time.'

'Yes, I understand,' Joey said evenly. 'I really appreciate the firm's belief in me. I'll give it my careful consideration and let you know.'

'Excellent!' Clive pumped his hand. 'I know you've put in for next week off,' Clive said, 'but I think I'm going to have to ask you to come in on Tuesday. Is that a problem?'

'No, of course not. I'll be stationed in Wicklow, so I can run up.'

'I could do the negotiation without you, but I'd prefer if you're in on any of the large projects going forward.'

'I appreciate that,' Joey said. 'I'd better hit the road now, though. We're flying along with the project I mentioned to you. You know my family estate in Wicklow . . . we've just been given the green light to use the old pile commercially.'

'Ah, super! We'll have to keep it in mind for some events in the future,' Clive said. 'Although, how the hell have you held on to it through the recession and all that? I mean, it's a big place, isn't it? Has to be a money-pit.'

Joey smiled, 'It is that. But we've poured everything into saving it. A while ago we'd thought we'd have to sell, but it's been in my mother's family for three generations, and we couldn't let that happen on our watch.'

'Are there other families involved or is it just your immediate family?' Clive asked, curious.

'My grandma actually ran the place after she was widowed at a young age. She was born there as an only child and kept it all going when her folks died. I guess there's a lot of pride attached to the fact that those women held on to it in spite of such difficult circumstances. So each generation wants to keep it afloat.'

'Of course. It's a heart-warming story, Joey. I like that sense of tradition mixed with tragedy. It's healthy that there's no awful feud going on in the background. That's the kind of thing that sets the rot. Good for you keeping it going. Let me know if we can help. Would it suit for one of our events, do you think? Would it pass the Janet test?'

'Definitely,' Joey said, nodding his head. 'The house was built in 1772 in the Georgian style and it retains all of its original features. It's really beautiful and classical and it sits on fifty acres, so there are views all round. It's really special.'

'Well then, maybe we could pencil it in as the venue for one of our bigger parties early next year. The Spring ball is always an awkward one to host as the weather can be dodgy. What's the capacity?'

'Well, we're looking at seating for up to two hundred. I'm negotiating a price on a second-hand luxury marquee at the moment. I'll keep you posted. We'd certainly appreciate the business.'

❄

As he drove out of Dublin and onto the N11 motorway, Joey was elated. He'd been hoping for a long time that the offer of a partnership would come and now here it was.

He was happy in love, work and family life. Things couldn't be better!

When he pulled up outside Huntersbrook an hour later, the view of the cherry red door against the two majestic pillars of the family home made him smile. So many memories and good times, and now they'd get the chance to add a whole lot more. He was so pleased he and Skye were getting to stay here for the whole week. He knew she'd fall in love with the place, too.

Skye and his mother were tending to some new boxus hedges they'd placed in pots on either side of the door. Like two peas in a pod, his girlfriend and mother were dressed in baggy tracksuit bottoms, mud-smeared quilted jackets and Hunter wellies. His mother had the added edginess of a red scarf tied around her head.

'Hey you!' Skye said skipping over to greet him.

'Hello, love,' Holly said, pulling off her gardening gloves and joining Skye. 'What do you think of our display?'

'Looking good, ladies!' Joey said. 'Love the outfits, too.'

Skye grinned and kissed him.

'You've got earth in your curls!' he laughed.

'That's what happens when you're a country gal. I've been counting down the days to this holiday,' she said happily. 'A whole week off work to spend at Huntersbrook. It looks like the weather is going to hold up, too. There's no rain forecast and if it stays as calm as it is today, we'll be flying with the work.'

'And you're the residing owners for the first time,' Holly said. 'With Dad and I fully moved into the gate lodge, you'll be in charge up here.'

'It's going to be a bit strange,' Skye mused, 'sort of like living in a hotel!'

'Speaking of hotel, come and see the new revamped entrance hallway,' Holly said. 'Lainey hired a steamer and it has brought the old floor tiles back to life.' They all went inside and Joey stood grinning with his hands on his hips.

'Wowzers,' he whistled. 'That looks fab. I adore the old style matt black and white look. I'm delighted you and Dad never gave in to all the interior fashion trends. I remember Pippa bending your ear about having them ripped up and replaced with something more modern.'

'Oh no, that'd be a travesty,' Skye agreed. 'The first time I walked into Huntersbrook, I was blown away by its classic beauty. The high decorative ceilings and chequerboard floor have the wow factor. Especially against the bright red front door.'

Holly smiled. 'I love that you feel at home here, Skye,' she said. 'Right. Chatting over. I'm going back outside to finish my jobs. I'll leave you two to get settled!'

As Joey carried his bags up the stairs to the room they'd decided to sleep in, he was quiet.

'What are you thinking about?' Skye asked.

'I never laughed with Sophia,' he said. 'I don't want to harp on about my ex or anything, but *we're* so different,' he said reaching over and taking her hand to kiss. 'I'm so different. I'm lucky to have you, Skye.'

'Aw, what a lovely thing to say,' she said. 'I think we're pretty great actually,' she grinned. 'We basically rock.'

'Joey?' Paddy's voice echoed in the hallway down stairs.

'Hi Dad, just coming.' He kissed Skye and raced down, taking the steps two at a time.

'How's it going?' Paddy asked, giving Joey a quick hug. 'Good to see you, son. Now, are you ready for some hard work? The gravel has arrived. Will you come out and give a hand? There are two men with rakes, but I want to make sure it's all put in the right place. If they drive off and leave us with enormous big mounds of it, we'll be goosed.'

'Let me grab some old clothes from the shed and I'll join you,' Joey said.

By the time he joined his father and the men, he found Paddy, as excited as a small child, directing the proceedings.

Joey got stuck in and helped ease the mounds of gravel onto the turning circle and paths that immediately surrounded the house. It finished the look of the place nicely. The old tarmac that lay beneath was full of potholes and weeds. The new surface added an instantly even finish. By the time the truck drove away, Holly and Skye had joined them and were examining the handiwork closely.

'I hope we get lots of parties booked in,' Holly said.

'You don't sound convinced,' Skye said gently.

'No, I am . . . it's just . . . well, while I think it's the best possible plan to use Huntersbrook as a venue, I'm still desperately sad that none of us is living here full-time. It was always a family home and nothing else.'

'I know, Mum,' Joey said putting an arm around her shoulder. 'But this is the way it has to be right now. Me and Skye will be here for the week, so at least there'll be many times like this. Just because it's becoming a rentable property won't stop us turning it back into a family home from time to time.'

'Maybe in a couple of years some of us will be back in residence full-time,' Paddy reasoned. 'But for now, isn't it better that it wasn't bought by a developer or someone who wanted to rip its guts out and make it unrecognisable?'

'I know,' Holly said. 'I'm just having a silly moment. Don't mind me.'

They chatted about the plans to creosote the fences.

'Lainey, Matt and Jacob are going to pitch in, along with a couple of the lads from Shaffrey's farm down the road,' Paddy told them.

'I can't wait to catch up with Lainey and Matt,' Joey said.

'They're over at the farmhouse right now, finalising the paper work for third party insurance and the alcohol licence,' Paddy said.

'Is Ely over there with them?' Skye asked.

'Yes,' Holly said, slightly snappily. 'But Sadie is over there minding him. I'll be having a word or two with Lainey when they join us later. Sadie is far too old to be dumped with a teething baby. Besides, she'd already promised to have my back this weekend. With all the helpers on board, we'll have quite a crowd to feed. I've asked her to make her world-famous lamb with garlic potato gratin,' Holly said.

'I can almost taste it already,' Joey said. 'It's worth coming down here for one of Sadie's delicious dinners. How is the old doll?'

'I don't mind the doll reference, but less of the old, thank you,' Sadie said, appearing from the pathway between Huntersbrook and the farmhouse with a happy Ely in her arms.

'Caught rapid!' Skye laughed. 'You tell him, Sadie. You're still a teenager up here, right?' Skye tapped her own head.

'Indeed, I am,' Sadie agreed. 'Although I thought I was spritely until I took charge of this little monkey today. He's full of beans, so he is.'

They all fussed over little Ely and commented on how like Lainey he'd become.

Joey took his nephew into his arms and swung him around, making him giggle. His infectious laugh made them all join in.

A pungent smell filled the air and Joey held the baby out at an arm's length. 'Who wants to do the honours?'

'Joey!' Skye laughed. 'Dirty nappies are part and parcel of minding little ones. Can't you do it?'

'You're joking, right? I'm a long long way off being ready to change smelly nappies. Until I absolutely have to, I'm choosing not to!'

'Come to me, pet,' Holly said, taking him and kissing his cheek. 'I'm sick of telling Lainey I can mind him. I've been pottering in the garden since early morning and he could easily have helped me. The fresh air would've done him the world of good. Still, I won't butt in when I'm not wanted.'

Sadie smiled softly at Holly and put her hand on her arm for a moment. 'Ah now, you know how it is with first-time mothers, Holly, have to keep the reins tight and keep it all to themselves. That's all it is.'

Clearly wanting to dispel the awkwardness in the air, Paddy chucked the baby under the chin and winked at Sadie and Holly. 'Two women in my life and I'm standing here parched. Any chance of a cup of tea, my darling ladies?'

Holly swatted him with her gardening gloves. 'You'd think you were helpless,' she said, teasing him. 'I'll get it for you.'

'Sure I'll help,' Skye said. 'Come on, Sadie, I'll mind Ely so you can have a sit down and a cup as well.'

The women headed off to the kitchen, and Joey was glad to have a few moments alone with his father.

'I'll have a little chat with our Lainey later,' Paddy mused. 'Your mother would love to see more of Ely. The two of them are like cats in a sack, though. Any time I think they're getting on, there's another spat. One's as bad as the other as well.'

'They've never been any different, Dad.' Joey sighed. 'Mum would say black and Lainey would say white and no one could back down. I have to say I feel sorry for Mum, though. I think she's feeling very left out.'

'I'll sort it,' Paddy said. He looked at Joey and smiled. 'So how is work going, son?'

'Busy,' Joey said. 'But it's all worth it now that I'm on such good money. I was blessed that they waited for me to get back on my feet after the accident last year. So many companies are giving people their marching orders, never mind waiting for them to recuperate.'

'You're brilliant at what you do. You deserve their loyalty,' Paddy said. 'Besides, it wasn't your fault the council left those road works uncovered. You could've been killed. I still shudder when I think of you lying in that hospital bed.'

'I know, it wasn't the most enjoyable time in my life,' Joey grinned. 'Between that and everything with Sophia, I think I can confidently sum up that I'm a hell of a lot happier now. *And*, as it happens,' Joey said, lowering his voice, 'Clive offered me a partnership this morning.'

'No way!'

'Yes way! I've to confirm or decline on Tuesday. I'd booked the week off as you know, but I'll have to shoot back up to Dublin for the day now.'

'I assume you'll say yes?'

'Totally.' Joey grinned. 'I haven't said a word to Skye or anyone. I wanted to discuss it with you first.'

'I'm honoured, Joey. Thanks.'

'Clive has pointed out I'll be expected to work even longer hours, but I don't mind that.'

'No, so you shouldn't. You weren't raised to be afraid of hard work. When are you going to tell Skye and the others?'

'This evening. I needed to mull it all over for a couple of hours and be sure it's what I want.'

'Well, the alternative at this point would be to move company or set up on your own,' Paddy said. 'Neither would be as lucrative and you'd be starting from scratch. In the current economic climate, as they say, I wouldn't see that as a good move.'

'No, I agree,' Joey said. 'I really want this, Dad. But I suppose

I'm just scared. It's a commitment and I guess it all feels very grown up! Am I really ready for that?'

Before Paddy could answer, the ladies appeared back with Ely in the buggy. Skye was carrying a tray of mugs and cakes.

'I thought we'd have a final fling at the outdoor table before we put it away in an outhouse,' Holly said. 'I can't believe the evenings have become darker already.'

'Yes, but the upside is that Halloween is around the corner,' Sadie said as her eyes wrinkled into a smile.

'Ooh, don't get me started,' Holly said rubbing her hands together in glee. 'Because we all know what follows Hallowe'en, don't we?'

'What would that be, Mum?' Joey asked.

'I was sitting at the gate lodge last night feeling a bit sad about the fact that the evening light is fading so much earlier, when it occurred to me that I could start thinking about my Christmas décor for this year,' she said.

'You crack me up!' Skye said. 'I've never met another woman who loves Christmas the way you do, Holly.'

'What's *not* to love?'

Joey accepted a cup of tea and stood back watching the ladies and his father cooing over little Ely as Holly attempted to explain Christmas to the baby. These were the type of scenes he remembered from his own childhood. No matter how old he was, nothing was as important as knowing he belonged. Work was mildly scary, in a good way. But here at home, he always felt secure and safe. A shiver ran down his spine. He was nervous and elated in equal measure about his new offer. But as he studied his father, Joey hoped most of all that he'd be as happy and self-assured as his father in years to come.

Lainey

LAINEY PHONED HUNTERSBROOK TO MAKE SURE Ely was OK. She grimaced when Holly answered.

'Hi Mum,' she said with forced cheer. 'Just wanted to check that Ely is OK for another hour? Matt and I are finally finished with all the business and we were going to get a couple of things done here at the farmhouse before joining you all.'

'Well, that's nice for you both, dear. Seeing as I'm not in charge of Ely, I'll pass you over to Sadie.'

Before she could reply, Lainey heard the phone being clunked down on the kitchen counter as Holly called out to Sadie. She came on the line and was discretion itself as she assured Lainey that Ely was snug in his buggy.

'Skye and Joey have taken him for a walk down the avenue. He was getting a bit grizzly, so he might have a little sleep, which will do him the world of good.'

'Thanks, Sadie. We'll be over in about an hour.'

She hung up and found Matt in the kitchen putting the paperwork in a file.

'All OK?' he asked.

'Super,' she said, sounding deflated.

'What's up?'

'Ah, nothing much. Mum answered the phone and is clearly in a total snit with me because I asked Sadie to watch Ely.'

'Holly *is* always offering to have him. Maybe you should take her up on it sometime,' Matt said easily.

'I know my mother, Matt,' she argued. 'She's full of hot air. She's great at offering, but I can guarantee you if I actually asked her to mind him, she'd be grumbling. You know what she was like during the pregnancy and his first weeks.'

'Ah she meant well,' Matt said. 'Remember what Sadie told you, that becoming a grandmother for the first time is just as overwhelming as becoming a mother for the first time. Sometimes, you need to see it from her side – cut her a bit of slack.'

Lainey decided to drop the subject, but she was damned if she was letting Holly poke her nose into her life. Before and after Ely was born, Holly had dictated and pontificated at her about what she should and shouldn't eat, drink and do. It really didn't help that Holly lived so close by and could 'pop in' whenever it suited her. By the time the child was born, Lainey was at her wits' end with Holly's constant advice. When Lainey finally snapped and told her mother to back off, Holly had nodded in a knowing way.

'You probably have postnatal depression, like I had with you. I understand. If you get much worse I would suggest you see a doctor, though. They can do marvellous things, you know? There's no need to suffer in silence.'

Lainey was exhausted, sore and just wanted to be left alone. 'I am not *you,*' she had pretty much screamed at her mother, something she felt guilty about to this day.

She understood that her mother had been plagued by postnatal depression. Back then, the support and treatments hadn't been great, so Lainey had no doubt her mother had suffered immensely. But Grandma had stepped in and practically raised Lainey single-handed. It wasn't as if Holly had been left in a flat all alone with a screaming child and nobody to turn to. Lainey couldn't help feeling as if her mother blamed her for her depression. But how could it be the fault of a little baby? In her heart of hearts, although she'd never admit to anyone, not even Matt, Lainey believed that Holly loved her less than Joey or Pippa because of the depression. And it hurt.

After Grandma Maggie died, when Holly and Lainey were equally, albeit differently, grief-stricken, things had been addressed, to an extent. Lainey had told her mother she wanted to forge a new and adult relationship with her, to try to ensure they didn't die with regrets – like Holly had about her treatment of Maggie in her final years. In fairness to her, Holly had agreed willingly. It was all easy to say, of course, but not quite as simple to implement.

Lainey knew she should probably allow her mother to bond with Ely a bit more. But every time she went near her, Holly couldn't help doling out unwanted and unasked-for advice.

'His cheeks look a little red, have you tried to rub something on his gums?' or her all-time favourite, if she couldn't find anything specific to pick on, 'he looks exhausted, did he sleep last night?'

Sadie, on the other hand, was so easy-going and always asked what Lainey wanted her to do.

'You're the Mammy, so I'll take my lead from you.'

Lainey didn't want to get into a slagging match against her mother or anything like that, but she often wished Sadie would at least acknowledge how difficult Holly could be.

It was an issue she felt she couldn't really raise with anyone, in fact. Joey was the apple of his mother's eye. The son and heir. And Pippa? Well, Pippa was just Pippa. Nothing much fazed her. In spite of the trouble she constantly caused, Holly seemed to forgive her completely. From where Lainey was standing, it was almost as if their mother admired Pippa's devil-may-care attitude.

Thinking of Pippa, she texted her sister quickly: *Hope ur week went well. Looking forward 2 seeing you over the wk end. Full steam ahead 4 getting the place ready 2 take guests. What time r u coming down?*

Pippa was normally very speedy with her responses, so Lainey was a bit miffed when she didn't answer. Figuring she was probably in the car on her way down, Lainey put her phone back in her bag.

By the time they'd finished clearing up, Lainey was gasping for some air.

'I think living in the country again has made me an air-a-holic,' she joked. 'I don't know how I managed so many years of living in my apartment and sitting in an office day in, day out.'

'You were at a different stage in life,' Matt pointed out. 'Now you're back where you belong. I feel the same way. I loved the years I spent in London and I probably wouldn't have come back when I did except that Mum was dying, but it was the right thing. This place fits me. And of course I bumped into you again,' he said with a smile.

Lainey smiled back. 'Well, husband dearest, I told Sadie we had a bit of business to attend to and we'd collect Ely in an hour.'

'Oh yeah?' He raised an eyebrow. 'And what are you saying, wife dearest?'

'Why don't you follow me?' Lainey said, leaning against him. 'Seeing as your father is in Wicklow for the day, I think we should see about making a little brother or sister for Ely.'

Matt hesitated. It was only for a second, but Lainey clocked it.

'Don't you want to make love?' she asked, making a bad job of hiding her hurt.

'It's not that,' he said quickly. 'I'm probably a step or two behind you with the family expansion idea, that's all.'

'Ely can't be an only child, Matt. And I'm not getting any younger, so I don't see what the problem is.'

'Yeah . . .'

'Matt, we've both said all along that we want a big brood. They're not going to appear by magic now, are they?'

She kissed Matt and ran her fingers through his hair. She giggled as he grabbed her hand and pulled her towards the stairs.

The landline started to ring, and she stopped.

'Leave it,' Matt said. 'If it's important, they can call back.'

'There could be a problem with Ely,' she said. 'I'll be really quick, I promise.' Matt went on up to their bedroom and she grabbed the phone.

'Hello?'

'Hey, Lainz! It's me!'

'Hi Jules,' she said, grinning instantly at the sound of her best friend's voice. 'How's it going?'

'Not too brilliantly, actually,' she said before bursting into tears.

'What's happened, sweetheart?'

'The usual. Girl trouble.' She sniffed. 'You know I was seeing Sylvia for a while, yeah? Well it turns out she was only testing the water to see if she wanted to be lesbian. She just phoned to tell me that she's grateful that I helped her dip her toe in gay waters, but she's not in the vagina business any longer.'

'She didn't actually say that, did she?' Lainey asked.

'She might have thought it was all a gay lark,' Jules said. 'But, straight up, Lainz, she's either an amazing actress or she's gay and doesn't want to admit it. But Christ, I liked her a lot.'

'Oh that's awful for you,' Lainey said. 'Why don't you come down here for the rest of the weekend? You can stay at the farmhouse with us, or else Skye and Joey are next door. I reckon Pippa's due down any minute too.'

'I might just do that,' Jules said, perking up. 'I can't face a weekend on my own. I'll end up drinking too much, forcing myself to watch *The Notebook* and bawling until my eyes look as puffy as a cloud.'

'Well, once you're ready to paint some fences, there's a place here for you,' Lainey said. 'And now, much as I love you, I have to run upstairs and shag my husband.'

Jules burst out laughing. 'Oh the empathy is overwhelming me, please stop.'

'I'll give you buckets of empathy when you get here,' Lainey said, laughing. 'And some gin, too, if it'll help.'

'It always helps,' Jules said. 'Now scoot, get going and do dreadful things to your man. I'll see you soon.'

Lainey put down the phone and raced up to Matt and they spent a delicious hour languishing in bed. It felt so bold to do this now they were parents – it made the sex even better.

'I suppose I'd better get up and present myself next door,' Matt said. 'The men will think I've abandoned them.'

'I'd better take Ely, too. Sadie will be busy cooking at this stage.'

❄

Lainey skipped across the grassy path, looking forward to hugging little Ely. Becoming a Mum was the best thing that had ever happened to her. Unlike Holly, who seemed to benchmark motherhood as a time when things began to fall apart for her, Lainey adored her newfound role in life.

She hoped so much that their efforts in the bedroom would pay off and she'd become pregnant soon. She wasn't going to harp on about it too much to Matt, but she'd decided five was her magic number. Imagine the picnics in the summer and bright expectant eyes around the tree at Christmas time with five children? The farmhouse only had three decent bedrooms and a box room as it stood, but there was oodles of space to build on. Lainey had been doing a bit of research on that score, and she was almost ready to share her plans with Matt and her family.

She was truly excited about her secret five-year plan. Yes, it was going to involve quite a bit of birthing and hard work, but Lainey knew it was what would make her happy.

The kitchen was a hub of activity as she opened the door. As soon as he saw her, Ely began to bounce up and down in the old high chair that Paddy had fished out of the attic.

'Hello baba,' she said stooping to kiss him.

'Hello Lainey,' Sadie said smiling. 'He's just woken up and I thought he might need a bit of tea. He's had toast and a boiled egg and he's set a little trend!'

'He's a man after my own heart,' Paddy boomed. 'We're all having dippy eggs now with toast soldiers!'

'What about dinner?' Lainey said.

'Ah this is just a little sneaky snack,' Paddy said cheerfully.

Lainey laughed as she hugged and kissed Skye and Joey. Choosing to ignore her mother's slightly grumpy expression, she kissed her too.

Joey's phone pinged and he read the text, then punched the air.

'I think I've managed to buy an incredible marquee just now,' Joey announced proudly. 'It's through a mate. He was in the party business, but since flamboyant do's have gone with the recession, he's trying to offload a pile of gear. The tent in question seats two hundred.'

'Would we need something that big?' Holly asked, looking shocked.

'If we're aiming to take weddings, we'd need to be able to seat that many at once, yes,' Lainey said.

'He has twenty round wooden tables and good quality fold-up

chairs too,' Joey said. 'I've priced the whole lot if we were to buy it new and he's cutting me a really good deal.'

'Is the tent properly lined?' Sadie asked, ever the practical mind.

'Totally,' Joey said. 'With cream floaty stuff.'

Skye laughed. 'I presume you mean tulle!'

'Yeah,' he grinned. 'Like net curtains, only floatier.'

'That's the stuff you want,' Sadie said. 'By the way, Lainey, those eggs are getting bigger and tastier by the week.'

'Thanks, Sadie,' Lainey said happily. 'The girls are really coming on. They take a lot of work to get going, but I'm glad I stuck to my guns.'

When she'd moved into the farmhouse, Lainey wanted to get hens again. Her late mother-in-law's flock had produced prize-winning eggs in her day, but Cynthia's illness and subsequent passing had meant all that had gone by the wayside. One by one the fox got the hens and the men hadn't the interest or time to replace them.

Then Lainey came along, with her big ideas and big energy. Jacob had been delighted to have a woman about the house again after his wife's death, and over time she'd worked her way to having free rein. She'd overhauled the farmhouse entirely. Matt and his father were about as far away from their feminine sides as it was possible to be. Without wanting to offend Cynthia's memory, she'd slowly redecorated the place, room by room.

She loved the idea of providing free-range fresh eggs for her family and wanted to take the whole concept a step further, so she'd invested in a polytunnel. Her idea was that they'd eventually have predominantly home-grown produce to eat. With a brood of children, she couldn't expect Matt to pay for everything after all. She didn't want his reason for a smaller family to be financial.

Jacob's arrival stirred a new flurry of musical chairs as everyone made room for Matt's father. He was an old-fashioned man of few words, but a total gentleman with it. Lainey had grown so fond of him since moving into the farmhouse. She'd been a little dubious at first, wondering how he might take to another woman muscling in on his turf. But he'd proven to be incredibly placid and so welcoming. He idolised baby Ely and never made Lainey feel as if she were intruding. The farmhouse truly was their home – all four of them.

As the lunch things were cleared away and Ely was released from his high chair, they began to plan the following day's work.

'Has anyone heard from Pippa?' Holly asked. 'I've called her mobile a few times and she's not answering.'

'She's probably on the way down with music blaring. I assume she still hasn't had a hands-free kit installed in her car. You know Pippa,' Joey grinned. 'She'll turn up at some point with a bag of dirty washing, starving and looking for attention.'

'Ah she's a great girl,' Sadie said. 'She doesn't take life too seriously, that's all. And why should she? Isn't she entitled to have a bit of fun while she's young?'

'She's twenty-five, Sadie,' Lainey said.

'Precisely,' Joey said. 'She'd want to start copping on soon before she makes a total bags of her life.'

'She's doing very well,' Holly said jumping to her defence, as usual. 'She's invaluable to that Brianna woman. And all she seems to do is get on Pippa's case. From what she's told me, she's a total dragon.'

'I'd say there are two sides to that story,' Lainey remarked.

'I'm sure she'll be here soon enough,' Sadie said happily.

'Oh I almost forgot, Jules is on the way, too,' Lainey said. 'Hope that's OK with everyone?'

'The more the merrier,' Paddy said. 'She always cheers me up.'

'That's because she wears incredibly short skirts, low-cut tops and gazes at you as if you're an oracle when you speak,' Holly said. 'The poor girl hasn't a breeze how to act around men after growing up without a father.'

'I don't mind her latching on to me,' Paddy said. 'And I take exception to you suggesting I'm being a lecherous old buzzard. She's the same age as my own daughter. I don't think that way,' he harrumphed.

'Really? I reckon you're the only straight man with a pulse who thinks that so,' Joey joked. 'She's all the more attractive because she bats for the other team. Just knowing I never have a snowball's chance in hell with her is wildly attractive,' he grinned.

'So I should resist your advances and bat my eyes at other women?' Skye joked. 'Now I know the way to your heart.'

'Dear Lord, what are you all like?' Sadie said. 'If I'd even *thought* half the things you lot talk about, I'd have been skinned alive as a young one.'

'Times have changed, Sadie,' Holly said. 'But I agree with you. There's too much baseline chat around here. We're all delighted Jules is coming down, Lainey, and nobody should be discussing her private life as if it's fair game.'

'We didn't mean any harm,' Joey said. 'Jules knows we all love her. Besides, she's hardly backwards about coming forwards. Remember the last time she was here? She sat and told Dad all about the fact she needed someone who loved her for her brains, not her body. She kept complaining about all the ladies who adore her body.'

'Poor Dad didn't know where to look!' Lainey burst into giggles.

'I only wish I'd had that problem myself as a young fella,' Paddy said with a grin.

'Enough,' said Holly, clapping her hands together. 'Or Sadie and I will have to wash your mouths out with carbolic soap.

Now, Joey, you go through the list and start handing out the jobs. There's still lots to be done. And will one of you please try Pippa again. I'm starting to feel worried about her.'

Lainey took her phone from her back pocket and tapped quickly: *Hey Pip, where are you? Mum getting frantic! And we need more help. Hurry up! xx*

Pippa

PIPPA HAD NEVER FELT SO INSTANTLY DRAWN TO a man. He was probably the coolest guy she'd ever set eyes on. In general, red-heads weren't her thing. In fact, they'd been a no-no, until now.

The cold had encouraged them to move from the beer garden they'd all frequented that summer to a pub with a back bar where music was pumping through the rafters. She was with the gang from work again.

Zach had been hounding her all week about buying the site and she knew she needed to sign it over to him soon or he'd lose interest. They'd had lunch together most days this week and she'd gotten to know him better. She had a lot of time for him and honestly didn't want to rip him off, but a few extra euros in her back pocket wouldn't go astray.

She'd been staring at this guy since they arrived. As she drank more, she became less discreet about eyeing him up.

She was meant to be listening to Molly from knitwear, who was rattling on with some tale of woe about some random guy she'd been dating. Pippa had never seen herself as a counsellor. She couldn't deal with sob stories and wasn't great at doling out advice. That was more Lainey's department. But this delicious man on the horizon meant she was done even feigning interest in Molly's romance problems. She could feel her pulse quicken as he grabbed his drink, held her gaze and walked straight up to her.

'Why don't you take a photo of me so you can stare at that instead?' he said. 'It would save you straining your eyes and craning your neck.'

'I beg your pardon?' she said haughtily.

He wasn't backing down. He gave her a wide smile and raised an eyebrow. 'Do you normally stare your victims down before you pounce?'

'I wasn't looking at *you*,' she said recovering swiftly and attempting to save face. Looking through him, she waved at nobody in particular. 'You got me all wrong, cowboy,' she said shaking her head slowly. 'I had my eye on a total dish who was standing by the bar and you've just blown it for me.' She sighed dramatically and flicked her hair, pretending to be furious. 'Nice one, now he thinks I'm with you and he's just left.' Planting one hand on her hip, she pouted and slowly raised her eyes to stare into his.

'Well sorry to wreck your buzz,' he said, looking obviously flustered.

'So, what are you going to do to redeem yourself?' she asked, twisting from side to side coyly.

He turned on his heel and marched away with such speed, Pippa almost shouted to him to wait. Expertly elbowing his way through the throng at the bar, he held up his hand and got immediate attention from one of the bar staff.

Within minutes he returned with a bottle of Moët and two champagne flutes.

'Is this good enough?' he asked as he popped the cork and poured.

'It's a start,' she said, raising an eyebrow. Her heart was thudding so loudly she feared her hand might shake as she lifted the glass to her lips. They sank the entire contents of their glasses in two large gulps.

'Jeez, you drink like you've just escaped from a week in the Sahara,' she said.

'I didn't see you lagging too far behind me, little lady.' He leaned in cheekily to kiss her. 'You taste great. I'm Danny.'

'Ditto, Danny, I'm Pippa.'

Within twenty minutes the bottle was empty and Pippa felt as if her belly would explode with fizz. She giggled and swayed slightly as the alcohol and bubbles had an almost instant effect on her.

'Let's get out of here,' Danny said as he pulled Pippa by the hand toward the side door.

'Hey, where are we going?' she said, suddenly nervous. She didn't know this guy.

'Somewhere fun!' he said, grabbing her hand again.

'Wait a second,' she said, releasing her hand from his grasp. 'I need to say *ciao* to my mates and for the record, I am going to take a photo of you and send it to Zach, so he'll know who you are, just in case.'

Danny cocked his head to one side and looked at her. 'OK,' he said slowly. 'If you need to do that, no problem.'

Pippa snapped a quick pic of him and texted it to Zach. Then she went over to her friends and told them she was heading off.

'You sure he's cool?' Zach asked craning his neck to look at him. 'Although what I saw of him while you two were sculling champers looks rather delicious.'

'He is, isn't he?' Pippa giggled. 'I'll call you. We need to talk business, yeah?'

'Sure thing. Don't do anything I wouldn't do,' Zach said kissing her on the cheek. 'God I'm jealous, he's divine.'

'And check your phone,' Pippa said, looking her friend in the eye. 'I've sent you a pic, OK.'

Zach frowned and looked down at his phone, then back at Pippa.

'Oh, I get it,' he said. 'I don't blame you after what happened
. . . the assault.'

'A girl just has to be careful,' Pippa said quickly.

Zach squeezed her hand quickly. 'If you need me, ring my
number. But he looks alright, I think.'

'Catch you later,' she said with a wink.

'Let's meet tomorrow and we'll try and get this transaction
sorted with the website, yeah?'

'Totally,' Pippa said. She went to find Danny, who had already
found a taxi.

'Come on, you're wasting precious time.'

'Where are we going?' she slurred as she fell into the back
seat. 'Ugh, I feel kind of woozy.'

'Not for long,' he said winking. As they pulled up outside
Dublin's exclusive Sumatra Hotel, she grinned.

'We'll never get into Fire and Rain nightclub at this hour.
You have to queue for hours and even then they look at you as
if you're scum.'

Danny paid the taxi driver and held the car door open, reaching
in to help her to her feet.

'Evening J,' he said to the bouncer.

'Danny. Madam,' he answered as he stood to the side and
unclipped the red rope. The club was heaving as they were sucked
into the heat. The dull thud of the bass beat made Pippa's stomach
lurch. Her eyes watered as she clamped her hand over her mouth,
praying she wasn't going to spew all over Danny's back.

Mercifully, she managed not to vomit as they were thrust into
a Perspex elevator she'd never even noticed before.

'Where are we going now?' she slurred as her head became
too heavy for her neck. 'Sorry, I'm plastered.'

'Poor pretty Pippa,' he said, leaning down to kiss her on the
mouth. 'Come with me and I'll sort you.'

'I'd like a pint of iced water,' she said as the elevator lurched to a stop.

Wordlessly, Danny scooped her into his arms and brought her to a small, dimly lit side room. It looked like a brothel. Not that Pippa had ever been to one. But this place was what she imagined one would look like. It was awash with dark burgundy and leopard-print accents and more velvet than a 1980s furniture showroom.

'A bottle of Evian with ice and a bottle of Moët, please, love,' Danny said to a hovering hostess. 'Give us five minutes' peace, yeah?'

Pippa looked over, longing to catch the girl's eye so she could at least apologise for being so drunk. But she'd vanished. Danny fiddled around in his pocket before producing a small silver box.

'Roll that,' he said handing her a fifty-euro note.

'Pardon?' Pippa said, licking her lips. Her mouth was bone dry and she needed to sit up straight. Inhaling deeply through her nose, she fought another wave of nausea.

'Shit, I'm shit-faced,' she said with a moan.

'Hey, you're in a bad way, kid.' He grinned, chucking her under the chin. 'Hang in there. Danny will make it all better.'

Groaning, she lay back on the squashy sofa and waited for her pint of water. Her eyes kept closing, much as she wanted to stay awake and say cute or flirty things, it wasn't happening.

'Here baby, lean forward. I've it all lined up for you.'

'Huh?' Pippa peeled her eyes open, willing her head to stop rolling. As she sat up and focused, the unmistakable lines of white powder on the table came into view.

'Oh no, I'm not into that shit,' she said waving her hand floppily. 'Never was and never will be. Uh-uh,' she said wagging a finger. 'It's a mug's game, honey.'

'And you're holding it all together so well right now?' said

Danny with a smirk. 'I actually think it's darn sexy that you clearly don't do this stuff. But believe me, it'll make you feel a hell of a lot better than you do this second. It'll sober you up in minutes.'

'I don't need sobering up,' she said. 'Not with that muck. I'll go home to bed and wake up tomorrow feeling like I've been hit by a lorry. That's the routine.'

'Doesn't have to be,' he said mildly as he leaned forward, shoved the rolled-up note in one nostril, covered the other and snorted. Without speaking he passed her the note and held her hair back. On auto-pilot, Pippa did what he'd just done.

The sensation as the powder hit her nose made her cough.

'Ugh, it's like sniffing swimming pool water as a kid.'

He roared laughing. 'You're so funny. That's the cutest comparison. From now on, I'll ask you if you'd like to go for a swim! That'll be our code for coke, OK?'

She knew she should feel dreadfully guilty and ashamed for what she'd just done, but Pippa didn't. Instead, she was instantly less ill and for some unknown reason she wanted to do it again. She pointed at the other lines on the table.

'Can I try another one?'

'Sure thing, pretty Pippa.'

By the time the waitress returned with the drinks the table was clear and they were sitting nonchalantly as Danny draped his arm over her shoulder.

'Thanks so much,' Danny said to the lady as he handed her cash.

'Pleasure,' she said with an easy smile. 'Call if you need anything else.'

Pippa drank most of the bottle of water and would've finished it if Danny hadn't pulled it away.

'Hey,' she said. 'What are you doing?'

'Don't glug it so quick. You'll be sick. Give your tummy a chance. Lots of people make that mistake when they're high. Kids have drowned.'

'No way! By drinking water too quickly?'

'Yeah, it's a condition called hyponatremia. All the water lowers the normal sodium levels in the blood.'

'Wow,' she said as the sounds of the club along with the flashing lights came back into her main focus. 'How do you know this stuff? Are you a doctor or something?'

'Hardly,' he said wryly.

'Oh yeah, sorry,' she smiled. 'Silly question considering what we've done.'

'I studied science in university,' he said.

'Ah ha! So you know exactly what's going on in my brain right now. God, I feel great.'

'That makes two of us,' he said with a smile. Instinctively she leaned over and kissed him.

'You,' she said holding his face with her hands, 'are amazing. I am amazing. This night is amazing.'

As if she was being controlled by a puppeteer Pippa stood up and walked, catwalk style, toward the balcony that overlooked the dance floor.

Raising her hands high above her head she began to dance with less inhibition than she'd ever experienced. Danny appeared with two full glasses of bubbly, which they downed swiftly before joining the frenzied crowd on the dance floor below. As the time slipped away, Pippa danced and moved like she'd never done before. With Danny's arms around her she felt as if she and the music were one.

She couldn't believe it when the club ended.

'I thought this place stayed open all night,' she said sulkily.

'It does,' Danny smiled. 'You danced till dawn, baby.'

'No way!' she said, wide-eyed as the overhead lights came on and the place began to empty.

They ran back upstairs and finished the champagne before wandering out into the murky, early morning half-light of Dublin city.

'This is terrible,' she giggled. 'People are starting their day and we haven't gone home yet.'

Pippa knew she was taking a chance going back to Danny's apartment. She didn't know the first thing about him, after all. But she couldn't stop herself – she was intoxicated by him.

His place was a five-minute taxi ride from the club.

'Wow, talk about central,' she said, as they emerged from the taxi and made their way to the lifts.

The apartment wasn't any great shakes. The décor was boring and there were no little personal touches to make it seem homely. He flicked on the heating.

'Who lives here with you?' she asked peeking around.

'Nobody,' he said, grabbing a bottle of beer from the fridge. 'The way I like it. I had a girlfriend but she treated me like dirt, so I walked away. Moved in here a couple of months ago. It's not the most amazing place, but it'll do.'

Danny turned on some music.

'Oh I love this song,' Pippa said closing her eyes and dancing. 'I'm having the best night of my life.'

'So I see,' he grinned.

Danny pulled off his shoes and sat on the sofa watching her.

'What do you do when you're not driving me crazy, pretty Pippa?'

'I work as a designer,' she said. 'But let's not talk about work. It's so not what I want to think of right now. Dance with me, Danny.'

He grinned and put his bottle of beer down and stood to

take her in his arms. It was Pippa who led him to the compact bedroom just off the living room.

She heard her mobile phone ringing in her handbag, but nothing was going to pull Pippa away from Danny. Before long they were in his bed, peeling off their clothes and pushing their bodies deliciously together.

After what felt like hours, she dragged herself into the shower. The bathroom was surprisingly clean and the towels were freshly washed. There was decent shampoo, conditioner and shower gel on offer too. As the hot water hit her back, Pippa's body felt suddenly tired. But she knew there was no possible way she could sleep.

By the time she emerged from the bathroom, Danny was in the kitchen making a pot of coffee.

'I'm wildly impressed by you,' Pippa said. 'You're very domesticated. I was half expecting a filthy slimy shower complete with a plug clogged with hair and no shampoo!'

'Ah no, not around here,' he said with a grin. 'Coffee?'

She nodded emphatically, feeling a bit scuzzy having to reappear in the clothes she'd had to pluck off the floor. They chatted happily as they drank their coffee. Pippa kept waiting for it all to feel slightly weird, but it didn't. Danny was articulate and funny and kept complimenting her.

'How long have you been working in IT?' she asked.

'Since I left college,' he said. 'I did a degree in computer science and marketing. I work for a multinational firm where there are massive benefits for loyalty. I'll be twenty-eight next month, which sounds so old.'

'I'm twenty-five and in ways I still feel eighteen, but in others I can't help thinking I'm getting old too.'

She told him all about Huntersbrook, growing up there and how she had fallen into her job at the department store.

'So your boss saw your designs online on your website and just called you out of the blue?'

'Yup,' she said.

'So you're clearly a gifted artist.' He nodded. 'That's cool. Being able to express yourself is really important. So many people are one-dimensional now. At least lots of the people in the computer firm where I work are. They're total techy wizards, but they don't do a darn thing outside of their field.'

Danny had grown up in a suburb not far from the city centre. As the eldest of four children, he'd been dying to move out of home and spread his wings.

'I'm one of those guys who had a summer job making burgers and came home to wash cars in the evenings. I always wanted to make money and be in a position to be my own person.'

'Yeah,' Pippa fibbed. 'Me too. I'm totally independent.'

'That's cool.'

Pippa finished her coffee and was immeasurably glad that none of her family were here. Lainey and Joey would bust a gut laughing if they'd heard what she just said. Of all the Craig family, Pippa was the one constantly in debt and getting into hot water. But Danny didn't need to know any of that. Pippa liked his vibe. He was totally different from any of the guys she'd met before. He had this burning ambition she found wildly attractive. As she sat chatting to him, she realised she was really into the idea of being her own person too. She had a job now, so she could build on it. Zach was looking to buy her website, so she'd make a killing on that and possibly ask Joey about investing the cash.

'I'm in the middle of selling one of my companies,' Pippa said nonchalantly. 'It's a fairly slow process, but I'm trying to build my resources as I go along.'

Pippa was thoroughly enjoying this newly invented corporate version of herself. More importantly, she loved how Danny was reacting to this image of her. He couldn't get enough of her. He was hanging on her every word and it wasn't because she was doing her usual sexy/cutesy and girly act either.

Pippa was the queen of getting what she wanted. Always had been. But she was growing tired of doing the same thing with the same crowd. It was time to take things up a notch. She wasn't looking for a house in the country with a dependable corduroy-wearing geek. She wanted a man about town. Someone who looked good, partied hard and knew how to make money. They'd only just met, but already Danny was ticking a lot of boxes. They moved into the bedroom where they got very little sleep. Pippa wasn't in the habit of sleeping with guys she'd just met, but somehow it seemed right with Danny. She felt like she'd only closed her eyes for a second when Danny climbed out of bed and disappeared to the shower. He returned smelling deliciously spicy with a towel wrapped around his waist.

'So I'm doing a bit of work this evening. How about we get a bite to eat and you can come with me?' Danny asked.

'I'll need to change, I feel yuck.'

'No time, my precious,' he said as his phone began to bleep with one text message after another. 'I've to hook up with a guy near Grafton Street. I'll do that while you grab yourself a new outfit.'

'Huh, I wish,' Pippa said. 'Soz darling, but I'm skint.'

'That's not a problem, I'll sort you out.'

'Pardon?' Pippa's heart lunged. 'Oh no, I couldn't. I barely know you . . . We've only met . . . I mean . . .'

'So you'll have sex with me and sit and bare your soul to me, but you won't allow me to buy you a dress? Hey, roll with the punches, pretty Pippa. Live life on the edge.'

Not wanting to seem like a nerd, she found herself agreeing.

'Can I have a quick shower?'

'Be my guest. Hurry though. I've people to see and things to do!'

She felt infinitely better as she rubbed her hair with a towel. Luckily she had her makeup bag and a fold up toothbrush with her so she did as good a job as she could in the circumstances. Her clothes smelled stale as she pulled them back on.

'Nearly ready in there?' Danny asked tapping on the door. 'Sorry to rush you, Pippa, but I've gotta shoot.'

They swapped phone numbers and Danny rummaged in his wallet.

'Here's a credit card, show me your hand and I'll write the pin number for you. Wash it off when you're done, OK?'

The short taxi ride was surreal. In one way, Pippa was on cloud nine. This was exactly what she'd always wanted. This guy was the bomb and he wanted to spend his cash on her.

Her voice of reason, however, was telling her this was only two steps away from prostitution.

As she was kissing him goodbye, her phone rang. It was Lainey. There were a pile of missed calls from Huntersbrook and from her mum, too. Knowing it would be easier to answer and say she was working, something stopped her.

She didn't trust herself not to blurt out something about Danny and her wild night. Deciding it was better not to chance it, Pippa planned to call her mother and text Lainey on Monday, saying she had an overnight work thing and had left her phone at the apartment. She knew she should be there helping. She'd already skipped last weekend, but she'd make it up to them again, she reasoned. There was so much to be done down there, it wasn't as if it'd all be done and dusted today. Besides the others loved all the activity. It gave them something to occupy their time. Unlike her, they were in need of a bit of diversion.

She didn't want to go near the department store where she

worked, so she hit the high street. All thoughts of family and Huntersbrook well and truly faded as she skipped about picking out something figure-hugging and sexy to wow Danny.

Wondering how much she could spend, she got totally lost in the game and ended up racking up a bill of several hundred euros. Suddenly unsure, she floundered and told the assistant she needed to run something by her boyfriend. Danny called before she had a chance to dial his number.

'Hey, I'm at the cash desk in Top Fashion boutique, but I've kind of binged. What's my budget?'

'There is no budget. Knock yourself out.'

'Seriously?' she giggled.

'I'm around the corner. I'll meet you there in five.' Danny hung up and she smiled at the sales assistant. As soon as she typed in the correct pin code, she licked her hand and rubbed vigorously with her thumb until the numbers faded.

Thanking the sales assistant she rushed to the door, where Danny was waiting.

'I need to go somewhere and change,' she said kissing him.

'We'll go to the Brasserie Hotel. Five star places tend to have plush bathrooms. You can change there while I order us some food.'

Pippa was relieved to find the ladies' room empty. She slipped into a roomy cubicle and changed quickly. The array of deodorants, hair sprays and creams on offer meant she could freshen up as well. She pulled out her make-up bag and touched up her face. Shoving her other clothes into the shop bag, she examined her new look. Satisfied she'd do, she found Danny.

'Jeez, you look amazing,' he said standing up from the table to kiss her. 'Please tell me you're not married or anything,' he said, looking suddenly paranoid.

'What kind of girl do you think I am?' she pouted. 'I've a good mind to walk right out of here.'

'Sorry,' he said. 'I just can't believe my luck. You're amazing. How are you single?'

Pippa softened. Danny really knew how to make a girl feel special. Their food arrived and although she hadn't eaten much in the past twenty-four hours, Pippa wasn't that hungry.

'Try to eat,' Danny encouraged. 'We're headed for another fun night. You'll be doubled over with stomach cramps if you don't get something into you.'

The bottle of white wine they shared helped with her appetite. It also perked her up considerably. The previously seedy feeling that had been creeping through her body lifted.

By the time they made their way to the trendy bar in the hotel, the hair-of-the-dog method had kicked in and Pippa was raring to go. Danny, chivalrous to the last, showed her to a high stool and ordered a bottle of bubbly.

'I should pay,' she said rooting for her credit card. 'I'm not comfortable with you doing all this.'

Danny was looking over her shoulder distractedly.

'Danny?'

'Huh?' he focused on her again.

'I said I'll pay for this. Put your money away.'

'Eh, no . . . Not at all . . . It's cool.' He nodded and waved over her head. Swivelling around she tried to see who he was engaging with.

'Put that on my tab,' Danny shouted to the barman. 'Hang tight here for a few minutes. Don't come looking for me, OK?'

'But Danny . . .'

He was gone. Pippa did as he'd asked and didn't follow him. She chatted to the barman as he poured two glasses of champagne from the bottle. The bar was filling up fast, most people were in groups hugging and air-kissing and chatting excitedly about the night ahead.

Pippa had drained her glass by the time Danny reappeared.

'Sorry, Pippa. I got caught chatting. You know the way it is?' Danny said sitting opposite her. Leaning forward, he kissed her. As soon as he picked up his glass to take a mouthful, his eye wandered to the far corner of the room. Turning around Pippa tried to follow his gaze.

'Apologies, babe. This won't take long.'

Before she could protest, Danny was gone again. This time when he returned, she pressed him for answers.

'Ah I just know a lot of people about town. It's business, that's all. I have to do the meet-and-greet thing. You know yourself?'

He was so attentive and charming when he was with her, that Pippa decided not to press Danny about his social butterfly habits.

By the time they arrived at Fire and Rain nightclub later that evening, she was more than ready for a dance.

'I have a few people to see in here and then I'm all yours,' Danny said, planting her in a booth similar to the one they'd shared the night before.

By one in the morning, Pippa was feeling like death.

'I need to get some sleep,' she said. 'I can't do this non-stop partying like you,' she grinned. 'I'm gonna head off.'

Danny looked so disappointed and begged her to stay.

'I wish I could, believe me, I'd love to stay here but like I said, I'm wrecked.'

'Here,' he said pulling a small package out of his wallet. 'This'll sort you.'

Pippa really didn't want to take any more drugs. Even though she'd done it the night before, it wasn't a scene she wanted to be part of on a regular basis.

'Thanks, but I'll pass. Why don't you come back to my place?' she suggested. 'We can chill out.'

Danny threw his head back and laughed. 'I'm not in a position to chill for quite some time,' he said. 'Haven't you noticed my eyes are popping? I'm buzzed up, baby.'

The voice in her head was screaming *no* as Pippa snorted a line of coke. Danny was so much fun and the music was so amazing that all guilt dissolved. By the time they got back to his flat in the early hours of Sunday morning, Pippa knew she needed to sleep. Peeling off her clothes, she curled up in his bed.

Moments later Danny joined her, stroking her hair tenderly and whispering sweet nothings into her ear. As Pippa drifted off, she had never been made to feel so coveted and precious.

❄

It was three in the afternoon before she finally surfaced. Danny was in the living room, working on his laptop.

'Hey, sleepy-head,' he said getting up to hug her. 'Nice sleep?'

'The best,' she said yawning. 'What time did you wake up?'

'Not long ago,' he admitted.

'What are you doing? Surely you don't work on Sundays?'

'I work every day,' he said. 'It's just a bit of bookkeeping. I like to stay on top of things.'

Pippa pottered around the kitchen and made a pot of coffee. Danny answered some text messages and finished writing in his notebook. Pulling the curtains shut, he grabbed the remote control and pressed a button.

'No way!' Pippa said giggling, as the mirror transformed into a TV.

'Cool, isn't it?' he grinned. 'I've had it for a while now, but I still get a thrill out of it.'

By four o'clock that afternoon, Pippa began to flag. She needed clean clothes and a few hours in her own bed. Her mother was probably doing her nut trying to contact her, but there wasn't a hope in hell she was going near Huntersbrook now. The thought of painting or hoofing stuff into sheds didn't appeal to her one bit. She guessed her family would be getting ready to sit down to a late Sunday lunch about now. Sadie and her mother would be fussing about as Lainey jigged Ely on her lap. The men would be discussing DIY jobs or sport. It was all so predictable and boring. Same shit, different day. Yawn.

'So I'm gonna split,' Pippa announced. 'I've a few things to sort. You know yourself . . .'

Danny instantly suggested they meet at Fire and Rain later that night, explaining he was meeting some clients.

'I won't be staying too long. I've to be in the office early in the morning. It'll just be a quick drink, if you're on for it?'

Pleased that he wanted to see her again, she decided to go with the upper hand. She gave Danny a hug and said she'd leave it for this evening, but promised to meet him again soon.

'I had the best weekend,' she crooned as he saw her out. Kissing him passionately, she wanted to make sure she left him longing for her.

'So much fun even though it was all a bit naughty,' she said.

'It's only naughty if it starts to interfere with your working life,' Danny reasoned. 'Besides, you said yourself, it was a lot of fun! Once you know how to be cool, you won't run into problems.'

Pippa nodded. It all seemed so simple when Danny put it like that. She'd only ever had a tainted and negative image of drugs. This was a whole new world for her.

She wasn't sure she would even do it again, but Pippa knew one thing was certain, she'd never forget her little dabble or the nights she and Danny had just shared.

'Don't work too hard, pretty Pippa,' he said as she pulled away from him and walked into the corridor.

She waved and walked as if she were modelling Chanel's latest collection. Knowing Danny was leaning against his doorframe staring gave her a little thrill. He was nothing like the other guys she'd dated before. This was a new and more grown-up guy. Ignoring the nagging inner voice that told her she was playing with fire, she stopped at the elevator and turned to wave. Seeing him wave back made her giggle. He was so damn gorgeous. As she stepped into the lift and the doors closed, she allowed a little gleeful *yes* escape her lips.

Lainey

MATT HAD OFFERED TO PUT ELY TO BED, SAYING he wasn't going to interfere with Jules and Lainey's chats. They'd had a delicious meal at Huntersbrook, which had led to Irish coffees and yummy chocolates.

'I know what you two are like when you get going. Us men will retire.'

'You're stuffed to the gills and I saw you having a sneaky second Irish coffee with Dad and Joey,' Lainey teased. 'You're going to conk out in our bed with Ely beside you like a little starfish while *In The Night Garden* is babbling in the background!'

'You know me too well. I admit it, I can't get enough of Igglepiggle.'

As he climbed the stairs babbling to Ely, Jules smiled. 'He's such a dote, Lainz. You're lucky to have him.'

'I know. Can you believe how different my life is now? Ugh, I was so miserable when we worked together at the council office in Dublin. I don't know how you ever befriended me!'

'Aw don't say that,' Jules said. 'You were so lovely to me when I started there. I know the others all thought I was some sort of brainless Barbie doll. You saw past my appearance and I'll always adore you for that.'

Lainey and Jules were like chalk and cheese in many ways. Jules' own description of a Barbie doll was pretty much on the button with how she looked. She was girly sweet and in many ways quite naïve. But Lainey had never met a more loyal and kind person. Lainey, in comparison, was far more conservative in style and all she'd ever wanted was to be settled down and living back in the country.

'How's Pippa?' Jules asked. 'I thought you said she was meant to be here this weekend?'

'She was,' Lainey said rolling her eyes. 'I think my parents are getting a bit fed-up with her lack of interest in helping.' Lainey bit her lip. 'Just let me text her one more time. I hope she's OK actually . . .'

Jules opened a bottle of wine and found two glasses and brought them into the living room as Lainey put her phone down.

'Any response yet?'

'No. Which is odd. Pippa usually replies instantly. I hope she's OK.'

'How has she been since the attack? I've barely seen her.'

'She's good, I think. She was very nervous for a while, I must say. She was down here most weekends and wasn't remotely interested in going out in Dublin. But it seems she's gotten over it all now.'

'It still gives me the heebie-jeebies when I think about it,' Jules said. 'I mean, taxi drivers are meant to be the safe option, right? Single girls don't go on night buses alone purely because it's not wise. Yet poor Pippa happened to find the one nutter who flipped out.'

'I know. It's scary as hell, but she was fortunate in a way that all he did was hit her. It could've been a lot worse,' Lainey said shuddering. 'I'm a bit worried about her, you know? She went from being like a scared little rabbit to having this *carpe diem* attitude of let's all live life as it comes.'

'That's a bad thing?'

'No, not if you're considering a level-headed person in the

equation. But our Pippa has always been impulsive and it usually gets her into hot water. That's who she is. Shock or no shock, I'm uncomfortable with her complete change in personality. Don't get me wrong, she's been doing so well, setting up her website and knuckling down at work. I just hope she's not drowning in it all now.'

'Maybe she's growing up and realising she needs to take responsibility for her own life?'

'Oh believe me, I'd be thrilled if that were the case,' Lainey said. 'But I know my sister and I think she's teetering on the edge at the moment. She's like a pendulum swinging. She went really high one way and was a total minx and now it seems she's gone totally the other way, channelling her saint Pippa guise. It's not sitting with me. Maybe she'll settle somewhere in the middle . . .'

'Where is she this weekend? Working?'

'No, I doubt it hugely. She didn't mention anything, so I reckon she's snapped and can't bear the goody-two-shoes act any longer. I hope she's not face-down in a pile of puke up a laneway.'

'Oh no, Lainz, don't say that,' Jules looked alarmed. 'Do you think she's in danger? Should we call the police?'

'Ah no. As we all know from Joey's accident, bad news travels fast. I reckon Pippa is fine. She's just having a blow out, if I know her. Anyway enough about Pippa, tell me about you. What's the story?'

Instantly, Jules' eyes filled with tears. 'Ugh, sorry, Lainz,' she said flapping her hands in front of her face. 'I'm an emotional wreck at the moment. I think living with my mother again has sent me over the edge. She's worse than ever.'

'Really? I thought you two had mended some bridges.'

'So did I. Otherwise I wouldn't have agreed to live there while my flat is being redecorated. But it's a nightmare. The first couple of days were lovely. We shared dinner after work and it was all very amicable. But as soon as it came to the weekend, the nasty comments started again.'

'Like what?'

'Oh the usual . . . Why can't I stop this "gay thing" and how I'd be much happier in the long run if I just married a nice man.'

'That's rich coming from her, considering she's never had a husband!' Lainey said crossly.

'Well,' Jules sighed heavily. 'That's the whole point, isn't it? Mum is so bitter about being alone that she's taking it out on me. She got quite irate the other night when I was going out to meet Sylvia. Said that I was a disgrace and she was ashamed of me. She came right up to me and said right into my face that she lies to her friends and tells them I have a boyfriend. That she'll never tell them I'm gay.'

'Oh Jules,' Lainey said, taking her hand. 'That's really narrow-minded of her. But you know it's just her own limitations that are holding her back? You can't tell her how to feel, but she's the one missing out. I wish I could grab her and shake her. She's raised the most wonderful daughter and she's too screwed up to see it.'

'Thanks, Lainz,' Jules took a big gulp of wine. 'When Sylvia said she didn't want to see me any longer, I crumbled. I stupidly told my mum and she was awful . . .' Sobs took over as Lainey's heart broke for her friend. Jules went on to explain how her mother had told her this was a sign that she needed to cop on and get over her "lesbian lark".

'How do I explain that I'm not doing this to annoy her? If I could fall in love with the boy next door and pop out some grandchildren, I'd do it. But I know I'd be miserable and she probably wouldn't be any happier with me.'

'Well I've done all of the above and my mother still treats me with disdain,' Lainey admitted.

'I know you're going to kill me now,' Jules said, holding her hand up. 'But I think Holly is a sweetheart. I'm not saying I don't feel your pain, Lainz. But your mum is a good person. She adores her family and all she wants is to be surrounded by all of you. My mother repels me like oil on water.'

Lainey hesitated for a moment. She honestly didn't want to poison Jules against her mother, but she needed someone to understand how she made her feel.

'Mum suffered with crippling postnatal depression when I was born,' Lainey explained. 'As a result Grandma minded me and you know how close we were. When Grandma died I honestly thought Mum and I had turned a corner. But she was horrendous while I was pregnant and she still treats me like a numbskull when it comes to Ely.'

'Are you sure you're not just being overly sensitive around her?' Jules asked honestly.

'Maybe I am, but I can't help the way she makes me feel, Jules. She's so different with Joey and Pippa and I can't seem to get past that.'

Jules nodded and said she understood. Not for the first time, the girls realised how lucky they were to have each other.

'Good friends are where it's at, aren't they?' Jules said as she lay back on the sofa. 'What would I do without you, Lainz?'

'I don't know and right back at ya,' she grinned. 'Hey, want to hear some exciting and slightly less depressing news before we fall up to bed?'

'Shoot!'

'Well, I have a five-year plan,' Lainey said with a grin.

'Tell me!'

'You already know I want a brood of kids, well, we've started trying again officially. I think Matt was a little reluctant at first but he's so into it all now. This place is going to burst at the seams if we don't add on, so I've an idea to build on some more bedrooms.'

'Ooh I like it! Will there be one for Auntie Jules?'

Lainey giggled and said that there'd be one for the time being, until she filled them all with babies.

'I'm glad one of us has a life that isn't a total car crash,' Jules said with a sad smile.

'Things can only get better,' Lainey said.

Jules burst out laughing. 'I used to love that song. It's true though. When you're at the bottom of the barrel, the only way is up.'

'I loved that song,' Lainey grinned. 'Maybe some night soon we'll go into Dublin and dance for five hours. What do you reckon?'

'Deal. As soon as my flat is ready we'll go out on the tiles.'

'You'd better tell the workmen to hurry up. I could have a bun in the oven very soon. I won't be any fun if I'm retching and sipping iced water!'

They finished the bottle of wine and decided to call it a night. As predicted, Lainey found Matt curled up in their bed with Ely beside him. The DVD had ended and the TV was showing a blank screen. While Jules was in the bathroom she slid Ely's cot from the spare room into theirs. Expertly, she slid her hands under Ely's warm sleeping body and lowered him into his cot. As she gazed down at his gorgeous cherubic face she felt a tiny shiver of excitement as she thought of the little brother or sister that would be joining their family soon. She hoped Ely would have as strong a bond with his siblings as she had with hers.

Fleetingly, she thought of Pippa. Lainey sincerely hoped she was OK. She'd have something to say to her when she got a hold of her. It was one thing avoiding helping, but it was quite another to ignore everybody's text messages and calls. Pippa needed to learn a bit of consideration.

As she pulled on her nightdress and climbed in beside Matt, Lainey was too tired to be angry. She fell into a delicious sleep, with dreams of babies and family occasions.

Joey

JOEY ALWAYS WOKE FEELING REFRESHED WHEN HE slept at Huntersbrook. He presumed it was the combination of fresh air and calm, but he was always on edge while in Dublin city.

'It's because you don't have to go to work,' Skye pointed out as she stretched lazily. 'I'm so glad we decided to stay here this week.'

'Me too,' said Joey. 'Oh by the way, I'll need to fly up to Dublin for the day tomorrow. It's no biggie. Just a meeting Clive says I can't miss.'

'But you booked a week off, Joey. What if we'd gone abroad?'

'Then I guess I'd miss the meeting. But we didn't go abroad, so I can go.'

Skye said she was planning a meeting with Lainey, as they needed to put the finishing touches to the website before it all went live.

'I think it's going to look really special when we're finished,' she said.

Joey pulled on a pair of old jeans and a T-shirt.

'Project Huntersbrook is going to work,' Skye said firmly. 'I feel it in my bones.'

Joey leaned over and kissed her.

'Have you much real work to do today?' he asked. The beauty of Skye's job was that she could do it anywhere once she had internet connection.

'I've a few things, but my aim is to try and take as much of the week off as possible. I want to enjoy the time with you and your family without feeling as if I've one eye on the laptop all the time.'

'OK, great. I'll see you later on. Help yourself to toast down in the kitchen. Sadie or Mum will probably be around at some stage, but there are always a few bits in the fridge.'

'Oh no, that's OK, I'm calling over to Lainey's house,' Skye said. 'I could happily stay here for the day though. It's so quiet and peaceful.'

'Oh yeah,' Joey stopped at the door. 'You know the black-tie ball for work that's coming up? I was thinking maybe you could borrow something from Lainey? It's going to be really swanky and I'd hate you to feel under-dressed. Growing up with two sisters I know what you gals are like . . .'

Skye stared at him with a look of confusion on her face.

'I have loads of clothes, Joey. I'll find something. Besides, I don't think either of your sisters' clothes would even go over my leg, let alone make me look good. You have noticed I am rather more curvy than Lainey, I take it?'

'It was only a suggestion. No worries,' he said.

Joey grinned and blew her a kiss before shooting out the door. As he bounced down the staircase, he couldn't help feeling a little uncomfortable. Skye didn't seem to be grasping the fact that the ball was going to be high-end. The girls at the office were all going to beauty salons to get their nails and make-up done. He didn't need Skye turning up looking as if she'd crawled through a time machine from Woodstock. He understood the floaty dresses she favoured were her style and usually he loved it. But there were certain times in the corporate world when a more structured dress code was required. Maybe he'd have a quiet word with Lainey again. She was fabulous at dealing with sensitive issues. Feeling better, he smiled as he heard Paddy's heavy-booted footsteps on the gravel out the front. Joey went to the front door and called him.

'Good afternoon, nice of you to join me,' said Paddy.

'It's not even nine yet, Dad,' Joey said.

'Ah you're on city time there, son. The sun has been up for a while. You'd want to make the most of the daylight. By this time next month, we'll be getting up and going to bed in the dark. Ah, the winter is pretty much upon us now.'

Joey grinned and told his father that he wasn't doing a single thing on an empty stomach, so Paddy followed him to the kitchen where they had fried eggs on toast and a mug of tea each.

'Where's your young lady?' Paddy asked.

'In the scratcher. She's off to Lainey's to finish the website in a while.'

'Super,' Paddy nodded. 'It's fantastic the way you're all pulling together on this, son. Your mother and I are so grateful. You know that, don't you?'

'We wouldn't have it any other way,' Joey assured him.

A knock at the back door was just the incentive they needed to get moving. Paddy had hired some of the local school-goers to come and do a bit of donkeywork about the place.

'They're thrilled with a few euros and they don't go in for the hourly rate nonsense,' he assured Joey. 'They do a good day's work as long as they're fed. They're all doing this transition year farce in school. Why they don't just get them studying for the final exams I've no idea. Apparently they're meant to be off out and about having a go at different jobs to see what they might like to become when they grow up.'

'I think that's a good idea,' Joey said. 'Most kids haven't the foggiest what they want to become. This way they can earn a bit of pocket money and who knows, maybe it'll give them a bit of hunger to succeed.'

'Beer money, more to the point,' Paddy chuckled. 'Whatever they do with the cash, they're a nice bunch of lads. Sadie will make a pile of sandwiches and a bucket of soup later on for them.'

❄

Once brushes were handed out and the creosote was poured into buckets, work began in earnest.

Joey decided to fire on ahead with the ride-on lawnmower.

'I'll keep the blades high and this'll be the last cutting until after the winter.'

As he fired up the mower, Pippa popped into his mind. Where on earth had she gotten to this weekend? Assuming she was with work colleagues, he didn't bother calling her.

She'd pitch up at some point. She always chose Dublin over a weekend at home. He knew that upset his parents a little, but she was single and enjoyed the impromptu nights out with her colleagues, and he could understand that.

'Hello there!' Holly called out.

Joey pulled the lawnmower to a halt as he waved to his mother.

'Morning, Mum! How did you sleep last night?'

'Very well, thank you dear.' She looked behind her and up and down the road.

'What's up?' Joey asked.

'I'm looking for your father.'

'He's creosoting the fences with the local lads. Will I give him a wolf whistle?' Joey went to lift his fingers to his mouth. His renowned whistles could be heard for miles.

'Oh no!' Holly said. 'Don't do that. I was only checking his whereabouts because I wanted to chat to you in private.'

'Really? What's up?'

'Well, I've been instructed by your father to keep my nose out of your business. And the dodgy thing is that I sort of promised I would.' She looked sheepish.

'I feel a *but* coming on.' Joey grinned.

'Um . . . but . . .' she smiled back. 'I have something I would like you to have.' Rooting in her pocket, Holly pulled out a small, slightly shabby looking, dull red velvet box. Before Joey could say another word, Holly popped it open, revealing Grandma Maggie's exquisite engagement ring. An oval, navy blue sapphire sat prettily between two sizeable ice-like diamonds.

'Wow, it's a real stunner, isn't it?' Joey did a low whistle.

'It's gorgeous,' Holly agreed. 'But it's Mummy's through and through. I never felt comfortable wearing it. I've tried it on many times and it doesn't sit with me. I grew up seeing it on her finger and I was so aware it was one of her only reminders of Daddy. So although I'd love to see it floating around again, I don't feel it's right for me to wear it, if you understand? So it's been languishing in the bottom of a drawer this past while.'

'That's a terrible shame really,' Joey said scratching his chin.

'Yes,' Holly agreed. 'Obviously I'm offering it for you to pass on to Skye.'

'Skye?' Joey was taken aback. 'But Mum, shouldn't Lainey or Pip have it?'

'Well I thought of all that of course,' Holly said. 'But how would I choose?' she reasoned. 'Lainey could have it because she's the eldest,' she said. 'Or equally Pippa could have it because she's the youngest. But Lainey has her own engagement ring and Pippa isn't really at that stage in life quite yet.'

'And you think I am?' Joey smirked. Holly nodded silently.

'Forgive me if I'm being a pushy Mum,' she said. 'I'd hate you to feel I'm being a pain. Your father told me to keep my beak out of your affairs. But I felt compelled to at least let you know I have the ring . . . should you require it,' she finished.

Joey pulled her into his arms. 'You're a star. Thank you, Mum.'

Holly looked intensely relieved. 'I'm glad you're not cross.'

'How could I be?' he asked. 'Just between you and me, I *have* been thinking of asking Skye to marry me,' he said. 'I know she's the one. I've never been so happy. I couldn't imagine my future without her in it.'

'Me neither,' said Holly. 'She fits in our family, doesn't she?'

'Certainly does.'

'Well, you know where this is if and when you decide to pop the question.'

'I might actually hold on to it, if you don't mind,' Joey said with a cheeky grin.

'I don't mind at all,' Holly said in delight. 'But you're not shoving it in a jeans pocket and mowing over it. I'll leave it in the bedside locker in your room, how's that?'

'Good plan,' he agreed. 'Just make sure Skye's not in the room, won't you? She was in bed when I left, but she's bound for Lainey's house.'

'Right, love.'

Holly waved as he started up the lawnmower once again. Joey couldn't keep the smile from his face as he put the machine into drive. His mother had always been amazing to him. Even as a teenager he didn't go through a stage where she annoyed or embarrassed him. His friends all adored her too and gladly stayed for weekends at Huntersbrook any time they were invited.

Holly didn't change for anyone and Joey admired that about her. What you saw was what you got with her. It made him so proud that when the chips were down for his parents, he was able to step up to the plate and help the family. His accident had been a nightmare, but when the compensation money came through, it was perfect timing. Just when all the talk was of selling

Huntersbrook up stepped Joey with a cheque and a plan. He hoped with all his heart that plan was going to work.

The person Joey was most grateful to, however, was Skye. She wasn't his type. Or so he'd thought. She was rather left of centre, quiet and not the girl most people would notice first.

Previously Joey had unwittingly gone for partners more like Pippa. The confident, funny, trendy party-girl sort. There were plenty of those around the Dublin clubs, all willing to dance the night away and allow him to ply them with cocktails and take them to parties. He'd been badly burnt by Sophia, though. He'd been totally blinded by her looks and charisma. But he'd learned that a bright and shiny exterior with an insatiably self-obsessed personality was not for him. When the chips were down, Sophia hadn't been there for him. Skye had.

Skye wasn't a showy girl nor did she want to go out on the town all the time. She liked the odd night out in the city lights, but she was more at ease at home.

Joey sighed happily as he continued cutting the grass. Skye was the love of his life and he couldn't wait to prove it to her.

Lainey

LAINEY SPOTTED SKYE PICKING HER WAY ACROSS
the path from Huntersbrook. Pulling the door open, she hugged
her and welcomed her inside.

'How did you sleep?' she asked.

'Like a log,' Skye said yawning. 'In fact, I found it so difficult
to get up!'

'The country air does that to you,' Lainey said. 'I used to crave
it when I lived in Dublin. Seeing as you grew up in the country
too, I'd say you're similar.'

Skye's face darkened momentarily.

'What did I say?' Lainey asked.

'Uh nothing . . .' Skye hesitated and looked up at Lainey. 'I
haven't mentioned anything to Joey just yet. But my dad has
been in touch. It seems he's not well. But he's decided he's not
going to a doctor as he feels he can cure himself with berries
and herbs.'

'Oh right . . .' Lainey wasn't sure what she ought to say. She
knew very little about Skye's family, apart from the fact that they
lived in a commune along with her uncle and aunt and several
other like-minded individuals. Lainey knew the children had been
home-schooled, which Skye had apparently hated. Eventually
they'd given in and allowed Skye and her cousin Echo to attend
mainstream school for their final years.

'My parents are free spirits and believe in the moon's phases rather than any government, or God for that matter. Doctors would be right up there with folk they don't trust.'

'Have you spoken to your mum?'

'Briefly,' Skye said. 'But it was all very sketchy, as usual. I only hear from them a few times a year. When they decide to go to a pay phone. Of course, those are disappearing at a rapid rate, so it's hard to know what's really going on there.'

'Would you think of calling to see them? I'm sure Joey would go with you. They live in the midlands, don't they?'

'Yeah,' Skye said biting her lip. 'I could get my cousin Echo to come with me, but he's even less tolerant of them than I am.' Skye and Echo had fled the commune at the first opportunity and set up home together in Dublin. Echo now worked for a graphic design and print shop and was forging a life completely separate from his family and past.

'Joey has never met my folks,' Skye admitted. 'And I'm not sure I want him to. They're bats, quite frankly,' she said sighing.

'But nice bats, I'm guessing?'

'Yeah, they're harmless and don't rely on anyone for anything. They're pretty much self-sufficient, growing their own food. They're all vegan, naturally,' Skye rolled her eyes. 'Mum and the other women make some cash by selling knitted things at markets.'

'What sort of knitted stuff?' Lainey said, smiling in spite of Skye's obvious disapproval.

'Random stuff like egg cosies and tea pot covers.'

'That's all back in vogue now, isn't it?' Lainey said. 'It might be nice to buy some things for Huntersbrook. I think guests would love little hand-knitted egg cosies to adorn their breakfasts.'

'Oh I don't know,' Skye said looking doubtful. 'You've no idea what they're like, Lainey. Really.'

Knowing Skye wasn't comfortable with the conversation, Lainey turned it to the matter in hand.

'So how's the website coming along?' she asked as a little noise from the pram made her smile. 'Hello Ely,' she crooned. 'Did you wake up?' Lainey picked him up and kissed his rosy cheek. 'He was up at the crack of dawn this morning so he nodded off just now. I'm a bit zonked to be honest. Jules and I had another bottle of wine after we left you all last night. She was up like a lark and headed up to Dublin to work. So we're all a bit tired here this morning aren't we?' she kissed Ely.

'Aw hello honey,' Skye said breaking into a smile. 'How's the best boy?'

The two women sat at the kitchen table, with Ely happily munching on a rusk.

Lainey rustled up an omelette along with toast and placed it in front of Skye while wrinkling her nose and waving her hand dramatically.

'What?' Skye asked a smirking Lainey.

'I've a feeling I might be pregnant again!'

'Really? And that's a good thing?' Skye ventured.

'Oh yeah, totally!' Lainey waved her hand again. 'I want at least four, if not five children. So I'm actually hoping this might even be twins. I have this really strong feeling I'm going to have a multiple birth.'

'You do?'

'Don't laugh,' Lainey said. 'But ages ago, Jules and I went to this woman who reads tealeaves. She's a full-on psychic and I know loads of people who swear by her . . .'

'Right,' Skye said sounding a little dubious.

'Anyway, this woman said I was going to have twins or even triplets.'

'Seriously?' Skye raised an eyebrow.

Lainey nodded emphatically. 'Matt and I have discussed having a brood of children and he's totally on for it. So fingers crossed,'

Lainey said looking really thrilled. 'I'm feeling quite nauseous, so I'd say I'm only a couple of weeks gone. But I've heard when a woman is pregnant with twins the morning sickness is way worse.'

'Either that or you're just hanging after the wine!'

'Nah, once you've been pregnant you *know.*'

'How will you all fit here at the farmhouse?' Skye wondered.

'Well, that's the thing. We'll have to build on at some point. So I'm thinking we ought to get going sooner rather than later. So I've asked Thomas Casey to drop over in a while.'

'He's the architect guy Joey went to school with, isn't he? We met him at the pub a few months back, at the beginning of the summer. Tall, thin chap with the glasses?'

'Yes, that's him!'

Ely was happy playing with some toys on the floor so the girls got down to business, knowing they'd be interrupted by Thomas at some stage.

Half an hour later, Skye was just satisfied that they were finally finished when the doorbell rang. Lainey went to let Thomas in.

'Hello, Skye,' he said as he entered the kitchen. 'Hello, little fella,' he said chucking Ely under the chin. 'He looks about a similar age to our twins.'

'You have twins?' Lainey said.

'Yeah, they've just turned nineteen months and they're a handful. A boy and a girl and they are like little demolition demons, but great craic.'

'I never even knew Niamh was pregnant,' Lainey mused.

'Ah that's because she wasn't,' Thomas said. 'We had the twins with a surrogate mother.'

'Oh gosh, I had no idea,' Lainey said blushing furiously. 'Sorry, I'm mortified.'

'Ah not at all,' Thomas laughed. 'We expected a bit of a shocked reaction to the new arrivals. Word will travel and by the time they get to school, I'm sure the world and its wife will know how they came to be ours.'

Lainey knew she couldn't turn around and tell Thomas that she was probably expecting twins right now. Instead she went for the more sensitive version of events and said they were looking to expand the house in case a little brother or sister might join them at some point.

Thomas asked if he could have a quick look around and make some notes. Lainey offered him tea, which he declined.

'I'll get going, if you don't mind? I've a few clients to see today. Thank goodness I'm pretty busy at the minute.'

'Sure, Skye and I will be here, so shout if you need anything.'

Skye was busily clicking away at her laptop getting the website on line, so Lainey allowed herself a few moments to enjoy a cup of herb tea. It tasted dreadful and the smell was worse. How could she drink this stuff and enjoy it ordinarily? Grinning, she patted her belly. There was no doubt in her mind now that she was pregnant. She was only a day late, but she prided herself on being very in tune with her body.

Besides, she'd been turned off many of her favourite things while expecting Ely, so it made perfect sense.

Thomas meandered into the kitchen a short time later brandishing an iPad.

'So here are my thoughts,' he began. 'Because this is such an old property and all the plumbing and shores are to the rear, it would cost a fortune to build on there. The best option would be to create a single-storey addition to the left of the front, just here,' he said pointing out the kitchen window.

'Would we need planning?' Lainey asked.

'If you were to build something fairly small, then no. But that's all depending on how many rooms you want to add. I'd like to make sure the new building is in keeping with the original one.

There's nothing worse than an extension that sticks out like a sore thumb.'

Thomas left, saying he'd drop over a quotation.

'You could email it to me either,' Lainey suggested. She needed to get Matt on side before drawings appeared. She also wanted to give him the great news that they actually *needed* the space now! He wasn't too brilliant with change and Lainey knew she'd have to speak to Jacob, too. He'd made it very clear that the farmhouse was as much hers as it was theirs, but all the same, she needed their blessing for all the plans she was eager to put into action. She could feel it in her bones – it was going to be a wonderful time for them next year. Huntersbrook and babies, what more could she want?

Pippa

PIPPA WOKE FEELING MUZZY AND CONFUSED. Glancing at her alarm clock, she was surprised. It was lunchtime already. She was mid-yawn before it registered in her brain that it was Monday. Cursing and almost doing herself an injury, she shot out of bed. Brianna was going to string her up. Stumbling toward the shower she grabbed the first thing she could find in the wardrobe.

Knowing she hadn't time to wash her hair, she pulled it into a high knot on the top of her head and dashed to the shower for a swift wash.

She was dressed and made-up in record time. Snatching her phone and handbag she rushed out onto the main road and flagged a taxi, a luxury she rarely allowed herself.

'Drive as fast as you can,' she begged the driver. 'You could be looking at a newly unemployed girl.'

The driver chuckled and shot off up the bus lane at high speed.

By the time she reached her office, switched her computer on and attempted to catch her breath, Pippa was in a state. What was she going to say to Brianna? A light knock at her door was followed by Missy's head. Groaning inwardly, Pippa put on her best smile.

'Hey, Missy. How's it going?'

'Good. Brianna and I are literally just back from that stupid fashion shoot. Apparently it'll generate a whole heap of publicity, but it was damn boring. In this tatty-looking warehouse with no heating and actual holes in the walls. Ugh, I can't imagine how couture clothes can possibly look good against such an awful backdrop, but the stylist was super excited about it all.'

'Yes, of course! I was wondering all morning where you two were and it totally slipped my mind,' Pippa lied seamlessly. She'd totally forgotten they'd be out that morning. Relaxing slightly, she thanked her lucky stars she'd gotten away with her sleeping beauty stunt.

'So, I was wondering if you're around tonight? Seeing as we're going to be business trip buddies, I thought we could have a little bonding sesh tonight?'

Pippa blinked, trying to think of a nice way of saying no. She could just about tolerate Missy. She knew it made perfect business sense to be in with the boss's daughter, but she was seriously annoying. While she'd never actually done anything to Pippa per se, it was common knowledge the girl only had a job because her Daddy owned the department store and she was a perfect example of what happened to Verucca Salt from *Charlie and the Chocolate Factory* twenty years on.

'Ugh, I'd love to see you, Missy. But I'm supposed to be going to Wicklow for a family evening,' she said.

'But you can do that anytime,' Missy said. 'I've got VIP passes for Fire and Rain nightclub. They're doing a champagne promo tonight and it's going to be the bomb.'

Pippa was just about to say she'd pretty much camped at Fire and Rain all weekend, but stopped herself when she saw Brianna approaching.

'It sounds like super fun,' Pippa said cheerfully, coming to the conclusion it'd be a seriously bad PR move *not* to go with Missy.

'Yay! You rock, Pippa. See you later. Toodles!'

As Missy was about to leave, Brianna marched right up to Pippa's desk.

'Hi Brianna, so how was the shoot? I'm in the middle of a design. It's been driving me crazy all morning . . .'

'Next time,' Brianna said sternly, 'next time you are leaving work early, have the decency to remember *not* to post photographs of yourself along with cocktails on Facebook.'

Oh shit, thought Pippa. She was well and truly goosed. Why on earth had she done that? She wasn't normally so stupid. Besides that was two weeks ago.

'I'm not on Facebook much but I decided to check in while we were in the taxi just now. I might not be that savvy with social media but I know when I've been lied to.'

'Brianna, I can explain . . . I went home and took painkillers on the Friday in question. I . . . I went to bed and slept, but it was my flatmate's birthday and I couldn't let her go alone so I . . .'

'Save it, Pippa. I'm not as stupid as you clearly think I am. Chalk it down. You're on thin ice with me. I don't like being made a fool of. Either cop on or cop out. Which is it to be?'

Pippa swallowed. Brianna was bloody scary at the best of times, but when she was annoyed . . .

'There won't be any more mix-ups,' Pippa said lamely.

Brianna didn't reply, instead she strode from the room, muttering and shaking her head.

It was just Pippa's luck to get into a mess like this with a business trip on the horizon. The prospect of spending two days and nights with Brianna hating her filled her with dread. Glancing to the right, Pippa realised Missy was still hovering. As Pippa was beginning to panic in case Missy reported the whole incident to her father the other girl rolled her eyes and stomped back over to her desk and leaned in close to Pippa's ear.

'Don't mind her, she's a total dragon. We'll give her the slip in Paris. You and me against the world, kiddo,' Missy said. She winked and spun on her Gucci heel and departed in a waft of expensive cologne.

Thanking her lucky stars they were having a night out this evening, Pippa was delighted to have Missy on side. If the boss's daughter liked her, Brianna would have to play ball.

Her mobile rang. Pippa sighed.

'Pippa, where on earth have you been?' Holly said crossly.

'Hey Mum,' she said holding her nose. 'I'm sorry I didn't call. I was stuck at a work promotion. The one I told you about? Yeah, then I've been in bed. I felt like I was coming down with a stinking cold so I literally hibernated yesterday. I meant to call earlier.'

'Oh,' Holly said. 'I didn't know you were doing a promotion.'

'I *did* tell you,' Pippa insisted rather convincingly.

'Oh sorry, love. I must have forgotten. I'm getting very remiss in my old age,' Holly chuckled. 'Will we see you next weekend so?'

'I'll do my best, Mum,' she said, still holding her nose. 'I have the Paris trip this week, so I'm not sure what state I'll be in by the weekend.'

'All the more reason to come home and spend some time in the fresh air.'

'I'll see Mum, yeah?' Pippa didn't want to get irritated with her mother but sometimes she really got on her wick.

'All right then,' Holly said sounding disappointed. 'Well stay warm and if you're feeling worse, just call. I could always come up for a little visit with Daddy tomorrow if you like? Bring you some chicken noodle soup?'

'Ah no, you stay put and don't worry about me. Talk to you soon. Gotta go.'

Pippa hung up feeling guilty. Turning her attention to her work, she knew she'd better sort some of the new designs she'd promised Brianna. Luckily, she'd had some strong ideas which she hoped her boss would like.

Totally engrossed, Pippa didn't notice the afternoon flying by. Pressing the Print button, she looked over the new pitch before slotting it all into a clear plastic sleeve. Rushing to catch Brianna before she left, she handed her the work.

Wordlessly, Brianna flicked through the pages.

'I'm impressed,' she said. 'These are so edgy. You've outdone yourself with this, Pippa. Every now and again I wonder why I employed you and then you pull this kind of stuff out of the bag and I remember. I really appreciate the hard work you've clearly put in. To this and to the Beau Chausseur job last week.'

'Hey, I'm just doing my job,' Pippa said smiling sweetly. 'About the Facebook thing . . .'

'Let's forget it,' Brianna said sighing heavily as she gazed at Pippa's work. 'Onwards and upwards, yeah?'

'Cool. See you tomorrow,' Pippa said, breathing a sigh of relief. Her job was a snitch. Brianna seemed to think it was rocket science coming up with new and fresh campaigns each season. But Pippa could do it with her eyes shut. She knew she could probably work a bit harder and secure an even better job in London or Paris. But right now, she was enjoying the work-fun balance too much to make any changes.

❄

Missy waved and squealed as she tottered on sky-high heels toward her.

'Ready?'

'Can you give me five minutes?' Pippa asked. 'I need to do a bit of a patch job on my make-up.'

Pippa locked herself in the ladies' and stared in the mirror.

She looked rough. Her eyes were dull and lifeless and her skin was the colour of putty.

Smoothing on some BB cream and a good shading of eye shadow she thanked God for the invention of make-up. Bright lipstick was the final touch. Stepping back to look in the mirror, she wasn't overly thrilled by how haggard she looked, but she'd have to do.

Missy was full of beans and chatted non-stop during the ten-minute journey to Fire and Rain.

'I don't know how you can walk in those heels,' Pippa said. 'They're gorgeous, but I know I'd end up in a cast with a broken ankle.'

'Oh I'm the opposite to most people, I can't walk in flats.'

Missy twittered on until they were greeted by a bouncer.

'Back again, Missy,' he said. 'Ah, it's yourself,' he said smiling at Pippa and nodding in recognition. She blushed and said a hurried hello. Luckily for Pippa, Missy was on a mission to find someone and wasn't in the least bit interested in her discomfort or the fact the bouncer had recognised her.

'You're such a doll for accompanying me tonight. I have my eye on this guy. His family own the Irish Fiddle pub chain and he's such a laugh.'

'Have you been dating?' Pippa asked, suddenly wondering if she was about to be either dumped or made to play gooseberry all night.

'No,' Missy said, 'sadly we've only spied one another, but I have it under good authority he's going to be here tonight. *And* he apparently thinks I'm cute.'

They were waved into the VIP entrance and although it was relatively early, the place was already filling up. Pippa sighed as she was offered a flute of bubbly. Down the hatch, she thought, feeling as if she were in the movie *Groundhog Day*. If champagne didn't cure her, nothing would. Oddly, she was barely able to stomach it. Even the smell made her retch.

Missy grabbed her hand and yanked her into the midst of the crowd. There was a huge kerfuffle as girls surged toward one person in particular.

'Oh my God! Is that the guy from those cult movies who did the crazy naked streak down the Champs-Elysées recently?' Pippa hissed.

'The very one,' Missy answered as she expertly elbowed her way into the centre of the throng. Pippa had to hand it to her, Missy was not used to taking a back seat and certainly wasn't backwards about coming forwards.

Before long the girls were stationed beside the movie star and his entourage. They even managed to muscle their way onto two of the precious high stools.

'Fancy meeting you here,' said a voice from over her shoulder. Pippa swivelled on her stool and came face to face with Danny.

'Hi,' she said surprising herself at how pleased she felt to see him. 'How are you?'

'Great, thanks,' he nodded. 'Hi Missy. How are things?' he asked, smiling brightly as he tugged her over enough to kiss her cheek.

'Better now you're here,' she said winking. 'So you two know one another I take it?' she grinned. 'Pippa, you devil. I'd never have guessed,' Missy giggled. 'Or maybe I did. I *knew* we were kindred spirits for more reasons than one.' Missy swatted her arm playfully.

Not wanting to show her confusion, Pippa giggled and shrugged her shoulders.

'Missy and I work together,' Pippa explained. 'We're going on a business trip with my direct boss this week.'

'Cool,' Danny said nodding. 'I didn't realise you work for the Hassett empire, Pippa.'

'Yup,' she said raising her eyebrows. 'And I'd love to continue working there for some time to come.'

'Oh don't worry about that,' Missy piped up. 'I'll make sure Daddy knows what an asset you are. We'll use the Paris trip as an example. If I'm good at nothing else in this life, I know I can shop. How hard can it be, buying stuff for two days?'

'I'm actually pretty darn fabulous when it comes to shopping,' Pippa said. 'So we'll make a great team.' Suddenly feeling a lot less nauseous, Pippa swiped a fresh flute of champagne from a passing tray. Missy and Danny followed suit.

'Drink up while it's free,' Danny winked. 'Not that we'll die of thirst later either.'

'Not on my watch,' Missy shrilled. 'So first things first,' she said, slipping Danny a wad of notes. In one swift movement he inserted the cash in the inside pocket of his jacket and pressed a tiny package into Missy's waiting palm.

'Save our seats, I can't stand being squashed when this place gets thronged,' Missy ordered.

'Not yet at least,' Danny laughed. 'Once you're powdered up you won't care how many bodies are squashed up against you.'

'Touché!' Missy giggled. 'Come on, Pippa. Don't sit gaping at me. There's no time to waste!'

Pippa found herself catapulted into the same cubicle as Missy in the plush, dimly lit bathrooms.

'Roll up a note and I'll get cutting,' Missy instructed.

'Well, I actually don't think I'll bother,' Pippa said. 'I had a couple of late nights over the weekend. I'm in the shits with Brianna as it is. I've to play it cool until we get this buying trip over and done with.'

'Oh sod her,' Missy said. 'She's got a chip the size of Everest on her shoulder. She's just jealous because you're younger, more beautiful and living life on the edge. Daddy thinks she's a genius, but as I told you earlier, I think she's a dragon.'

Pippa felt immeasurably grateful that Missy was taking her side.

Looking down at the cistern of the toilet, Pippa was impressed. Missy was in a hurry and seemed to be very au fait with this drill. In no time she'd used her credit card to chop up the white powder and arrange it into neat lines.

'We'll have two each for starters, yeah?' she asked, looking wide-eyed with anticipation.

'Sure,' Pippa heard herself saying. 'But only if I can give you some money towards this. I don't want you thinking I'm a sponger.'

'Ah don't sweat it, Pipps. You can buy a bottle of bubbles or something. I'm just so grateful you came out with me tonight.'

'Who do you normally hang around with?' Pippa asked.

'A gang from school, but they're all away or doing boring couple stuff. So many of them are getting married. They're dropping like flies.'

'I know what you mean,' Pippa agreed as she leaned in and copied Missy. She was still terrified of the coke thing. Besides she'd been hammered each time she'd done it before, so she honestly didn't trust herself to do it right.

'Wow,' she said, relieved she'd managed the snorting without spluttering and making a total eejit of herself.

'Yeah, seriously good shit, isn't it? So clean and pure.'

'Totally,' Pippa said, grateful she hadn't sounded foolish.

'Danny's the most reliable guy I've found. There are so many scumbags around lately. I only buy from him unless I'm totally desperate.'

Pippa computed the information and remembered to close her mouth. So Danny was a dealer? Surely not? He wasn't a gouger. He spoke nicely and was dapper and well dressed. He was articulate and funny. He had a job. He'd been to university. People like him weren't drug dealers surely?

'How long have you known Danny?' Pippa asked.

'Um . . .' Missy flushed the toilet and smiled. 'Just in case there's anyone in the bathroom, you know it's always better to play the game and pretend we were peeing!'

'Oh yeah!' Pippa smiled back. 'So how long did you say you know him?'

'About two years,' Missy said. 'Yeah, it must be that. You?'

'I only met him recently,' Pippa said.

'He's a nice guy, but I wouldn't want to hang around with him or anything,' Missy said, pulling the door open and strutting back towards the bar.

Pippa was totally confused. This didn't fit. She needed to talk to Danny. She figured this was probably just a small-time weekend thing where he bought stuff from a mate and supplied a few people he knew well.

As they were handed yet another glass of champagne and the music seeped into her bones, Pippa forgot to feel puzzled about Danny. He'd kept their seats but as soon as they arrived back, he'd waved and grinned and said he'd see them later. The dry ice and laser lights swallowed him as the girls got down to some serious fun.

Pippa had never felt better. Well, at least not since the last time she was this wasted the other night.

'I adore your dress, Missy,' she said impulsively, leaning over to hug her. 'You must have the most enviable wardrobe *ever.*'

'I have tons of dresses,' she agreed. 'But the sheen kind of wore off a while back,' she admitted. 'I'm not as thick as people think,' she said dryly. 'I know most of them look at me as if I'm some spoilt brat.'

Pippa was going to wave her hand and tell her that wasn't true. But she felt a sudden confidence to say what she thought.

'A lot of people *do* think that,' she began, wondering what on earth was coming from her mouth. 'But feck the begrudgers. They're just jealous of you and haven't gotten to know the real you.'

'Aw thanks, Pipps. Well I can tell you for nothing that Brianna despises me,' Missy rolled her eyes. 'She totally hates me.'

'Yeah, I think she hates me too,' Pippa grinned. 'Great that we're going to Paris together, eh? I'll have your back and you have mine. We'll be just fine.'

Missy squealed and tottered toward her and looped her skinny arms around Pippa's neck. 'We're going to be BFF's from here on in. I can just tell . . . You can be my bridesmaid and oh . . . godmother to my child.'

'No way! When are you getting married?'

'Oh not yet. I'm not even dating. I'm just saying you *will* be all those things.'

'Well when ever you decide. You need to have your wedding at Huntersbrook, our house. It's going to be the dog's once it opens to the public. When I say it'll be the coolest venue from here to Vegas . . . I mean it's gonna rock it.'

'Deal,' Missy said, looking thrilled about the non-existent wedding plan.

The night was better than Pippa had ever imagined. They got so much attention from men it was a joke. At one point Pippa went to the bathroom to check her make-up. Staring at her reflection, she scrutinised her face. She wasn't bad looking. Her hair was pretty fabulous at the moment. That mocha colour the hairdresser had suggested was actually gorgeous.

Once she'd fixed her eye shadow and reapplied her lipstick, Pippa sauntered back to find Missy, feeling as if she could take on the world.

'You're looking hot,' a voice said from behind her.

Pippa spun around to face Danny.

'Aren't you busy dealing, Danny-boy?' she asked, with a little more sneer in her voice than she'd intended.

'Hey,' he said as his smile faded. 'I didn't see you objecting to my extra-curricular activities as you downed the bubbly and filled your nostrils this weekend.'

He looked her up and down angrily and walked off. Her heart was pounding in her chest as Pippa chased after him through the crowded nightclub. Grabbing the back of his shoulder she stopped him.

'I'm sorry, Danny. Don't go. I was just shocked earlier when Missy told me what you do. As you well know,' she cupped her hands around his ear so nobody else would hear, 'Friday night was the first time I've done any of this stuff . . . I'm not up on the scene. I didn't think a guy like you would be doing . . . this,' she finished sweeping her hand.

He led her to the side of the club where there happened to be a couple of free tables. He motioned for her to sit.

'I work in computers during the day as I told you,' he said. 'Up until recently I earned a pittance, even though I have a degree in computer science. I wanted more, Pippa. I'm like you. I'm hungry for success. This is merely a bit of weekend work. It's fun, harmless and means I can have the lifestyle I deserve having graduated from college and played by the rules my entire life.'

Pippa nodded. It made so much sense as she looked into Danny's eyes. So why was that bloody niggling voice in the back of her mind whispering that it wasn't *really* OK? As Danny cupped her face in his hands and kissed her, Pippa's previous protests seemed petty.

'I'm sorry,' she said suddenly. He looked so desolate.

'I really thought we connected,' he said, raising his hand to stroke her hair. 'Fine, what I do isn't something I'm proud of. But it's a stopgap. It won't be forever.' She nodded. 'I really like you, Pippa.'

She couldn't help leaning in and kissing him again.

'I really *really* like you too,' she said. 'But I . . .'

'Shush,' he said placing a finger on her lips. 'We'll work out the details another time.' He took her into his arms and although the music was at a similar tempo to a jack-hammer, he swayed her gently from side to side.

'You're cool,' he said.

'You're cute,' she responded.

'You're amazing,' he said.

'You're killing me!' she laughed.

'Pippa . . . will you go out with me?' he asked looking suddenly shy.

She actually thought she was going to collapse. 'Yes,' she whispered. 'Are you my boyfriend now?'

He nodded and grinned. They kissed and danced, in a world of their own until the main lights came on. He took off his jacket and draped it over her shoulders and pulled her over to where Missy was busy doing shots with a group.

'We're off, you coming?' he asked.

'Nah, we're going to Jimmy's. He's got decks and we're having a party,' Missy said.

'You OK if I split?' Pippa asked.

She couldn't have been more delighted to be dumped by Missy. As she flagged a taxi and pulled Danny in with her, Pippa knew she was smitten.

Holly

THE FOLLOWING MORNING HOLLY AND PADDY
were enjoying a light breakfast at the gate lodge, when the landline
rang.

Paddy scrambled to his feet. 'Ah good morning, Sadie,' he said
cheerfully. 'I might have guessed it was you. Hardly anyone has
this number and the children never call it. It's all texts with silly
cartoon pictures of a yellow man with his tongue out or a glass
of beer. Why don't you come and have a cup of tea with us? It's
glorious here.'

'Would that suit you, Paddy? I don't want to intrude but I'm
taking part in the final fete before the Christmas one at the
village. I told do-gooder-Gloria I'd man the cake stall. Holly said
she'd do a few buns for me.'

'Right you are,' Paddy said with a grin. 'The buns are here
cooling and I've been told I'm not allowed eat them before my
breakfast. You'd think at my age I could have what I want! Still
if they're ear-marked for do-gooder-Gloria, I'd better not touch
them.'

They were all terribly fond of do-gooder-Gloria and she did
marvellous work within the community, but the woman was a
force to be reckoned with. Holly took the phone and chatted
for a few minutes. 'There'll be plenty of buns,' she assured Sadie.
'Or cup cakes as I'm meant to call them now! I didn't commit

to a stall, but I did promise to come and lend a hand where ever I'm needed.'

The two women chatted for a while longer before Holly put the phone down with a smile.

'No doubt Gloria will be running the event like clockwork,' Paddy said. 'Crusader with a clip-board that woman.'

'I worried about Sadie after Mummy died. She's on her way over by the way,' Holly said wistfully. 'It must be scary as hell when all your contemporaries start dropping like flies.'

'Yes,' said Paddy. 'And swiftly you and I are elevating toward "elderly" status. We're almost at the top of the barrel you and I.'

'Speak for yourself,' Holly said. 'I'm still a young slip of a thing in my own mind. I might even remove all the mirrors from the gate lodge so I can continue to fool myself.'

'Ah that'd be a travesty,' Paddy said. 'Why wouldn't you want to see your beautiful reflection?'

Paddy filled their cups with fresh tea and Holly gazed at him. He'd always remained steady, her Paddy. Even when she'd suffered with postnatal depression and they'd gone through that annus horribilis with the house, Paddy hadn't faltered. He'd accepted the idea of living at the lodge without so much as a blink of the eye. He'd told her relentlessly that she wasn't to consider him in any of the decisions.

'So long as you're happy, I will be too. I'll go with the flow, you know me.'

It was still strange without Maggie. She'd been such a formidable presence, yet they'd all adored her.

As she thought of Lainey, Holly smarted. Much as she tried, she couldn't shake the feeling that she and her eldest child would never be anything other than civil to one another at best. She was still feeling unusually pensive when Sadie arrived moments later. Paddy had gone off with his pliers to fix a bit of fencing.

'Hello, love,' Sadie said kissing her and patting her back the way she'd always done. Holly placed a cup of tea in front of her and perched on a high stool.

'Penny for your thoughts,' Sadie said.

'Well there's a redundant phrase,' Holly said with a tired smile.

'Fine, cent for your thoughts,' Sadie corrected. She smiled and reached over and stroked her hand.

'I'm thinking about Lainey. She must miss Mummy even more than I do. They were more like mother and daughter than grandma and grandchild,' she mused. 'Mummy would've loved Ely . . .'

'Indeed she would,' Sadie said, clearly choosing to ignore the previous statement.

'I was thinking we might offer Lainey and Matt a dinner out. They've done an astonishing amount of work on the business and I think it would be a welcome treat. We could offer to have Ely for the night.'

'That's a lovely idea,' Sadie said.

Holly was miles away. Biting her lip she looked up at Sadie with tears in her eyes. 'Would you put it to her? She might agree if it comes from you.'

'Sure. But try not to look so down-trodden, love. I'm sure you and Lainey will find a common ground over time.'

'You don't mind if I don't hold my breath, do you?' She gave a shuddering sigh. 'I'd love the opportunity to spend more time with Ely. He's a little angel. But it's so hard not to feel hurt by how little Lainey rates me.'

'What do you mean?'

'Sadie, she barely allows me to hold him. I know I was a mess when she was a baby. But I was crippled by postnatal depression. I couldn't help it.'

'I know, love,' she said patting her hand gently. 'I remember. Sure wasn't I there?'

'I can't help feeling that Lainey is punishing me now. It wasn't as if I left her screaming in a cot. I knew Mummy was minding her. You were there too. I didn't mean any harm, Sadie. I simply couldn't cope.'

'Of course you didn't mean any harm, love. None of your children could ever say they weren't loved. Between you, me, your mother and Paddy they were doted on. I suspect Lainey's reluctance to let you mind Ely is more down to first-time mother's overprotectiveness. That's OK too. She needs to find her feet. Perhaps if she has another little one, she'll have less time for fussing over Ely.'

'I suppose you're right,' Holly said. 'I can almost hear Mummy telling me to buck up and stop worrying unnecessarily,' she said as she smiled bravely. 'Let me rephrase that. You *are* right. Things will work out for the best.'

All of a sudden it was as if a dam had burst in Holly's heart. Big fat tears began to course down her cheeks and she became engulfed in sobs.

'Hey,' Sadie said getting to her feet. 'Let it out, my girl . . .' She rubbed her back and said nothing more.

'Look at me! Crying like a school girl. I'm a grandma and I'm behaving ridiculously.'

'You're never too old to cry,' Sadie said. 'Besides, you were very ill all those years ago. Don't underestimate the power of postnatal depression, Holly. You were like an empty shell. It was heartbreaking for Maggie and me to watch. You used to try so hard to hide it.'

'I didn't think I'd tried enough.'

'Oh believe me you did. You used to go through the motions and force a smile on your face. But your mother and Paddy and

I knew you were feeling dead inside. Lainey was a good baby, God bless her. But she was a baby none the less. Like any other she required undivided attention 24/7. You weren't in a position to provide it. Simple as.'

'You know, if I hadn't had Joey and Pippa, I would've lived out my days convinced it was all my fault. That I'm simply a terrible mother with no maternal instincts and no ability to love my own offspring.'

'Of course that's not the case,' Sadie said gently.

'No. I realised that when Joey came along,' she said staring off into the middle distance.

'Well you got the help you needed at that point, thank God. The doctors were much more in tune with those things and they recognised postnatal depression as being an illness.'

'For a long time I hated myself,' Holly mused. 'I couldn't look in the mirror without seeing a total failure. I will never forget the pain and emptiness. It was pure torture, Sadie.'

'I can only try to imagine. It wasn't easy for those around you either. Paddy is a rock steady man. He never wavered once. He never gave out about you or grumbled that you were hard to reach. Because you were, love. You changed from a can-do kind of girl to a sullen and sad little creature.'

'I wasn't exactly little back then,' Holly shot back. 'I piled on the weight while I was pregnant with Lainey. Then all the sitting about feeling numb meant I was eating food as fuel and not burning it off.' Shuddering she sighed deeply. 'It was without a shadow of doubt the worst time of my life.'

'I'm sure it was,' Sadie said kindly. 'But it's fantastic that you were able to crawl back. You should be proud of yourself. It can't have been easy to venture into another pregnancy. Now that we're talking about it, you must've been terrified.'

'Oddly enough, I found the time of Joey's birth incredibly

freeing. I had the medication I required straight after the birth so I was able to bond with him. God, I thought he was the most wonderful thing on earth. In a way I reckon he helped fix me.'

'So you've forgiven yourself for your bout of depression then?' Sadie asked.

'Yes Sadie, I think I have. It took me a long time to do that though. If I'm honest, it only really happened when Pippa was born. I still remember that final push as she was delivered. I prayed she'd be another boy.'

'Why?'

'Because I felt I wasn't good at girls . . . I'd made such a botch of things when Lainey was a baby . . . And she was Mummy's in many respects. Joey and I were close and I knew that no matter what, he'd always come running to me. I was his sun, moon and stars and that felt so good . . .'

'So when you knew Pippa was a girl?'

'Ugh, I used to physically shake if I was in the room on my own with her. For about the first two weeks I was terrified . . . But she was such a little angel. She fed when she was meant to, slept from six weeks of age and did all the doe-eyed gazing at me that Joey had done. So I knew I'd got it right with her too.'

'I'm glad you felt able to put those demons to rest,' Sadie said. There was silence for a few moments as both women were lost in their own thoughts.

'Can I ask you something?' Sadie said.

'Sure.'

'Have you forgiven Lainey?'

'For what?'

'For being the one who happened to be born first. Because clearly it wasn't her fault that you ended up with postnatal depression. But that's the way it happened, right? So do you forgive Lainey for being the unwitting catalyst in your depression?'

Holly gasped. She'd never thought of it that profoundly. Her immediate instinct was to poo-poo Sadie and tell her she was being a fool. Of course she didn't *blame* Lainey. Did she?

Skye

SKYE WAS SWEEPING THE DOORSTEP WHEN PADDY arrived. Autumn was well and truly in full swirl. The trees along the avenue had transformed from shades of sage to a symphony of burnt orange, fiery reds and murky browns. The last of the leaves were fluttering to earth, making rusty piles. The damp chill in the air had encouraged Skye to pull on her puffa coat over her pyjamas.

'Hello, dear,' Paddy said smiling. She hugged him.

'Morning, Paddy. How are you today? Excuse my attire.'

'I've seen worse,' he chuckled. 'I'm well, thanks,' he said.

'Will you come in and I'll get you a mug of tea?'

'Sure,' he said. 'I need to nip inside to Joey as well.'

'Oh he's not here,' Skye said. She hadn't meant to sound so sad.

'Really?' Paddy gazed at her. 'I thought he had the week off?'

'Um,' she said. 'So did I. But it seems Clive couldn't do without him today. So he's gone . . .'

'Ah, he did mention it to me now that I think of it.'

'He didn't tell me until this morning,' Skye said.

'I'm always putting my foot in it,' Paddy began. 'Especially with you girls. I have a habit of saying things I shouldn't. Holly gets terribly cross with me,' he grinned. 'But you seem very down, pet. Is everything alright?'

Skye heard her own sobs before she even realised she was crying.

'Oh dear, I'm sorry. I'm being such a nit-wit.' She put the sweeping brush down and flapped her hands in front of her face. 'My God, where did that come from?' She forced a giggle through her tears. Using the cuff of her coat she wiped her eyes roughly, willing the tears to dry up.

'There now,' Paddy said pulling her into a bear hug. 'Let's get you inside and we'll make some nice hot tea and see if we can get to the bottom of all this.'

Skye nodded and followed him. Chewing the inside of her cheek, she tried to remain calm. But the damn tears kept coming. As they sat at the warm Aga in the kitchen, she watched as Paddy set about making tea and toast.

'It's so lovely to have a fatherly man in my life,' she said sadly. 'I get on better with you and Holly than I ever did with my own parents.'

'I'm glad you feel comfortable with us,' Paddy said. 'We think of you as one of our own, too.'

'I never knew what a proper family life was like until I came to Huntersbrook. I remember the first time I stepped into this very kitchen. It was a hub of activity with Holly and Sadie orchestrating a fantastic Sunday lunch.'

'My favourite,' Paddy said patting his round tummy.

'I was instantly drawn into the sense of camaraderie. The fun and easy banter between you all was mesmerising. But what really struck me was how much you guys adore one another. You asked each other questions . . . You were interested in what had gone on that week. Who had met who and how work was going, what was planned for the week ahead. It was like being in a movie for me.'

'It was? Why was that now?' Paddy asked, taking care to keep his gaze fixed on the teapot and the buttering of the toast.

Skye sighed. 'My parents are free spirits. That sounds like it should be warm and tender, right? Well it roughly translates as a bunch of adults who behave like selfish teens without so much as an inkling of responsibility or regard for their kids.'

'I'm sorry to hear that, love,' Paddy said looking flummoxed.

'Sorry, Paddy,' she said smiling. 'I don't know what's come over me today. I think I'm having some sort of a mental breakdown. I'll be fine. I'll stop acting like a lunatic now, promise.'

They both sat down and he poured their tea and looked thoughtful for a while.

'It never really strikes me that Holly and I have lived in a sort of cocoon here at Huntersbrook. But we have . . . In a way we could be accused of having our own little commune right here.'

'No, Paddy,' she shook her head. 'It's totally different. You've both been here for all your children's lives, but you join in with community events. You host parties all the time. Your children bring friends in and out of here. You're nothing like my parents. Besides, you know your children and want them around.'

Skye sipped the tea and gazed around the kitchen. This was such a welcoming space. The notice board in the corner was still crammed with notes, childhood drawings and reminders going back years. Ely's scribbly first attempts at art were adding to the memories. Even with just the two of them sitting at the table, it felt like a family gathering.

'But what has you so down today?' Paddy asked gently. 'Is it Joey?'

'I don't think so,' Skye said, feeling stupid that she couldn't decipher her own emotions. 'I think maybe it's because I know my dad isn't well. And I know he won't do anything constructive about it. I just feel so . . . helpless. Maybe it's getting older, you know, I'm thinking about my parents differently, thinking of the future without them, that sort of thing.'

Paddy nodded, then he smiled at her. 'Only one cure for sad

thoughts,' he said, 'and that's to fill up your day. There's a cake sale going on at the village today. Sadie is doing a stall and Holly is helping out. If you fancy a walk about later, we could drop down and lend our support.'

'That sounds nice,' Skye said.

'I'd really appreciate the company. Holly and the ladies will be fussing and I'll be left like a spare part . . .'

Skye smiled over at him. 'In that case I'd be delighted to accompany you. Thank you, Paddy.' There was an awkward silence and Skye couldn't help smiling to see the blush creeping up Paddy's neck.

'You know what,' she said, saving him from any more of this talk, 'I think I'll go for a walk. Joey and I shared a bottle of red wine last night after you all left and I'm feeling wretched.'

'Ah, hangovers are a demon. Fresh air will do you good.'

The sound of the kitchen door opening made them look around. Matt walked in with Ely in his arms.

'Hello, son!' Paddy said taking the baby and kissing him.

'Lainey said she'll be over shortly, Skye. Would you mind taking Ely for a few minutes? I need Paddy to give me a lift with some plants out the front.'

'Of course,' Skye said. 'We'll play here until Lainey comes.'

The distraction of Ely was just what she needed. His happy chirping and delight in finding the toys he always played with lifted her spirits no end. By the time Lainey arrived, she was feeling much better.

❄

Up in Dublin, at the office, Joey was thoroughly enjoying the presentation he was making. As he rounded off, he could tell the prospective clients were impressed. Clive gave him a discreet nod as he sat back down.

'I've no doubt you gentlemen have spoken to other accountancy firms, but I can assure you the service and level of expertise you will find here is second to none.'

Joey resisted the urge to leap about like a jack-in-the-box as the clients told them there and then they would like to work with him. This deal was worth in excess of three hundred thousand a year to the firm. They chatted for a few more minutes before the clients stood up to leave.

'We'll have the contract drawn up and couriered to you as soon as possible.'

'We'd like to have this on our desks by Friday.'

'I can sort that,' Joey said confidently. 'Welcome aboard. You won't regret this.'

As the client pumped Joey's hand up and down, he clapped him on the shoulder.

'I love the energy you bring to the table, Joey. You're an asset to this company. I hope Clive here is paying you well.'

'I've actually just been offered a partnership,' Joey said. 'Which I haven't had time to accept officially.' Joey glanced sideways at Clive, hoping he hadn't said the wrong thing. Clive gave him another quick nod.

'Good on you. We look forward to seeing that paperwork by Friday.'

As the men shut the door behind them, Clive loosened his tie and sat down.

'Good work, Joey,' he said. 'And I'm delighted you're accepting our offer.'

'Not as delighted as I am,' Joey said with a grin. 'This is just the type of account I need to really get stuck into. Hey, I hope you didn't mind me divulging the news, but I figured it seemed appropriate.'

'This is what I like most about you, Joey,' Clive said. 'You trust your instincts and go with them. Obviously we can't ever allow private business matters to be divulged, but letting those guys know you're a permanent, highly thought of partner was spot on.'

'Cheers,' Joey said beaming.

'The Christmas ball in a couple of weeks will be a good opportunity for you to schmooze this lot too. Get your PA to send them a set of invitations from you. In fact, offer them a table for ten.'

'Good plan,' Joey said. 'I'm going to get going on that paper-work right away. I'll deliver it all personally on Friday.'

'Excellent,' Clive said. 'And for my part, I'll get *your* paperwork sorted too. Welcome to the firm, partner!'

Joey was elated as he strode to his office. He ordered a soup and salad from his PA and instructed her to have the invitations sent to the client. Glancing at his watch he realised he'd probably be here until at least seven. But that couldn't be helped. Skye would be stoked when he told her the news. He was about to call her to share the great news when Clive arrived in for another quick chat.

✽

Skye had finally sorted the last glitches in the Huntersbrook House website and it was live. Lainey, Holly, Paddy, Jacob and Matt were all crammed into the kitchen at the farmhouse, peering at the screen of her laptop.

'This is wonderful,' Holly said getting teary. 'It makes the place look so inviting. If I were seeing it for the first time, I'd book in immediately.'

'It really does look impressive,' Lainey said with a smile. 'Well done Skye!'

Before they could protest, Jacob popped the cork on a bottle of bubbly.

'We all have things to do this afternoon and we don't want to drive into a ditch, but a little mouthful each won't hurt. We must mark the moment.'

'Not too much for me,' Holly warned. 'I've to go back to the fete shortly. There are a hundred and one things to do there.'

They didn't want to upset Jacob, who was busily pouring the bubbly from a great height into coffee cups. In the end it really was only a mouthful. It was also flat.

'Yum,' said Skye as she clapped her hand to her mouth. Turning around she discreetly retched and mercifully managed to swallow. Her eyes watered as she fought the urge to vomit.

Lainey winked at her as she poured hers into Skye's glass while raising her finger to her lips.

Skye wanted to cry.

'Aren't you having yours, Skye?' Jacob looked crushed.

'Yes of course. I was miles away thinking about all the wonderful events that are going to take place in Huntersbrook,' she lied. Gingerly, she drank Lainey's share. Her stomach growled as she felt the liquid burn. Suddenly, it hit her – she realised what had been wrong with her this past while. Her ulcer must have returned, worst luck. Last time, she'd had special liquid to drink for the problem and it had sorted everything. She'd go to the doctor and get a repeat prescription.

She took out her phone and texted Joey: *Hey you, take a look at the site. It's live! Wish you were here to share the excitement xxx.*

Pippa

THE SOUND OF PIPPA'S VOICE IN THE HALLWAY of the farmhouse silenced them momentarily.

'We're all in here, darling,' Holly called back in surprise.

In true Pippa style, she burst through the door of the farmhouse amidst a flurry of hugs.

'Hi all! These are my friends, Missy and Danny,' she introduced. 'Hope you don't mind us landing down, but I told them about our new, uber-cool party venue and they wanted a look! We've had a snoop next-door and I figured you were all over here.'

'You're both more than welcome,' Holly said, standing to greet the guests. They all introduced themselves to one another as chairs were offered to Danny and Missy.

'It's only a flying visit,' Pippa said. 'We've zoomed down during lunch break and we're all pretending to be at a meeting so we have time to get back up to Dublin.'

'I see, well we're thrilled to see you all,' Holly said. 'Now I'm sorry to be so rude, but I have to run. The fete is today and I have to go lend my support.'

'No worries, Mum,' Pippa said kissing her hello and goodbye at the same time.

'How are you feeling today, Pippa?' Paddy asked. 'Mum mentioned you were coming down with a cold?'

'Uh, yeah. Soo much better, thanks Dad,' she said, shooting

Missy and Danny a warning look. 'The early nights over the weekend did the trick.'

Without missing a beat, Danny busied himself shaking hands with everyone.

'Let me make you all a cup of tea before I go,' Holly said.

'I can do it, Mum,' Lainey said. 'Seeing as you're in a hurry and besides, it *is* my house after all.'

Pippa sighed loudly. 'Would you two stop behaving like a pair of alley cats? I'll make the tea.' She proceeded to tell them all about the impending trip to Paris.

'Please don't tell me any more,' Skye groaned. 'Paris would be wonderful. I'm so jealous!'

'That'll be a fabulous experience I'm sure,' Lainey added with a smile.

'I'm sure it will, but God, I'm so relieved Missy is coming,' Pippa said. 'I couldn't think of anything worse than being stuck with Brianna the ball-buster on my own.'

'I thought you and Brianna got on really well,' Lainey said. 'When did all that change?'

'Ugh, she's one of those people who's never satisfied. No matter what I do, she's of the opinion it's not enough.'

'She's like that with everyone,' Missy said, backing her up immediately. 'She particularly hates me, though.'

'Why?' Holly asked. 'What's your crime?'

'She's the boss's daughter,' Pippa said, winking at Missy. 'So even if she was Coco Chanel herself, Brianna would despise her. She's the most chippy, jealous dragon on the planet.'

'That's not nice talk now, Pippa,' Paddy scolded. 'You know how I dislike nastiness.'

'Yes, quite right,' Holly said. 'I'm out of time,' she said checking her watch. 'Bye everyone.'

'See you, Mum,' Pippa said hugging her.

'Lovely to meet you,' Danny said standing to shake her hand.

'Yes, enjoy the fete,' Missy said. 'No doubt I'll meet you again soon.'

Pippa grinned as she watched her father take over with the guests. Eagerly, he filled Danny and Missy in on the details of their new venture. She didn't know if Danny was just putting in an Oscar-winning performance, but he seemed to be hanging on her father's every word.

'All we need is a few bookings to get ourselves going,' Lainey explained.

'After that, word of mouth will help, we hope,' Matt said.

'I know loads of people about town,' Missy said. 'And I'm actually looking for a venue for my thirtieth birthday party. I was telling Pippa earlier and she suggested Huntersbrook. That's why we landed upon you unannounced.'

'Oh I see,' Lainey said, side-glancing at Pippa.

'I didn't want to commit without seeing the place,' Missy said. 'I have quite a reputation to uphold,' she sighed, rolling her eyes. 'I mean, people will expect something pretty special considering who I am . . .'

'And?' Lainey said.

'Oh yeah, I totally love it,' she said. They breathed a collective sigh of relief. 'So the catch is that my birthday is, like, just over three weeks away.'

'That's not a problem, though,' Pippa said. 'Sure it isn't?'

'Of course not,' Lainey said lightly.

'How many were you thinking of inviting?' Paddy asked.

'Um . . .' Missy put her finger to her chin. 'Two hundred anyway, possibly more.'

'I don't see why we can't accommodate that,' Lainey said.

'No, it won't be a problem,' Matt said sounding certain. 'The only issue that jumps to mind is transport. There aren't many taxis in this neck of the woods, as you can imagine. But we could organise a couple of buses to ferry guests here and back?'

'Ooh good plan, Matt,' said Pippa. 'There's nothing worse than being stuck somewhere with no way home.'

'If it wasn't so cold, we could suggest camping,' Paddy said. 'But I think it'd be too messy.'

'We'd need all sorts of insurance for that too,' Matt said. 'The bus idea is better.'

'Wow, it'll be the party of the year, Missy,' Danny said. 'I think Huntersbrook is the most amazing spot for a shin-dig. The scenery is breathtaking. The main house is totally awesome, too. It's the perfect venue for a party or wedding.'

Pippa thought she might melt into the chair as Danny looked over at her and smiled as he said the word wedding. She sat back and folded her arms, observing as Danny chatted easily to Matt and her dad. It was really early days, but she had such a strong feeling that he was *the one*.

There was the small matter of the drug dealing. Much as she wanted to be, Pippa really wasn't cool with that whole scene. But she figured that it could be sorted with time. Nothing in life was totally perfect and she wouldn't like it to be. But this was the first time Pippa could actually appreciate why her sister had dropped her job and life in Dublin for Matt. Love was a powerful word and one she'd pretty much tried to steer clear of until now, but when Pippa looked over at Danny and another shiver ran through her, she knew something very special was happening here.

Baby Ely was becoming fractious, so Pippa offered to take him outside for a bit of air.

'Want to come for a little tour?' she asked Missy and Danny.

'I'd love it,' Missy said, standing up.

'Ah thanks, Pippa,' Lainey said. 'Ely would love to spend a bit of time with you.'

'Hey, no worries,' Pippa said, scooping her nephew into his stroller.

'By the way, Missy,' Matt said, 'we have a fabulous luxury marquee arriving in the next few days. It will have space to seat two hundred guests as well as a fantastic dance floor.'

'Cool!' Missy shrugged her shoulder in delight.

'Sounds wonderful,' Lainey said happily as Matt came over to put his arm around her.

'Obviously I'll need to run it by my parents,' Missy explained. 'But take it that it's a goer, yeah?'

'Sounds to me as if Huntersbrook has just got its first booking,' Paddy said, sounding delighted.

'Yay me!' Missy sang, doing a little happy dance.

'Are you coming?' Pippa asked Danny.

'I'm happy here for a few minutes, if that's OK?' Danny replied.

'Sure,' said Pippa, rejoicing a tiny bit more. He was slotting in. He was actually a perfect fit in the family, she mused. Just like Matt and Skye, who looked like they'd always been here, Danny was totally at his ease. She was stoked that he wanted to sit and chat to Matt and Lainey and her dad.

'You might like to borrow some wellies or a pair of crocs, Missy,' Lainey said, eyeing her expensive-looking stilettos. 'You're in the country now!'

Missy kicked off her shoes and slotted into a pair of mucky crocs. Making them all laugh, she kicked her leg backwards and pouted.

'The style is eclectic here in County Wicklow,' she said pretending to be a fashionista. 'Wow, this feels truly odd. I never go about in flat shoes.'

'There's a gap in the market,' Danny joked. 'High-heeled wellingtons. You could make a killing.'

Pippa giggled and waved to Danny as she led Missy out along with the buggy. First stop was the stable area, with the vast expanse of green paddocks beyond. Instantly, Pippa noticed all the amazing work her family had done. Guilt prickled at her conscience. She should've been here helping, she thought. Instead she was off doing stuff her parents and family would certainly not approve of.

Suddenly, the naughtiness of it all made her giggle.

'What's so funny?' Missy asked.

'Jeez, I was just thinking about the contrast between here and our nights out lately. It was a wild weekend, wasn't it?'

'Hell, yeah,' Missy laughed. 'I really enjoyed it, though. Oh I meant to say it, but Danny's a great guy. I never really spoke to him before I realised you and he were an item. He's smart and classy and he's *way* into you, Miss Pippa.'

'D'ya reckon?' Pippa asked unable to stop smiling.

'I think the guy is totally smitten,' Missy said.

'Is he a total bad-boy though, Missy?' Pippa wondered. 'Am I being totally stupid even considering getting involved with him?'

'No,' Missy said immediately. 'He's not like one of those gangland criminals or anything. He only dabbles and as far as I can see, he just sells to a small circle of regulars. That's totally fine. He's just providing a service, you know? And he's not doing dangerous drugs like heroin or any uncool stuff. It's all fine,' Missy said dismissing any form of doubt.

'He says he's only doing it until the economy picks up and he can get paid more for his job. He has a college degree and everything,' Pippa said.

'Yeah, totally,' Missy agreed waving a hand limply. 'It's all fine for people like us, who come from big houses and have, like, a ton of money behind us. But he's from a regular house in the suburbs and there isn't the cash to back him up, poor love.' Missy's head dropped to the side in sympathy for Danny.

Pippa chose not to point out to Missy that the Craig family fortune was non-existent and they were currently doing their best to scrape through. It also irked her to hear Missy being so bloody condescending about Danny and his perfectly normal background.

As they walked around for another few minutes, Pippa's energy began to fade. She was enjoying the fresh air, but her limbs were aching. She'd only slept for a couple of hours last night. And although her mind was fairly alert, her body was crying out for sleep.

'Are you not gonzoed after last night?' she asked Missy in confusion.

'God, yeah,' she said flinging herself onto the grass. 'But I don't feel half as shit as I would if I'd just been drinking. At least with coke the hangover doesn't hit home until later tonight. Then I can crash.'

Pippa wasn't sure she liked this feeling one bit. Slowly she began to feel shaky and cold even though the sun was shining and she was wearing a warm coat. She needed to get away from the brightness and although she adored Ely, his constant high-pitched chirping was starting to get in on her.

'Let's go back inside. Nanny McPhee I certainly ain't. I'm going to suggest to Danny that we split. I can't do the happy family thing for too long. We need to get back to the shop as well. We don't want Brianna going off on one today.'

'I guess you're right,' Missy said reluctantly. 'It's so beautiful here though, Pippa. You're lucky to have grown up in such an amazing spot.'

As they joined the others at the farmhouse, Pippa couldn't help feeling yet another rush of pleasure as she saw Danny nattering and looking like he'd known her family forever.

'I'm just regaling your family with all your dark secrets,' Danny said, winking at her.

Pippa felt a rush of guilt, then realised he was joking.

'He's going to keep an eye on you for us,' Paddy said. 'He's good and solid, this man, whereas you, Pippa, are a bit flighty. Still.'

'Don't believe a word he says,' Pippa said, pouting.

'No, I'm with Paddy on this,' Matt said, grinning at her. 'Danny seems a good bloke to me. Next time we have a weekend of work to do, I'll be texting him, not you.'

'Ah now, I'll drag her down with me,' Danny said, laughing. 'But seriously, Matt, don't hesitate if you need an extra pair of hands. I'm falling in love with this place by the minute, and I'd be delighted to help out.'

Pippa smiled at him, pleased that he was starting to feel the same way about Huntersbrook as she did – even if she didn't want to actually spend all her time down here, mucking out.

'Good news,' Lainey said, putting down her phone. 'Jules is on her way and we're all going to drop by the cake sale. This is the last one before the Christmas market. I don't suppose you can swing the afternoon off, Pippa? I feel like we haven't done anything together for eons.'

'Sounds awesome,' said Danny hopefully. 'Lots of country stuff and I've been promised faithfully there'll be apple tart. I can almost taste it!'

'You've just eaten a massive sandwich on the way down in the car,' Pippa said grinning.

'Ah leave the lad alone,' Paddy interrupted. 'If he wants an apple tart, I reckon that could be arranged.'

'I can think of nothing I'd love more than to hang out with you guys for the afternoon,' Pippa said, 'but I don't know if I'll have a job any longer if I push Brianna too far.'

'Let me make a quick phone call to the shop. I think it's time for me to pull my boss's daughter card!'

'I don't think that's wise,' Pippa said, looking worried.

'Ah chillax, Pip,' Missy said as she got through to Brianna's desk. In a couple of clipped sentences she explained that she and Pippa were detained with a job for her father.

'So we'll be a while. I reckon we won't be back before closing time . . . Yeah I'll tell her . . . OK then, Brianna . . .' She hung up and grinned at Pippa. 'Sorted.'

'What about you, Danny?' Pippa asked.

'I'll swing it. I do quite a bit of outside work. No hassle. Besides, none of it is important in comparison with apple tart.'

Paddy chuckled and banged him on the back convivially.

'Where's Skye?' Pippa asked, looking around the room.

'She's gone to have a lie down,' Lainey said. 'She's been pale as a ghost all day and she says her stomach ulcer has returned.'

'Shame,' said Missy, looking totally uninterested in poor Skye.

'And seeing as you haven't even noticed,' Lainey said to Pippa, 'Joey had to go to work today, but he'll be back later.'

'Cool,' Pippa said, smiling sweetly at her sister. 'And for the record, I *did* notice he wasn't here.'

Paddy coughed and they all knew he was going to attempt to defuse the situation.

'It's a shame he didn't get to meet you, Danny. I think you boys would get on like a house on fire. Wouldn't they?' he asked Matt.

'Totally, hey, maybe we can arrange to go for pints over the next couple of weeks?' Matt suggested.

'Yeah, sounds great,' Danny said grinning. 'Do you take a pint, Paddy?'

'Indeed I do. Especially if I'm being invited,' he chuckled.

'Sounds like a boys' night in the making,' Danny said rubbing his hands together.

'You've only met my family and already you're organising social events without me,' Pippa said pouting.

'Ah don't be like that, Pippa,' Paddy laughed. 'Maybe you'd bring Danny down for a proper weekend and we'd have time for a sneaky pint before dinner.'

'I'll see how he behaves,' she said winking at him.

'I'd better be nice in that case,' he said. 'Sneaky pints are the best kind, especially when they're followed by a delicious dinner.'

They helped Lainey lock up the house and then drove to the fete in two cars.

As they all pitched up at the field a short time later, Pippa finally began to relax. Missy was full of praise about Wicklow and was clearly loving the idea of stamping around a field in Lainey's crocs for a change. Danny fell into step with her dad and Matt and continued bantering with them. The only person who was being decidedly frosty was Lainey.

'Everything alright?' Pippa asked.

'I saw your post on Facebook last weekend,' Lainey whispered. 'You're a witch for not bothering your ass to come and help out. Then you have the gall to arrive here pretending you'd been ill.'

'It wasn't like that, Lainey,' Pippa hissed.

'Really? So how was it then?'

Pippa's heart sank. Lainey could dob her in to her parents and make her look like a right cow. She needed to get her back on side.

'Missy is my boss's daughter and she'd been having a really hard time of it lately. She asked me to go out with her and I couldn't say no. I knew Mum and Dad wouldn't understand so

I *had* to lie. I'm really sorry, Lainey. But maybe this party booking can go toward showing you how much I'm rooting for project Huntersbrook? I promise I'll be on hand to help out. I won't let you down again. I'm really sorry. Can you forgive me?'

'Pippa, you've dug yourself into holes before. Don't go back there. I can't bear lies and right now, I'm very close to exploding with you. I love you, but sometimes you make it very difficult to like you.'

Pippa's hangover had kicked in big style. He heart and head were pounding in stereo. She longed to curl into a ball and hide away. She hadn't enough clarity of mind to argue.

'Please, Lainey,' she said, sounding piteous. 'I'm so sorry. I love you and I'd never intentionally do anything to upset you. You know I wouldn't . . .'

Lainey sighed and looked at her.

'You do look sorry,' she conceded. 'All right, Pippa. Clean slate? But don't let us down again, right?'

'I won't, Lainey.' She hugged her sister and felt immensely relieved that particular spat was over. Lainey could be fearsome when she got her back up about something.

'Try and think outside your own little bubble, yeah?' Lainey said.

Pippa nodded fervently. 'I'm trying to be more like you, Lainey, but I suppose I still have quite a way to go . . .'

'Now you're being ridiculous. I almost believed you were truly sorry for a moment,' Lainey said with a grin.

'I am!'

'Sorry you got caught more like it. Come on, let's enjoy the fete and forget about you and your bloody Facebook antics.'

'Whatever you say, big sis,' Pippa said, putting on her most earnest face.

Lainey strode on ahead shaking her head and muttering, but

Pippa knew she wasn't that cross any more. They found Matt and Danny.

'Hey, beautiful girl,' Danny said putting his arm around her. He pulled her close and whispered in her ear. 'This is awesome. I totally love your family, by the way. Such cool people. And your house! Wowzers. I'd no idea you were a lady of the manor!'

'I'm not,' Pippa said. 'We're just a regular family.'

'Yeah right,' Danny said shaking his head and grinning. 'I've never been anywhere like this,' he said waving his hand around. 'It's like some deadly series on telly. Like a modern version of that *Downton Abbey* thing.'

'We're nothing like that,' Pippa laughed, in spite of her misgivings.

But Danny wasn't listening. He was pulling her by the hand towards do-gooder-Gloria's baking stall and the apple tarts he'd spied.

Across the hall, Pippa saw Lainey's best friend Jules come through the door and look around for them. When she spotted Lainey, she rushed towards her, grinning madly and arms out to engulf her friend in a big hug. She was her usual bubbly, jazz-hands self and Pippa gave silent thanks for the warming impact she knew Jules would have on Lainey. It had been an absolute age since the three of them had shared a drink and laugh together, and Pippa made herself a promise that she would organise it soon.

❋

The afternoon dragged for Pippa. She couldn't shake the crawly hung-over feeling inside. The others seemed to be loving the fete, though. Danny won a crappy, cheap-looking teddy bear, which he presented to her with a lopsided grin.

'Ah he's a keeper, Pip,' Jules said, then seeing she was getting no response, she wandered off. Normally Pippa had great fun with Jules, but today, for some reason, Pippa found her irritating. In fact, the entire world was beginning to irritate her.

'Jeepers, that's a scary expression,' Paddy said elbowing her and following her gaze. 'You do remember Jules is our friend, I take it?' They looked over at Jules, who was bouncing up and down clapping as Danny tried to pin the tail on the donkey at an over-sized cardboard cut-out.

'She's also gay, remember.'

'What's that got to do with anything?' Pippa asked her father crossly.

'I figured that you were giving her those dagger looks because she's being so enthusiastic with your fellow Danny,' he said.

'Jules is welcome to him. Gay or not.'

'I thought you liked him,' Paddy said in confusion. 'He seems very keen on you. When you were out with Missy earlier on back at the house, he was waxing lyrical about you. Saying you're the most fun-loving and smart girl he's ever met.'

'Really?' Pippa said, turning to look at her father. 'Did he really say I'm smart and fun?'

'He certainly did,' Paddy said. 'Which of course I agreed with whole-heartedly.' Paddy puffed his chest out proudly. 'I told him I expect him to mind you and treat you well or he'll have me to answer to.'

'Oh Daddy, you didn't!'

'Indeed I did,' Paddy said indignantly. 'Now I didn't tell him this,' he leaned in and whispered, 'but I think he's a good guy, Pippa. What you see is what you get. He's better than any of the previous offerings you've turned up with, that's for sure!'

Pippa hugged her dad and smiled. She *had* liked Danny before her hangover kicked in. He was great fun and easy to be around. But Pippa wasn't so sure her dad would like him quite as much if he knew what Danny did on the side. In fact, none of her family would be half as welcoming if they knew the truth.

Deciding there and then she was going to fix the little drugs problem with Danny, Pippa felt better. She wasn't going near coke again. It had been a fun few days, but she'd made a mistake and she'd just about gotten away with it. She needed to step away from the danger and count her blessings. She couldn't take the risk of her family finding out the sordid truth. It'd devastate them. She just hoped Danny might like her enough to follow suit.

Knowing her energy, patience and put-on smiles had all run out, Pippa marched over to Missy and Danny and told them in no uncertain terms that she needed to go back to Dublin – immediately.

She found her mum behind a craft stall and said goodbye.

'Bye, love,' Holly said. 'It was great seeing you. Danny seems like a lovely chap, too. I think he's even curried favour with your father, which is really saying something.'

'Yeah,' Pippa said. 'He was telling me that. I'm not sure if that makes me like him more or less,' she said grinning.

'Oh go on and don't be such a so-and-so,' Holly grinned back, hugging her tightly. Pippa closed her eyes. The familiar scent of her mother and the warmth of her embrace brought with it a sudden rush of emotion that almost made her cry. She felt like a heel for lying and being so unhelpful. Her parents were decent people who adored her and she'd behaved like a total madam lately. Out of the corner of her eye she saw Lainey watching them. She didn't want to cause any awkwardness between her mother and sister. Inhaling sharply, she pulled herself together and pulled away from Holly's warm embrace.

'Thanks for bringing Missy and encouraging her to make a booking for the party,' Holly said. 'You're a great girl, and Dad and I are so proud of you. This is just the break Huntersbrook needs to put us on the social map. Your father looks ten years younger since this morning. Well done, pet.'

'Thanks, Mum. It's nothing. I'm not giving Huntersbrook the business, Missy and Mr and Mrs Hassett are.'

'Aw now, credit where it's due,' Holly insisted. 'Take care, love, and the best of luck in Paris. I can't wait to hear all about it.'

'All right, Mum. I'll call when I return.' She found her father, who was holding Ely as he shouted and clapped at the rubber ducks that were bobbing around in a little pool so people could try and hook them for a prize.

'Bye, Dad,' she said kissing Paddy.

❅

Pippa knew she shouldn't be driving. Her eyes were burning and she was beyond exhausted. She and Danny had been very active for most of the night.

Luckily, the road was so familiar, she didn't need to concentrate too much. Missy and Danny raved about Huntersbrook and the surrounding area for the entire journey back to Dublin.

'Your party is going to be the bomb,' said Danny. 'You'll be the first *ever* person to hire the place. Nice one.'

'Ooh I love the sound of that,' Missy said with growing excitement. ''Cause as soon as the Dublin crowd see your place, it's going to be *the* venue. Be a trendsetter not follower I always say.' Missy decided to phone her father there and then.

'Hey Daddy,' she said, putting on a little girly voice. 'So, great news! I know where I'm having my thirtieth birthday party . . . I know I *said* Fire and Rain was the place. But I've changed my mind, as is a girl's prerogative. But I think you're going to love it.'

Pippa listened in amusement as Missy instructed her father on how her party was going to be.

'Yeah . . . I know . . . OK . . . Call you later. Love you. Yup. I know. Love you more, Daddyyyy.'

She hung up and punched the air.

'Looks like that's the final confirmation I needed,' she said smugly. 'Pippa, I'm so happy! My party's totally happening at Huntersbrook!'

'Yay!' said Pippa as she tried not to swerve the car. 'That's amazing! I can't believe it. This is so cool!'

Pippa pulled up at Missy's apartment a short time later. They hugged and she tried not to yell at Missy to just hurry away. Danny wanted to go to his office so she dropped him off too.

Knowing she could easily fall asleep at the wheel, she rolled the windows down and turned up the radio. The sun had dropped and the early evening chill in the air was just what she needed.

As soon as she arrived at her apartment, Pippa peeled off her clothes and got into her pyjamas. Before crashing out she figured it would be good PR to call Lainey and confirm that Missy had spoken to her father and that Mr Hassett had agreed to the party at Huntersbrook.

'That's super,' Lainey said.

'Do you reckon it'll be ready on time?'

'It'll mean some hard work,' Lainey said. 'But since when have us Craigs shied away from a challenge?'

Pippa gave Lainey all Missy's details and phone number.

'I'll give her a call tomorrow to chat about food and the other details.'

'Great,' Pippa said, rubbing her head. 'So I'd better go. I've a hundred and one things to organise for work and my trip to Paris.'

'OK, Pip,' she said. 'Well done.'

As she dropped her phone on the bed and curled into a ball, Pippa was genuinely delighted about Missy's party. But she needed a good night's sleep. She didn't care about the fact it was only five in the evening, she simply couldn't stay awake. Danny's T-shirt was strewn on her bed as she flopped down. Clutching it to her face, she inhaled his scent. He was the most intoxicating boy she'd ever come across. Sod the cocaine, she thought with a happy sigh, I'm addicted to you, Danny!

Joey

JOEY WAS FINALLY IN HIS CAR, SPEEDING BACK TO Wicklow, when his mobile phone rang.

'Hi Clive, is everything OK?'

'Yeah, I meant to mention a little detail about the ball. It only came back into my mind as I'm headed home. You have a significant other, right?'

'Yes, Skye is her name and she'll be there.'

'Oh good. Janet is looking for a couple of ladies to give her a hand on the night. I take it we can count on your Missus to pitch in?' Knowing it was more of a statement than a question, Joey agreed instantly.

'Yeah, certainly . . . I'm sure Skye would be delighted to help out.'

He hung up and gripped the steering wheel a little tighter. He guessed Skye was going to have heart failure when he mentioned this. She wasn't exactly comfortable about the idea of coming, let alone being involved.

The mood when he arrived at Huntersbrook made him forget all worries of Janet and her need for assistance. His parents were in the kitchen, chatting animatedly to Skye when he walked through the door.

'Great news,' Skye said, beaming at him.

'We got our first booking, and it's a biggie!' Paddy said. 'It's from the boss's daughter at Pippa's work. She's having her thirtieth birthday party here. There'll be two hundred people all wanting food, drink and a place to dance.'

'Wow,' Joey said. 'My God, that's terrific news! I'd better get back onto my source about the marquee and make sure it's arriving. When is this party happening?'

'That's the slight hitch,' Paddy said. 'We literally have three weeks to get the entire place organised.'

'No bother,' Joey said, pulling a stricken face. 'I'll get onto it pronto. At least Skye and I are here for the rest of the week. We'll pull together and it'll be the event of the season!'

By eight o'clock that evening the celebrations at Huntersbrook were in full swing. Lainey, Matt, Jacob and Ely had come over to help plan the event in detail.

'It's incredible to have our first booking!' Lainey said. 'Good old Pippa. She's a messer, but yet again she's managed to come up smelling of roses.'

'Why is she a messer?' Matt asked with a grin. 'What's she done now? I thought she was keeping her head down of late.'

'Ah, no reason. Don't mind me,' Lainey said with a wave of her hand.

'Please don't be so nasty about your sister,' Holly scowled. 'It's not nice. Anyone would think you're jealous of her.'

'I'm not . . . I . . . Ah, forget it,' Lainey said.

'Let's focus on the positive news,' Paddy said hurriedly. 'This is the break we needed. I'd reckon that Missy has a huge gang of potential customers on her party list. This couldn't be better.'

'I agree,' Holly said. 'This is the best advertising we could wish for.'

'Which means we can hold off on blowing any unnecessary cash on advertising for the moment,' Matt said sensibly.

The wine was flowing and the crackling log fire made for perfect relaxation.

'I love the summer, don't get me wrong,' Joey said. 'But nothing beats sitting in this room with the fire blazing and a delicious glass of vino.'

'Yes, Huntersbrook has always come into its own during winter,' Holly agreed. 'Before we know it, I'll be planning this year's decorations. Ooh I can't wait! I wonder if we'll have any Christmas parties booked in?' She held out her glass for Joey to top it up.

'Only a drizzle left. Will we all have another drop if I open a new bottle?'

The nodding and thumbs up from around the room made him smile. This was what it was all about. Coming home to a great atmosphere and planning ahead.

As they charged their glasses Joey decided to make his announcement.

'So Clive and I had a serious discussion today . . .' he began. 'It seems my job is no longer available to me.'

'What?' Skye looked stricken.

'Because they're making me a partner! It's official! I accepted and it's all being drawn up.'

'Good work, bro,' Lainey said, going over to hug him. Matt clapped him on the back as did Jacob and Paddy pulled him into a bear hug.

'You're never too old to have a hug from your dad.'

Holly dabbed at her eyes and told him she was bursting with pride. Skye looked pale and slightly down at the mouth.

'Aren't you happy for me?' Joey asked, feeling stung by her muted reaction.

'Of course I am,' she said, flushing wildly as she glanced at the others. Holly swiftly struck up a casual conversation with the others while Joey and Skye talked quietly.

'What's up?' he asked.

'Nothing at all,' she said. 'I think the wine is literally burning the hell out of my ulcer. I should probably lay off the booze for a bit.'

Joey felt as if Skye had popped his bubble. He couldn't believe how furious he felt.

'Lay off it? You never drink! It's a special occasion for crying out loud. We're on holiday.'

'I know . . .'

Joey didn't know what to say as Skye looked like she'd been thumped. Tears welled in her eyes and he instinctively put his arm around her. 'Why don't you go on up to bed if you're not well?' He wanted her to protest and say she'd be fine and hold out her glass to join in the party. Instead, much to his dismay, she nodded and did as he'd suggested. Anger spiked and he shot off out of the room after her. She was at the bottom step of the stairs when he caught up with her.

'What's up with you?' he asked accusingly.

'I'm in bits with this ulcer of mine. I've been trying to clear it up using herbal teas, but I think I'll have to admit defeat and go to the doctor tomorrow.'

'I see.'

'Why are you so cross?'

'Why are you being so weird?'

'Joey, if you really want to know, I'm pissed off with you for not telling me your news in private. I can tell you already told your father. He wasn't a bit surprised. I've no problem with you talking to Paddy, but I'm meant to be your partner. You could've discussed it with me first. You already work non-stop. Where is this promotion going to lead to? Will we become one of those couples who see one another once a year at Christmas?'

'Oh my God!' he said throwing his hands in the air. 'I didn't tell you because I wanted to surprise you. I stupidly assumed you'd be happy for me. I'll be on much better money and it'll mean we can move out of your horrible flat and find somewhere nicer.'

'My *horrible flat* as you so delicately put it, happens to suit me just fine. I like living there and I thought you did too.'

'I did . . . I do . . . But it's not exactly luxurious is it?'

'Well I'm sorry that my standards are so low,' she said as tears began to soak her face. 'Maybe we're not as compatible as we first thought, Joey? Maybe you need a girlfriend who likes staying up drinking all night with a penthouse apartment in a better postcode than ours. Hey, why don't you start dating Pippa's friend Missy Hassett? Her daddy owns a department store and she thinks life is one constant party.'

Joey didn't bother following her as she ran up the stairs. All he wanted was a fun night with a small celebration among his nearest and dearest. He was hardly suggesting a private jet to Vegas for the weekend. Skye was usually so sweet and calm. The girl he'd fallen in love with had his back and treated him like gold-dust. This new crabby anti-social version wasn't easy to be around. He didn't want to break up the party. The remainder of his family seemed really happy for him, so he'd go back into the living room and pretend this stupid spat hadn't happened. With a bit of luck, Skye would wake up feeling differently in the morning. Bloody women.

As soon as he went back into the room, Ely started howling.

'I'd better get this little man to bed,' Matt said. 'I've to go to Galway early tomorrow to see a new client. So I'll take him if you want to stay a while longer?' he asked Lainey.

'I won't look a gift-horse in the mouth,' she joked. Jacob accompanied Matt, leaving Joey, Lainey, Holly and Paddy.

'When it's like this, it feels as if we've never left,' Holly said sadly. 'It hits me from time to time that we've lost this old girl.'

'We haven't lost Huntersbrook,' Joey said forcefully as he

opened yet another bottle of wine. 'Quite the opposite. We're giving her the makeover of her life!'

He topped up his own glass along with his parents'.

'Lainey?' he offered wagging the bottle in her direction.

'No, you great big goon,' she laughed. 'You're so inebriated you haven't noticed I wasn't drinking.'

'Why not?' he asked looking confused. 'Jeez, nobody wants to celebrate my promotion with me,' he said.

'I'm all about celebrating at the moment,' Lainey said. 'But there's a good reason why it can't be with alcohol . . . It's not public knowledge yet,' she said with a wicked grin. 'But I'm expecting again. I won't know until my scan in twelve weeks' time, but I've a feeling it might be twins. I'm already getting a bump.'

Joey stood to hug her.

'Good on you, sis. I couldn't think of a worse scenario right at this moment in time,' he grinned. 'But I know you're looking to expand your brood, so congratulations.'

'Well done, love,' Paddy said and Holly joined in.

'Any time you need a lie down, just call us. We'd love to mind Ely any time,' Paddy added.

'Thanks, Dad,' Lainey said. 'I might take you up on that.'

'Actually, love,' Holly said. 'We'd love to have Ely for a sleepover some time. We've never had the little fellow come for a night at the gate lodge. What do you say?'

'Eh . . .' Lainey hesitated. 'I'll think about it. But thanks.'

Joey couldn't believe his ears.

'Are you insane?' he shouted, draining his glass. 'If I were you, I'd take all the opportunities for chilling out. What about Matt? Wouldn't he like a night out some time?'

'I guess,' Lainey said looking thoughtful. 'I haven't told him my news yet, by the way . . .'

'What, that you're preggers?'

'Yeah, I wanted to be sure first.'

'And you've taken a test?' Holly said.

'No, but I don't need to, Mum. My trousers are tighter already and all my weight is right here,' she said lifting her jumper.

'Yup, that's pretty unmistakable for sure,' Holly agreed.

Everyone bar Lainey continued drinking the wine and by the time the last bottle was empty, Joey feared his parents might end up head-first in a ditch.

'Why don't you crash here?' he slurred.

'We're not teenagers. We're going home,' Holly said as she weaved her way toward the front door. Lainey disappeared across the garden and Joey locked up. Feeling quite muzzy, he crept up the stairs to Skye. Hoping to nudge her awake, he changed his mind when he saw her. She was curled into a ball, wearing those God-awful purple flowery pyjamas he detested. He'd told her a million times that she had the sex appeal of a leper wearing them, yet here she was again . . . He made quite a few thumping noises in the hope of rousing her. He didn't want to go to sleep without resolving the row. But she was either genuinely out cold, or she wanted to ignore him. Sighing heavily, he climbed into bed and lay awake.

It had been a very productive day. Clive was treating him like a confidant and now Huntersbrook was about to be put on the map. It was all fabulous, apart from Skye's black moods and the stupid argument. The bed was spinning a little so he realised he was far too drunk to even attempt a conversation, so he sank under the covers and fell into an open-mouthed slumber.

Lainey

LAINEY WAS CLATTERING ABOUT IN THE KITCHEN, looking for ingredients to make scones, when Matt appeared looking bleary-eyed and grouchy.

'I take it you're hungover to hell?' she smirked. 'You snored like a walrus last night.'

'I wasn't that drunk,' he said. 'But I feel like I was drinking petrol. Red wine isn't my friend. How come you're so chirpy?'

'I wasn't drinking,' she said smugly.

'Weren't you?' he asked in confusion as he scratched his head. 'I thought we were all pretty much laying into it. What's made you so sensible all of a sudden?'

'I'm pregnant!' she said triumphantly.

'You are?' Matt blinked slowly, looking totally bewildered now. 'But I thought we were only at the discussion stages with all that.'

Lainey's heart sank.

'We had a chat, yes, but I didn't realise when we were chatting that I was already expecting.' A rush of emotion washed over her like a tsunami and she dropped the metal baking bowl on the counter and fled the kitchen, sobbing.

Knowing she was behaving like a total lunatic, she dived onto the bed and buried her hotly embarrassed face in the duvet. She hadn't planned on delivering their wonderful news in such an explosive manner. She'd wanted Matt to light up with delight and take her tenderly in his arms, telling her she was the most clever and precious being on earth.

With Ely in his arms, he appeared moments later.

'I'm sorry,' he said sighing. 'I'm a dreadful idiot. I shouldn't have said any of that stuff to you. I always suffer when I drink red wine. You know I do. I should've had beer last night . . .'

'It's OK,' she said sniffling. Not sure of what else to do, Lainey crawled off the bed and scurried to their bathroom to fetch the home pregnancy test she'd carried out that morning.

'Look,' she said holding it up for him to see. He recoiled as she shoved it close to his face.

'Thanks, hon, but I'll pass on sniffing or indeed licking it if that's OK with you?'

They both burst out laughing and he hugged her with Ely still in his arms.

'You're going to be a big brother, Ely,' she crooned as she took him and planted a big kiss on his soft doughy cheek.

'I've a feeling it's twins, too,' Lainey said. 'I'm huge already,' she pointed to her belly. 'And I've been feeling dreadful.'

She concealed a giggle as poor Matt looked a little green.

'I'd better go, love. Sorry to dash off while you're busy trying to frighten the living daylights out of me and all that . . .'

She kissed him and tried to flatten some of his matted hair.

'You might want to brush your hair before you go near any customers. You look like you've crawled out from behind a rock.'

Matt managed to find his briefcase and laptop and the over-night bag he'd packed the night before. Lainey and Ely waved as he pulled away from the house.

'Daddy's gone until tomorrow night,' she said to Ely. 'So we'll have to manage together, won't we?'

She'd made porridge earlier on, but it looked and tasted too much like frogspawn, hence the idea to make scones. Now even the scones seemed like far too much trouble. Not sure what she wanted to do, Lainey returned to the kitchen. All the ingredients were weighed up so she reluctantly mixed the dough, giving some to Ely to play with.

'Don't eat it like that, pet,' she said. 'That's yuck. We'll bake it first.' She showed him how she was shaping the dough. Ely watched in awe and proceeded to squish his piece through his fingers animatedly. Grinning, she put her finished product in the oven and began to wipe the surfaces clean.

By the time she'd made tea and taken the scones from the oven, Lainey felt wrecked again.

Matt called on the phone to check in and sounded much happier.

'Great news, I've just spoken to a guy who owns several mobile phone shops and he needs a new accounts package for his computer. I'm going to set him up.'

'Great,' said Lainey. 'Will he take you on as his accountant going forward?'

'Yeah, looks like it,' Matt said. 'It's a family company and he's just taken the reins from his parents. Seems the previous accountant was reliable but very old-fashioned. He wants to move with the times and that's where I come in.'

'Super,' said Lainey.

'And what's even better is that he wants me to link all his branches so the tills are all synched. So it'll be a nice bit of work. I'm having a bite to eat with him this evening and fingers crossed I'll check out his shops first thing in the morning.'

'That's great, love,' she said.

'Listen, I'm sorry I was such a dim-wit this morning. I'm a bit shocked by the news, but I didn't want you to think I'm not happy. Ely is amazing and I'm sure the next baby will be too.'

'Or babies,' she said with a giggle.

Things were really starting to look up for her and Matt. They were a great team. Life was good, but they could certainly do with some extra cash. They'd ploughed almost everything they owned into saving Huntersbrook. Lainey still had a small 'rainy day' fund and they could certainly use that now.

'Did my dad turn up?' Matt asked.

'He went off in the jeep with my dad and Joey early this morning. They took an empty horsebox and they're picking up the marquee and the tables and chairs Joey bought from his mate, remember? You were all talking about it last night?'

'Are you certain you'll get the money back from that kind of an outlay this early in the proceedings?' he said sounding worried.

'Yes, Mr Accountant, I'm sure,' Lainey grinned. 'Thanks for your concern, but we can't do this party for Missy without the equipment. Besides, we could easily add a zero to her bill and she wouldn't even notice.'

'We're hardly going to have many future clients if we behave that way. But aside from Missy, will we have a lot of people wanting to use such a huge marquee in the future?' Matt worried.

'Maybe not all the time, but Joey reckons it'll all pay for itself fairly quickly. We'd only need a couple of large bookings a year to make the marquee worth buying. Besides, Missy keeps saying all the "It" guys and girls are going to want their parties and weddings here once she does it.'

'Let's hope she's right,' Matt said 'Right, I've to fly. I'll be back late afternoon tomorrow.'

'OK, bye love,' she said.

It was a dull day and for the first time that year Lainey really appreciated the central heating. Knowing Matt probably wouldn't approve, she turned on the television and found Ely's favourite cartoon.

With him entertained, she sat at the table with a mug of tea and a fresh scone and proceeded with the party plans for Missy.

She made great progress, but the biggest problem she was facing, as it turned out, was finding a reasonably priced caterer. Missy hadn't yet specified what type of food she wanted, but it was becoming apparent to Lainey after several phone calls that buffet style was the best option to suit the kitchen facilities they had to work with.

Her mother had insisted last night that they could do the food. 'If it's turkey and ham with some salads, we could manage,' Holly mused. 'Or even a hot chicken dish with rice and maybe beef bourguignon as a second option. Sadie and I could rustle that up with our eyes shut.'

But Lainey had a sneaking suspicion it wouldn't be quite as simple as her mum thought.

'I'm not sure it'd work, Mum . . .' she'd said tentatively.

'We've done so many supper parties at Huntersbrook,' Holly said, becoming a little affronted. 'I've fed umpteen hunts and New Year's Eve goers in this house and none of them ever complained of being hungry.'

While Lainey took her point, she knew deep down that this was a different kettle of fish. It all needed to be incredibly professional and it *had* to run smoothly.

One thing was for certain, Lainey wanted the food to make a lasting impression on the guests – a good one at that. When she and Matt had a rare opportunity to eat out, they expected to savour each mouthful. Missy clearly had money to burn, but Lainey suspected the majority of her guests wouldn't be in the same boat. They needed to make the best impression possible so Huntersbrook would appeal to everyone and entice them back to spend their hard-earned cash.

An idea came to her. She opened her laptop and clicked into

the search engine: *cookery schools southeast Ireland.* She knew there was one in Wexford, a seaside town that was less than an hour's drive from Huntersbrook.

The phone was answered on the second ring and a very jolly-sounding lady chirped down the line.

Lainey explained she was looking for a budding cook who might like to take on the job of catering person for the new venture. Lainey outlined in detail what she needed. She clearly impressed the lady with how specific she was.

'You've certainly done your research.'

'Yes, well it's a family venture as I said and I don't want our standards to slip. We've put our hearts and souls into transforming Huntersbrook and we hope it'll be a thriving business that will provide for the next generation of Craigs.'

'I have a couple of people I could certainly recommend for this job,' the lady said. 'But having heard your plans and taking all your blood, sweat and tears into account, I have a proposition for you.'

'You do?' Lainey said in surprise.

'I'm Sally and I own the school. You should come and do a course. Learn how to cook and do all the catering yourself. You'd save a fortune, Lainey, and let's face it, nobody will do as good a job as you would because it's your business. I'm usually booked up well in advance, but as it happens I got a last-minute cancellation yesterday. I haven't had time to offer the place to a name on my waiting list. We're a family business too and we feel passionate about our work. I'd love to offer you the last place on my course.'

'Wow,' Lainey said. 'That sounds like a lovely idea, Sally. I'd have to talk it over with my husband and the rest of the family.'

'The full-time course runs Monday to Friday for four months. I know that sounds pretty full on, and believe me it is. But you'd come out the other end perfectly equipped to make delicious fresh food for your guests.'

'I know I'd love it,' Lainey said. 'But there's another fly in the ointment,' she said. 'I've just found out I'm pregnant and I have a little boy already.'

'I have a crèche on site and your little boy can go there. How far along are you with your pregnancy?'

'I've literally done the test this morning.'

'Right, well that all depends on how you feel. The course begins in January.'

'I see,' said Lainey. 'Can you leave it with me, Sally, and I'll call you back before four this afternoon.'

'Sure.'

Lainey put the phone down and her head was reeling. She adored being a mum and she couldn't imagine ever going back to work in an office like she'd done before. But she was all too aware that Ely and the baby, or babies, would go to school before she knew it and she didn't want to end up feeling redundant. Huntersbrook House, the venue, would hopefully take off nicely, but Lainey would love a specific job that she could really get her teeth into.

Picking up the phone, she dialled Matt's number, knowing he'd still be in the car.

'I think it sounds like a brilliant opportunity, love,' he said immediately once she'd outlined it to him. 'I can absolutely see you in your navy and white stripy apron!' he chuckled. 'All jokes aside, I think it would make sound business sense too. We're growing so many veggies and herbs on the farm already. So if you were trained to turn them into delicious dishes, we'd be flying. Sally's right, it could help us save a fortune, and hopefully make a fortune.'

Next she called Pippa, who sounded slightly pained.

'What, Pippa? Come on, spit it out!' Lainey said with a grin.

'Ah nothing, don't mind me,' Pippa said clearly attempting to brush over her hesitation. 'I just couldn't think of anything worse than spending day in, day out peeling spuds and making trifle.'

'Eh, I think there might be a bit more to it than that, Pippa,' Lainey laughed. 'This school has a huge organic farm attached to it and they teach cuisine from all corners of the globe. It's not exactly four months of boiled cabbage and pigs' trotters.'

'Yeah,' Pippa said, not sounding convinced. 'Do you know what, Lainey? I think you should totally go with your gut feeling on this one. If you want to go to cookery school, that's cool. Go for it, sis. But you're kind of talking to the wrong person. I'm trying, but I can't muster up lots of pretend delight at the thought of pot walloping for the day.'

'Thanks, Pippa,' she said dryly. 'Anyway, I just wanted to keep you in the loop with the thoughts and decisions down here.'

'Great,' she said, feigning enthusiasm badly. 'So I'll talk to you at the weekend or even next week. I'm off to Paris on Thursday and I can't wait.'

'Of course,' Lainey said. 'Enjoy, and behave yourself. Remember that Brianna is your boss at the end of the day, so don't get hammered and tell her all the secrets of your soul.'

'As if,' Pippa scoffed. 'She's such a weapon. I'll be hanging with Missy.'

'I see,' Lainey said guardedly. 'Be careful, Pip. It's one thing for Missy to act like a diva when her dad owns the store . . . But you're a plain old employee. Brianna could have you out on your ear in no time.'

'I suppose,' Pippa said.

They said goodbye and Lainey couldn't help feeling dubious about Pippa's new friendship with Missy. Her younger sister had always been easily led and she wasn't sure that Missy Hassett was exactly the most grounded individual for Pippa to pal around with.

She couldn't put her finger on it, but her little sister was acting more strangely than usual right now. She understood that her life was probably Pippa's worst nightmare in many respects. The hubby, baby and cooking wasn't her scene. But Lainey couldn't help feeling there was more to it. Pippa was up to something and Lainey sincerely hoped it wasn't all going to end in tears.

Dialling Joey's number, she figured she'd get a slightly less negative reaction to her new venture from him. He was hugely enthusiastic.

'Yeah! That all sounds amazing, Lainey. Go for it.' He passed on the information to Paddy and Jacob, who were in the jeep beside him.

'Good on ya, love,' Paddy shouted from the passenger seat.

Joey made her giggle as he told her about the men who they'd just bought the marquee from. 'They're crazy as a box of frogs, but seemed sound at the same time.'

'They sound hilarious,' she giggled. 'Good plan to ask them to come and help erect it, though.'

'They're real Arthur Daly types,' Joey said. 'Count your fingers after you shake hands with them. You know the sort?'

'Well, they've met their match with you lot,' Lainey laughed.

Deciding to take the bull by the horns, she phoned the cookery school back.

'Hello, is that Sally?' she asked.

'Yes. Lainey? Have you made a decision already?'

'Yes I have and I'd love to snatch that place, if I may?'

'I'm delighted,' she said. 'I hope you'll enjoy the course. I promise it'll be enlightening and you'll be a great asset to Huntersbrook for the future!'

Lainey took the details and promised to send on her payment

by post. Feeling slightly shell-shocked, she crouched down and kissed Ely.

'Mummy is going to be really busy for the next while,' she said. Life was moving at a rate of knots, but Lainey was so excited, all that mattered was to keep moving.

Pippa

THE PAST COUPLE OF DAYS HAD DRAGGED FOR Pippa. She was sick of being in the shop and was dying to be immersed in Parisian life. Danny wasn't quite as enthused by her impending departure, however. Last night she'd been attempting to pack strategically, laying out her clothes and making sure she looked stylish both in the exhibition hall and at dinner. She was almost organised when her buzzer sounded.

'Hey, it's just me,' said Danny. 'I couldn't let you run away to Paris without a kiss.'

She giggled. 'Did you come all the way over here for a kiss?' She pressed the buzzer and let him inside.

He must've sprinted up the steps and down the corridor because he was there seconds after Pippa opened the door.

He picked her up and swung her around before planting a large smacker on her lips. She giggled and wriggled free.

'You're a nutter,' she said taking his hand and bringing him to the tiny, messy living room.

'I had one of those days where everything went wrong and all my colleagues seemed to have a bone to pick with me,' he sighed. 'I needed to see my girl and know I have at least one ally.'

'Aw diddums,' she said curling her bottom lip. 'I need to get my stuff ready. If I'm not on top of things for the next couple of days, Brianna will have my head on a stick.'

'Forget her,' he said. 'The only thing you need to be on top of is me.'

He picked her up and balked slightly at the sight of her room. 'Bloody hell, Pippa, was there an explosion in here?'

'I'm packing, I told you.'

'Using gelignite?'

❄

After they made love, Danny pulled her into his arms.

'Don't rush off. Lay here with me, please.'

'I have stuff to do, silly,' she said. 'You can wait there and once I'm organised, you can hold me all you like. Wanna stay for a sleepover?' she asked.

He nodded. 'I brought my clean shirt and shorts for tomorrow.'

'For a drug dealer, you're very pernickety,' she joked.

'Hey,' he looked crestfallen. 'Don't call me that.'

'Sorry,' she said, looking sheepish.

He rolled onto his back and sighed. 'I never thought about the future before I met you, Pippa. Now I think about it all the time. I want us to be together for donkey's years. I want to see a fuzzy-looking photo of us as white, fluffy-headed little old people gazing proudly at the camera as our grandchildren take a family photo at our ninetieth party.'

'Ah, now there's an issue with that image already,' she said. 'I'll have shocking pink hair when I'm old.'

'Of course you will,' he said, smacking the heel of his hand off his head.

When she eventually finished packing and joined him in bed, Danny was scrolling through his Facebook page.

He turned his phone for her to see. He'd updated his status to say he was in a relationship with Pippa. Grinning, she kissed him and snuggled into his arms. She'd never been a particularly soppy girl, but somehow all the romance stuff seemed so much more fitting when it was connected to Danny.

✱

They parted ways outside her flat the following morning.

'Don't forget me, darling girl,' he said, gesturing wildly and pretending he was in an old-fashioned movie and she was leaving him forever.

'Paris will be cold without you, but I'll never forget you, Danny,' she said, playing along with the charade. He moved on down the road and turned dramatically.

'Don't let them poison your mind against me. I will always love you,' he shouted. 'No matter what they do, we will always have last night.' An elderly lady from across the street stopped and stared at them in confusion. As Danny ran around the corner, Pippa giggled uncontrollably.

She was still smiling as she lugged her wheelie case into work and made sure she was organised for their flight.

'You're in a good mood,' Missy said, making a fleetingly grumpy face.

'I had so much fun with Danny last night,' she said giggling. She was just about to tell Missy about this morning when the other girl flapped her hand and looked disgusted.

'Ugh, don't tell me anything else about your drug baron boyfriend. Actually, Pippa, I'm a little concerned about you. Danny is fine to bring to a party and most certainly good to know. But he's not *our* ilk. He's a scumbag, sweetie. Don't get confused here . . .'

When Missy was gone, Pippa staggered to her chair and flopped down. Feeling as if she'd been physically slapped, she tried to take stock of what Missy had said. It was completely different from her enthusiasm about Danny out at Huntersbrook. What had gotten into her since then?

'Ready to go?' Brianna asked, poking her head around the door.

'Eh sure,' Pippa managed.

❄

By the time they reached the airport, Pippa's head was pounding. Missy was clearly oblivious to the hurt she'd caused Pippa, which in turn led her to assume one of two things. Either Missy was correct and Danny was a total waster, or Missy was insanely jealous and wanted to curb the relationship she was building with Danny . . .

Hoping the style and general suaveness of Paris would ease her addled mind, Pippa tried to envision herself walking down the Champs-Elysées with a parasol and a poodle. As the plane took off, she could see Danny in her mind's eye, grinning at her; but she could hear Missy's affected voice dismissing him. For the umpteenth time, she wondered if Danny really was just a lowdown dealer at heart, not worthy of her time and certainly not worthy of her love?

The plane journey was fine, until Brianna ordered sparkling water from the refreshment cart.

'Give me a break!' Missy said, rolling her eyes. 'We're headed for gay Paris! Let's have bubbles. It's almost four o'clock in the afternoon, for crying out loud. We're not even going to be buying things until tomorrow.'

'You can if you like,' Brianna said with a tight smile. 'But I need to remain clear-headed for the moment. I don't think your father would appreciate it if we were all hung-over tomorrow and end up buying a dodgy winter collection for next year.' Brianna reiterated her order to the air hostess. 'I can't bear drinking alcohol on planes anyway. It makes me too dehydrated.'

'You'll have bubbly with me, won't you?' Missy asked Pippa while glowering across at Brianna.

'Eh,' she glanced over at Brianna, who shook her head crossly. 'I'd better not, Missy. As Brianna said, this is a working trip. Perhaps we should wait until later?'

'*Perhaps we should wait,*' Missy mimicked mockingly. 'Don't be such a pair of losers,' she said. 'Three snipes of champagne and three boring waters to keep the pair of goodie-two-shoes here happy,' she ordered the air hostess rudely.

Pippa could barely swallow the champagne. Missy had snatched all three tiny bottles and poured them into plastic cups before handing them out. As she was sitting in the middle, Pippa could feel the tension from her boss on one side and the fury from Missy on the other.

'Let's compromise and have half a glass each!' Pippa said, hoping to smooth things over. Brianna didn't touch her champagne but guzzled her water instead.

'I'll have a glass of wine with my meal later, but I don't want this now, thank you,' Brianna said picking up the offending glass and placing on Pippa's tray. 'I'm an adult, Missy, and I get to choose what I do *some* of the time.'

Missy muttered obscenities under her breath and swiftly worked her way through the three snipes.

Brianna pulled out a file and proceeded to show Pippa a list of labels and fashion houses.

'If we start at the top left-hand corner of the exhibition hall and work our way back, that way we're methodical and with purpose. There's nothing worse than wasting time on things we don't need or indeed missing out on a possible exciting new label.'

'That's a lot of fashion houses to view,' Pippa remarked.

'I know,' Brianna said. 'Which is why I'm not even contemplating getting squiffy before we land on French soil. Romantic and wonderful as Paris sounds, this is a very important business trip.'

Missy kept elbowing Pippa and making barely audible snorting noises to show her disapproval.

As they disembarked in Paris, Brianna continued to brief the girls on what would happen over the next couple of days. Pippa was fascinated. They most certainly had a lot of work ahead.

'Brianna, sweetie,' Missy said, as they were waiting at the carousel for their luggage. 'It's no wonder you're single, darling. No man could possibly keep up with you. It's all work, work, work. It's exhausting.'

'I enjoy my job and I've climbed the ladder of success by working hard. With all due respect, dear, *I* didn't have a choice.'

Missy had finished all three glasses of bubbly singlehandedly and was utterly oblivious to Brianna's hurt or annoyance. Pippa, on the other hand, was sweating and wanting to grab her bag and dash for the nearest exit.

'Great that all our cases have arrived safely,' she said chirpily. 'Let's get going, yeah?'

Brianna marched toward the taxi rank and gave precise instructions in flawless French.

'Nicely done, Brianna,' Pippa said as their taxi wormed its way out of the airport toward the city centre.

'I did a course many years ago. Paris is not the place to turn up and find oneself unable to communicate. It shows a total lack of education and the locals are quick to judge if you can't converse at a basic level.'

Pippa was seriously impressed. Brianna could certainly hold her own. Again, she felt Missy's elbow digging into her ribs as she giggled into her sleeve and mocked their boss.

They stepped out of the taxi and looked up. The hotel wasn't quite what Pippa had in mind. She'd been expecting a classy boutique style boudoir with a gorgeously decorative frontage, complete with antique revolving doors. Where was the divine-looking doorman dressed in a navy costume with red and gold accents, bowing politely as he welcomed them with a sexy French accent? Instead they were greeted by a grey building with a shabby paint-chipped door that weighed a ton. Pippa prised it open and struggled under its weight as she tried to hold it ajar so the others could get their bags inside.

The reception area was no great shakes either. The desk was dull and ancient-looking with an uppity woman standing there in an ill-fitting trouser suit and no sign of a smile.

Brianna gave their names and took the keys to their rooms.

'You're on the second floor,' Brianna said handing them their keys. 'I'm on the first, so how about we meet back here in half an hour?'

The girls agreed and both looked momentarily horrified when Brianna picked up her case and began to haul it up the stairs.

'Where's the elevator?' Missy asked. 'They don't expect us to hoof our bags up several flights of stairs?' she scoffed.

'You can leave them there, if you'd prefer,' Brianna called over her shoulder.

The two girls followed as Missy cursed and complained.

'If my father knew we were staying in a dump like this, he'd be livid.'

Pippa didn't comment, but she hoped the rooms were going to be more impressive. She anticipated crisp white linen and a dressing table with a pretty spoon-backed chair covered in luscious damask fabric that matched the curtains and four-poster bed.

She found her door, shoved the key into the slot, took a deep breath and pushed open the door. Alas, it was more like a nasty motel, with dingy carpet tiles and a sad, saggy single bed.

Throwing her bag on the ugly wooden chair, she hung her suit cover in the wardrobe, which smelled decidedly like cat pee.

Brianna was insisting they go to a bistro around the corner. She'd been telling them all about it during the flight.

Missy had thankfully agreed and said it sounded like a perfect plan.

Pippa was secretly quite glad that Missy wasn't going to have the upper hand this evening. If they were left to Missy's devices, Lord only knew where they'd end up.

The bathroom was the size of a broom cupboard so Pippa didn't bother having a shower. Instead she fixed her make-up, pulled a brush through her hair, brushed her teeth and made her way back down to reception.

Brianna was out front, looking around with a smile on her face.

'All OK?' she asked as Missy brought up the rear.

'This place is a kip,' Missy spat. 'I suggest we find somewhere better. Does my father know you booked us into this dive?'

'Yes, he's the one who showed me where the place was all those years ago. It's not five star, but it's very central. We can walk everywhere and it's near the exhibition hall. Once you immerse yourself in Parisian life, you'll *get* it,' Brianna said as she waltzed down the street, looking thrilled.

Missy looked at Pippa, curled her lip, shrugged her shoulders and followed.

The restaurant was typically Parisian, with small square tables shoved together in such tight proximity they had to be pulled out to allow people to scooch in and sit on the opposite side.

'It's lucky we speak a different language,' Pippa hissed. 'I'm not into the idea of all the tables practically touching. You wouldn't want to be having a private conversation, would you?'

'Ah this is what I love,' Brianna said, continuing with her theatrical stance. 'Wait until you taste the steaks. They cut like butter.'

On Brianna's rather insistent recommendation, they all ordered a simple meal of steak, rustic potatoes and green salads along with a bottle of red wine.

Moments later, three plates were banged down in front of them.

'Jeez,' said Missy. 'Why don't they just throw the plates from the kitchen and be done with it? This is bordering on violence.'

'This is totally *raw*,' Pippa hissed as she cut into her meat. 'The outside is vaguely charred and the rest looks like it might still have a pulse.'

'They don't believe in over-cooking meat here,' Brianna explained knowingly. 'Taste it. I promise you'll love it. Washed down with the red wine, which is at the perfect temperature, you'll be blown away.'

The two girls cut around the outside of their steaks and couldn't bring themselves to eat the really rare bits. Brianna carefully chewed hers, looking as if she were on the verge of orgasm.

'*Excusez moi*,' she said, heading for the bathroom some time later.

Missy leaned across the table to Pippa and whispered. 'She's lost the plot. She thinks she's a local. Look at her floating about with her arms outstretched!'

'She's used to coming here, that's all,' Pippa defended.

'Play along for another fifteen minutes and we're out of here,' Missy said. 'Here, I'll fill up her glass and hopefully it'll knock her out. It's like drinking ink, whatever the hell it is.'

'Yeah, I thought it was just me,' Pippa said. 'I like most red wines, but that stuff is rough.'

By the time they got Brianna back to the hotel, via a couple of cobbled side streets, where she pointed out coffee shops and other things the girls had zero interest in, Pippa could tell Missy was getting antsy.

'So, nighty-night then, Brianna. Thanks so much for the guided tour and the gorgeous meal,' Missy said. 'I'll be certain to tell Daddy what a super hostess you are. Sorry about my cribbing earlier on. You're dead right. I needed to see Paris like the locals do. I'm bushed. Don't know about you gals, but I'm off to my scratcher. See you both in the morning for breakfast. Shall we say eleven o'clock?'

Brianna snorted with laughter. 'Missy, you *are* a hoot! Let's agree on seven-thirty, yes? They do a very basic breakfast here at the hotel. But *entre nous* it's not exactly delicious. So I suggest we stop by a superb patisserie I know of. They do melt in the mouth pastries that are worth every last calorie! Then we can trot on across town to the exhibition hall. That way we should be there in plenty of time for the nine o'clock opening.'

'Seven-thirty!' Missy whined. 'Ah seriously, Brianna. Let's not get carried away. Nobody expects us to be up *that* early, for God's sake.'

'Well it's only a quarter past ten now,' Brianna said in surprise. 'So it's not as if we'll be lacking in sleep,' she yawned. 'And I think I'll be out like a light after that divine wine.'

'Uh yes, it was gorgeous,' Pippa said, rushing toward the stairs. 'See you in the morning, ladies.'

They all trooped toward their rooms. As soon as Brianna was gone, Missy grabbed Pippa's sleeve and pulled her up to the second floor.

'Let's go to my room for a few minutes until the coast is clear,' Missy said, fishing her room key out of her handbag.

As soon as Pippa saw Missy's room, she burst out laughing.

'Dear Lord, your room is worse than mine. I thought the dark maroon colour in mine was bad, but this is just gross. Who would have thought of doing up an entire space in mustard?'

'Isn't it like a migraine?' Missy said, pulling her wash bag from the bathroom. 'Still, things will be so much better in a minute. Quick sneaky line before we head out for a few scoops?'

'What?' Pippa nearly choked. 'Please tell me you didn't bring drugs on the plane, Missy!'

'Only a tiny amount,' she said, looking at Pippa mockingly. 'Relax! Bloody hell, you're acting as if I'm a gangster. Chill out, Pippa. It's a pinch, I'm hardly Nidge from *Love/Hate*.'

'Chill out? Missy, if you got caught with that, you'd be gonzoed. Coke is illegal, in case you've forgotten. Can you imagine how much trouble you'd be in if you were caught?'

'I don't look like a drugs mule, Pippa. There's enough here to keep a mouse going. The customs people aren't interested in people like me. They'd get more excited about someone smuggling unpasteurised milk than this.'

As she laid out two lines on the dressing table and helped herself to one, Missy seemed totally at ease with what she'd done.

Pippa actually thought she was going to be sick. She walked to the window and opened it gently.

'Careful!' Missy said. 'You'll blow this all over the floor and I don't know about you, but I wouldn't fancy snorting anything off those rancid carpet tiles.'

'I'm actually good for tonight,' Pippa said. 'I'm not really that into powder. It's only an occasional thing for me and I'm still a bit hung over after the weekend. You go ahead.'

'What do you mean?' Missy asked standing up and walking over to Pippa. 'You're making me sound like some sort of lowlife here. I don't appreciate your tone, Pippa. Besides, little-Miss-holier-than-thou, you're the one screwing the dealer, not me.'

Her heart was thumping in her chest as Pippa saw the flaring anger in the other girl's eyes.

'Danny's not ...'

'Not a dealer? Ah get off your high-horse, Pippa. He's a nice enough guy, I'll give you that. But he's a wolf in sheep's clothing. He can talk the talk and he looks great. But don't be fooled by him, darling.'

There was silence for a moment as Pippa struggled to contain her boiling anger. As if on cue, her mobile rang. She couldn't snatch it off the bed quickly enough to conceal the name that was flashing up.

'Ha! Speak of the devil and he'll appear!' Missy said. 'I'll go into the bathroom and touch up my make-up while you speak to your dealer boyfriend.'

Pippa wanted to hit Missy. Instead she answered the call through gritted teeth.

'Hey, what's up?' Danny asked sounding really concerned.

'Yeah, Missy is just popping to the en suite to do her make-up while we have a little chat.'

'OK, you're surrounded,' Danny said. 'Is she driving you insane?'

'You could say that,' Pippa said trying to keep her voice even. 'We were out for dinner with our boss. She's gone to bed and Missy and I are going out for a couple of sneaky drinks.'

'Nice,' Danny said sarcastically. 'As long as she doesn't go off hunting for powder, you'll be fine. It's too dodgy to partake in any of that abroad, you do know that, right?'

'No need to go out looking, she brought some in her bag,' Pippa hissed.

'Pardon?'

'You heard,' Pippa whispered as Missy flushed the loo. 'I've about thirty seconds before she's back in the room. She brought the shit with her and now wants me to go out clubbing. This is a disaster, Danny.'

'Shit!' he said. 'Pippa, I'd no idea she'd be that stupid. Can't you say you're sick or something? You have to be careful doing any of that stuff over there. The police there lock you up, throw away the key and *then* ask questions.'

'Don't you think I know that?' She wanted to cry. This was insane.

'Play along with her. Keep her sweet and after tonight, don't get caught on your own with her. Lie, say Brianna was annoyed at being left out.'

'She doesn't know . . .'

'You'll think of something. But keep her sweet until this trip is over and after that, you'll need to distance yourself from her slowly. She's bad news, Pip. Everyone in Dublin dreads her.'

Missy appeared from the bathroom looking ready for action.

'Right, let's go. Say kissy-kissy to lover boy and let's go.'

'God, she's a bitch,' Danny said down the phone. Pippa grimaced, knowing she really wanted to cry.

'I'd better get going,' Pippa said.

'Mind yourself. No dodgy situations, OK? I . . . I love you Pippa.'

'OK . . .' She closed her eyes wanting to tell him she loved him too. But she was too scared of talking in front of Missy. She'd only go off on one, teasing her for being in love with a scumbag. And besides, it was private. Between her and Danny.

'I'll call you tomorrow,' she managed and hung up.

'So hurry up!' Missy demanded. 'It's late enough already. We don't have all night. Especially if the dragon wants us ready for work at bloody half seven.'

Pippa looked over at the white powder.

'Why are you looking at it as if I'm trying to poison you? You should be grateful I risked life and limb to bring it. I'm sharing with you and that's the thanks I get?' Missy's nostrils were flaring and her face had turned a dangerous shade of violet.

'Listen, I don't want you thinking I'm totally sponging off you all the time,' Pippa said in an attempt to recover the mood.

'We're mates.' Missy closed her eyes and clenched her fists. 'I don't want to fight with you, Pippa, OK? It's cool. Besides, you can buy the gear for my party, so it's no biggie.' Missy handed her the rolled-up note and stood with one hand on her hip.

Pippa took it and closed her eyes as she inhaled through her nose. Pippa wished she could click her heels three times and go home.

She still felt uneasy as they walked into a heaving, noisy bar a few minutes later.

'Now this is more like it,' Missy said as she started to sway her hips to the beat. 'Look, six o'clock,' she said out of the corner of her mouth. 'Delicious French men and they're staring in our direction.'

'*Bonsoir*,' one of them said, advancing instantly. As he babbled in French, Missy giggled and flicked her hair.

To her astonishment, Pippa could actually understand him. Delighted with her memory skills, she soon forgot her inhibitions and woes. Channelling her school-girl French rather expertly, she oozed confidence as she began to speak like a true linguist.

'You're seriously good at this,' Missy said, looking wildly impressed. 'Those guys are totally melting. Your accent is mega.'

'I never thought I was that brilliant in school, to be honest I was always a bit embarrassed about doing the accent. But I suppose it's so much easier to speak a language when you're in the country, right?'

'Or when you've had a line of Charlie to boost your confidence!'

Either way, the girls were an instant hit. They found themselves welcomed with flailing arms, *ooh-la-la's* and *mon dieu's*.

A carafe of wine appeared from nowhere and the conversation flowed. No matter what the guys said, Missy was smitten.

'Their accents are dreamy. I could get used to this lot,' she said. 'Look at their hair and skin and their clothes. They're so sophisticated and . . . manly . . .' she finished.

'And so animated and passionate,' Pippa said, knocking back her wine. 'I'm loving the wine here, too. It doesn't seem to make me drunk, unlike the awful monkey wee they serve in the bars at home.'

'Yeah, I know. But I guess it's because these people totally invented wine, didn't they? Also,' she elbowed Pippa. 'Don't forget you've got a little bit of help from your friend Charlie. It always makes drinking easier. Just part of the magic, I guess.' Missy flashed a bright smile.

Pippa felt a sudden jolt as guilt revisited her once more. She also felt suddenly nervous and suspicious. Under normal circumstances, she'd be hammered by now. Instead she was feeling sharp as a razor, not to mention on top of the world. Knowing it was all down to the effect of the drug, she became totally panic-stricken.

'I think we need to go, Missy.'

'Your teeth are all black,' she grinned back. 'I guess you're right, we need to get a couple of hours' sleep or Brianna will tell Daddy on us,' she said blowing a childish raspberry.

'What time is it?' Pippa asked.

'It's half-past five,' Missy sighed. 'We really will get into serious trouble with the teacher.'

'Whaat?' Pippa said lurching sideways. 'How can it be that time already?'

'Time flies and all that, sweetie,' Missy said, grabbing her bag. The men all protested and acted as if they were being stabbed in the heart with a wooden stake at the thought of losing the girls' company.

'They're wildly enthusiastic, bless them,' Missy grinned. 'But we gotta go, Pippa girl.'

They waved and had their cheeks kissed until they were dizzy. Linking arms, the two staggered up the road.

'I'm glad you seem to know where you're going,' Pippa said, squinting into the dark. 'I'm totally lost. I'd happily lie on the road and have a quick snooze. In fact, that seems like a seriously marvellous plan,' she said attempting to sit down.

'Come on, you floozy!' Missy giggled. 'You crack me up, you crazy mad thing! You need to get into bed and sleep off some of that alcohol.'

'I was fine a minute ago, but I'm so so so tired now, Missy.'

Pippa wanted to howl as Missy pulled her up and dragged her back to the hotel.

As they made their way up the stairs, Pippa swayed dangerously backwards.

'Jeez, are you trying to flatten me and kill yourself in the process?' Missy said. 'I think you should crash with me. Otherwise you'll never wake up and we'll be up shit creek without a paddle.'

Pippa nodded. Her head felt too heavy for her body and her legs were cramped and achy. She was ridiculously chilled and had an urge to curl into a foetal position.

'I'm broken,' she whinged. 'I can't walk anywhere else.'

'You'll be tucked up in a jiffy,' Missy said, 'here's the room. You need to make it to the bed and you'll be home and dry.'

A few seconds later, Pippa was vaguely aware of her friend pulling her shoes off and unzipping her dress. On autopilot she grabbed at the blankets and sheet and rolled into a little cocoon.

❋

When the alarm clock went off, Pippa wanted to die. Impressively, Missy staggered out of bed and into the shower without even thinking about it. Pippa conked off to sleep again as she listened to the trickling of the shower. Before she knew it, Missy was standing above her, shaking her angrily.

'Get up, sleepy-head,' she said, pulling the blankets off Pippa.

Knowing she would be fired if she stayed in bed, Pippa dragged herself out and into her own room. Miraculously, she managed to present herself at the front door at the allotted time. The pastries Brianna had raved about tasted dry and flaky to her. The coffee burned her mouth and made her want to do open-mouthed howling.

Feeling shockingly awful, she trailed pathetically behind Brianna and Missy for the most of the day.

Danny called three times before Pippa answered.

'It's really noisy in here,' she said. 'I'm dying, Danny. We had about an hour and a half of sleep and I feel like I'm going to have a heart attack.'

'I hope you weren't off with sleazy French men,' he said.

'No,' she said miserably.

'You're in a really bad way,' he said. 'Take some painkillers and get a double espresso. You can't let your boss see you acting like a washed-up junkie.'

'I know, I've been trying really hard to act upbeat all day, but I feel so terrible. I'm never taking drugs again.'

'Shush,' he said loudly. 'Don't say that kind of stuff on a mobile phone or within spitting distance of your bloody boss!'

'Sorry, Danny. I'm not as experienced as you are with all the deception.'

She hung up as tears of self-pity burned her eyes.

'All OK?' Brianna asked from directly behind her.

'Eh, yes. Of course,' Pippa said. Sweat ran down her back and the sensation of sheer panic terrified her. Had Brianna heard her on the phone?

'How are you?' Pippa asked. 'Should we have a coffee break?'

'Good plan,' Brianna agreed before striding toward one of the coffee docks with the stand-around tables.

Pippa bought cappuccinos for the others and a double espresso for herself. Popping two painkillers into her mouth, she downed both in one gulp.

'Have you a headache?' Brianna asked suspiciously.

'Yeah,' Pippa said. 'I'm never great in these huge enclosed spaces. Country bumpkin that I am.'

'I thought you were unusually quiet all day,' Brianna said. 'I thought it was partly down to madam, too,' said referring to Missy, who was at the loo.

'Ah, she's not a bad egg.'

'No, I'm surprised by how chirpy she is actually,' Brianna conceded. 'Anyway, we're nearly finished for today. There's a lot left to see tomorrow, but we don't want to feel burnt out either.'

Even though she was dying inside, Pippa was careful to nod and make the right noises at the right times. She caught sight of her reflection in a mirror. She was the colour of putty.

'Are you still not feeling any better?' Brianna asked an hour or so later.

'I'll be fine tomorrow. A good night's sleep and I'll be raring to go.'

If it weren't for the fizzy energy tablets Missy slipped her, Pippa knew she'd be horizontal on the floor by now.

Missy, on the other hand, was absolutely fine. Pippa hadn't the energy to work out how she was still so chirpy.

By the time Brianna decided enough was enough and called it a day, Pippa felt close to tears.

'So do you girls want to eat here at the exhibition hall or will we go back to the hotel to freshen up and go out for a proper meal?' Missy asked.

'I'd prefer to get out of here,' Brianna said. 'We've got the other half of this place to walk and shop in tomorrow. I reckon a change of scene is called for. Pippa?'

'Yeah, I need to get back to the hotel for some sleep.'

Brianna had been ready to walk back, but Pippa had begged to be allowed to take a cab. As she collapsed against the car seat, Pippa felt like she could sleep for a week.

'Pippa?' Brianna said, nudging her gently. 'Are you positive you're OK, honey?'

'Oh, sorry,' Pippa said peeling her eyes open. 'I'm really sorry about this girls,' Pippa said. 'But I'm totally out of sorts today. I think I might have to retire. Get a sandwich sent up by room service.'

'I know from past experience that the hotel doesn't do room service,' Brianna said. 'All they offer is coffee and croissants and they're vile, which is why I suggested we have breakfast on the way this morning.'

'I don't care,' Pippa murmured. 'I don't need food, just sleep.'

'You're very pale,' Brianna said worriedly. 'And you had an early night . . . Unless you two snuck out without me?' She raised an eyebrow.

'Oh no!' Missy said throwing her head back and giggling. 'As if we'd do that!'

Pippa couldn't even join in with the banter. She needed to

crawl into bed and nothing was going to make her change her mind.

'So,' Missy said as they walked through the hotel lobby toward their rooms, 'let's take forty minutes. That's enough for a shower and the usual calls home and we can meet here. I'm starving.'

'Well, I think it'll be just you and me,' Brianna said, looking at Pippa.

'I'll bet you'll be fine once you freshen up,' Missy said, linking Pippa's arm. 'Besides, you really need to eat. You've barely eaten a bite all day.'

'That's true,' Brianna said. 'Unless you want me to run to the nearest patisserie and buy you something?'

'Ugh, no! The only place near here is that dump over there,' Missy scoffed as she pointed to a rather dank looking building. 'You'll end up with a tapeworm or something. We'll go to a bistro nearby and I promise you'll be tucked up in bed at a decent hour.'

Pippa thought she was going to do open-mouthed ugly crying. She hadn't felt this miserable or vulnerable since the time she'd fallen and split her lip in Kindergarten.

'I don't know . . .' she tried to protest.

'Ooh, I still have your hair spray,' Missy said, knocking her forehead. 'Silly me! Come to my room and I'll give it back to you. I'm not washing my hair now and I think you said you are . . .'

'It's fine,' Pippa said, not even aware enough to pick up on Missy's ploy.

'I insist,' she said, widening her eyes at Pippa.

'Uh. OK,' she said, traipsing after Missy. 'See you in a while, Brianna,' she said, mustering up as much strength as she could to wave.

As soon as they closed the door in Missy's room, Pippa flopped onto the bed.

'Missy, I feel like I'm going to die,' Pippa whined. 'I can't go out tonight. I'm so exhausted. I've never felt this awful in my life. Every inch of me hurts.'

'Pippa, you *really* need to get it together,' Missy snapped. 'Brianna is going to smell a rat here. Are you trying to get us both into trouble? All I need is for her to report to Daddy that the two of us were falling around Paris, acting like wasted drunks.'

'Sorry,' Pippa said softly. Swallowing hard, she felt incredibly nervous all of a sudden. Missy was incensed and it was scary.

'Not good enough, Pippa! Get with the program here. If you can't be cool, I have a serious problem with that. Believe me, you don't want to make an enemy of me. Now go and tart yourself up and stop acting like a diseased dog.'

Pippa half staggered, half crawled from the room. Clamping her hand over her mouth, she bore down on the inside of her cheek and willed her tears to hold off. Fumbling with her room key, she eventually managed to spring the door open and fall in. Knowing she had very little time, she made for the bathroom and turned on the shower. Much to her dismay it was ancient and dribbly, a far cry from the therapeutic needling of a power shower that she so desperately needed.

Reaching for the tiny complimentary bottles of shampoo and shower gel, she hoped their scent might help lift her flagging spirit. When she opened them, they smelled alarmingly like washing-up liquid and her hair seemed to react accordingly, as it instantly matted into a tangled and knotted bird's-nest on the top of her head.

Turning off the cruddy shower, she wrapped herself gingerly in a towel. Even that wasn't at all what she'd had in mind. Longing to feel fluffy, cosy comfort, the scutty, threadbare offering was like another slap in the face.

Due to the liquid restrictions on the plane, Pippa hadn't brought any hair products along, so the process of yanking the travel-size rigid brush through her tresses was painful. Pulling open the musty drawer on the dressing table, she found a joke of a hairdryer. As she flicked it on, she cursed. It was one of those annoying ones that needed the button held in place all the time to keep it turned on.

The sheer effort of pushing the button and attempting to style her hair made her feel exhausted. The muscles in her arms screamed in pain as she tried to smooth her hair. She was also bathed in sweat by the time she was finished.

Knowing the clock was against her, she patted her face with the damp towel and applied her make-up as best she could. Scrutinizing her reflection in the mirror, she hoped she didn't look as freaked or wrecked as she felt.

'There you are, slow coach!' Missy said as she eventually joined the ladies in the lobby.

'Ah she's only five minutes late,' Brianna said with a smile. 'How are you feeling? You certainly look a lot better.'

'Yes, fine thanks, Brianna,' Pippa said, unable to look her boss in the eye. 'Looking forward to a bit of dinner.'

'And a glass of wine,' Missy said, linking both their arms and marching them out into the night.

The conversation was light as they swapped thoughts on the show that day.

'I'm very happy with the day-time looks,' Brianna said as they were shown to a table in a massive buzzy restaurant. Missy ordered a bottle of champagne.

'It's on me,' she winked. 'Go on, Brianna,' she said politely. 'You love the day looks. So do I detect a thumbs down for the evening wear?'

'Well,' she said helping herself to a bread roll. 'I can't say I've been blown away by any of it. There are the usual gorgeously tailored black dresses, but I'm waiting to see some pops of colour that excite me.'

By the time they'd ordered and the sommelier had poured the champagne, Pippa was feeling marginally better.

'Cheers,' said Missy with a bright smile. 'Here's to a great day's work.'

'Yes indeed,' Brianna said. 'And I'm sure we'll find some amazing pieces for the evening wear section tomorrow.'

'Hear, hear,' Missy said. 'Have you gotten lots of design ideas, Pippa? It must be an Aladdin's cave for an artist such as yourself.'

Pippa made a huge effort to chat and constantly reminded herself to smile. She didn't want to draw any more attention from Brianna. Choosing the most plain and comforting food possible she knew she was simply counting down the minutes until she could bolt back to the hotel and flop into bed.

Missy excused herself and went to the bathroom just after the main course.

'She's not being too bad,' Brianna whispered as soon as the other woman left the table. 'I think I've been rather judgemental of her. She's a nice girl and well able to put in a day's work.'

'I'm fond of her,' Pippa said with a frozen smile. 'Maybe she gets some unfair bad press in light of her dad's wealth.'

It was like musical chairs for the next while. As soon as Missy returned, Brianna excused herself.

'You've started a trend,' Brianna laughed. 'No doubt you'll need to run to the ladies now too,' she said to Pippa.

'I'll wait with Missy until you return,' she said.

Pippa finished her glass of white wine. It was probably very expensive seeing as Missy ordered it, but right at that moment it could easily have been battery acid.

'Pippa, Pippa, Pippa,' Missy said shaking her head. 'You're totally flagging, my girl.'

'Yeah, sorry,' she grimaced. 'I'll be fine once I get a good sleep tonight.'

'Well, that won't obviously be happening for some time,' Missy winked. 'Here, take this to the loo. There's enough to pep you up.'

'Oh, thanks so much, Missy,' Pippa protested. 'But I'm beyond help today. I won't be out on the tiles this evening. I simply couldn't.'

'You will and you can,' Missy answered coldly. 'I didn't come all the way to Paris with the view to having Mrs Brianna-bore as my party buddy. But right now, she's more fun than you are. Go to the bathroom, powder your nose and quit whining. I thought you were fun, Pippa. You're beginning to piss me off.'

Swallowing hard, Pippa was just about to tell Missy where she could stick her coke and her faux friendship, when the other girl narrowed her eyes.

'I got a text from your sister earlier. Seems they've bought the marquee and all the stuff for my party. I'm going to put your family's business on the map, Pippa. *I'm* being a true friend. The least you can do is come out with me for an hour.'

'Please, Missy. I'd love to come out with you any time . . . You know I would. But I'm too exhausted right now.'

'How would your family feel if I told them I was worried about you?' Missy said as she nonchalantly glanced at her nails.

'Pardon?' Pippa's blood ran cold.

'Imagine if I rang Lainey or your mum and said that I didn't want to cause any upset, but I'm *so* worried about you dating a drug dealer . . .'

'Jesus Christ, Missy, you wouldn't . . .'

'Ah there you are, Brianna,' Missy said brightly. 'Right Pippa, your turn, off to the ladies room with you and then we'll pop off for a little nightcap. How does that sound to everyone?'

'Where are we off to?' Brianna said as she sat down with a smile and her lipstick reapplied.

'Where would you suggest?' Missy asked cheerfully.

Pippa scurried to the bathroom and slammed the cubicle door shut. Leaning against the door, she tried to stifle her sobs. She was tempted to hurl the tiny package Missy had pressed into her hand in the toilet bowl. But the thought of staying awake for even another hour was torturous. Pippa also needed to be on her guard. If Missy started spouting about Danny and calling him a drug dealer, she could lose her job along with her family's respect.

One thing was certain, she couldn't possibly go on another bender tonight, and there was no way she would. But as she eyeballed the foil container, she knew she was goosed. If she didn't keep Missy sweet, Huntersbrook could end up in debt before it even got going as a venue. She could lose her job, and Danny could end up in jail.

Sitting on the closed toilet seat, Pippa jigged her foot up and down trying to stop her tears. Scrolling some loo roll from the dispenser, she patted her face dry and blew her nose. Checking her phone, she saw three text messages had come through earlier. One each from Joey and Lainey, and another from Danny. Missy hadn't been lying. They'd bought a ton of stuff for this party.

Buy Missy a drink from us tonight! She deserves it, just look at all the great equipment we've got!

Pippa's tears returned as she gazed around the tiny cubicle. Lainey would be so disappointed with her if she knew the truth. Pippa couldn't bear the thought of her sister's beautiful features crushing into an expression of bewildered hurt. She'd never felt so alone. Texting Danny, she poured her heart out to him, telling him Missy was blackmailing her. Mercifully, he texted instantly.

Play it cool until you get back. She's a bunny boiler and always was. Keep her sweet and you'll be fine. Don't drink and keep your wits about you. If I could, I'd get on the next flight to be by your side. I'm sorry if I've caused any trouble for you. Things will change. We'll get through this. Love you xx D

Sighing, Pippa opened the foil and fumbled with the contents. Terrified she'd do something wrong now that she was alone without a guide, Pippa did her best to control the shaking in her hands.

What felt like a week later, she rejoined the ladies at the table. 'There you are,' Missy said raising an eyebrow. 'Oh you look pretty. I love that lip-gloss. You'll have to point out which one it is in duty-free.'

'You certainly are an ad for it,' Brianna agreed. 'It lights up your face!' As the waiter arrived with the bill, Missy whispered, 'So does a line of Charlie!'

Pippa tried not to stiffen her muscles when Missy linked her arm as they walked. Astonishingly, it appeared they were back to being best friends all of a sudden.

By the time they found a bar they all deemed suitable, Pippa was feeling decidedly better, but still incredibly wary of Missy.

'I love this song,' Missy said as she danced her way to a round table. 'This place is the bomb.'

'What's everyone having to drink?' Brianna said with a smile.

'Ooh, let's have a cocktail!' Missy suggested.

'Good call,' said Pippa knowing she needed to play her cards right. 'My round!'

Pippa had learned a long time ago that it was lethal to use a credit card in bars, especially while inebriated. But all sense went out the window as the cocaine relieved her inhibitions and restored her confidence.

She should have known she was racking up quite a bill when

their table was pretty much covered in empty glasses, but Pippa was unstoppable.

'I'm showing my age here, ladies,' Brianna slurred. 'But I cannot even smell another drink. I need to go back to the hotel and crash. Lord only knows what kind of shopping we're going to do tomorrow at this rate. This,' she hiccupped, 'is the most unprofessional I've been in twenty years. You two are a dreadful influence on me. But your enthusiasm is contagious!'

'Let's get you back,' Pippa said wobbling slightly. 'We should probably all go to bed. As Brianna says, we're in danger of buying hideous gear tomorrow otherwise.'

The two younger women had to practically drag Brianna back to the hotel.

'Are you certain you're OK from here?' Pippa asked as she fell in her hotel room door.

Brianna waved and clunked the door shut.

'I'm going to hit the hay too,' Pippa said with conviction. 'I was such a mess today and I'm probably going to be as bad tomorrow.'

Much to her relief Missy agreed. Pippa took off her make-up with shaky hands and pulled on her shorts and T-shirt, ready for bed. When she lay down, her body throbbed and her eyes burned, but her brain was still whirring like a hamster on a wheel.

She hadn't really taken Danny's advice to heart. She shouldn't have downed so many cocktails.

Anger soared through her. What would he know? He was a bloody druggy, after all. Pippa thought of Lainey and Joey, who were putting their heart and soul into getting Huntersbrook off the ground, and felt utterly ashamed in comparison.

Pippa loved fun and entertainment, but she hated this awful feeling that she was doing the wrong thing. She would curl up and die if her family knew the truth about Danny.

The Heart of Winter

As tears seeped onto her pillow, all anger at Danny melted. She wished she could stay angry at him. She wished he didn't make her heart do flips. She wished he wasn't funny and clever and charming. She wished she wasn't falling head over heels in love with him . . . .

Joey

JOEY COULD BARELY CONTAIN HIMSELF AS HE
tucked the basket into the corner of the back seat of his car.
He'd heard about the picnic basket hiring company when they'd
come to the office to pitch for business a couple of weeks ago.
When he called them, wondering if they'd deliver to Wicklow,
it turned out their premises was a fifteen-minute drive from
Huntersbrook.

He'd ordered the most luxurious version, which promised to
be a feast. It included champagne, caviar and napkins to match
the picnic rug. Every detail had been thought about and perfected.
If this worked out well, he could see Huntersbrook using the
hire company's services in the future to wow guests.

He needed this day to be perfect. Skye was being so helpful
to Lainey and he couldn't fault her enthusiasm over project
Huntersbrook, but he also was aware that she was going to be
under a bit more pressure to come to corporate events over the
next while as he established his career as partner. He felt they
needed a day away from work and Huntersbrook so they could
reconnect. He adored Skye, but there was a niggling feeling in
the back of his mind that they were getting a bit lost in trans-
lation as a couple of late. She hadn't mentioned their argument
the other night and neither had he. But he knew they should
clear the air.

Having agreed to meet the delivery van at the main gate, Joey was confident about today's surprise. When he'd last spied her, Skye was in a backroom working on a website for a customer. Although they'd had high-speed broadband installed, it seemed to work best at the rear of the house. His palms were sweating as he tried to act nonchalantly. Having taken delivery of the basket, he stowed it in the car and drove back to the main house, then walked through the house to find Skye.

'Hey.'

'Hi,' she said looking surprised. 'I thought you said you were going into Wicklow town for a bit. Did you forget something?'

'Yeah,' he said. 'I forgot you! Come on with me and we'll go for a bit of lunch. What do you reckon?'

Skye stretched and yawned.

'I've been rooted to the spot here for the morning,' she said, gazing longingly out the window. 'Sure, go on then. It is meant to be my week off after all.'

❄

Skye was quiet until they drove in the wrong direction out the main gate.

'Aren't we going to Wicklow?' she asked.

'Not today,' he said evenly. 'I've heard of a place that does amazing lunches. Ones like you've never experienced before. One you'll never forget,' he added.

'Have you been drinking?' Skye asked with a grin. 'You're in a very odd mood today.'

'Am I?'

As they pulled up at the wooded walk they'd been on many times before, Skye opened her seatbelt and sat to face him.

'Joey, have you lost your marbles? I'm hardly wearing walking gear and there's nowhere to get food here unless we're planning on doing it Bear Grylls style.'

'Follow me,' he said with his nose in the air. 'In fact, you go and stand over there,' he said pointing to the little wooden stile. 'I'll be with you in a sec.'

He watched as Skye walked over, shaking her head. He pulled the picnic hamper and fold-out stools from the car and followed her.

'What the . . .'

'No questions,' he said firmly. 'I'm in charge and you're going to do what you're told.'

Laughing, she walked alongside him as he heaved the large basket.

'Have you a dead body in there or what?' She tried to catch a peek inside.

'Ah-ah,' he warned. 'Walk on ahead.'

'At least allow me to carry the stools. Where did you get all this from?' she giggled.

As soon as they came to a little clearing with enough space to spread a blanket, Joey stopped. Laying the basket down gently, he opened it and took out the pretty rug and folded out the two stools.

'Wow, this is awesome!' he said staring inside. 'Look at all this.' The delicious quiche and salads were in easy to open containers and the matching gingham-patterned plates and cutlery were delightful.

'Where did you get this?' Skye asked. 'It's amazing!'

Joey explained and said he wanted to test the product before they considered buying more from the company as corporate Christmas gifts.

'You wouldn't give picnic hampers at Christmas, though. It'd be freezing out and nobody would use them. This is pushing it,' she shivered, 'and it's only just November.'

'True,' Joey agreed. 'But they do the usual Christmas fare of puddings and cakes and mince pies along with pâtés and other seasonal food. I suppose people could eat them inside!'

Skye tucked into the quiche. Joey's mouth was dry and he honestly thought he was going to have to bolt off behind a tree and be sick.

'What's wrong?' she asked mid-munch. 'Don't tell me you're feeling sick?'

'No.' He didn't look or sound convincing.

'Well you're as green as Yoda.'

He felt Skye staring at him as he made several attempts to speak. He gulped, coughed and then stared again.

'Joey, what's happening?'

'I . . . I had all sorts of things to say. I wrote it down and practised it in the back shed . . . About how I appreciate all the support you've given me since we got together . . . How happy I am that you get on with my family. That we've been doing really well at living together and all that . . . But . . .'

'Did you bring me here to break up with me?' Skye asked, her eyes starting to well up. 'I . . . I thought we were OK? I know we had that awful row the other night. But I felt so mean afterwards. I know I should've apologised . . . I was raining on your parade. It was wrong of me. But I was genu- inely feeling ill . . .'

'No!' he shouted, sitting onto his hunkers. 'I've made a total bags of this and I'll have to try and do the speech properly later, after several pints of gin or a shot of adrenalin to the heart, but Skye . . . will you marry me?' He fumbled in the side of the picnic basket and found the little box Holly had given him.

Now it was Skye's turn to look dumbfounded and sit in stunned silence. By the time Joey managed to prise open the ring box, tears were sliding down her cheeks.

'Will you marry me?' he repeated, crawling closer to her on his knees. All she could do was nod as she threw her arms around his neck.

'I'm stunned,' she said eventually. 'Wow that's some ring. It's gorgeous.'

'It was Grandma's. Mum gave it to me at the weekend.'

'Does she know you're giving it to me?' Skye asked in astonishment.

'Ding-dong!' he laughed. 'That was the general idea. She hardly thought *I* was going to wear it now did she?'

'But what about your sisters? Won't they be annoyed I'm getting your grandma's ring?'

Joey explained what Holly had said and how she was certain Skye was the right woman to wear it. Fumbling somewhat, Joey removed it from the box and slipped it onto her finger.

'It fits!'

'Just about,' she said, blushing.

As they kissed, Skye began to sob.

'Hey, I hope they're happy tears,' he said.

She nodded.

'Sorry. I don't know why I'm being such a ninny. I'm not usually this ridiculous.'

'What? All the other times you've gotten engaged,' he teased.

'You know what I mean,' Skye said. 'Well one thing is for certain, I *won't* ever forget this lunch.'

'I'm sorry I made such a hames of it all. It was meant to be romantic and perfect. I had the speech all ready . . . I wanted you to have an amazing start to the rest of our lives.'

'And giving me a bespoke picnic and a glittering rock isn't?' Skye said. 'If you feel this was a bad start, I'm looking forward to the bits you think are great! It was a marriage proposal, Joey, not a work pitch. Besides, you got your client,' she teased.

'Yeah,' he grinned. 'By the way, speaking of clients and all that . . .' A small voice in his head was shouting at him that this wasn't the time, but Joey was desperate to know that Skye would be on side. He needed her to understand what being Mrs Joey Craig would entail.

'This ball that's on next week . . . Clive's wife, Janet, is doing most of the organisation and she needed some extra pairs of hands and I sort of volunteered your services,' he said. 'Hope that's OK. It's a great chance to—'

'You what?' Skye looked horrified.

'Well, Clive didn't give me much choice, if I'm honest. He was fairly adamant that you pitch in seeing as I'm about to be a new partner and all that. It's kind of expected, sweetheart.'

Skye nodded silently.

'It'll be cool,' he said kissing her.

Joey didn't want to ruin their special moment, but he wasn't impressed by Skye's reluctance to back him up.

Skye gazed at her ring. A feeling of warmth and safety crept through her. No matter what the world threw at her from here on in, she'd manage. Before this, she had always felt so isolated. Her childhood had been so odd and she couldn't really explain it to anyone. It had left her feeling very alone in the world. But meeting Joey, and his family, finding Huntersbrook . . . it was the family she had always wanted. She looked up at Joey and kissed him again.

She didn't want to ruin this moment, but she knew the time had come for her to introduce Joey to her family. She'd have to call to their commune and share the news. But what if they wanted to come to the wedding?

They weren't *bad* people. There was nothing nasty or evil about them. But they existed in a bubble where the rest of civilization was blocked out entirely. They could be described as alternative, at best, and just plain odd, at worst.

Skye was terrified Joey might see her in a different light when he saw where she came from, but at the same time she needed him to know, to have that insight into her. Joey tightened his arms around her and rested his head on her shoulder.

'Will we phone my parents?' he asked. 'Seeing as Mum gave me the ring, I'd like her to be the first to hear our news.'

'Sure,' Skye smiled. 'We might have to think about making a journey to my parents at some point, too,' she said carefully.

He nodded happily.

As Joey spoke to his parents on speaker-phone, Skye knew everything was going to be just fine for them. The excitement she could hear down the line was so touching.

'Skye, I'm so thrilled you're going to be a permanent part of our family, love,' Holly said and Skye could hear the tears in her voice. 'You and Joey are a wonderful couple and I couldn't be happier.'

'Thank you for giving me Maggie's ring,' Skye said as tears began to fall. 'I'm so honoured to wear it. I can't believe you've entrusted it to me. If you ever feel you'd like it back, just say so.'

'Indeed I will not,' Holly said. 'It's yours now, pet. I wouldn't dream of taking it away from you.'

'Thank you, Holly,' she said.

'Will you have a wedding in Huntersbrook?' Paddy shouted out.

'We literally haven't had a chance to think about anything,' Joey answered. 'Leave it with us. We need to tell Skye's family too.'

'Are you telling your sisters and Echo?' Holly asked. 'Or do you want us to keep it quiet?'

Skye and Joey looked at one another and smiled.

'Maybe we should wait until Skye's parents know before we spread the happy news,' Joey suggested.

As soon as they put the phone down, Skye sat onto her fold-up chair and faced Joey. She had a strong sense that they had to do this, quickly, before she lost her nerve and never showed him her past.

'I'd like to go see my parents sooner rather than later,' she said.

'Well we have the rest of the day, why don't we go now?' he asked. 'Clearly it's going to mar your enjoyment of our engagement until you tell them. So shall we go?'

Skye was totally taken off-guard.

'Why not leave it until tomorrow?' she asked, suddenly panic-stricken at the whole idea.

'Ooh, I meant to tell you,' Joey said. 'I have to go to work for a bit tomorrow . . . So let's get it over with while we have the chance.'

Joey was right, Skye mused. Better to get it over and done with. Best not to have it hanging over her, dulling their happiness, but she hadn't missed the fact he'd said he was going back to work again tomorrow.

They finished their picnic and packed the car. The cottage was situated in the midlands, about two hours' drive away. Joey chatted easily as they sped from Dublin. He was so pumped about his new partnership, and Skye knew it meant the world to him.

'I know it's going to take me away from home for longer hours at times, but I can't remain stagnant,' he reasoned. 'I need to move onwards and upwards, you know?'

She nodded and said she understood. But a tiny spark of uncertainty was taunting at the back of her mind. *He's not going to have time for you* . . .

❄

As they neared her parents' commune, Skye tried to act nonchalant. She rarely divulged much about her family and her childhood was a time she didn't particularly want to recall. Nothing dreadful had happened to her, but she couldn't help feeling slightly resentful of the fact that her parents had turned her out into the world completely unprepared for modern life.

This visit would be as swift as possible, with little or no encouragement on her part for her family to get involved with the wedding.

'Looking forward to seeing your folks?' Joey asked as they neared the site.

'Not really,' she said honestly. 'They're really left of centre, Joey, so be prepared.'

'Ah, they can't be that bad,' he said with a reassuring pat of her leg.

'They're not like your family,' she warned. 'I hope my dad has reconsidered and visited a doctor.'

As soon as they drew up outside the cottage, Skye regretted coming. The small thatched building had a plethora of lean-to add-ons badly made from breezeblocks and corrugated iron roofing. The watery sunlight did nothing to make the yard and surrounding land any prettier. Although there were unspoiled meadows out the back as far as the eye could see, the immediate area was like a junkyard.

Scrawny chickens pecked at the muddy earth and picked their way around, looking disgruntled.

A weary mongrel with matted hair waddled over to sniff them.

'Bernard!' Skye said, looking fleetingly pleased.

'Bernard?' Joey looked mildly amused.

'Yeah, Echo and I were desperate to have what we deemed normal names so all our pets were called John or Mark or Mary. Bernard was only a pup when I left for Dublin. Now, as you can see, he's a grizzly old man.'

'Hello there.' A woman with exceptionally long grey woolly hair appeared, dressed in an elongated caftan style dress in rainbow colours.

'Hi Mum,' Skye said as she and Joey turned to look at the woman.

'Skye!' she said, holding her hand up to her eyes to shield the sunlight. 'You're welcome,' she said. 'And your man friend. Welcome,' she repeated clasping her hands and nodding vehemently.

Joey stood and stared as neither woman made any attempt to gravitate toward one another. He saw his own mother constantly, yet each time she saw him she hugged and kissed him as if he'd been missing in action for a hundred years. He found the lack of warmth from Skye's mother unnerving.

'I'm Joey,' he said offering his hand. She gazed at it in confusion until he retracted it.

'I'm Heaven,' she said. 'Come this way.'

'Sorry, Joey,' Skye said looking desperate. 'She's probably stoned out of her mind.'

Joey shrugged his shoulders and followed silently.

Inside, the small stone cottage was dark, damp and horribly chilly. Joey dreaded to think what it might be like when the really cold winter weather set in later in the winter.

'Hi, Auntie M,' Skye said. 'This is Joey.'

'Hey,' said a woman who looked similar to Heaven, with pepper and salt curly hair. 'What brings you kids around? Is Echo with you?' she asked peering around Skye.

'No,' Skye said, 'we came on a spur of the moment visit. He doesn't even know we're here.'

Bar the wooden kitchen table and chairs, there was very little proper furniture. Auntie M was slouched on a corduroy beanbag, knitting.

'So you still sell your knitted stuff I see,' Skye said clasping her hands together awkwardly. Joey looked over at his girlfriend, not really recognising the harsh tone in her voice.

The two women nodded.

'So Joey,' said Heaven. 'It's lovely to meet you.' She held out a hand that looked as if it should belong to a ninety-year-old. Her fingernails were yellowed and clogged with dirt. Joey shook it. He was totally confused by this woman. She certainly didn't conduct herself the way his mother did.

'Is Dad around?' Skye asked.

'Nope,' said Heaven. 'He took off after your uncle died,' she said without much emotion.

'What?' Skye looked stricken. 'When did Uncle Henry die?'

'Six weeks or so ago,' she said.

'Is that Echo's father?' Joey asked feeling upset too.

'Oh no,' said Heaven. Nobody seemed to want to expand on that, so Joey decided to remain quiet.

'Is Dad coming back?' Skye asked.

'Some day,' Heaven nodded. 'He needed to be with the moon and see the dawn in a different destination. He'll come home when he's ready,' she said easily. 'He's sick, too. He told you, didn't he? Seems his lungs are struggling to work.'

'Has he been to the hospital?' Skye asked, swallowing hard.

The two women shook their heads. 'He doesn't need to be incarcerated. He'd rather live freely for the time he has left.'

'But what if he has cancer? He needs treatment,' Skye said angrily.

'He's doing it his way,' Heaven said. 'I support him. Me and M support him.' She nodded and gazed into the middle distance.

'How are you supporting him when you're here rotting and he's God knows where slowly choking?'

'You let those emotions out, Skye,' said Auntie M. 'No sense in keeping it all bottled up. Let it fly . . .'

Joey was standing with his mouth open. He glanced over at Skye. His heart went out to her. She really looked as if she wanted the ground to swallow her.

'So, the thing is . . .' Skye looked at her shoes. 'Joey and I are engaged.'

'Nice,' said Heaven with a smile. 'Isn't that nice, M?'

'That's nice, you two,' she said as she paused momentarily before continuing to twiddle furiously with her knitting needles. The rustling noise from overhead made Joey look up.

'Hamsters live up there,' Heaven said following his gaze. 'They like the warmth of the thatch. We put a couple up there during a cold spell many years ago. We thought it would be a warm nesting place to see them through the winter. Now there are little families. They're reassuring when the nights are long and dark. The tiny squeaks are company for me and M.'

There was an awkward silence as Skye moved over closer to Joey. Neither of the older women made any attempt to offer them a drink or even a seat.

'Right, well Joey and I need to be getting back to work,' Skye fibbed. 'I'll write my mobile number on a card for you,' she said rustling in her bag.

'Will you do a wedding or what's your thinking on it all? No pressure, mind. I'm just asking, seeing as I'm your mother,' Heaven said, grinning to reveal a grey, gap-toothed mouth.

'There are no decisions yet,' Skye said. 'It all just happened. I thought we'd come and tell you . . . That's all.'

'Great,' said Heaven without so much as an ounce of enthusiasm.

As Skye spoke through gritted teeth, Joey knew she was struggling to remain calm.

'We'll be in touch. Tell Dad I said hello if he comes back. You'll let me know if you hear from him, won't you? That's my mobile number, OK?' Heaven nodded. M made a lame attempt to stand up.

'Don't get up. We'll see ourselves out. Bye, Auntie M. Bye, Mum.'

The women waved and blew kisses into the air and pretended to catch them and release them to the universe before joining hands and making an odd humming noise.

'We are asking the elements of the earth to come together and watch over you,' Heaven said. Skye tugged Joey's arm and led him back to the car. He was like a gawker at a car accident – appalled, but unable to look away.

It was a couple of minutes after they'd left the compound before Joey spoke.

'What the hell was all that?' he asked looking utterly traumatised.

In spite of her previous edginess, Skye burst into snorting laughter. Joey glanced over at her and back to the road as she actually cried with laughter. Clearly his confused grimacing was making Skye even worse. Eventually she calmed down and managed to speak.

'I tried to tell you how removed from reality my family is. You judge everyone by your family's standards and I know you never quite got what I meant . . .'

'Well I hear you now,' he said, finally starting to laugh too. 'Loud and clear. Christ Almighty, Skye, how are you so normal?' They both giggled as he tried to hide his utter shock at the scene he'd just witnessed.

Once her laughter subsided, Skye opened up to Joey about her childhood. It had literally been a fug of grass (the smoking variety rather than meadows) and dried fruit, with the odd book thrown in for good measure.

'How did you even learn to read or write?' Joey wondered.

'Actually Echo's mother was less insane than mine and she was originally a Montessori teacher. So we were lucky. Once we hit early teens, we insisted on going to proper school.'

'But you didn't live in that awful dark hamster hellhole for long, did you?' Joey shuddered.

'Yeah, for quite a while,' she said smiling. 'It didn't seem quite so dank back then. I guess it was less dreary when there were kids running about. Besides, we didn't know any different.'

'So Auntie M isn't Echo's mother?' Joey said, attempting to piece it all together.

'No,' she said. 'But he and M always got on well.'

'Where is Echo's mother now?'

'She left with Dino, her partner. They live on one of the tiny islands off Thailand, apparently.'

Joey shook his head. 'It's all bananas. I don't understand why they're so removed from you guys, though. If they're all about embracing the land and being free spirits, shouldn't that mean they hold the fruits of their loins close to their hearts?'

'You'd think, wouldn't you?' Skye said sarcastically. 'Maybe if they stopped smoking weed and had a vague reality check, they'd cop that they're missing out on our lives. But I can't see the moment of realisation dawning any time soon.'

'No,' Joey agreed. 'I wouldn't hold your breath if I were you.'

❋

By the time they got back to Wicklow, Skye was looking less stricken. Joey, on the other hand, was feeling decidedly disturbed. He stopped the car outside Huntersbrook, and sat back with a ragged sigh.

'You look boggle-eyed,' she giggled. 'We don't have to go near them again,' Skye said. 'I don't think we'll tell them any details of the wedding. Can you imagine how awkward it'd be having to introduce them to your family?'

Joey wasn't worried about his family. He was mentally taking colleagues and clients off the wedding list. There was no way in the world those two worlds could ever mix.

'Ah well, of course we'll have to invite them. Blood is thicker than water and all of that,' he said, hoping he sounded convincing.

'Joey,' Skye took his hand and stared at him intently. 'Please don't start having second thoughts about me.'

The look of raw terror that marred her pretty features made Joey love her even more than he had before.

'I don't share any of their crazy notions,' she said. 'You know that, right?'

'Ah damn,' Joey said, before grinning. 'You've spoiled my dream of living like hippies as we grow old disgracefully,' he said. 'Shucks.' He clicked his fingers.

When Skye didn't smile, he pulled her close and kissed her hair.

'Nothing matters but you and me,' he said. 'We've no immediate plans for the wedding, so let's take it one step at a time. If you want your family there on the day, then that'll be fine.'

'Just so long as they don't bring a bag of grass and a clay pipe,' she grinned.

Joey hugged her for a while longer and tried not to shudder as he thought of Heaven. More like *Hell* he mused. He certainly understood why Skye had wanted to start a new life away from her childhood home. On the up side, Joey was certain that Skye would be eager to stay with him at Huntersbrook, rather than suggesting they tear off and live elsewhere.

The Heart of Winter

Joey had never appreciated his home as much as he did that moment as they walked back into the welcoming warmth of Huntersbrook. Banishing all thoughts of crazy Heaven and the hamsters, he focused his mind on celebrating their engagement.

Lainey

LAINEY WAS FINDING IT DIFFICULT TO BECOME motivated today. Fair enough, they'd had a late night celebrating Joey and Skye's engagement, but she'd only had a single small glass of champagne and they'd been sitting down the whole time.

A dull ache crept into her heart as she thought of Grandma's engagement ring. She could never admit it to anyone, not even Matt, but she'd fought back tears when Skye held her hand up shyly for her to see.

She hoped she hadn't betrayed her true thoughts to Skye. She felt she'd gotten away with it because Skye hadn't flinched or retracted her hand swiftly. But Lainey knew she'd stared at the ring agog before recovering herself and forcing a smile. She'd actually wanted to crumble to the floor and sob in grief-stricken sadness. Why had her mother given Skye Grandma's ring?

Lainey didn't begrudge Skye at all. She adored her and was thrilled Joey was making her a permanent part of their family. But how could Holly give away Grandma's ring like that?

She'd considered asking for it over the past couple of years. It had been on the tip of her tongue to say it so many times. But Lainey knew she'd risk sounding like a selfish grabber. Besides, her mother clearly hadn't seen fit to offer it.

It wasn't the monetary worth of Grandma's beautiful diamond and sapphire ring that Lainey craved. It was the familiarity and the sense of Grandma that it carried.

From the time she was a toddler, Lainey had adored that ring. She'd fiddled with it and twirled it around Grandma's finger any time she'd sat on her lap. Grandma was her primary carer in those years, when Holly wasn't together enough to be a proper mother. It was Grandma who had made her feel safe and special and loved. She loved Maggie so much, and it was so horrible when she died. Ever since, Lainey privately kept hoping for the moment when Holly would call her aside and press the old red velvet box into her hands. Now, that would never happen.

Lainey hadn't made a big deal of the ring recently because her Mum never wore it. It had been hidden away in its box until now. Blaming her pregnancy hormones for her emotional reaction, Lainey knew she needed catch herself on and stop gazing at Skye's finger like a stalker.

But no matter how hard she tried, every time she caught a glimpse of Grandma's ring last night, it had jarred her. To Lainey, it was the very essence of her beloved Grandma, and now it was going to be worn by somebody else, somebody who'd never even met Maggie.

'Are you feeling OK?' Skye had asked her last night.

'Yeah, I'm ridiculously tired,' she'd said as tell-tale tears crept down her cheeks. 'Ugh sorry, Skye. I'm an emotional wreck right now. I'm just so happy for you and Joey.' She had hugged Skye and forced a smile. 'Silly me! Don't pay any attention. I'm giggling one minute and sobbing the next. I'm a disaster! So,' she said pulling herself together. 'Do you think you'll change your name? Will you become an official Craig?'

'Definitely,' Skye had said nodding. 'I'm not close to my own lot, as you know. You guys have been my family well before today. I'll be honoured to take Joey's name.'

Lainey had stayed for as long as she could last night. In fact, she would have gone to bed a lot earlier except she was terrified of drawing attention to her miserable status.

Jacob took Ely away to bed and she knew she could have used that as an opportunity to escape. But she felt grinning and bearing it and putting on a brave face was a safer bet.

She'd assumed her ploy was working a treat, until Holly cornered her and gave her a hushed dressing-down.

'What's wrong with you, Lainey? Don't think I haven't noticed you giving poor Skye the most seething glowers. Can't you at least pretend to be happy for your brother and his girlfriend?'

'I am,' she hissed. 'I'm thrilled for both of them. I adore Skye, you know I do . . .'

'So what is it then? Why are you acting as if you'd rather be anywhere but here?'

'I wouldn't,' Lainey said weakly.

'If it's because of Grandma's ring,' Holly began. 'I discussed it with Joey. We decided it wouldn't be fair to give it to you or Pippa. I had an equal amount of reasons as to why it ought to go to either of you. So I figured the safest thing would be to let Joey have it.'

Lainey had opened her mouth to say something in protest but realised no matter how she put her argument across, she would only sound horribly spoilt.

'I'm just a little shocked to see the ring again. I'm used to it being on Grandma's finger and it makes me sad. I'm sorry if you think I'm being awful. That wasn't my intention . . .'

'No,' Holly sighed deeply. 'I'm sure it wasn't. I should have mentioned it to you. But I didn't know Joey was going to propose today. I suppose I thought he'd wait a while. I only gave it to him the other day.'

'It's not your fault, Mum. Besides, this is a happy occasion. We all adore Skye and I know I'll get used to seeing the ring on her. It's hers now and I honestly wish her the very best with it.'

'That's good,' Holly said. 'Why don't you get off home? You look exhausted.'

'No, I'll stay a while,' Lainey had said stubbornly. 'I'm actually feeling great,' she insisted, even though bed was all she could think of.

Now, as she struggled to even exist, she berated herself. Why did her mother make her act so obstinately? Nobody else had that effect on her. She should have come home to bed last night and maybe she wouldn't be feeling so rotten today. Her whole body felt odd. Nothing specific, just an oddness that wasn't going away.

Suddenly longing to speak to Pippa, she dialled her number, hoping to catch her for a couple of moments while she was in Paris . . . The foreign ring tone ended and Pippa's voicemail message clicked on. Lainey left a brief message saying she was missing her and wished her a good trip.

It was misty and grey outside and heavy sheets of squally rain began to pelt against the window.

'Yucky day out there,' she said to Ely who was busy emptying a cupboard of all its contents.

'I hope you're going to tidy that all away again,' she said grinning. He chirped away, totally content with his game. She ruffled his silky hair and sat down at the kitchen table, forcing herself to turn her attention to something positive. She'd fill in the forms for her cookery course and send them off to Sally.

With Sally's recommendations she'd found some former cookery school students to do the food at Missy's party, but she was hoping it would be the last time she'd need to pay such extortionate money for catering.

She couldn't believe the party was now only a fortnight away. Time had flown and she was really excited to see how the venue would play out.

As she checked over the form to ensure she'd written all the necessary details, Lainey's head began to swim. She carried on regardless and wrote the payment cheque and popped the whole lot into an envelope. She'd licked the stamp and secured it when she began to feel really strange. It was as if a furnace had been ignited inside her. The intensity and swift onset of the pain that seared through her belly was terrifying.

Gripping the table, she struggled to breathe through the pain, just like she'd been taught to do for labour.

The kitchen door opened and she heard a voice.

'Lainey? Are you OK? What is it?'

She knew it was Jacob, but she couldn't see him. The sounds in the room began to drawl and she knew she was fainting before it actually happened. Lainey heard the thud as she hit the floor. After that, things became blurry.

She felt several people lifting her and knew she was being wheeled. The sound of the siren zoned in and out of her consciousness as she fought to stay awake. Her eyes were too heavy and she couldn't muster the strength to speak. A voice she didn't recognise kept repeating something, but she wasn't able to decipher what it was saying.

Bright lights came and went and the droning voice continued. All of a sudden it ended. The need to sleep was too much to fight and she felt her body relaxing. The wonderful soft comforting feeling that engulfed her was like none she'd ever experienced before.

As she floated, she was met by the most beautiful scenes. She was sitting on an animal that seemed similar to a horse, yet she knew it wasn't one. The crystal clear colours of the valley below were like nothing she'd ever seen. There was blue water that seemed so pure and sparkly, it made her call out in joy. Tiny fragments of multicoloured iridescent light surrounded her as she came to a halt. A figure began to walk toward her. With its arms outstretched, it coaxed her forward. Encouraging her and making her feel more loved than she'd ever thought possible.

With all her being, Lainey wanted to run to the figure and follow it to the gorgeous valley. But something was holding her back. She glanced behind and saw a face. It was blurred at first and she couldn't recognise who it was. She rubbed her eyes vigorously and focused hard.

'Ely!' she called. 'Come with me.'

His image began to retreat and fade. He moved backwards and away from her.

'Wait,' she said. Fear and sadness drenched her. 'Help,' she screamed. 'I need to be with my baby.'

Torn, she looked at the wonderful valley once more. Hesitating, she closed her eyes and balled her fists. If she went there, she knew she'd be happy. But her longing to be with Ely was stronger. He needed his mother and she wanted to be there for him. Reluctantly she blocked out the image of the magical valley before turning and running after Ely, her boy.

As her eyes fluttered open, the harsh lights made her wince. The scent in the air was sharp and it stung her nostrils. The sounds were clattery and harsh. She groaned, wanting to claw her way back to the beautiful utopia she'd just left. She tried to call out, to say she'd changed her mind. That she wanted to see the beautiful valley once again. But her mouth was dry and leathery. Her voice was paralysed and her chest felt as if it were lined with lead.

'Lainey? Can you hear me?'

She turned her head to the side and squeezed her eyes shut, hoping the awfulness would disappear. Loud swishing noises made her stomach lurch. The voice came back.

'Lainey? Please answer me, love.'

She licked her lips. They were flaky and her tongue was spongy.

'Lainey?'

She needed to tell the voice to stop annoying her. Maybe then she could return to the lovely floaty state. Instead, her eyes popped open as an image of Matt hovered right there above her face.

'Matt.'

'Thank God,' he said lowering his head to kiss her tenderly. She smiled. Even though she wasn't in the paradise she'd visited, it was wonderful to see him.

She tried to sit up so she could tell Matt about the place. He'd love it. She could try and take him there. But none of her muscles wanted to engage. She couldn't direct her spine to curl forward so she could sit up.

She felt Matt's touch on her forehead as he stroked her hair gently.

'It's all going to be OK,' he said, his voice croaking with love.

She focused on him. He looked drawn and exhausted. There was deep sadness in his eyes that told her something awful had happened.

'What is it?' she managed.

A single tear escaped down his cheek as he tried to give her a brave smile.

'You're going to be fine, and that's the main thing.'

Confusion was an added pain she simply couldn't deal with. She closed her eyes again, willing sleep to take over. The journey she'd been on was incredible. But she needed to sleep now. She couldn't bear to hear the tale of woe Matt was clearly burdened by. Perhaps when she'd had a little sleep, then she'd be able. Or better still, maybe the problem might go away. She drifted away again, leaving it all behind, embracing the quietness and the darkness.

❄

What seemed like hours later, Lainey woke again. A team of doctors were standing at the end of her bed. One stepped forward and came round to the side of the bed.

'Lainey, I'm Dr Cumisky,' he said. 'I need to tell you what happened.'

'OK,' she managed as she tried to sit up.

'I'll get the nurses to help you into a more comfortable position. But for now, you'll need to lie still.'

'What happened to me?' she asked.

'I'm afraid I had to perform a full hysterectomy on you.'

'No . . .' She wanted to cry, but her body was too exhausted and numb. The words washed over her like a wave of icy water. 'My baby . . .'

'That's the thing,' Dr Cumisky said. 'You weren't actually pregnant, Lainey.'

'But I did a test,' she said.

'You had a cyst. Let me explain . . . There is a type of rare ovarian cyst that can occasionally produce HCG, which is the hormone present during pregnancy. That's why your home-testing kit gave you a positive pregnancy result.'

'Do I have cancer?' she whispered.

'I don't know the answer to that question just yet,' Dr Cumisky said. 'I've removed the mass, which is called a teratoma or a dermoid. These cysts can be either benign or malignant. I have no way of knowing which until pathology test it.'

Lainey was numb. She had no words. Dr Cumisky talked a bit more, but she'd already zoned out. She managed some level of small talk while remembering to thank him for saving her life before he moved off with his team.

Left alone in the room with Matt, she tried to make sense of it all.

'I'm sorry,' she suddenly said turning to him.

'Hey,' he crooned. 'What are you apologising for?'

'I've killed our chances of having any more children,' she said as her voice cracked. Her body shook violently as she sobbed.

Matt said all the right things and reassured her over and over again that he loved her and nothing else mattered.

'We have Ely and most of all we have *us*.'

She nodded. He was right. But she couldn't shake the hollow, lonely, bitter ache that was snowballing inside of her.

'Where's Ely?' she asked suddenly.

'He's with Holly. She was brilliant. As soon as the ambulance arrived she took him and said she'd keep him as long as we need.'

'I don't want her near him,' she said loudly.

'Lainey,' Matt sighed. 'We need all the support we can get right now. It's going to take a while before you're back on your feet. We need to know the test results. This could be a long road ahead, love. Let's not shut anyone out . . .'

Anger shot through her like a runaway train. The thought of her mother commandeering Ely galled her. Knowing Holly, she'd change his routine and poison him against her. She was about to voice all of that to Matt when she glanced up at his stricken face. Knowing he was on the edge and had clearly been through the mill, she gritted her teeth and remained silent.

'It's better for Ely if he's being minded by Holly rather than shunting him from Billy to Jack while you're incapacitated,' Matt said pleadingly.

She nodded.

Matt sat back in the chair and she looked over at him. He'd actually aged since this morning. He was pale and pinched looking and all she felt was guilt. How could she shout at him and make a fuss? The poor man looked worried sick.

'Why don't you get off home?' she suggested. 'It's been a much longer day for you than me. I was asleep for most of it. You've been through the mill.'

'I'm fine here,' he said.

'I'd rather you went.' She put her hand out for him to clasp.

'It won't change anything if you sit here uncomfortably for the entire night. Go and get some food and a proper night's sleep.'

'If you're sure,' he said, looking doubtful.

'I am. Thanks for everything. We'll be OK, darling. As you rightly said, we have each other. We'll get through this.'

Her ploy worked and Matt's worried face softened slightly. He leaned over and kissed her before walking out. He turned around as he was about to enter the corridor and waved. She blew him a kiss and smiled.

Once she was certain he was gone, Lainey allowed the tears to fall. Her sight blurred as she lay on her back, staring up at the ceiling. A hot angry trickle coursed down either side of her face as she gulped. The tsunami of grief that engulfed her was so fierce, it threatened to stop her heart. Grief for the baby she thought she was carrying. Grief for the other babies she would never have. Grief for Ely, who would be an only child. Grief for Matt, who had a defunct, useless wife.

Pippa

PIPPA WAS ALMOST ON HER HANDS AND KNEES. She'd had hangovers before, but none came close to the ones she'd been experiencing lately. Her eyeballs felt like they'd been peeled, her limbs ached, but most of all it was as if a fog had descended on her brain. Even the most menial task was difficult to carry out. When they'd returned from Paris, Missy had bamboozled her into going clubbing. Right now she felt as if her liver were beginning to fail. She needed a week of early nights so she wouldn't be in a coma by the time Missy's party came round.

'Seriously, Pippa,' Missy said crashing in the door of her office. 'You look like hell. This isn't going to work. Daddy is on his way in here and we've to sit with Brianna and go through the events of the trip to Paris.'

Pippa swallowed hard. The thought of having a conversation with Mr Hassett, let alone fill him in on what they'd bought and how they proposed selling it all, was terrifying.

'Here, get your ass into the bathroom and powder your nose,' Missy said tossing a small leather purse at her. 'It's in the tiny zippy part.'

'Oh no, thank you Missy but I couldn't . . .'

'Your eyes are hanging out of your head, Pippa. You look like shit. I am not about to raise any suspicions with my old man. He knows you and I go together like ham and eggs right now.

If you're looking this horrendous, he's going to start scrutinizing me. I don't need to be in the firing line today. Daddy thinks I've turned over a new leaf. He's delighted I'm finally showing an interest in this sorry excuse of a store. So don't you even dream of messing this up for me, you hear?'

'I'm sure he won't even notice me . . .' Pippa began.

'My father isn't some old buzzard who has no idea of life, Pippa. I need him on side. I've had enough of his and Mum's lectures and tutting to last me a lifetime. You're not going to make me look bad, you hear?'

'I'll pop to the loo and put on some more make-up. That'll do the trick.'

As she went to walk past, Pippa felt Missy's long gel nails digging into the top of her arm.

'Do what I tell you, Pippa. I won't allow you to screw things up for me. Even if you hired the world's most talented plasterer, he wouldn't fix your sorry hungover face.' She grabbed the purse from Pippa's desk and thrust it into her hand. 'Hurry up, you don't need to be late and make an entrance.'

By the time she secured the cubicle door shut Pippa was sweating. Panic pricked at her, giving her goose bumps all over. Her eyes burned with unshed tears as she fumbled with the purse. She hated the thought of taking more coke, but she couldn't figure out any alternative choice. She'd become quite the expert by now and she swiftly snorted two lines. She was washing her hands when her mobile rang. Grabbing it up from the side of the sink, she saw Matt's number flashing up.

'Pippa,' he said sounding strangled. 'I have some bad news about Lainey. The worst, really.'

She listened in horror as he filled her in on Lainey's condition and the emergency surgery she'd had the day before.

'Oh no! Poor Lainey,' she managed.

'I tried calling your mobile last night. So did Holly. But we couldn't get you.'

Pippa sucked in air sharply. She'd been out with Missy and hadn't wanted to answer the phone in case she sounded totally out of it. The commotion with Missy this morning had sidetracked her and she'd forgotten to ring anyone back.

'She's really low, Pippa. She was trying to put a brave face on things, but she's struggling like I've never seen her before. It broke my heart to leave her there last night,' he said. 'I think she's grieving the baby she thought she had and all the others she wanted.' His voice dropped to a ragged whisper. 'It's just awful.'

'Will you call me when you get to the hospital this morning?' she asked. Her head was spinning and she could feel her pulse racing. Her temples throbbed and she struggled to focus on what Matt was telling her.

'Pippa, I think she'd love to see you,' he said.

'What?'

There was a pause at the other end of the line and Pippa knew Matt must be shocked by her reaction. 'Lainey needs you. Would you be able to leave work and go to her, even for an hour?'

'I . . .' Pippa clunked her head against the wall. 'I'm in the middle of something at the moment. Can I call you back?'

She hung up and ran the cold water tap. Splashing it onto her face, she prayed the shock would sober her. The door burst open.

'What's up? You look like you've just been shown Santa's grave,' Missy said. 'Come on. Brianna and Daddy are waiting. I'm not sitting in there on my own. Jeez, Pippa, fix your make-up for crying out loud.'

'Missy, it's Lainey,' she said and quickly filled her in.

'I hope this isn't going to affect my party,' Missy said immediately.

'Pardon?' Pippa asked, narrowing her eyes.

'Uh, like . . . 'cause it's all costing your family a pile of cash. So it really needs to go ahead. And besides, soo many people are coming . . .'

Pippa wanted to thump Missy. She really was the most selfish and spoilt creature she'd ever met.

'My sister is lying in a hospital bed and she might have cancer,' Pippa said through gritted teeth. 'Are you seriously telling me that the first thing that jumps into your head is your party?'

'Now you're twisting my words,' Missy said. 'I am just as concerned as you are about Lainey. *I'm* the one who's helping your family business don't forget,' she said. 'Talk about biting the hand that feeds,' Missy sneered.

Pippa took deep breaths, attempting to calm herself.

'I'm sorry, Missy,' she said. 'I . . . I'm just so scared.'

'OK,' she conceded. 'I'll get you a taxi. We'll both go to the hospital and see Lainey.' As she turned to walk away, Pippa felt as if she were swimming through syrup.

'I can't see Lainey while I'm buzzed off my head,' Pippa blurted out.

'Would you keep your bloody voice down,' Missy hissed. 'I don't get you, Pippa. All I've done since this morning is try and help. First I try to dig you out of looking like shit at our meeting and now you're acting like a diva for no reason. I'm offering to accompany you to sit at your sister's bedside and you're throwing it all back in my face and behaving like some deranged idiot. Sometimes I wonder why I bother with you . . .'

'I'm so sorry, Missy,' Pippa said as her heart pounded. The last thing she needed was Missy turning on her and taking it out on her family.

'Friendship is a two-way thing,' Missy said with her hands on her hips.

'I know,' Pippa said. Her pulse was racing and she longed for a drink of water. 'Thank you for being so good to me,' she said attempting to say what she thought Missy wanted to hear.

Pippa's phone rang again. Bracing herself, she prepared to tell Matt she'd be there later in the afternoon.

'I'm still in a meeting,' she said answering it without looking.

'Oh . . . Sorry, Pip. I just wanted . . .'

'Lainey!' Pippa wailed. 'Oh God, are you OK? Of course you're not. Oh Lainey, I'm so sorry to hear what's happened. Matt just called.'

'It's been so scary, Pippa.' Her voice sounded so weak and far away, not like her sister at all. Tears streamed down Pippa's cheeks as her entire body began to shake.

'I'll come as soon as I can,' she promised.

'Thanks, Pippa,' Lainey said. 'I'd like that.'

'Hang in there, Lainey,' Pippa said as she hung up.

'Ugh, the drama of it all,' Missy said and pulled Pippa towards Brianna's office. 'There's been a crisis,' Missy announced.

By the time Pippa explained the situation to Brianna and Mr Hassett she was having trouble controlling her heaving sobs.

'Oh Pippa, that's terrible,' Mr Hassett said. 'You must go to your sister at once. Missy can organise a cab for you. Take as much time as you need.'

'Absolutely,' Brianna agreed. 'Would you like me to come with you? I can stay in the waiting room. I wouldn't want to crowd your family.'

'Oh gosh no,' Pippa said. Her hands were shaking violently. Her jaw was clamped and her teeth began to grind horribly.

'You're really in shock, love,' Brianna said, taking her arm and guiding her to a chair.

'I'll be fine in a minute,' she managed. She knew she needed to stop crying, but her emotions seemed to be operating independently of her brain. Looking up at Brianna, she heard herself saying she'd like to go home and fetch some things.

'Will I take you?' she offered.

'Thank you. You're being so wonderful,' Pippa said as she finally managed to reduce her bawling to a shuddery version of hiccupping. 'But I think it'd be best if I go alone. Missy has been amazing too,' she said looking over at her. 'But the hospital where they've taken Lainey is a small regional one and they wouldn't be able to cope with a crowd. Lainey is very weak too . . .'

'Of course,' Brianna said.

'If you need us, just call,' Missy said sweetly.

Pippa strode to her desk and gathered her things. As she made her way down the escalator and out into the dewy air she felt completely bug-eyed. There was no way in hell she could pitch up at Lainey's bedside in this boggled state.

Half running and half walking, she made it to the end of the street and jumped on a bus. The journey to her apartment seemed to go on forever.

Her phone rang as Lainey's name danced on the screen. Her vision was oddly blurred. She let it ring out. Bile rose in her throat as she disembarked and staggered from the bus to the safety of her apartment.

Not sure of who else she could call, she dialled Danny's number.

'Hey,' he answered in a whisper. 'I'm with a client. Can I buzz you back in a few?'

'Danny,' she said sounding strangled. 'I need your help . . .'

'What's happened?'

'It's Lainey . . . She's in hospital and I need to go to her but I'm buzzing off my face . . .'

'What? Now? How?'

Haltingly, she filled him in.

'Oh bloody hell, Pippa,' he said. 'Listen, I've stepped outside my office for a minute. But I'll have to go back in. I'll get to you as soon as I can. But it's going to be at least half an hour. Stay calm, yeah?'

'I have to go to Lainey,' she wailed.

'Are you insane?' he shot back. 'You can't go near a hospital in that state. A doctor would take one look at you and know you're out of your mind. You'll have to wait a few hours until you're in a fit state.'

Pippa hung up and perched on the edge of the sofa. Hoping it might help, she peeled off her clothes and got into the shower. Slowly moving the temperature dial she made the water as cold as she could bear. Shivering violently she stepped out and pulled a towel from the hook on the back of the bathroom door. Wrapping herself, she plunged onto the floor and sat huddled like a cornered rat.

Lainey

LAINEY FELT DESOLATE. SHE KNEW MATT WOULD be there soon and she honestly wanted to see him. But sometimes a girl just needed her sister.

Pippa would be here as soon as she could. Lainey knew she was under a lot of pressure at work and she'd just come home from Paris. But it was comforting to know she was on her way.

Pippa would pull her out of this dark hole she felt she was slipping into. Nobody could nail things in a sentence like Pip. She'd have some sort of logic as to how all this awfulness would be fine in the end . . . She was probably gathering her bag and coat and clearing her sudden departure with her boss. Lainey closed her eyes and thought back to how different Pippa used to be. She was the typical youngest sibling really. She got away with murder at school growing up. Lainey wouldn't have dared do half the things Pippa had gotten away with. But now that they were adults, their relationship had become one of acceptance and mutual admiration.

Unlike Pippa, Lainey would never know the exact accessory to brighten up an otherwise dull outfit. In turn, Pippa would never see the fascination with researching twenty varieties of potatoes to ensure the right one was planted and made to thrive. But that was why Lainey loved her so much – Pippa was entirely, uniquely herself.

The pain was definitely worse than it had been earlier. Lainey knew the nurses were rushed off their feet, but she couldn't take it any longer. Pressing the call button she waited, almost holding her breath and afraid to move a muscle.

'Hello dear, everything OK?' the nurse asked as she breezed in.

'I'm in a lot of pain. Could I have something to help?'

'Yes, you're due some medication as it happens, so you're bang on,' the nurse smiled. Lainey watched as she read her chart and made a little note.

'I'll be back in a jiffy.'

The other three beds in the ward were empty, which was a relief for the moment. Lainey wasn't sure she could conduct a normal conversation with a stranger. She wasn't sure she could say out loud what had happened to her either. All her energy was being sapped by just behaving normally – what she really wanted to do was fling herself onto the cold tiles and bash her head against them to block out the pain in her heart.

Suddenly, a hotly stabbing shot of pain coursed through her. Crying out involuntarily, she attempted to curl into a ball. The stitches in her lower abdomen along with the thick wadded bandaging restricted any movement.

'Here we are,' the nurse said as she returned. 'I'm going to check your blood pressure first.' As she fastened a black Velcro cuff around the top of Lainey's arm, the machine kicked in. Although it was only gentle squeezing pressure, it made Lainey groan.

'You poor love,' said the nurse reading the numbers. 'Your blood pressure is up a little.' She took her temperature and scribbled on her chart again. 'You really are very sore, aren't you?'

Lainey nodded miserably.

'On a scale of one to ten, ten being the worst pain you've ever endured, where would you reckon you are right now?'

Lainey blinked. She knew this numerical idea must be a very

clear method of gaining accurate information most of the time. But her head was so muzzy and the pain so awful, she honestly couldn't choose a number.

If she said nine, the nurse might give her heroin. If she said two, she'd probably only get paracetemol.

'It's only a ball-park figure,' said the nurse, patting her arm. 'If it's easier, you can use an adjective.'

'I'm in agony,' Lainey said weakly.

'I guessed, pet. I'm going to give you a little injection along with a couple of tablets. That'll make you feel a bit like having a snooze. But you're in the right place for that.'

Lainey hated needles. Who didn't? But at that moment she'd never been so delighted to be stabbed by one and was hoping the magic liquid it contained was going to lift her out of this excruciating pain. She swallowed the tablets and tried to close her eyes. She'd have a little rest and Pippa would be here soon. Knowing her sister, she'd cheer her up. She'd probably say completely the wrong thing, but that was why Lainey needed her there.

❄

Back at the apartment, Pippa had forced herself to get dressed and put on makeup. She styled her hair and it looked glossy and bouncy, in total contrast to how she felt. The effect of the drug wasn't fun or even confidence-boosting today. She longed for the unnatural sensation to depart. She leaned into the bathroom mirror and stared. Her eyes were like two snooker balls. There was no way she could see her family or Lainey yet.

Figuring she could walk some of it off, Pippa pulled on her puffa coat and left the apartment. Her mobile rang again. This time it was Missy.

'How's Lainey?' she asked.

'Eh, I haven't made it to the hospital yet,' she said.

'OMG, you are not going to *believe* this,' she shrieked. 'Daddy has just told me I'm to stay on late tonight along with Brianna. He wanted you to be here too, but seeing as we thought you were at the hospital he'd said not to bother you . . .'

'What?' Pippa said. 'Why? Did we do something wrong?' she asked nervously.

'Nuh-uh,' Missy said, 'quite the opposite. Daddy seems to think the three of us are a buying and sales powerhouse. Brianna talked us up to him so much at the meeting just now. She totally loves us, Pippa,' she said triumphantly. 'And now Daddy thinks we're totally the bomb. It seems there's an A lister celeb coming in to do some after-hours shopping tonight! Daddy said not to even mention it to you if you're busy at the hospital, but I know I'd totally kill you if you didn't tell me about this one!' she said squealing with excitement.

'Really?' Pippa said as her interest spiked. 'Who is it?'

'Guess,' Missy said raising one eyebrow.

'Eh, is it a man or a woman?' Pippa asked. She stopped walking and leaned against a wall, gulping in fresh air.

'Woman.'

'Is she a singer or an actress?'

'I can only answer yes or no,' Missy insisted. Pippa rolled her eyes. She couldn't cope with all Missy's antics, but knew better than to snap at her.

'Is she an actress?'

'Yes!' Missy said in delight.

'Um . . .'

Missy sounded like she was about to explode. Pippa sighed and rubbed her face, trying to feel less out of it.

'I'll give you a few clues. She's the living end, has starred in *all* the biggest must-see movies of the past ten years. She used to be married to the most gorgeous man in Hollywood. She's the only person on the planet who seems to genuinely have an amicable public divorce. She's totally stunning and doll-like. Every girl wants to *be* her and all the men want to be *with* her . . . Oh and she's Irish!'

'Not Jodi Ludlum,' Pippa said in awe.

'Yes, Jodi Ludlum!'

'Shut up!' Pippa said nearly collapsing. 'And she's coming into the store tonight? To buy stuff?'

'You got it, genius,' Missy teased.

'Oh holy God,' Pippa said. 'I have to phone everyone I know and tell them.'

'No you don't,' Missy said. 'Daddy says we can't breathe a word and we're not to have phones or cameras near her.'

'Shoot,' said Pippa chewing the inside of her cheek. 'Bummer. I'd love a pally looking selfie photo for my Facebook page. Could you imagine how jealous everyone would be?'

'I know!' Missy said. 'This is so cool. I actually feel like I'm going to have a heart attack!'

'I still haven't gone to see Lainey at the hospital,' Pippa confessed. 'I was so off my face I couldn't go. I came home and had a shower and now I'm wandering aimlessly about trying to sober up.'

'Well get your ass back in here and we'll pass the time and use your energy to pick out the most amazing clothes for JODI LUDLUM!' Missy yelled.

Pippa was greatly relieved to have a valid reason why she couldn't go and see Lainey. She could tell her sister tomorrow exactly who the 'secret shopper' was . . . Lainey would understand . . .

Pippa still felt like a complete bitch as she texted her sister: *Lainey I'm so sorry honey, but I've been detained at work. We've an A lister celebrity coming to do personal shopping and I can't leave. It'll be too late by the time I get out. I'll be there first thing in the morning. Promise. Love you xx P*

Lainey had just drifted off as her phone beeped with a text message. The sickening raw pain was beginning to subside as she tried to focus on the text. Her heart sank as she read Pippa's words. Knowing her sister couldn't possibly help not being here, she felt like a spoilt child as her tears began to fall once more. Not wanting Pippa to feel any worse than she already did, Lainey sent a brief message: *Hey no worries Pip. I know you'd be here if u cud. C u 2moro xx*

❄

Pippa read Lainey's text and stuffed her phone into her coat pocket. Shame and guilt taunted her as she strode back toward the city centre. Pippa knew she deserved to be hit by a truck or have a bird poo on her head right now. Karma would be well within its rights to bite her on the ass this minute. She was the worst sister on the planet and a total mess.

Her throat hurt as she gulped in cold air and forced her burning leg muscles to move faster. Her phone rang yet again.

'Hello?' she panted.

'Pippa, where are you? I'm at your apartment.'

'Danny! Shit, I'm sorry. I've had to go back to work.'

'I thought you were off your trolley? What about Lainey?'

'I'm sorry, Danny. I've been called back into work. It's an emergency and I've had to tell Lainey I'll see her tomorrow.'

'Didn't you tell your boss you have a family situation?'

'Yeah, they know. But this is . . .'

'What? More important than your sister?'

'Fuck off, Danny,' she said, hanging up on him. Tears fell down her cheeks as she picked up her pace. As the store came into sight her mobile rang in her pocket. She snatched it out and gazed at the screen.

Cursing under her breath she pressed the red button, cutting her mother off. Switching the phone off, she tried to block the entire situation with Lainey and her family from her mind. All she could cope with was the here and now. Everything else was far too complex.

Lainey

LAINEY THOUGHT HER HEART WOULD BURST OUT her chest as she saw Jules approaching from the hospital corridor.

'I came as fast as I could. Matt rang. Oh sweetheart, how are you?'

'I'm fine, Jules. You're so good to come. You must've driven like a bat out of hell.'

She nodded. 'I parked on the grass out there too. There weren't any proper spaces left and I needed to see you.'

'Don't make me laugh,' Lainey said wincing. 'Your car might get towed away. Should you not move it?'

'Nah, sod it. If anyone wants to steal it, I'd be thrilled. It's on its last legs and I doubt if it'll make the NCT.'

Jules didn't want to say it to Lainey, but she looked like a corpse. She had so many tubes and scary machines hooked up to her. Her eyes were heavy and she was clearly fighting to stay awake.

'You sleep for a while, pet. I'll be right here. I'd prefer to sit on this chair with you than spend another evening with my mother. So you'll be doing me a favour.'

Thankfully, Lainey drifted off into a deep sleep. Jules couldn't help taking a small brush from her own bag and gently teasing her friend's hair into a less nest-like state. She plucked some facial wipes from her enormous bag and cleaned her skin. Lainey was seriously hot and looked an odd shade of green.

The nurse came by to check on her and insisted they must stay quiet.

'It's after official visiting hours, so I'll be shot if a doctor comes past.'

'I'll say that I snuck in,' Jules said. 'She's my best friend in the whole world. I can't leave her alone.'

'She's lucky to have you, love,' said the nurse kindly. 'I'll turn a blind eye.'

By the time Lainey woke, Jules had transformed her. She'd even massaged hand cream onto her arms.

'I smell like you,' Lainey said with a weak smile.

'I gave you a little bird-bath while you were sleeping. I resisted doing your make-up figuring you'd only have to take it off again tomorrow.'

'Thanks, Jules.'

'How are you feeling now? Is the pain bad?'

Lainey shook her head saying she was OK. They chatted a bit about Jules' mother and both agreed she was a dragon who would end up alone.

'She won't even be a cat woman. No cat would want to live with her . . . Still my flat will be ready to move back into in a couple of days. So no harm done.'

'Doesn't it all make you feel ill?' Lainey asked. 'You know . . . Knowing that your own mother doesn't . . .'

'What? That she doesn't really love me?' Jules said. 'I used to cry myself to sleep over that very fact . . . But since I've been back living with her, I've come to feel sorry for her, Lainz. She's a sad, bitter, twisted, little-minded woman. It's not actually *my* fault and I've realised that I can't fix her. If she wakes up to reality some day, I'll be there for her. But for now I need to get on with my life as best I can.'

They sat in silence for a while until Lainey tried to sit up.

'Ouch.'

'Don't move. I'll call a nurse.'

'No. I'm OK. I'll stay like this . . .' Jules actually jumped in fright as an animalistic noise emanated from Lainey.

'Aw babes, will I get them to give you more painkillers?'

'No, Jules.' She reached over and covered her hand with her hot clammy one. 'It's not the physical pain that's crippling me. It's in here,' she banged her chest. 'How am I going to carry on, Jules? Everything I hoped for is gone . . . I thought . . . I thought it was all falling into place.'

'Something will work out. You have Matt. And your parents.'

Lainey's head shot around as she gazed at Jules with such anger it blew her away.

'I told Matt to keep my parents out of here.'

'Why?'

'Dad would be too upset and he wouldn't know what to say or do, bless him. Mum would be insufferable. She'd have some barbed comment about how I deserve this and how it's my own fault.'

'Darling, nobody could possibly blame you for this terrible situation.'

'You'd think so, right? But I'll bet you a fiver my mother will have convinced herself I should've done something differently. Sometimes I catch her looking at me, Jules . . . I swear she hates me.'

'Oh I'm sure that's not true. Why would she hate you, honey?'

'Your guess is as good as mine. But I know what I see.' Angry tears choked her momentarily as she tried to stay calm. 'It's ironic, Jules. You look at both of our mothers. Yours treats you like shit and mine hates me. Why were they given babies if they behave that way? My mother has three children, but she acts as if she only wanted two. It's so fucking unfair . . .'

'Eh ladies,' the nurse popped her head in the door. 'I'll have to ask you to keep it down . . . Oh, sorry love. Is everything OK? Are you in pain?'

'No. Sorry, nurse,' Lainey said. 'I'm just having a total brain melt here.'

'That's understandable in the circumstances, Lainey. Just try not to yell the "f" word at the top of your lungs if possible.'

She smiled through her tears and apologised again to the retreating nurse.

Jules held her hand and sat convivially in the chair with her head tilted as she thought about things. Lainey wasn't imagining it, she concluded. Holly was slightly snappy with her when she spoke. She put pressure on her to take Ely all the time too.

'Hey, what if your mother is upset because you won't really allow her to mind Ely that much? Would she be better if you handed him over a bit more?'

'Why would I want to do that? She makes it clear she has no respect for me. She questions my mothering skills and belittles me at every given opportunity. So I'm hardly going to give her the chance to poison my own son against me. She so spiteful at times, I wouldn't put it past her to tell him I'm a bad mummy.'

'I'm sure she wouldn't do that, Lainz.'

'She has him right now,' she said. 'Poor Matt doesn't know whether he's coming or going. So he dropped Ely to the gate lodge. Mum had the cot brought down and he's staying there. I hate the thought of it. It churns me up inside.'

'Why don't you ask Pippa to help out for a bit then? Ely loves her. Where is she by the way?'

'She's stuck in work . . .'

'What, at seven o'clock? Isn't the store closed by now?'

'No, I'm sure she's finished now. But she was meant to come

earlier on and she had to see some celebrity at the shop. One of those private opening things they do at the store.'

'Who was coming in – not that they're more important than you?'

'She didn't say . . .'

Jules knew she needed to change the subject. Lainey had enough negative thoughts shooting around her head with adding Pippa's selfishness to the list. Jules had to literally sit on her hands. She didn't doubt for one minute that Holly had a profoundly harmful effect on Lainey's happiness. But right at this moment in time, at least she was mucking in and helping. Pippa, on the other hand, was proving to be a self-centred little wench. When she got a hold of her, Jules was going to give her a piece of her mind. She'd noticed Pippa being rude and off-hand with her at the fete the other day. She'd let it go, but this was the final straw. Lainey bent over backwards for her younger sister and the least Pippa could do was be there in her hour of need.

'How about I call to Huntersbrook tomorrow and take Ely for a while?'

'Would you?' Lainey asked.

'It'd be my pleasure. I'll be discreet and tell your folks I'm giving them a break.'

'I don't care what you say to my mother, quite frankly,' Lainey said hotly. 'Make sure she's not poisoning my son against me, OK?'

Jules encouraged Lainey to lie back and try to relax. Her body had been through so much and she needed to rest. She stroked her hair until she was certain her friend was deeply asleep before tip-toeing out the door.

As she drove back toward Dublin, Jules realised that she wasn't the only one with a fractious relationship with her mother. She'd meant what she said to Lainey earlier. She was blocking her own mother's negativity from her life. That would certainly help her situation. But she sincerely hoped Lainey could somehow build new bridges with Holly. Unlike her own mother, Lainey's was a good person deep down. There was obviously some deep-rooted pain that needed to heal. Jules wanted both women to be happy.

Pippa

BRIANNA LOOKED ASTONISHED AS PIPPA WALKED back into the shop.

'Hey, how did it all go? Is Lainey OK?'

'Yeah, I couldn't get to see her after all,' Pippa lied. 'She's not well enough for visitors so I'm going to see her in the morning. I figured I ought to come back to work.'

'OK, if you're sure,' Brianna said looking at her. Pippa was so paranoid. She prayed Brianna would let it drop and stop staring.

'I'm sure you're very worried,' Brianna said. 'If you'd prefer to go home to Huntersbrook, we'd all understand?'

'No!' Pippa almost shouted. 'But thanks, Brianna. You've been so kind. I'd rather be here. If I'm working, the time will pass quicker.'

Mercifully, Brianna patted her on the shoulder and began to gather some pieces in Jodi's size. Guessing she'd be a bit of a diva and probably wouldn't even talk or make eye contact, Pippa relaxed a little, figuring she could simply stay in the background. All she hoped was that she didn't make a total fool of herself in front of the actress.

'Pippa, that's a size ten,' Brianna said as she lifted a pale blue silk shirt. 'Would you mind grabbing me the size eight?'

'Sure,' Pippa said, glad to have something to focus on. Much as she tried, she couldn't shake the awful nagging in her head that she was letting Lainey and her family down. Missy fell into step beside her.

'Pippa, you're all over the place. You can barely string a sentence together, for crying out loud. Jodi Ludlum is about to walk in here. You may not care about the reputation of this store, but I do.'

'I'll grab a pint of water and I'll be fine. I won't mess up with Jodi Ludlum.'

'Here, give me the shirt and I'll get the right size,' Missy said bossily. Pippa strode toward the back room and filled a glass. Drinking thirstily, she prayed she'd pull this off.

'OK? Feeling better?' Missy asked poking her head around the door.

Pippa nodded. Missy hugged her tightly before shoving the shirt in the correct size at her.

'Let's get back to Brianna before she smells a rat. It's so brilliant having you as my besty,' Missy said. 'We're going to be so buzzed up once Jodi leaves. Let's go out for bubbles afterwards! Yay!'

Missy shot off across the shop, leaving Pippa reeling. She began to sweat. She felt totally claustrophobic and terrified all at the same time. She didn't like being ensnared by Missy. She'd never met anyone like her and Pippa honestly hadn't the first idea of how to deal with her.

Pippa placed the shirt on the clothing rail and grabbed her handbag and did a quick patch job on her make-up in front of one of the full-length mirrors. Sighing, she examined the bags under her eyes.

'Gosh it's exciting, isn't it?' Brianna said as she came to join Pippa at the mirror. 'I've met a few celebs in here over the years, but none as famous as Jodi Ludlum.'

'I'm sure she'll barely speak to us, but I'm stupidly trying to look my best,' Pippa said.

'I know what you mean. Just be yourself and I'm sure she'll be fine,' Brianna said as she squeezed Pippa's hand. 'She's here to see the clothes after all, not us!'

'Ha,' Pippa laughed unconvincingly.

'Are you sure you're able for this in light of your sister being in hospital?' Brianna asked kindly.

'Yes of course. I'm really worried about Lainey, to be honest, and I'm bricking it. I've never met anyone this famous before. I'm scared I'm going to mess up and say something really stupid.'

'She's just a person at the end of the day,' Brianna said smiling. 'You're well able for this. Have a bit of faith in yourself! And it'll be a superb story to tell Lainey when you see her tomorrow.'

'Thanks,' Pippa said appreciatively. As Brianna rushed to straighten a dress, Pippa felt a fresh wave of guilt. She and Missy had been such little witches to her in Paris. Brianna was a genuinely decent woman and didn't deserve the childish way they'd treated her. Pippa hoped she didn't know they'd gone off without her.

At the exact allotted time, there was a rap on the back door.

'She's here,' Brianna said, exhaling loudly. 'Be cool now, girls.'

Missy rolled her eyes at Pippa and made a face behind Brianna's back as the other woman opened the door. Jodi appeared. As Brianna was about to introduce them all, Missy barged forward and grabbed Jodi by the hand, pumping it up and down.

'So lovely to meet you. I'm Missy Hassett. My father sends his apologies for not being here to meet you, but he knew he could leave you in *my* capable hands.'

'Thank you,' Jodi said smiling sweetly. She glanced over at Brianna as her gaze rested on Pippa.

'Hi, I'm Pippa,' she said shyly.

'Hey,' said Jodi. 'What a gorgeous name. I longed to be called something pretty like that when I was younger.'

Pippa was rooted to the spot. Sweat was pouring down her spine in a chilly, uncomfortable trickle.

'Thanks,' Pippa said knowing she sounded kind of silly and wishing she could've come up with a more punchy answer. 'This is my boss, Brianna.' She motioned toward her and stepped back a bit.

'Hello Brianna, lovely to meet you,' Jodi said calmly.

As they began to walk along with Jodi's entourage, which oddly enough only consisted of two people, a quiet man in jeans and a pale grey T-shirt and a larger bouncer-type, Pippa felt very wobbly.

'You must get totally sick of shopping all the time,' Missy said. 'Well hopefully you'll find some stuff here that you like. I led a junket to Paris a few days ago and we've some incredible pieces on the way in.'

Jodi's smile never faltered.

'Daddy says I've an amazing eye for design. But I've always been totally brilliant at spending money, *if you know what I mean*,' Missy said dropping her voice an octave and winking.

'I'm actually the world's worst shopper,' Jodi confessed. 'I didn't have the funds when I was growing up and I guess I never developed much of a talent at it.'

Brianna took charge of the situation and asked Jodi if there was anything in particular she needed.

'We have a stunning selection of evening dress or plenty of day wear if that's more along the lines of what you were thinking.'

'It's really the less dressy stuff that I'm looking for,' Jodi said. Her voice was so much softer than Pippa expected. Jodi wasn't brash or abrasive and certainly didn't act like a diva. As she trailed to the rear of the group, Pippa had a good look at Jodi. She was absolutely tiny. So petite and yet so perfectly proportioned. Her long wavy hair was glossy and bouncy, just like one of the shampoo adverts on TV, only more natural looking.

As they congregated at the personal shopping area, Brianna invited Jodi to sit.

'Can we offer you a glass of champagne?' Missy asked stepping forward with her hands clasped, taking on the hostess-with-the-mostest role.

'Sparkling water would be fab if you have it,' Jodi said with an easy smile.

'That's right, you don't drink do you?' Pippa said before slapping her hand over her mouth. 'Sorry. I didn't mean for that to be said out loud. I'm a huge fan, Ms Ludlum,' she said apologetically.

'Aw thanks, Pippa,' she said easily. 'No, you're right, I don't drink or do drugs. I'm not a very cool movie star now am I?' she grinned. 'And call me Jodi, please. I can't bear formalities. It makes everyone unnecessarily uncomfortable.'

'I . . . Oh sure. Thank you, Jodi,' Pippa stuttered at the mention of drugs. 'I . . . I actually think that's kind of refreshing,' she said. 'It must be hard to stay sober at some of the mega parties you go to though.'

'I never drank. My mother did enough to last us both a life-time. I don't *get* the draw with alcohol or drugs. Besides I've done OK without both so far,' she said with a shrug. Pippa wanted to laugh out loud. That was the understatement of the year. Jodi was probably the most successful actress in the world right now. Pippa held her gaze for a second before looking at the floor. Did Jodi know she'd done coke that morning? Was she trying to warn her off it? Paranoia crept through every fibre of Pippa's being. She wished she could somehow stick a pipe cleaner up her nose and remove all traces of the dirty drug she'd inhaled.

Missy, on the other hand, seemed utterly unperturbed by the conversation and floated away from Jodi oozing with confidence.

'So water it is then. I'll pop to the canteen and get that for you. Would the gentlemen like a drink?'

The broad security man with the earpiece shook his head and didn't speak, placing himself at a lean against a wall. The other man said he'd have water too.

'The last of the crazy ravers,' Missy whispered to Pippa as she walked toward the back room to get the drinks.

'By the way, this is Harry,' Jodi said, 'and that's Markus. He doesn't do conversations. We call him Marcel after that famous mime artist, Marcel Marceau,' Jodi said with a giggle. Markus grinned and remained in the background like a protective blockade.

'So we have lots of lovely day wear,' Brianna said professionally. 'If you'd like, Pippa could model some things for you?'

'Oh no, I wouldn't put you through that,' Jodi said smiling at Pippa again. 'Let's all have a look at what you have.'

Brianna wheeled the first rail toward Jodi and nodded at Pippa to pick some things out.

'I love jeggings and jumpers for when I'm at home,' Pippa said. 'Perfect for throwing on under a wax jacket, yet stylish enough to make sure you don't look like you've come in from a day's work in the fields! This sweater is so soft it makes me want to pet it all the time. It's a silk and cashmere mix and I think the purply grey colour would be amazing on you too.'

'You're obviously a country girl,' Jodi said holding her head to the side.

'Yeah, I'm from Wicklow.'

'That's where I live when I'm not filming,' Jodi said. 'I bought the house a couple of years ago so my son Saul could go to school in Bakers Valley.'

'Well I'm from a place called Huntersbrook. It's an estate not a million miles from you, actually. We're in the process of turning it into a venue for parties and weddings,' Pippa said. Talking about home brought on a fresh wave of guilt.

'I think I know that place,' Harry said. 'It's got a big horse livery yard, hasn't it?'

'Yes!' Pippa said delightedly. 'But sadly the economic down turn meant my family were forced to change direction. We lost too many of our livery customers to keep going. So this is our way of holding on to the property.'

'Good for you,' Jodi said. 'We'll have to come and have a look some day,' she said kindly.

Pippa tried not to fall over in surprise and reminded herself that Jodi was an international superstar and was probably just being polite.

The time flew as the women fussed and Jodi picked some clothes.

'She's a cool customer in every way, isn't she?' Brianna whispered to Pippa a while later as they packed the clothes in tissue paper. Missy was making it very clear that she was in charge and the others were only there as lowly minions. Pippa and Brianna were leaving her to it.

'I'm amazed by her,' Pippa said in awe. 'She's not *up* herself at all is she? She's certainly not a diva.'

'She has that *je ne sais quoi* though, doesn't she?' Brianna said stealing another look across the room.

'She's so beautiful,' Pippa breathed. 'I wish I could be her best friend. I feel like asking if I can go home with her!'

Brianna laughed. They handed the bags to Marcus and Harry who thanked them and hung back, allowing Jodi to lead them toward the door.

'Thanks so much for staying late to see me,' Jodi said to them all. 'I really would love to see Huntersbrook some time,' she said stopping by Pippa.

'It's the coolest place,' Missy oozed. 'I'm having my birthday party there this weekend. You should come!' she said. 'In fact, I'll give you my mobile number and you can call me.'

Jodi turned to face Missy and held her head to the side.

'You're so kind to invite me to your party, Missy,' she said. 'But without wanting to sound like an awful bore, I'm really not a party girl. I hope you have a fabulous night though.'

As she turned to leave, Pippa felt Jodi press a piece of paper into her palm. Jodi was gone before she could even react. Knowing she shouldn't say a word, Pippa shoved it into her pocket before Missy or Brianna noticed.

As soon as the limousine pulled away from outside the store, Missy did a little dance on the spot.

'That was totally awesome!' she said punching the air. 'Let's pop a bottle of champers. Dad will assume Jodi or her people drank it.'

Brianna was just as excited as Missy and rushed after her to collapse on the plush chaise longue in the personal shopping section. Pippa followed, feeling a little dazed.

'She's *stunning* in reality, isn't she?' Brianna said. 'Those green eyes! I always thought they made her wear tinted contact lenses on screen. But they're real. She's so down to earth, too.'

'Apart from blowing sixteen and a half grand in one fair swoop,' Missy said. 'God she's so bloody cool. Now that's what I call style. No fuss, no grand gestures but wow, can she shop?'

'Who's the fella she was with do you think?' Brianna asked. 'He seemed quite dull. I wonder if he's her accountant? He's not exactly Darius Drew material.'

'Well there aren't many men in the world like her ex-husband in fairness,' Pippa pipped up. 'I thought Harry seemed nice.'

'Yeah, that's just it though,' Missy said handing out full-to-the-gills glasses of bubbly. 'He was too normal.'

'Maybe that's what she wants,' Pippa argued. 'Maybe she's fed up with Hollywood divas and high maintenance men. Who knows, maybe she wants someone ordinary to hang out with after hours. Like that movie, *Notting Hill*.'

It had made worldwide headlines when Jodi Ludlum and Darius Drew announced their divorce. They'd cited 'location differences' as the main reason and said they would always be close on account of their son, Saul. Jodi had released a statement saying Darius was her best friend and she would always love him, but it was time to go separate ways.

'I wouldn't care if Darius was residing in Pluto, I'd fly over every ocean and travel light years to find him,' Missy said dreamily. 'He's probably one of the most divine men alive, don't you agree?'

'It's not that simple if you're Jodi Ludlum,' Pippa defended. 'Her career is as strong as his. They really were the golden couple of Hollywood. Maybe it all became too much. Hollywood job . . . Hollywood husband . . . Hollywood overload . . .'

'There's been surprisingly little mud-slinging since they split, now that you mention it,' Brianna mused. 'They really do seem to have managed an amicable divorce.'

As they drank their champagne Missy called her father to let him know how it had all gone.

He instructed Missy to put him on speaker phone.

'Well done, ladies,' Mr Hassett boomed down the line. 'Needless to say you'll be rewarded with a nice bonus each in this month's pay cheque.'

Hearing their exhilarated boss sounding so thrilled down the phone line made Brianna quite giddy.

'Well done you,' she said patting Pippa on the leg as they sat on the sofa. 'She was well on for chatting about the Wicklow hills. Good one. It's always a fantastic plan to pretend you're at one with the customers. Even if it *is* Jodi Ludlum. And you were a bag of nerves as she was arriving. You're a pro, Missis.'

Pippa wanted to point out that she wasn't putting on a show. She'd genuinely enjoyed chatting to Jodi. The champagne went straight to her head as she struggled to act normally.

As soon as she hung up from her father Missy threw her hands in the air and danced around like a loony.

'Woo-hoo, we rock. Daddy thinks we're amazeballs. But we've to keep schtum about the bonuses or the other workers will be bummed with us.'

'Jeez, Missy,' Pippa said, sounding rather more scornful than she'd intended. 'The *other workers* aren't some sort of sub-species!'

'Pardon?' Missy stopped bouncing and narrowed her eyes at Pippa.

'Joke!' Pippa said, leaping off the sofa and doing a forced little dance. 'Joke, you silly ninny!' she said again, rushing over to hug her.

Missy took the bait and giggled again too. 'We rock,' she said swigging the remainder of the champagne from the bottle.

By the time they were ready to leave, Pippa's heart was racing once more. She was wired to the moon and knew there was no way she'd get a wink of sleep, but she needed to be alone. The sound of poor Lainey's voice on the phone earlier was playing on a loop in her head. First thing tomorrow morning she was getting in her car and zooming straight to the hospital.

'Let's go for a quick celebratory bite to eat and a glass of vino,' Missy suggested as the security company came to check the alarm was fully set.

'I'm out of here,' Brianna said. 'Regretfully, I have a house full of relations who are probably dining on pot noodle as it is.'

'No worries, Brianna. Thanks for everything and see you in the morning,' Missy said. 'Yes,' she hissed while winking at Pippa triumphantly. 'Just you and me, chick!'

Pippa thought she was going to cry.

'I . . . I can't come out, Missy. I'm sorry. I'm really upset about Lainey.'

'Don't be retarded. You can't go home now! You're lit up like a lamp, Pippa. Your eyes are like two beacons in your face.'

Missy linked her arm and literally frog-marched her toward a bistro as Jules' name popped up on her phone. 'Hi Jules,' Pippa said as Missy whooped and shouted in the background. 'Any news on Lainey?'

'Well yes, as it happens. I was just at the hospital.'

'OK,' said Pippa. Before she could say another word, Missy snatched the phone.

'Hi Jules, sweetie. We've had the most amazing day and we're about to celebrate. So don't wreck our buzz by talking about hospitals and all of that.'

Pippa stood motionlessly with a dropped jaw as Missy continued a very cheery, one-sided conversation. She wanted to click her heels and be home in Huntersbrook with her family. She needed to be near Lainey and know what was happening.

Pippa had never felt so trapped. The worst part was that it was all her own doing. She'd isolated herself into a horrible bubble of drink and drugs and had let Lainey down in her hours of need.

Missy nudged her in the door of the bistro while concluding her very loud and screechy conversation with Jules.

'Tell them we want a table for two,' she mouthed to Pippa.

Numbly, she did as Missy asked and before long they were seated in the window. Pippa knew she couldn't eat a bite, so when Missy pointed to the Prosecco on the wine list and did a thumbs-up sign, she ordered it.

She sent Jules a quick text to say she was sorry Missy was behaving like a lunatic and that she was as drunk as a skunk and she'd call first thing in the morning.

There was a cold silence from Jules.

The bubbly arrived and Pippa downed a full glass. It numbed her momentarily, which was a welcome relief.

'Let's have a Caesar salad each,' Missy said beckoning to the waiter and ordering it.

'That was such a buzz, wasn't it?' she asked. Pippa nodded. 'I'm going to pursue Jodi Ludlum. Could you imagine the envy of my guests if she turned up?'

'Yeah it'd be amazing,' Pippa said noncommittally.

Pippa excused herself and made for the ladies. Pulling the piece of paper from her pocket, she was astonished to see Jodi's handwriting.

I'd genuinely love to see your family home. I'm actively looking for somewhere to host an event. Could you give me a call tomorrow? Thanks, Jodi.

Pippa stared in shock. She read the note over and over in disbelief. She actually had Jodi Ludlum's mobile number! This was insane. She tucked the note back into her pocket. Gazing in the mirror, she scrutinised her face. She looked better than she had earlier. In fact, she felt awesome compared to earlier. She couldn't wait to tell Lainey and the others about Jodi. Trying to calm down before she faced Missy, Pippa knew she'd have to keep quiet about the note. If Missy got wind of it, she'd hound Jodi and ruin any chance Pippa had of getting to know the star.

She briefly considered calling Skye or Joey to fill them in on the news, but she couldn't risk Missy hearing. Her gut instincts had been right. Just as she was about to return to the restaurant, the ladies room door flew open and Missy popped her head around.

'Hurry up, great news! I've just had a return text from Danny. He's on the way to meet us with his friend, Charles.'

'Who?' Pippa asked.

Missy rolled her eyes and pointed to her nose as another lady came out of a cubicle.

'Oh right, that Danny,' Pippa said, copping on and following Missy out to the restaurant. Just as the waiter served their salads and topped up their glasses, Danny arrived. Pippa stared at the table, suddenly horribly aware that her last words to him had been 'Fuck you, Danny'. She had no idea how he was going to behave with her now.

Missy stood and held her arms out. 'Darling! Fancy meeting you here. Sit!' She beckoned to the waiter to bring another glass. When he did, she asked for a fresh bottle of bubbly too.

'So Pippa's gonna sort you this time, right, Pip?'

Pippa felt her cheeks flush.

'Ah no, that's not going to work,' Pippa said.

'What?' Missy shot her a deathly stare. 'It's your shout, Pippa. Friendship requires give and take. Don't be the one to take, take, take all the time,' she warned.

'Of course,' Pippa said with an uneasy smile. 'I've no cash, so I'll nip across to the hole in the wall.'

'Well Danny doesn't take credit cards,' Missy said guffawing. 'So off to the drink-link with you,' she said. When Pippa realised Missy meant right now, this second, she fumbled her bag onto her shoulder and walked out in a daze.

Danny followed her.

Just as she was about to key in her pin number at the machine, he stopped her.

'Hey, I'm not taking your money. I'll give Missy what I have left. Then I'm done with this game. I literally have enough to keep her smiling and then I'm stepping away from this dodgy crap for good.'

'Are you sure?' she asked. 'I don't want to do you out of your money.'

'Pippa, please. You're my girlfriend. I'm hardly about to fleece you now, am I?'

She looked him in the eye for the first time. 'Am I still your girlfriend?'

He smiled at her. 'It'll take more than one expletive to get rid of me,' he said, leaning in to kiss her lightly. 'I know it was the coke talking, not you. Are you OK?'

Pippa nodded, feeling if she opened her mouth to speak, she'd start wailing.

'I won't quiz you about stuff now,' Danny said quietly. 'Let's just deal with dragon lady then try to get away from her.'

Feeling wobbly, Pippa made her way back to the restaurant. Danny put his arm around her to steady her. When she looked up at him, his smile made her heart flip.

Missy was ecstatic when Danny handed her the small bundle.

'Nice one, Pippa,' she said as she immediately rushed to the ladies. Pippa exhaled. She knew the stress she felt was showing on her face.

'I always thought of myself as a decent bloke,' Danny said pulling his fingers through his hair. 'In the cold light of day, I'm a drug dealer. There's no dressing it up. I can have as many degrees as I like, but at the end of the day, would any judge look upon me favourably and say that I'm a better calibre of dealer than any other? I doubt it.'

Pippa nodded. She wanted desperately to believe Danny, but she couldn't help feeling doubtful. Missy returned looking incredibly animated.

'That's special gear,' she said. 'Here, Pippa, knock yourself out.' She handed the bundle over.

'I'm good for the moment,' she said guardedly. 'Let's get out of here and have a quick drink somewhere, yeah?'

Missy skipped out the door as the waiter waved the bill in Pippa's face.

As the payment went through, Pippa followed the others outside. Missy was dancing to the music in her own head, flinging her hair around like a rocker.

'Wow, I feel great,' she said giggling. 'I need to dance. Let's go to Fire and Rain.'

Pippa groaned, she couldn't think of anything worse. Danny looked at his watch.

'I'm not great on school nights, Missy,' he warned. 'I'll come for an hour, tops.'

'OK, Danny-boy. Your loss. Pippa and I will be making the most of the night.'

'Does she know about Lainey?' Danny whispered. Pippa nodded. 'Christ she's selfish,' he said shaking his head.

'I need to keep her sweet until after this party. After that, believe me I've no desire to spend time with her again.'

They'd only arrived and ordered drinks when Missy looked at Pippa sheepishly.

'Could I have a teeny bit more Charlie?' she begged.

'Sure,' Pippa said, relieved to get the stuff out of her handbag.

'Will you come with me?'

'Eh, right. But I'm not going to partake this evening. I've too much on tomorrow and I'll be zombified. I've got to get to Lainey first thing.'

'Now you're just being silly,' Missy said. 'You'll be grand tomorrow and if you're not, just take a small sniff and you'll be right as rain. Easy peasy lemon squeezy!'

Pippa glanced over at Danny, who seemed to be a million miles away. Reluctantly, she followed Missy.

'I've got to pee,' Pippa said. 'You get set up and I'll knock on your cubicle door in a minute, yeah?'

The club was quiet seeing as it was midweek, but Pippa couldn't be certain there was nobody else in the other toilets. Missy rushed in, delighted with the whole thing.

Pippa went to the cubicle furthest away and shut the door. As far as she was concerned, this was the end of the coke line for her. She waited a suitable amount of time before flushing and exiting. Missy peeped her head out the door and beckoned to her.

'You go on,' Pippa said. 'It's well dodgy in here tonight because it's so quiet. We don't need anyone asking why we're stuffed into one cubicle when most of them are free,' she whispered.

'Ooh good point,' Missy said. 'I'll go wash my hands.'

Once alone in the cubicle, Pippa swept the powder into her hand and shook it into the toilet bowl. The sound of the music was suddenly louder as the door opened and a couple of girls came in. Throwing the five-euro note into the sanitary disposal unit, Pippa wanted to ensure there was no evidence on her person. Remembering to flush, she joined Missy at the sinks.

'Good?' Missy asked. Pippa nearly gasped when she saw the other girl's eyes. Her pupils were like saucers and jet black.

'Great,' Pippa said injecting as much enthusiasm into her voice as possible. 'Let's get back inside.'

'Ooh, I sense a little love affair with you and Danny boy!'

'Ah we're just friends,' Pippa said.

'Like hell. I don't look at my friends the way you look at him. And he's like a love-sick teenager with those puppy dog stares in your direction too. It's cute. I approve. Besides, he's a handy guy to have on side. Nice one, Pips.'

Pippa wanted to say so many things to Missy, but none of them were going to please the other girl, so she simply followed in silence.

Pippa knew there was a God when twenty minutes later a group of Missy's *set* appeared.

'Pips, would you mind if we share a bit of your stash?' Missy asked with bug-eyed excitement.

'Not in the slightest,' Pippa said. 'You keep it all. I owe you. This way we're quits, yeah?'

'Are you sure?' Missy said looking as if she'd just been told the winning lotto numbers.

'Totally sure. Knock yourself out, Missy.'

Knowing Missy wasn't going to miss her one jot, Pippa whispered to Danny that she was slipping off home. Looking relieved, he grabbed his jacket off the back of the chair and followed.

'You don't have to leave just because I am,' she said.

'I know. I want to. I told you earlier, I don't stay out late on school nights. Besides, I was only there to see you.'

Her stomach flipped as he pulled her into his arms. She didn't want to fall in love with Danny. He was a bad boy. He'd told her tonight he was going to change and she desperately wanted to believe him. But Pippa was torn. If any of her family found out what he was really like, they'd be horrified.

Joey

JOEY COULDN'T HELP NOTICING HOW QUIET SKYE
was being. But he had so much on his mind with organising
Missy's party, worrying about Lainey and trying to keep up with
the constant emails from Clive that he hadn't been able to focus
on her.

'I'm going to drop over to see Lainey for a few moments and
go from the hospital into work,' he said.

'So much for your week off,' Skye said dryly.

'I know. I'm sorry. Honestly I am, but I couldn't say no to
Clive. I doubt I'll be there all day. I reckon it'll only be a few
hours. I'll be home here by five at the outside. Why don't we go
to the village for some pub grub and a couple of drinks tonight?'

'No thanks,' Skye said. 'I'd rather be here. I'm going to visit
Lainey this afternoon. The weather is so awful and according to
the forecasters, this rain is down for the next few days. We've too
much to do for Missy's party as well.'

'OK,' he said feeling oddly awkward. 'How about I bring a
takeaway then?'

'Sure,' she said despondently. 'Might be nice to invite Matt
and Jacob with baby Ely, too.'

'Good plan,' he said. 'I'll say it to my folks as well. We'll light
the fire and have a cosy evening. Love it,' he said clapping and
rubbing his hands together. 'See you later on.'

Joey couldn't put his finger on it, but Skye was being quite odd. He was putting it down to shock over Lainey's surgery. It really was a horrible situation. He hoped with all his heart that his sister would get good news from the doctors.

As he pulled up outside the hospital, his mobile rang.

Clive was up to ninety and said he needed him at the office, pronto.

'My sister is in hospital and I'm outside there now. I need to run in and give her a quick hug and I'll be there.'

'OK, fair enough Joey. Oh and I need you to come with me tonight. These guys are looking for a night on the tiles. I've booked that Michelin star place in the city centre and we'll take them to the members only bar afterwards. A few scoops are the order of the day, my man!'

'Sounds like a plan!' Joey said enthusiastically. 'See you shortly, Clive.'

Feeling truly hassled Joey climbed out of his car and dashed into the hospital. By the time he located Lainey's ward he was in a sweat.

To his dismay, her bed was empty.

'Excuse me,' he said flagging down a passing nurse. 'I'm looking for my sister, Lainey. She should be here.'

'She's down having an ultrasound scan. She just left. It'll only take around half an hour to forty minutes. There's a chair beside her bed. You can wait there.'

'I'm already late for a meeting up in Dublin,' he explained. 'Would you possibly be able to give her a message that her brother Joey was here?'

'Fair enough, Joey. I'll let her know.'

Joey vowed to return the following day, knowing he had no choice but to leave. He could envisage Clive pacing up and down as he waited for him to get there. He couldn't risk his boss feeling he wasn't reliable, not in these key early stages of his partnership.

Once he was on the main motorway he called Skye. The phone at Huntersbrook rang out. Thumping the steering wheel in frustration, he berated himself for not setting up the answering machine. Yet another niggly job he'd thought he'd get to this week, but it had slipped under the radar.

Dialling Skye's mobile, he shook his head as it went directly to voicemail.

The mailbox on the mobile phone you are calling is full. Please try again later.

Clive's second call distracted him.

'Hey Clive, I'm on the way. I'll be with you in fifteen minutes, tops.'

'Great stuff, thanks Joey. The group are here. Head straight to boardroom five when you get here, yeah?'

'Sure. See you shortly.'

Joey felt bad for bailing on Lainey, but he couldn't keep the meeting waiting. Forgetting all about everything but his clients he zoomed toward Dublin.

Sadie

THE SIGHT OF THE HOSPITAL MADE SADIE WEAK at the knees. She'd only taken one course of antibiotics in her entire life and medical people terrified the life out of her. Up until now she'd managed to avoid these places since that time . . .

Taking a deep breath she forced her feet forward and presented at the reception desk. Holding her head high she asked for Lainey's ward and made her way to the lift.

She'd often heard that smell was the one sense that evoked a thousand memories. By the time she reached Lainey's floor, it was as if she were stepping back in time. Sounds and scenes shot through her mind like a movie reel in slow motion. Only for the fact her beloved Lainey was lying in tatters in a hospital bed, she'd have bolted and run for the hills.

Gingerly she found the right door and pushed her way inside.

'Hello there, pet.'

'Sadie!' Lainey said. Her voice sounded different. Deeper and bereft of joy. The poor girl's face said it all. She looked positively beaten.

'Don't suppose there's much point asking you how you're feeling?'

'Not really,' Lainey forced a smile. 'I've been having scans and tests all day. I feel like exhibit A at this point. You're so good to come, Sadie. I know you hate hospitals and doctors.'

'Um.' She gazed around at the high ceilings remembering the

last time she'd done the same in a similar building. Blinking slowly, she focused on the present. Remembering the envelope in her bag, she fished it out and handed it to Lainey.

'What have you brought?'

'It's from your mum. She wanted you to have a little smiley face to gaze at.' Sadie clasped her petite hands under her chin as she watched Lainey. As she slid the photo from the envelope, tears began to cascade from her eyes.

'Your mum took it last night and Skye printed it off. A team effort,' she said in delight. The photo was of Ely as he burst out laughing.

'Aw he's such a little darling,' Lainey said. 'I love him so much it hurts.'

Sadie patted her hand. Comfortable silence descended as Sadie did what she'd always done best and waited until Lainey wanted to talk.

'It's an odd one, isn't it?'

'What's that, dear?'

'The relationship between Mum and me . . .'

'It is really, dear.'

'You know where I'm coming from, Sadie, don't you?'

Sadie didn't want to come between Holly and Lainey, but she was in no doubt of how she felt about both women.

'Your family are the only family I've ever known. Well since I was sixteen at least. Once my brother left for America in the nineteen forties I would've had nobody if your Grandma hadn't offered me a job.'

'We were lucky to have you all these years, Sadie.'

'Your grandma Maggie was more than just any old friend,' she said sighing. 'She was the only one who really knew me.'

'How do you mean?' Lainey asked, sliding the photo of Ely back into the envelope.

'Maggie and I could've talked for Ireland. We were like two old crows cackling away to one another. Most of the time it was mindless. Easy talk as I'd say. But every now and again the subjects became darker. Like when her Stanley died suddenly. It rocked her to the core. I honestly thought she wouldn't come back from it.'

'But she had Mum,' Lainey stated.

'Yes, love, she did. And believe me I was the first one to remind her of that fact.' In spite of years of practice, Sadie's resolve suddenly dissolved. She allowed the tears to fall. She didn't even raise a hand to mop them away. Lainey glanced over and clearly assumed she'd be fine in a moment. Sadie knew a dam had just burst. Emotion she'd held in a tightly locked box in the very recesses of her heart had been let free.

'Sadie?' Lainey looked terrified. 'What is it?'

'Lainey,' she took her hand. 'I know you're angry at Holly. She's always been a bit angry at you, too. I could see it.'

'You could?' Lainey said feebly.

Sadie nodded. Her tears still hadn't abated. 'You've so much going on right now though, love. You need to let those old wounds heal. Concentrate on the here and now.'

'How can I when I've no idea what's happening to me?' she said crossly. 'I'm asking over and over again for answers and the doctors keep saying they're waiting for pathology results. Until then I'm meant to lie here and go slowly insane . . .'

'You won't go insane, love. We're all here with you.'

'Thanks, Sadie, but with all due respect, my biggest fear is something I can never explain to you.'

'Try me.'

'It's to do with Ely . . .'

'Go on . . .'

Lainey took a deep breath. 'What if I die, Sadie? What if I

leave him with no Mum? He's only a tiny baby. He won't remember anything about me. All I'll be is a couple of framed photographs that other people cry over at Christmas and birthdays. He'll have no recollection of me.'

Sadie paused for a moment. Her heart was thumping so loudly, she felt it could beat right through her chest.

'The way I'm feeling is something that happened the minute I became a mother. From that first nano-second I held Ely in my arms it began. It's a feeling I can't begin to explain . . .'

'You're right, dear. That feeling cannot be explained . . .' Sadie knew it was time to finally tell the truth. 'I agree that it can't be put into words. Nothing would or ever could come close to making a person understand what it feels like to be a Mum . . .'

'I'm sorry, Sadie,' Lainey said suddenly. 'I'm being very selfish and stupid. How would you possibly know what I'm talking about? I'm talking gobbledy-gook.'

'No love, you're not . . .' Sadie closed her eyes momentarily. 'Sixty-eight years ago I gave birth to a beautiful baby girl.'

'Wha . . .' Lainey's voice trailed off in shock. 'I had no idea . . .'

'I was sixteen years old. The only person outside of my ailing father who knew about the baby was your Grandma Maggie.'

'Oh my God,' Lainey managed as her voice cracked. 'Sadie . . .' She held her hand out and clasped Sadie's. 'Please tell me all about it.'

'She was like a tiny doll. The nuns allowed me to hold her for what felt like a matter of seconds. I was in labour for three days. They didn't think I'd survive . . .' She fished for a tissue in her bag and blew her nose. 'But I managed eventually. Nothing could've been as bad as the abuse and torture I'd endured at the mother and baby home before she was born . . . From the day my father knew I was pregnant, I was sent there.'

'Where was it?'

'It was outside Galway. In a huge grey God-forsaken building with cold floors and endless corridors leading to countless rooms where terrified young girls like me were forced to wash, iron and fold clothes. When our time came we were ushered to cubicles where we were left to give birth with little or no assistance.'

'Oh Sadie, I had no idea.'

'The worst part was that the man who made me pregnant was a man of the cloth. He brutalised and raped me and yet I was the one to be punished. That punishment has stayed with me for every day of my life.'

'Didn't you tell your father what had happened?'

'Oh no. Priests were royalty at that stage. Ireland was a bowing servant and the church was her bidding master. Nobody would've believed me and the beatings would've been far more fierce had I blasphemed against a priest.'

Sadie knew she needed to keep talking, bile rose in her throat as she forced her mind away from the horrific images that only came to light when she was too tired to stop them.

'My little girl arrived and she managed to erase all the damage, hurt and pain,' Sadie said smiling. 'But without a shadow of doubt, the most horrific, cruel and debilitating moment was when Sr Laurence plucked her from my bosom and marched her away. They brought papers and I refused to sign them, so one of the nuns did it for me. Two days later I was turned out onto the street. When I arrived home, I met Maggie.'

'And she took you to Huntersbrook?' Sadie nodded.

'I lived there with her and Stanley until my father died. His cottage became mine.'

'Do you know where your little girl went? Did you get to give her a name?'

'I called her Elizabeth. I thought it sounded regal and it would make her strong and able. But I don't know where she was taken or what her adoptive parents named her.'

'How have you lived with this?' Lainey asked.

'What choice had I? I was up against an authority that was backed by the medics, government and many ordinary people aside of the clergy. I was powerless. I knew a long time ago that I had a choice. I could allow it to cripple me and rob me of any future happiness or I could bury it all and never revisit it again.'

'Until now,' Lainey said.

'It was your expression when I walked in here,' she said. 'You looked similar to me and the other girls back then. You talked about that feeling when you hold your own baby. I agree with you. It's universal. So too is it that haunted look, when your baby is stolen. It's like having your soul removed by a great invisible vacuum.'

Lainey leaned forward in the bed, oblivious to her wounds or any physical pain and held her arms out. Sadie rose from the chair and moved to the bed. As they hugged and rocked, the grief that they shared united them in a way that nobody would ever understand.

Eventually, Sadie managed to calm herself. She wiped her face and took a clean tissue and did the same for Lainey. She patted the younger woman's hair and sighed.

'This is what women do, Lainey. We mop up the tears, pull our shoulders back, raise our chins and move forward. I did it and I know you can too. Can I beg you to do one thing for me?'

'Anything,' Lainey said sadly.

'Try again with Holly. She loves you. You love her. You need to learn to like one another. Do it while you have the chance. Don't waste the opportunity to own that mother and daughter relationship. There's nothing else in the world like it. Even though I only experienced it for a matter of minutes, I know it's powerful.'

Lainey nodded.

'Meanwhile you mind yourself. What will be, will be. No matter what those test results say, you have so many people who want to help. For many years I thought there was no such thing as a loving God. I've come to the conclusion I was wrong about that. There are too many wonderful things on this earth to argue that point. I know it's tough, Lainey. But try not to allow the fear to win.'

'I'll try,' she said.

'Your mum took that photo so she could cheer you up,' Sadie said. 'She doesn't know what to do. She's dying to come in and see you, but she won't come where she's not wanted. I know you asked Matt to keep her away and believe me I understand why, but time is precious, my dear. Don't waste it.'

Lainey looked totally lost. For that, Sadie was sorry.

'It's ironic, Lainey. You and your mother live right next door to one another and you barely communicate. I'd move heaven and earth to see Elizabeth again. Even for a moment. I know you're grieving for the baby you thought you were having and all the little ones you'd planned for the future. But don't forget to stop and look around at what you still have, love.'

Sadie stood up from the bed. She bent to kiss Lainey on the forehead.

'I'll see you soon, OK?'

'You bet,' Lainey said. 'Thank you for sharing your story with me. I bet Elizabeth is just like you. Strong, wise and incredible.'

'Thanks, love.'

As she walked out of the hospital, in spite of the pungent smell that reminded her of the mother and baby home, Sadie felt lighter inside. In a way she wished she'd told people before now. But she also knew that there was a right time and place for everything. Today was the right time to talk and Lainey was certainly the best person she could've told.

'I know you're sitting back in your armchair sipping a cup of tea and smiling down on me, Maggie. I can just picture you,' she said as she got into her car.

❄

Back up in the ward, Lainey was reeling. She'd known Sadie all her life. She'd never suspected the hurt or sorrow that had lain dormant in her heart. It baffled Lainey how she'd stayed for so long in Huntersbrook, caring for and helping with her and Joey and Pippa. The only conclusion she could come it was that it had somehow made life more bearable to be part of the family.

Lainey thought about Holly. After hearing Sadie's revelations their petty arguments seemed to pale to insignificance. Lainey vowed she would try and make amends. It was time to grow up. Besides, she may not have very much time left.

❄

Sadie prided herself on being quite savvy when it came to technology. Joey had bought her an iPhone for her birthday and she pulled it from her bag now, before starting the car. Selecting the group text option, she sent a message to Pippa and Joey.

Lainey needs you all at the moment. Life is precious. Every now and again we are thrown a curve ball. Please try to be there to help Lainey catch this one.
Sadie.

Pippa

PIPPA WOKE EARLY WITH DANNY'S ARM AROUND her. As she peeled her eyes open, Lainey was her first thought.

'Hey,' Danny said stroking her arm. 'You OK?'

'Not really, Danny,' she said. 'I have to get to my sister. I let her down so badly yesterday and I can't forgive myself.'

'You didn't know she was going to call. Besides you were working.'

'Danny,' she sat up and stared down at him. 'This is where we differ. You think it's fine to deal drugs in order to fast track yourself into a bigger and better apartment. You feel there's a way of reasoning as to why I couldn't go to my sister when she desperately needed me. I don't accept any of that as being OK. It's *not* OK. It's not the way I was raised.'

She got out of bed and marched to the shower. She washed her hair vigorously and soaped her body. Pippa was certain of one thing. She was well and truly finished with behaving like an idiot. Missy was a nightmare and she wanted nothing more to do with her. Hopefully her party would be a roaring success for Huntersbrook, but once it was over, that was it. Pippa knew it was time to grow up and start taking responsibility for her own actions. The time for blaming other people for the messes she ended up in was over. She felt a clarity in her head she hadn't had for weeks. And with it came shame. She was ashamed that she'd allowed herself to fall headlong into coke, which in turn made it feel OK to be manipulated by a class A bitch like Missy Hassett. Enough was enough.

Danny went for a shower as she dressed. Thankfully, there wasn't much time for chatting as he needed to get to the office.

'Will you call me as soon as you've seen Lainey?' he asked.

'Yeah,' she said absentmindedly.

'Pippa?'

'I'll talk to you later at some point, OK, Danny?'

Pippa was glad that the traffic was predominantly going in the opposite direction as she made her way to the hospital. Brianna had told her to take the day off and be with her family. A fresh wave of shame washed over her as she thought of how shabbily she'd treated Brianna in Paris, and generally. She was a hardworking and extremely nice woman who didn't deserve to be the butt of her and Missy's stupid jokes.

Knowing she shouldn't pitch up at the hospital empty handed Pippa stopped off at a small shopping centre en route to the hospital. Knowing it wouldn't change anything but it might ease her guilt slightly, Pippa set about choosing a nightgown with matching dressing gown and slippers.

'Can you gift wrap it for me please?'

As the lady was busying herself with tissue paper and ribbon Pippa's mobile beeped. Sadie's message popped onto her screen and she had to bite her finger to stop from screaming out loud.

'Forget the ribbon and stuff. I have to go,' Pippa said shoving money at the alarmed assistant. 'Sorry, it's an emergency.'

❄

As she parked and rushed into the hospital, Pippa braced herself for the worst. Lainey had been so low on the phone yesterday and the last thing she needed was Pippa gawping at her with glassy eyes and a wobbly lip. Entering the ward she spotted what was left of poor Lainey. She looked pale and frightened as she curled uncomfortably under the thin papery hospital blanket. All plans to be calm and collected went out the window as Pippa rushed to her sister.

She was surprised to see Jules sitting there.

'I'll give you two some space,' she said, glowering at Pippa with her back to Lainey.

'Aw Lainey,' Pippa said stooping to hug her. 'I'm so sorry I couldn't get here sooner.'

Both women sobbed as Pippa eventually pulled over a chair.

'I'm sorry. I'm not used to you acting as if the world is ending,' Pippa said. 'But you look terrible.'

'Thanks,' Lainey smiled momentarily. 'In a way the world is ending,' Lainey said listlessly. 'They've taken my womb and my ovaries, Pippa.'

'Oh Lainey,' Pippa said taking her hand. 'I'm so sorry. You must be reeling.'

'We had it all planned, Pip. Matt and I were going to have a brood of children. It was going to be idyllic. Now Ely will be on his own with no brothers or sisters to play with.'

'He'll be fine,' Pippa said firmly.

'Well he hasn't much choice, has he?' Lainey spat.

Pippa recoiled in shock. She'd never heard her sister sounding so defeated. 'And it doesn't end there. What if this mass they removed is cancer, Pippa? Then Ely will have no mummy either.' Lainey thumped the bed. 'I've wrecked everything. I'd never have married Matt or brought Ely into the world if I'd known I was going to leave them high and dry.'

'Lainey, don't . . .' Pippa began.

'It's true, Pippa,' she said jutting out her bottom jaw. 'I've ruined their lives. If I die poor Matt is going to be abandoned and left to raise Ely alone. Jacob and Mum and Dad will help for a couple of years. But they're not getting any younger. So ultimately it'll all be left to Matt.'

'Honey, we don't know that you have cancer for sure. Besides even if you do lots of people survive it now.'

'Lots die too.'

Pippa didn't want to get into an argument with Lainey. But she guessed this wasn't the moment to try and reason with her either. 'I know it's really hard. But you've got to try and think positively. I hope you'll get better and all this can seem like a bad dream . . .'

'A bad dream?' Lainey scoffed. 'This is a total nightmare, Pippa. And even if I don't have cancer . . . Even if I'm not dying, I've saddled Matt with a wife who can't bear him any more children. He's going to hate me, Pip. Everything is going to crumble and fall apart one way or the other . . .'

'OK!' Pippa said raising her voice. 'That's enough. You are not going to die, you hear me? And . . . and if you do, God damn you . . . I'll mind Ely. I know my track record hasn't been great and I barely managed to mind myself. But I'll step up to the plate. He'll have me, OK?'

'Pippa, you can't bear being in the countryside. I know you think the whole married with kids and living in the back end of nowhere thing is your idea of hell.'

'I don't hate it *that* much,' she grinned. 'And the point is that if Ely needs me, I'll be there. Nothing else matters more than family. Even if I don't know anything else . . . I know that.'

'Thanks, honey,' Lainey said and smiled weakly.

'Now enough of the death talk and the depressing stuff. Guess who I met yesterday? There was a reason I didn't get here.'

'Go on,' Lainey said smiling. Pippa filled her in on Jodi's visit to the store and how she'd given her the piece of paper with her number on it.

'Wow!' Lainey said.

Although she still looked hollow around her eyes Pippa knew the story was taking her mind off her situation for a few minutes.

Just as they'd finished chatting about what Jodi had bought Joey arrived looking completely flustered.

'I came as quickly as I could . . . I had to run out on a lunch. Clive was staring at me like I was crazy . . . But who cares? I'm here now.'

'What in the name of God is wrong with you, Joey?' Lainey asked half smiling, half nervous.

'I . . . I guess I had a moment of clarity just then. I was sitting talking shit with two fat balding men when I realised my sister is sitting in a hospital bed while her insides are being poked in a Kilner jar.'

'Nice,' Pippa said rolling her eyes. 'Could you have put it in a more graphic and gross way?'

Lainey laughed for the first time since she'd collapsed.

'What?' Joey and Pippa chorused.

'You two are a tonic. I know you clearly came in here to try and help. But nobody else could come in and act so panicked. I'm meant to be having the meltdowns not you two!'

'But don't you see?' Joey said. 'That's the way it works, Lainey. You're the big sister.'

'You're the only ones I really needed to see,' said Lainey. 'Thanks for coming in, you guys.'

Pippa glanced over at Joey and looked back down at the floor. She'd never felt like such a bitch in all her life. She should've been here this time yesterday. Looking at Joey's expression, she sensed he felt exactly the same way.

'I called in first thing this morning,' he said. 'But you were off having a scan. The nurses couldn't tell me how long you'd be. I should've waited. I'm sorry, Lainey.'

'Hey, don't be silly,' she said. 'I know you're both up to your eyes. Besides there's so much going on right now. Anyway, look at us! We're all here now. That's all that matters.'

Less than an hour later one of the nurses arrived with a blood pressure monitor and some tablets.

'Sorry to break up the party, folks, but Lainey needs to have her vital signs checked and I'll administer some painkillers. Could I ask you to call back another time? I think perhaps she's had enough too.'

'Sure,' said Joey. 'We'll be back soon. I'll keep in touch with Pippa and we'll rotate it so you're not bombarded.'

'Or left on your own,' Pippa added.

They both bent to kiss her and moved off toward the door. Just as they were about to say goodbye to one another, Jules walked over.

'Hey. Can I have a quick word in private before you two zip off?'

'Sure,' said Pippa.

They followed her into a door marked 'family room'.

'So how did you find Lainey?' Jules asked.

'She was in great form thankfully,' Joey said pulling his fingers through his hair. 'I was really hassled coming down here. I've so much on right now. But Sadie sent this text earlier and I knew I should come . . .'

'Me too. Well I was on the way. But it jarred me, I have to admit. I was expecting to see Lainey on life support or something,' Pippa joked. 'She's not exactly jumping about, but she's doing really well. We had a good chat and I think she's fine now.'

Jules marched up and down clenching her fists.

'Are you two quite finished?'

'What's eating you?' Joey asked, as his smile faded.

'Are you serious?' Jules seethed. 'I cannot get my head around you two. You're so full of what's going on in your own lives and how hassled or busy or up-your-own-asses you are. Stop and take a look around, why don't you? Lainey needs to be the centre of attention right now. She could die. Have you actually thought about that?'

'Jules, we're all aware that Lainey is in a really scary place right now,' Joey said. 'But there's no need to be so aggressive.'

'Isn't there?' she shouted. 'I have one relation. My mother. Who happens to hate me. She despises the fact that I still exist. But you know what? At least she's straight up and honest about it. Whereas you lot are so lovey-dovey at times and yet now when the chips are down and your sister needs you, neither of you are anywhere to be found.'

'That's not true,' Joey said. 'I came this morning . . .'

'Yeah and couldn't wait for five minutes until Lainey came back from a scan. Joey, you're so obsessed with saving Huntersbrook and climbing the career ladder that you've forgotten what really matters. If Lainey dies, it'll be too late. No money, house or job will ever replace her.' Jules couldn't manage to say any more.

'I'm out of here,' Joey said through his teeth. 'Jules, I know you mean well. But I don't appreciate you telling me how to behave with my own sister. Lainey knows she means the world to me. Thanks for the dressing down, but I think you should sort your own messed-up life before you start trying to organise mine. See you later, Pip.'

As he marched out and slammed the door, Jules collapsed onto a chair.

'I give up,' she said weakly. 'I'm brilliant at killing relationships . . . I only wanted to protect Lainey. I thought you were all ignoring her . . . I know she helped you two years ago,' she said sheepishly to Pippa. 'I see the effort she puts into being a good friend to Skye and how she nursed Joey after his accident. I couldn't bear the fact that neither of you seemed to care. I was wrong . . . I'm sorry,' she said bursting into tears.

'Hey,' Pippa said quietly. 'Don't cry, Jules. For the record, you're right. Everything you've just said is true. Joey is on some arrogant bastard buzz right now. So leave him to his door slamming and being a stroppy git. But I'm not afraid to admit that I've behaved like a total witch.'

'Pippa,' Jules said. 'I didn't mean to attack you . . .'

'I've been so bloody stupid, Jules,' she said.

Bit by bit, Pippa explained the situation with Missy and how she'd been blackmailing her.

'Pippa, have you been taking drugs too?'

Silently she nodded, having the grace to look utterly ashamed. 'That's why I couldn't come to see Lainey last night. I'm so disgusted with myself, Jules. I knew she needed me and I was so off my face, I couldn't come.'

'Wow,' Jules whistled. 'That's not ideal, Pippa.'

'Not ideal? It's a bloody fiasco,' she said throwing her arms in the air. 'I cannot believe how stupid I've been. I knew all along that I was playing with fire. I knew it was wrong. It goes against the grain and I can't think of any reason to justify what I've done. But all I can say is that I want to change.'

'That's a start,' she said. 'Listen, Pippa. I'm hardly Mother Theresa. Nobody's perfect. But you can turn this around, yeah? You can disentangle yourself from Missy as soon as this party is over. You can walk away. You're lucky. Lucky that it hasn't impacted on your life any further.'

'Why do I keep getting myself into stupidly dangerous situations, Jules? I don't intend to do it. But it seems to happen. Why can't I be normal?'

'What's "normal" anyway?'

The two girls hugged.

Jules knew she wasn't going to find it quite as cosy next time she saw Joey. But she didn't regret shouting at him. She'd do it again, ten times over, if it meant he'd think more about Lainey.

'Are we friends?' Pippa asked.

'You bet,' Jules said. 'I love all you guys. You're the closest thing I have to family. That's clearly why I think I can hide in hospital rooms before jumping out and yelling at you all.'

'Lainey's lucky to have such an amazing friend,' Pippa said. 'I'm envious. I don't know anyone who'd do that for me.'

'Lainey would.'

'Touché. You know, Jules, I thought I was living my life on the edge. I honestly didn't face up to quite how emotionally disturbed I've been since that attack. I was terrified to go out for ages. Then it was as if I took off in a totally different direction. It was like I was trying to give my fear the two fingers. That game is over now, I can tell you. Everything to do with that seedy drugs world is being culled from my life.'

Pippa

PIPPA DIDN'T FEEL LIKE RETURNING TO DUBLIN.
She couldn't face seeing Danny or anyone else. She needed some
time out, to think and plan. Jules' words had hit home, and she
knew she had to rethink her life. Instead she pointed the car in
the direction of Huntersbrook.

She called into the gate lodge to look in on Holly and Paddy
who were busy with Ely.

'So I've just been with Lainey,' she said.

'What?' Holly asked rushing to her. 'But Matt told us that
she's not accepting visitors. How come you went in there? Paddy,
we need to go in there right now.'

'Let's just hear what Pippa has to say,' he urged, trying to
restore calm. 'We need to keep things on an even keel for this
little man,' he said pointing to Ely.

'She's OK, considering,' Pippa said. 'She's doing her best. But
I reckon she must feel like a ticking time bomb.'

Holly began to twist the napkin she was clutching.

'Matt is still insisting she doesn't want to see us. Pippa, do you
think we could go anyway? I'm going stir crazy here. I know
she's angry with me at the moment . . . Well, I know our relationship is . . . But I'm her mother. And it isn't right that we're
not in there with her. And . . . and Paddy shouldn't be punished
because Lainey is angry with me.'

Skye arrived and knocked on the door.

'Hello love,' Holly said. 'Pippa's just come from the hospital. It seems Lainey is a little brighter today,' she said with forced cheer.

'That's good,' Skye said. 'I'm planning to visit her in a while. I'll let her rest a bit and then go over. Joey texted to say he was there and that Jules is still in there. Did she need anything brought in?'

'I'm not sure,' Pippa said. 'Maybe give her a text before you leave.'

'Right, that's it,' Holly said. 'I'm going in now.'

Paddy stood up and moved over to place his hand on her shoulder. 'Lainey has asked us to mind Ely. That is the most important thing right now. We need to make sure he's happy. The others can trot in and out of the hospital. That's fine. Let's do what she needs us to do and that way things are as stress free as possible. Am I right?' he asked the two girls.

'Totally,' Pippa nodded in agreement. 'Dad's right. Let's all try and rally around. Besides if Skye is popping in and Jules is already there, it'd be like a zoo. The ward isn't that spacious, so I think your best policy is to stick with Ely.'

Skye changed the subject by telling them about the takeaway idea and asked if they'd join.

'Sounds lovely,' said Holly. 'We'll bring this little man along and it'll be cosy.'

'Great. I'll make tracks now then,' Skye said. 'See you all later.'

'I think I'll go on up to the house too. I'll give you lift, Skye.'

'I can walk down the driveway. You don't have to leave on my account.'

'It's cool,' Pippa said easily. 'See you both later. Bye Ely,' she said as the baby waved happily.

Pippa glanced over at Skye a couple of times as she zipped down the drive. Normally Skye would make a smart comment about her not being a rally driver and slowing down.

They got out of the car and walked into Huntersbrook in total silence.

'So I know things aren't exactly zippity-do-dah around here right now,' Pippa said. 'But what's going on with you, Skye? It's not like you to be so quiet.'

'Oh, I'm fine thanks, Pippa. Just worried about Lainey.'

'Are you sure?' Skye nodded, but the tell-tale tears gave the game away.

'Please tell me what's wrong. You can trust me,' Pippa said. 'I don't want to upset you any further than you already are, but I'd like to help if I can.'

She was still smarting from Jules' outburst. The idea that she was so completely selfish had hit her hard. She wondered how many other people saw her as a self-centred shallow wagon.

'You have enough problems on your plate right now,' Skye said attempting to fob her off.

'Listen, there's always room on the plate for another pile of crap. So don't be shy.'

'I thought all my prayers had been answered when Joey proposed. I still can't quite believe that Holly wants me to wear her mother's ring. But it's almost like the universe is trying to burst my bubble in as many ways as possible ever since. First, this awful thing is happening to Lainey. Then I go home to try and have a civil conversation with my insane mother and she's more out there than ever . . .'

'You don't have much to do with her though. So it's not really something you should worry about, right?'

'But I do, Pippa. I'm supposed to be the child and she's the adult. But it's always felt as if it's the other way around. My father is off God only knows where, probably dying unnecessarily because he won't take the medicine he requires . . .'

'And?' Pippa raised one eyebrow.

'And Joey is like a different man . . . Since he's been offered this partnership I feel as if he's slipping away from me. I barely see him and when I do he's full of work jargon and who is making the most profit. I'm pleased for him that he's being rewarded at work. He deserves it. He's very dedicated . . . But I don't know where I fit in any more.'

'Oh Skye,' she said hugging her. 'I'm sorry that you feel side-stepped by Joey.'

'Do you know what's bothering me the most?'

'What?'

'Any time I broach the subject, Joey tells me he's doing it for us. For our future. For our benefit. But what's he's really missing is that all I want is him. I've no interest in material things. I never had. I don't care about labels or price tags. None of those things matter when push comes to shove. What use will it be to find myself in some plush home with a shiny big car in the drive and nobody to talk to?'

Pippa felt as if she'd had a bucket of freezing water dumped over her head. This was all echoing exactly what Jules had said earlier. Both the girls were right too. Pippa had an urge to run and grab her brother and shake him until the advice he'd been given by Jules spun about like bingo balls before landing in the right slots and creating a jackpot win. The prize being a great big dose of let's-cop-the-hell-on.

Pippa made tea and they shared a slice of Sadie's chocolate cake.

'God this is good,' Skye said. 'Worth the calories.'

Just then a loud rumbling noise from outside made them jump.

'Oh Skye. You've got to see this.'

As they peered out the window a large flat backed truck came into sight with a huge mound of poles and fabric on top.

'Ooh, the tent!' Skye said. They pulled on coats and ventured to the side of the house where Matt, Jacob, Holly, Paddy and Ely were congregated.

'That looks massive,' Pippa whispered. 'Who are the band of merry men?'

'The ones Joey bought it from. They only wanted a few quid in cash to erect it, so we thought it was wiser to pay.'

Hammering and dragging went on for the entire day. Men kept arriving until there must've been over two dozen of them on site.

'I can't believe we actually considered not paying the vendor to have his team put this up,' Paddy said shaking his head in awe. 'It's a massive construction.'

'And well worth every penny these lads are charging,' Matt agreed.

'It's so exciting now,' Holly said. 'I can almost hear the corks popping and the animated chatting of a party.'

Holly noticed Pippa standing off to one side, arms folded tightly across her chest, looking distracted. She stepped across to her.

'Hi love,' she said. 'Are you feeling OK?'

'Yeah,' Pippa said rather too quickly. 'All great thanks. You?'

'Ah I'm worried sick about Lainey, but dad and I are trying to keep ourselves busy. Having little Ely is a blessing,' Holly said. 'He's such a darling boy. Lainey and Matt have done a marvellous job with him, you know . . .'

They looked over at Ely, who was clearly thrilled with all the action. She waved over at him as he stamped his feet gleefully on the section of dance floor that was already laid.

Pippa was rubbing her temples and exhaling. Holly knew she wasn't hearing a single word she was saying. Trying a different tack, she tried to engage her daughter in conversation.

'How are things going with Danny then? He's still on the scene I hope?'

'Um,' Pippa said distractedly. 'I'm looking forward to getting this party over and done with.'

'Why?' Holly laughed. 'Is Missy going on and on about it at work?'

'Something like that,' Pippa said as she walked over to talk to Paddy.

Holly watched her go with a sense of apprehension. Pippa wasn't a bit like herself lately, she seemed to have lost her spark. And she'd lost a lot of weight. Of her two daughters, it was Lainey who wouldn't miss a few pounds. Pippa's hair was usually glossy and her skin had a velvet-like sheen that Holly had always admired. Today, she looked almost scraggy and hollow.

Paddy hugged their youngest child and showed her his new toy, an electronic tape measure that extended and reeled in with the push of a button.

'I'll get great use out of this,' he said.

Pippa couldn't help smiling at his enthusiasm. 'So what are you going to measure first?' she teased.

'This dance floor,' Paddy said. 'I have to make sure we're getting every centimetre we've paid for.'

'You do that, Dad,' Pippa said, clapping him gently on the back. 'I think I'll go make a round of coffees and teas. I'm sure the men could do with a break.'

Holly watched Pippa leave her father and walk in the direction of the house. At least Paddy had been able to make her smile. She would have to try to get Pippa alone again and see if she could get a feel for what was behind her sad face.

Something was definitely eating away at her, that was plain enough to see.

With a sigh, Holly turned her attention from Pippa and went to find little Ely. At first she thought he must be with Matt. She scanned the marquee, then spotted Matt high on a ladder tying some of the tulle to the roof.

Her heart started to beat faster, but she told herself to remain calm. Paddy was busy measuring; Pippa had gone to the house alone. Where was he?

She dashed from the marquee and looked left and right. No sign of him. She ran to the house. In the kitchen, Pippa was setting out mugs and biscuits and Sadie was chopping vegetables.

'Do you have Ely here with you?' she asked in as calm a voice as she could muster.

'No, love. I thought he was with you.'

Holly ran back toward the marquee, calling his name loudly. No answer.

Back inside the tent, she called out, asking if anyone had him.

'He can't have gone far,' Paddy said, turning around with a smile.

'Ely!' Holly screamed as she ran from one end of the marquee to the other. Realising he wasn't there, panic set in. Matt climbed down from the ladder as everyone dropped what they were doing and joined Holly outside.

Matt was brilliant as he sent different people in each direction, instructing them to yell loudly when they found him.

Blood rushed through Holly's ears as she ran toward the farmhouse. Praying that he'd simply gone home, she felt a wave of nausea when she reached the property and he wasn't there.

Turning on her heel, she rushed back, looking left and right frantically as she went. She could hear the others calling his name and the answering silence.

She met Paddy at the rear of the marquee. Stricken, she fell into his arms.

'Jesus, Paddy, what will we do if something's happened to the child? Lainey will never let us near him again.'

'Hush now,' Paddy said, hugging her. Holding her away from him, he spoke firmly and slowly. 'We will find him. He's only tiny. He can't have gone far.'

Nodding, she wiped her tears away and took his hand as they continued to search.

What felt like a decade later, they found themselves on the main road circling the estate. Holly's screams rang out across the road as she noticed a stationary car with the driver's door wide open.

'No!' she called out, running frantically toward the scene. Paddy got there before her and fell to his knees. The lady driver was crouched on the ground, chatting to Ely. Seeming totally at ease, he was gabbling away to her as if he did this all the time.

'Oh thank God,' Holly said stooping to scoop him up in her arms. Squeezing him and twirling around joyfully she made him giggle.

'I was driving down and saw this little fella scurrying along,' the lady said. 'He's lucky a truck didn't come around the corner and flatten him.'

Holly gasped and buried her face in his soft downy hair.

'Thank you. Thank you so much. Oh my God, Ely,' she said as tears of relief soaked her face. 'We were all frantic looking for him. He was there one minute and the next he was gone.'

'Where is his mother?' the lady asked. There was a tone in

her voice that suggested she wasn't entirely happy about leaving him in the care of Holly and Paddy.

'Our daughter, Lainey, is in hospital at the moment. Ely's father is back there, at the house. It was one of those things where we each thought the other was minding him.'

The lady regarded them for a few moments. 'Make sure you keep a closer eye on him,' she said coldly. 'He could have been killed here today and you would only have had yourselves to blame.'

Holly's face burned at the woman's words. Paddy nodded curtly. Holly thanked her again and they stood to the side to allow her to drive away.

'Bit sharp,' Paddy said tightly as he lifted Ely and set off for home.

Holly put her face in her hands and wiped away her tears.

'What do you expect?' she said. 'We let a toddler run on the road. We were meant to be minding him and he could've been killed. We're lucky she didn't insist on calling social services.'

Paddy told her not to overreact. That things like this happened all the time. That it was all fine now. But Holly was shell-shocked. She knew Lainey would hit the roof when she heard what had happened. The last thing Lainey needed right now was more stress and more reason to feel out of control.

They were welcomed with hugs and relief when they returned to the marquee. Poor Matt looked like he'd been hit by a bus.

'I'm so sorry, Matt,' Holly said and burst into tears.

'Hey,' he said putting his arm around her. 'It wasn't your fault. He's a little maggot. He's here one second and gone the next. All's well that ends well and sure we'll all have to realise that he's fast enough to make a run for it now.'

'Thanks, Matt,' Holly said gratefully.

Ely seemed oblivious to the chaos he'd caused, giggling as his daddy tickled him.

No matter how kind Matt was or how Paddy and Pippa tried to reassure her, Holly knew she'd have flash-backs of that awful moment she realised he was gone for some time to come.

Pippa

AFTER THE SHOCK OF ELY'S ESCAPE FROM THE safety of Huntersbrook, things settled down again as the men got back to working on the marquee. Skye left to visit Lainey, so Pippa decided to do what she couldn't believe she was going to do: phone Jodi Ludlum to arrange to see her again.

She went to her old bedroom at Huntersbrook and fished the precious piece of paper out of her purse. Her hands were shaking as she dialled the number. Holding her breath, she almost wished it would go to voice mail.

'Hello?'

'Hello . . . J . . . Jodi . . . It's Pippa Craig here. I met you . . . Eh I was there when you were shopping . . . I was the sales assis . . .'

'Oh hello, Pippa, how are you?' Jodi said. 'Thanks for calling, I really appreciate it.'

'Oh, no problem,' Pippa said, feeling as if she were having an out-of-body experience. 'Thanks for your note. I was totally stunned, if I'm honest.' Pippa managed to laugh. 'It's not every day someone like you gives me their mobile number.'

'Well it's not every day I meet someone with a lovely home that sounds perfect for my requirements,' Jodi shot back. 'I was chatting to Harry after we left and we'd really love to come and have a look around at Huntersbrook, if you were on for it?'

'Seriously?' Pippa's voice sounded like a squeaky toy. Clearing her throat, she tried to be cool. 'You're welcome any time, Jodi. You and Harry.'

They chatted about potential dates and settled on the following day.

'I'll be here trying to get things ready for Missy's party. My whole family are getting really excited now.'

'I'll bet,' Jodi said. 'I don't want to sound like a total diva here, Pippa. But would it be possible to keep it quiet that I'm coming? I know it must sound totally contradictory for a movie star to say this, but I'm not crazy about folks knowing too much about my private life.'

'Of course,' Pippa assured her. 'The only people who might be there bar my family are a couple of catering staff. But we can avoid them if you'd prefer. Put it this way, I won't be calling the newspapers.'

'Aw that's great, thanks Pippa,' Jodi said. They settled on two o'clock as a meeting time and Pippa clarified exactly where the house was. She hung up and sat motionless staring at her phone in a daze. Had that really happened? Was Jodi Ludlum actually coming to Huntersbrook?

She was just putting her phone in her back pocket when it vibrated. She looked at the name on the screen and contemplated not answering, but that wasn't going to solve anything.

'Hi Danny,' she said evenly. 'Listen, I won't stay on long if you don't mind. I'm up to my tonsils here. We've had a couple of setbacks and I need to keep my head down.'

'That's OK,' he said. 'Will you be back in Dublin before Missy's party?'

'No,' she said firmly. 'My family need me here to help out. With Lainey so unwell, I need to take on some responsibility, so I've arranged time off with Brianna.'

'Listen, I want to be there with you, Pippa. You can rely on me and I need you to know that. You don't have to do things on your own any more. I can come down after work and be there tomorrow to give a hand, if you like?'

'Eh I'm not sure, Danny. I think maybe we need some family time. I can't afford for there to be any shenanigans either.'

'There won't be,' he said sounding stung. 'I wouldn't dream of pitching up at your family home with any of that shit on my person.'

Pippa sighed heavily

'Pippa, please believe me,' he said. 'I did some bad things. I made money in an awful way, but I'm not a liar. I want to get to know you better. I want us to try and have a proper relationship . . .'

'Right now, Danny, I need to concentrate on sorting some family stuff.'

'I understand.' He sounded crushed and Pippa wanted to cry. 'You go and do what you have to do and I'll call you in the morning, yeah?'

'OK, thanks,' she said.

'Take care, pretty Pippa,' he said and hung up.

Pippa smiled. The stupid nickname should probably annoy her, but much as she hated to admit it, she found it quite endearing.

She pushed Danny out of her mind and decided to focus entirely on Huntersbrook and what she could do here. She smiled as she thought of Jodi and went to find her family.

She found Matt, Ely, Jacob and her parents in the almost-finished marquee, sitting at a round table chatting.

'You'll never guess who's coming here tomorrow,' she said.

'Paddington Bear!' Paddy jibed.

'Jodi Ludlum,' Pippa deadpanned.

'I beg your pardon?' Holly gasped.

'You heard me correctly,' Pippa said coolly. 'Huntersbrook is going to play host to the hottest movie star around, and it's happening tomorrow!'

'Oh Jesus Mary and Joseph,' Holly said jumping up out of her chair. 'Oh dear, I think I need to sit down again,' she said flapping in confusion. 'This has to be one of the most unnerving days I've ever had in my life. Now tell us everything,' she said.

Pippa told them the whole story of how Jodi had come to the store and given her a note.

'That's unbelievable,' Paddy said shaking his head. 'Only you could charm Jodi Ludlum,' he grinned.

'She stressed that she wants to keep it all low key,' Pippa said. 'So I think we should keep it between the family for now.'

'Of course,' Paddy nodded. 'I'm sure the poor girl is sick of the world nosing into her movements.'

Pippa looked at her mother, who was clearly very shaken after the awful shock of losing Ely. She hoped things were going to improve. Between Lainey being ill and the house turning around, Pippa worried about her. She wasn't getting any younger. Imagine if she knew about Danny? It'd kill her. Pippa couldn't risk adding to her mother's stress.

Her mobile started to ring again and she expected to see Danny's name flash up. It was even worse: Missy.

Pippa closed her eyes and wished she could wave a magic wand and make Missy go away.

'Eh yes, of course it's OK for you to drop by,' Pippa said loudly. The others looked up in alarm. 'Ah isn't that a coincidence that you're at the gate. Sure . . .'

'She's not here this second?' Holly said. 'Tell me I'm hearing things.'

'Sadly not,' Pippa said. 'Let's just get this over with and then we can collapse in a heap.'

As the cough medicine pink convertible Mercedes pulled up outside Paddy was the first to comment, much to Pippa's amusement.

'Now that's a travesty if ever I saw one. Who knew you could do that to a Merc?'

'Daddy, you can do what you like when you have Missy Hassett's bottomless pit of cash,' Pippa said dryly.

She rushed to greet Missy as her mother climbed out of the car. She was literally a slightly more worn looking version of her daughter without an ounce of surplus body fat.

'Hello, Mrs Hassett, it's lovely to meet you. I'm Pippa.'

'Who?'

'Mummy, this is the girl I was telling you about. My friend. The one who works for us but isn't common.'

'Is this your house then?' Mrs Hassett said.

'Yes, well, my family home. These are my parents Holly and Paddy, my brother-in-law Matt, soon-to-be sister-in-law Skye . . .'

'Skye? What kind of a name is that?' said Mrs Hassett. 'You poor child. No wonder you look drab. I would too if I had to cower away from my name my whole life.'

'Muuuum,' Missy said.

Pippa raised an eyebrow. She'd never seen Missy cringe before. As Pippa introduced the others and showed them the marquee, Mrs Hassett hadn't a nice thing to say about any of it.

'Obviously the marquee is still under construction, but it'll be stunning on the night of the party,' Holly said. 'Can I offer you ladies a cup of tea or coffee? I could go on ahead to the kitchen and have it ready for you?'

'Coffee or tea?' Mrs Hassett said. 'I sincerely hope you'll be serving something a little more edgy at the party!' she whooped with laughter, clearly seeing herself as some sort of a comedian.

'Would you prefer a pint of whisky or a shot of adrenalin?'

Paddy asked, jumping to Holly's defence. His wit was totally lost on the two.

'Ooh bubbles would be lovely,' said Missy as she clapped. Paddy wandered off in the direction of the kitchen mumbling under his breath.

'So what colours do the interiors come in then?' Missy asked.

They all looked at one another. 'The base colour is cream,' Pippa said. 'But we can decorate with whatever colour scheme you have in mind.'

'I thoroughly enjoy flower-arranging and I could do some under-stated yet beautiful centrepieces for your tables with some larger ones near the entrance,' Holly offered.

There was a slight pause before Mrs Hassett spoke, while smiling.

'I don't think you lot are getting the point here. Missy wants the wow factor. A few daisy chains and lame accessories are just not going to cut the mustard. Us Hassetts are known for our taste. We need to make this a party to remember. We have a reputation, you know.'

'Oh I can tell,' Holly said nodding. 'I absolutely get you now.'

'Yes I think we all do,' said Matt.

'What did you both have in mind?' Pippa said, stepping in swiftly before someone attempted to show Mrs Hassett how effective the lump hammer could be.

'Balloons!' Missy said clasping her hands together. 'Millions of them. In big bunches. Then an archway of them around the door, oh and over there,' she pointed to the stage. 'I want a net of them over the dance floor too, with glitter and flower petals.'

'Are you all writing this down?' Mrs Hassett asked.

'No need,' said Holly cheerfully. 'We won't forget a single detail. Carry on Missy, please do.'

'Now, obviously it's all going to be pink. The same colour as my car. Do you like it, by the way, Pip? Dad got it for me.'

'Love it,' Pippa said pursing her lips and nodding slowly. 'I'm sooo envious.'

'Yay! I know.'

'So we're going for that pink,' Holly coughed. 'And a paler one perhaps?'

'Yeah but not too much paler. We're not looking to tone things down here. It's to be bling bling all the way.'

'All our table linen is white, but we can do pink napkins and perhaps you'd like glittery centrepieces?' Pippa suggested. 'I've seen some really choice ones. They're almost like a fountain for all the world, with little hearts shooting out of them on the end of thin sparkly shards of ribbon.'

'Yes!' said Missy. 'Now you're getting it.'

'It'll be fairly cold, so how about an ice sculpture at the door,' Mrs Hassett suggested scratching her chin.

'No, Mummy,' Missy said dismissing her rudely. 'That'd be tacky.'

They discussed the menu in finer detail and thankfully they weren't that interested in arguing about it.

'We don't really eat much,' Mrs Hassett said. 'A minute on the lips and all that. I'll just be surviving on champers!'

Skye and Matt stayed in the marquee as Pippa and Holly brought the ladies to the main house where Paddy was pouring some champagne.

'This is Sadie,' Holly introduced. 'She's been our housekeeper for over forty years and is part of our family.'

'Oh you are a gas character!' Mrs Hassett said swatting Holly's arm. 'Part of the family. As if! We changed over to a fully foreign staff a few years back. God, it's a relief. They don't speak much English yet they get the job done. Far easier to deal with too.'

Holly opened her mouth but no words came out. Pippa patted her gently on the back and led her to Paddy and Sadie so they could huddle together like startled chickens. She noticed Sadie's grip of her metal whisk tightening so hard that her knuckles whitened. Holly mouthed 'S-O-R-R-Y,' to Sadie.

'I'll show the ladies the rest of the house,' Pippa suggested. 'You all have menial tasks to get to, I assume?' They nodded wordlessly.

The house tour was much of the same. The comments were thick and fast, in every sense of the word, and Pippa was expecting them to cancel by the time they reached the front door.

'Well, that's pretty much all I can do for you,' Pippa announced as she snatched the two empty champagne flutes from them. 'Do you want to get back to me on anything?'

'No, I don't think so,' Mrs Hassett said looking more cheerful than she had. 'It's not as plush as our home, obviously. But it'll do nicely. It has that olde-worlde charm thing going on. I couldn't live here. It's all too crumbly and ancient. I like new shiny things. But I know there are lots of people on our guest list who will be wildly impressed by the whole thing.'

'It's old money, Mum,' Missy said matter-of-factly. 'People will know this furniture didn't come flat-packed and things like the staircase are amazing. I love all the squiggly-looking stuff in the ceilings too. It's like very professional cake icing, isn't it?'

'Can you do pink lights in the marquee?' Mrs Hassett said, clearly not interested in talking about the icing on the ceiling or any of the period features of the house.

'I'm sure we can,' Pippa said.

'Good. Well, how about I write you a cheque for fifteen thousand euros to keep you going? You'll need to buy all the balloons and things. Don't scrimp on them now. There's nothing worse than walking into a room and thinking the people were on a tight budget. No piddly little bunches now. Think OTT! It is a party after all!'

Pippa thanked her for the cheque and showed them out the main entrance. The other family members congregated and entered into air kissing and frozen smiles.

'We look forward to welcoming you and your guests for Missy's special party,' Paddy said. 'We hope it's going to be a night to remember.'

'Uh, it'll be the bomb!' Missy said. 'Bye, Pippa. See you soon and thanks for showing us around. Yay me! This is going to work brilliantly!'

'Yay!' Pippa responded injecting as much enthusiasm as she could muster. As they were reversing away, Pippa said through her teeth without moving her lips, 'She just handed me a cheque for fifteen grand to buy balloons. Wave more enthusiastically.'

Instantly, they reacted with renewed vigour and waved as if their lives depended on it.

Huddling close to one another just inside the marquee, they all said nothing for a moment. Holly broke the silence.

'Never in all my years have I met a woman like that.'

'Which one?' Paddy asked looking genuinely traumatised.

'Does Mrs Hassett's face move at all?' Skye asked.

'No,' Pippa said. 'But it's given me a real insight into Missy. She's a complete angel compared to her mother. Poor Mr Hassett. He's actually a really lovely man.'

'I'd say they tie him up and threaten to poke him with a cattle prod until he does what they want,' Paddy said.

'I agree,' said Matt. 'No wonder Mercedes did that to one of their cars. I'd say they'd have painted *My Little Pony* on it just to get rid of those two.'

Pippa phoned a couple of balloon suppliers to get some prices.

When she phoned Missy back, she discovered they'd already called a man they'd used before.

'I'll hold on to your cheque then,' Pippa said.

'Yeah, take it off the end price or something,' she said.

Darkness brought a chilly dampness with it so the family decided to call it a day.

'I'm going to take Ely home and give him a quick bath and put him in his pyjamas,' Matt said. 'Dad is already at the farm-house, so I'll bring him back over with me. Shall we say an hour to reconvene?'

'Perfect,' said Holly. 'We'll go to the gate lodge and freshen up too.'

Pippa and Skye went over to Huntersbrook.

'I'm going to have a shower and try to block Mrs Hassett from my brain until I absolutely *have* to think about her again. She gets my vote for "Horrible person of the year award".'

'She's kind of offensive, isn't she?' Skye agreed.

✳

Skye waited another half an hour. She tried Joey's mobile number one last time. It was still going to voicemail. She guessed he'd turned it off for the meeting earlier and had forgotten to switch it back on again. He was probably on the motorway right now, speeding his way back to her, oblivious to the fact.

She set the table and threw another couple of logs on the fire. She was just ready when the back door opened and Holly and Paddy arrived.

'No sign of the neighbours yet?' Holly asked, searching for Ely.

'No, and Joey isn't back yet either,' Skye said casually.

'What time is he meant to be here?' Paddy asked.

'I'm not sure. Actually his mobile has been off all day.'

'Bet he doesn't realise,' Holly said.

'Yes that's what I figured,' Skye said. 'He'll land back in looking blankly at me!'

Matt and Jacob arrived with Ely looking clean and cosy in his onesie.

'Well I don't know about anyone else, but I'm Hank Marvin,' Pippa said. 'I can't wait another second to be fed – not after the day we've had. I'm not waiting for Joey to fall in the door looking confused in two hours' time. I'll call the new Chinese restaurant in the village. They deliver.'

Skye looked over at Pippa flushing with embarrassment. She knew there was probably a perfectly reasonable explanation as to why Joey hadn't been in touch all day and currently had his phone off, but she was cross with him for putting her in such an awkward position with his family.

Paddy opened a bottle of wine and shortly after that the food arrived. The landline rang and Skye ran to answer.

She did her best not to sob or yell in fury when Joey said he'd had a few drinks and would be staying in Dublin.

'I see,' was all she could manage without causing a scene with his entire family listening. 'We need to have the marquee set up by lunch time for another prospective client, so maybe you'd try and get back in time to help with that . . .'

Skye listened as Joey covered the mouthpiece on the phone to call out to Clive. The sound of laughter and clinking glasses was almost deafening.

'OK, gotcha, Skye. Chat to you tomorrow. Sleep well, hon. Love you.'

She was still holding the phone after he'd hung up. Plastering a smile on her face, she turned to face the others.

'He's not coming home as it turns out.'

'Bloody men,' Pippa said crunching into a prawn cracker. 'Sod him, Skye. We'll have a girls' sleepover!'

'Just as well you're here, Pippa,' Holly said. 'Joey's an imp to leave you here like that, Skye.'

'Ah not at all,' she said trying to make light of it. 'I figured he'd probably have to stay up. With being made a partner and all that, I knew he'd be in demand.'

The rest of the evening was a trial. Skye longed to curl up in bed. She wanted to call Joey and yell down the phone at him that he was a selfish git and he could bloody well stay in Dublin and never come back.

Mercifully, the others were completely done in after all the excitement of the day and weren't in the mood for a late session, so they helped her clean up and said goodnight.

'Large bucket of wine?' Pippa offered as she pulled a bottle of white from the fridge.

'I'm actually too full to drink. I ate enough for three grown men just now,' Skye joked.

'Well I'm having one glass and then I'll go to bed. I'm so tired. You wouldn't believe the couple of weeks I've had, Skye.'

'How's Danny?' Skye asked. 'He seems great, Pippa. I'm so glad you've found a good guy.'

'Yeah, me too,' she said, but it didn't sound convincing.

If Skye wasn't so exhausted, she would've pushed Pippa to know why she seemed so hesitant about Danny all of a sudden. But that issue would have to be put on hold.

'Sorry to be such a party pooper,' Skye yawned. 'But I have to hit the hay. I'm completely wrecked.'

'No worries . . . I'm dying to get into bed and crash too. I don't want to look like a corpse when I meet Jodi Ludlum again tomorrow. She's so cool, Skye. You'll love her.'

'I can't believe she's really coming here. It's bananas!'

Skye waited until she'd firmly shut her bedroom door before she allowed herself to cry. She knew Joey adored her. She gazed at her gorgeous engagement ring as proof. But she was terrified this new role as partner was going to change him.

If he turned into an alpha male powerhouse businessman, where would she fit in? She loved Joey with all her heart, but she wasn't prepared to be treated like an afterthought. She'd had enough of that with her own family. She had no choice about being related to them. But she wasn't about to marry a man who did the same.

Joey

JOEY WAS UP AT QUARTER TO SIX THE FOLLOWING morning. He'd had a restless night. There were too many thoughts shooting around his head right now. Between work, home and Lainey, he was addled. The skin-full of drink hadn't helped matters either.

The pressure of getting the place ready for the party was weighing heavily on his already burdened shoulders. Still, it was all taking his mind off waiting for Lainey's news.

Reaching over for his mobile phone he groaned. He'd noticed there were missed calls when he got to the pub last night, but now as he realised Skye had tried him six times during the course of yesterday and his parents twice, he felt like such a sod. He'd left his damn phone on silent during the meetings and had totally forgotten to switch it back. He'd meant to call her to say he wasn't coming home. He'd tried after being at the hospital and had clearly registered in his own head that he'd done it.

It was too early to phone now, so he kicked his legs out of bed and into the shower. He'd zoom straight down to Wicklow and make Skye a lovely breakfast. She was a sweetheart and he knew she'd be fine once he explained.

Besides, the meeting and subsequent dinner and drinks last night had gone swimmingly and Clive was ecstatic with him. Skye would understand that he was looking after the best interests of his job. He was building a future for them. She'd be pretty darn proud of him, in fact.

It was only seven-thirty when he drove down the avenue at Huntersbrook. The sun was rising and the fields were blanketed in a soft woolly grey mist. Frost crystallised the grass, making it look as if it had been sugar-coated. Several large birds rose from the remnants of the cornfield and traversed the land. Joey drew to a halt, climbed out and inhaled deeply. The freezing air filled his lungs, cleansing the fug of his hangover. Rubbing his hands together he realised just how cold it was. He'd go inside, make breakfast for Skye and perhaps head out for a jog.

He turned his key in the lock, but when he shouldered the door it remained firmly shut. Skye had clearly put the inside bolt across for extra security. He went around to the back door, fiddled with his bunch of keys and selected the right one. The key was in the lock on the inside. He was blocked out.

Not wanting to wake Skye and risk frightening her, he considered going for a run straight away. He might have the makings of a running kit in the car. To his dismay, he had everything bar trainers. With no alternative he returned to the front door and rapped firmly with the knocker.

When he'd knocked three times and there was no answer he reluctantly climbed into the car and drove back to the gate lodge. Guessing his father would be up and about by now, he sighed with relief when he saw the kitchen light on.

Paddy looked up cheerfully as he tapped on the window.

'Good morning, early bird. Are you having a cuppa and a slice of toast?'

'Yes lovely, thanks Dad. Brrr, it's seriously cold out there.'

'Well it would be, standing about in a shirt and that measly excuse of a jumper with no sleeves,' he teased. 'Where did you get to last night, then? Skye was calling and calling you. We were all sitting with our knives and forks and our napkins tucked into our tops waiting for our take-away.'

'Shoot,' Joey said. 'I totally forgot about the take-away. Em, well it was all a bit of a mess. But it was good business-wise in so far as that all went brilliantly. I totally nailed it with the clients and Clive thinks I'm a star.'

'Good for you, son,' Paddy said.

'But I'm guessing I'm in the bad books with Skye?'

'Ah you know Skye. She's about as calm as they come. But it might have been nice to call and let her know you weren't coming back. I think she was embarrassed, to be honest.'

'Poor Skye,' he said, feeling really bad. 'I intended to call. I tried her in the morning and didn't get her and after that the day and evening just ran away with me. I'll make it up to her today. We might go for lunch or something like that.'

'Can't see that happening today with Jodi Ludlum coming.'

'I beg your pardon?' Joey said laughing.

'Oh you haven't heard, of course,' Paddy said and proceeded to fill him in on the new developments.

'Well I'll be damned,' he said shaking his head. 'Pippa is some operator, isn't she?'

Paddy nodded happily as he tucked into his toast. 'Yeah, it's a lovely bit of positivity for us all. It might help to balance the other awful woman. Missy Hassett came for a quick nose around with her mother yesterday evening.'

'What happened?'

'Nothing detrimental. She's just a garish woman whose brain isn't connected too tightly to her mouth.'

'Are they still having the party with us?'

'Yes, although I'll have to keep your mother's hands tied behind her back on the night in case she tries to anaesthetise Mrs Hassett with a large vase!'

'So it was a productive day all in.'

'Yes, but that didn't stop your mother being awake half the night. She's in a heap over Lainey.'

'I know, we all are.' Joey felt another stab of guilt as he remembered yesterday's hospital visit.

'So let's turn this around and get some good stuff going for the Craigs again. It's about time we grabbed life by the horns.'

Joey grinned, encouraged by his father's glass half-full attitude. He drove back to the house. It was still in darkness, so he made his way to the farmhouse. Hovering at the back door momentarily, he heard Matt chatting to Ely.

Knocking on the door first, he lifted the handle and walked in.

'Good morning, uncle Joey,' Matt said cheerfully. If it weren't for his two day old stubble and the dark circles under his eyes, Matt might have been convincing in his good humour.

'Sorry to intrude,' Joey said. 'How are you doing?'

'Ah so-so,' Matt said sighing. 'I'm trying to keep things upbeat for the little fella.'

'I know,' Joey sympathised. 'I don't suppose you've heard from Lainey yet?'

'Nah, it's a bit early. I didn't want to phone in case she's sleeping. She'll ring as soon as she wakes up, always does.'

Joey filled him in on all his exciting business advancements and they got chatting about Jodi's impending visit and the plans.

'I'm obviously minding this little man and I've to go over and see Lainey. But I'll do what I can.'

'I spoke to Dad and between her and Sadie, they'll be delighted to take Ely. Sadie is due in at around nine. Pippa appeared last night and apparently she's on board too.'

'Pippa's been great,' Matt said. 'She was in with Lainey yesterday and seemed to calm her down greatly. Apparently they had a great chat.'

Joey nodded and said nothing.

'I'm going to walk Ely across to Huntersbrook in the buggy,' Matt said. 'Care to join us?'

'Sure,' Joey said.

By the time Matt and Joey arrived at the door, Skye and Pippa were up and dressed.

'Morning,' Joey said stooping to kiss Skye. She smiled fleetingly and didn't answer.

'Where the hell were you last night?' Pippa fired across the kitchen. 'It's lucky I arrived or Skye would've been on her own here. Did your phone fall down the toilet or something? We all tried calling you.'

'Said the pot to the kettle,' Joey shot back. 'Pippa, you're hardly in a position to shout at me about not telling people where you are. You go AWOL on a regular basis and we're all meant to put up and shut up.'

'It's different for me,' she figured. 'Nobody expects me to act responsibly and besides, I didn't leave my fiancée sitting like a fool.'

'I'm so sorry, Skye,' he said, deciding to give up on arguing with Pippa. 'I got side-tracked and before I knew it, it was too late to call.'

'There's no point in going on about it. You're here now.' She smiled tightly. 'We have a lot of work to get done this morning. Did you hear who's coming?'

Thrilled at being thrown a lifeline, Joey grasped the positive change of subject and ran with it.

'I know, Dad told me. I can hardly believe it.'

'Oh and Lainey just called,' Pippa said to Matt. 'Seems she rang the farmhouse, got no answer and immediately called here. Obviously while you were en route. Give her a buzz there, Matt. She sounded tired.'

Matt disappeared to the landline. Pippa and Joey exchanged a look, but now wasn't the time to talk about Lainey – or Jules, for that matter.

'Right,' Pippa said. 'Matt can call Lainey and we can all get this show on the road,' she said clapping her hands loudly and making for the kettle and toaster. To Skye and Joey's astonishment, she whipped up a great big pot of buttery scrambled eggs, along with a mountain of toast and a large pot of coffee.

'Sit and eat,' she instructed as Holly arrived.

'It's a feast! Did you do all this, Pippa?'

'Yes! Why is everyone acting as if I've committed a crime?'

'You're not exactly a domestic goddess in general,' Holly said, stifling a giggle.

'And you're usually only up at this time if you're on the way home from a night out,' Joey reasoned.

'People in glasshouses, brother dear,' she said, poking out her tongue at him and then sitting down to help herself to some breakfast. Joey and Paddy decided to keep quiet about their previous tea and toast and sat to eat more.

Matt came back in with the wireless phone. 'Lainey wants to chat to you all,' he said, and put it on speakerphone.

'Hi guys. I just wanted to let you know that Sally from the cookery school will pitch up mid-morning with the other cooks. So will one of you promise to stick with her and help her find stuff?'

'I'll do it,' Holly said.

'Thanks, Mum,' Laincy said. 'She needs to get her bearings so she can have everything organised for the party.'

'Lainey, you've got to promise me you're not going to fret. We'll do everything we can to ensure things run smoothly at Missy's party. We won't let you down.'

'Thank you,' Lainey said, as her voice cracked.

'We miss you and we wish you were here,' Skye added. 'But you are to concentrate on getting well. You are more important than any party or even Jodi Ludlum's visit.'

'I'll call in quickly later,' Pippa added.

'No, Pippa, don't worry about it,' Lainey said. 'You have to have everything set up perfectly. You'll be up to your eyes.'

'I'll be there,' Pippa replied quietly.

❄

Once the table was cleared, they all jumped into action. They needed the place looking party perfect for Jodi's visit. Skye took Ely to the marquee, where she was in charge of laying the table-cloths and placing the pretty silk flower arrangements in the centres. Missy may not like the subtle look but they were hoping Jodi might. The boys unstacked the chairs and got the bar set up. There was a hum of busy activity that soothed Joey's nerves and made him feel like he was reconnecting with the place again. It was an odd division in his life at the moment – it felt like he had to be an entirely different person depending on whether he was in Dublin or in Huntersbrook. As he stacked bottles of spirits on the shelves behind the bar, he realised that, for the first time, he wasn't sure which one he'd liked being most. Before, he would have said Huntersbrook Joey, no contest. But work was so exciting now, and the places he was eating in, socialising in – it was all so vibrant. He felt a little shot of panic as he wondered if perhaps Dublin Joey was starting to take over.

'Morning!' called out a voice from the entrance. A man was standing there holding the biggest balloon Joey had ever seen. It was a three and zero in glittering silver and it dwarfed the grinning man who was holding it.

'Morning, come in,' Joey called as he walked over.

'Hope you don't mind me coming this morning instead of

this evening?' the balloon man said. 'But I was sure I'd get lost. The girl who ordered the stuff made out the house was on the furthest peninsula of the country. She had me convinced if I took the next right turn, I'd be in New Zealand!'

'Ah we're not that remote,' Joey said.

'I know that now,' he said grinning. 'This is an amazing set-up, by the way. I thought I'd been to all the fancy venues in the area.'

'We're new!' Joey said, grabbing a bunch of brochures from a table. 'So if you'd be able to put some of these in your shop, we'd really appreciate it?'

'I'll certainly help spread the word,' he said. 'Have you just bought the place?' he asked looking around with interest.

'No it's been in our family for three generations,' Joey said. 'But opening it up to the public is new for us.'

'I'm in business fifteen years. I'm *the* Bob from Bob's balloons,' he said pointing to the van emblazoned with his logo. 'You'd be surprised how many people ask about suitable places for parties. I'd be happy to give you a mention.'

Joey offered to help Bob unload the van before showing him the main house. He called out for help and Skye, Holly and Pippa came over. They took the many bunches of balloons and distributed them around the marquee.

'She certainly spared no expense with these,' Holly commented. 'Mind you she did mention quite a few times that she wanted it all to look OTT.'

'Should we hide these behind a screen or something until Jodi's been?' Pippa wondered.

'What kind of screen had you in mind?' Joey asked. 'One the size of Canada? Have you seen how many balloons Bob has?'

All they could do was giggle as the room was taken over with a sea of bobbing pink. Bob set up the roof net and filled it with Joey's help.

'They won't all be saggy by tonight will they?' Holly asked.

'No, I put special gel stuff in each one before I add the helium,' said Bob.

The pièce de résistance or more notably, 'the final straw' as Paddy put it, was the archway. Once constructed it would span to the full height of the roof from the floor and back down again.

'Why would you want that?' Holly asked. 'It's such a waste of money.'

'And it's hideous,' Pippa laughed.

'Hey, I'm not complaining,' Bob said cheerfully.

'Missy isn't exactly known for holding back with anything,' said Pippa dropping her voice so only Skye and Holly could hear her. She didn't want to openly dis Missy in front of Bob. 'Her dress for tonight cost two and a half thousand euro.'

'That's obscene!' Skye said. 'How could you justify that?'

'It's a drop in the ocean for Mr Hassett,' Pippa whispered.

'Even if I had that sort of cash, I wouldn't buy a dress for that price,' Holly said. Her expression changed from a scowl to a smile as she looked toward the door.

'Hello Danny,' she said walking over to welcome him. Pippa jerked around to stare as he greeted Holly and waved shyly across at her.

Joey watched his sister and judging by her face, he didn't think this guy stood a chance of staying in the picture for long.

Pippa

PIPPA'S HEART SANK WHEN SHE TURNED AND SAW Danny standing there. Actually, it flipped and sank. It flipped when she saw him, even though she wished it wouldn't, then it sank as she realised he was forcing her hand. She didn't want to talk things over right now, but it looked like she had no choice now. She walked over to him with one eyebrow raised.

'I tried calling your mobile and couldn't get you, so I thought I'd drive down. I hope you don't mind?'

'I said I'd be in touch,' Pippa said pointedly.

Danny blushed and looked uncomfortable. 'I know,' he mumbled.

'Come on,' Pippa said. 'I'll make you a coffee in the house and we can talk.'

There were silent as they strode across the yard to the house, but once inside and beyond the radar of her family, Pippa couldn't help showing her annoyance.

'You shouldn't have appeared here,' she said as she let him into the kitchen.

'Pippa, I'm sorry if I've done the wrong thing by coming here.'

'You have,' she said. 'I said I'd let you know the score. I don't appreciate your impatience.'

Danny stared at her. 'I don't want to lose you,' he said simply.

Pippa hesitated. She was so confused. Now that he was standing in front of her, all she wanted to do was rush into his arms and stay there forever. But the warning voice in her head was too strong. She'd had so many awful relationships in the past and she wasn't about to add another to the pile.

'Please give me a chance,' he said, reading her mind. 'I know I haven't exactly given the best first impression. But you make me want to straighten out my life. For the first time, I've woken up and realised what a stupidly dangerous game I've been playing. I could've ended up behind bars. I've been an arrogant idiot.' He dropped his arms heavily by his sides and exhaled loudly.

'Now that I say it all out loud, it actually sounds farcical. Why on earth should you consider a future with me? You're not from the same tainted mess of a life as I am. I shouldn't have come. I'm sorry for bothering you.'

'Wait,' she said quietly. 'I'm certainly not perfect, Danny. So don't think I'm princess Fiona and you're Shrek. I've made a total mess of my life, several times over in fact.'

She looked at him, weighing up the pros and cons, trying to decide what was best, for both of them.

'All right, cards on the table time. I don't want to like you Danny, but I do. You're a bad boy. But I'm not a teenager any longer. I need to get my life together. I was doing quite well until I started hanging around with Missy.' She shook her head. 'The truth of the matter is that I've been a bit of a disaster and I've made stupid mistakes. I'm not a hotshot business woman with everything worked out. I'm a girl who has behaved like a spoilt child most of the time, but I'm lucky enough to have a family that loves me and continuously forgives me. But they don't need me causing any more hassle . . .'

'I understand,' he said.

'Wait,' Pippa said, holding up her hand. 'I need to just get this said. In my good moments, Danny, I can see a future with you.

You're brilliant in so many ways and I love hanging with you. We have lots in common and I think Dublin with you could be fantastic. But – and it's a really big but – right now you're known all over town as a drug dealer. You're part of a set that are messed up and horribly manipulative. I was stupid enough to allow Missy to take charge of me and it ended up with me being too wasted to be with my own sister when she needed me most. Lainey is so good I know she'll forgive me that, but I'll never forgive myself. I've been utterly blind, Danny, and you've been part of that blindness. Right now, I'm thankful for my health and for my job and for my family and I'm not going to get mixed up in anything again that threatens those things. I know I'm a bit old to be saying it, but I have to grow up, Danny. There's things I want to do and achieve and it won't happen if I'm snorting powder off the back of a toilet. I want change. I need change now. And if I have to drop you as part of that change, well, it'll break my heart, but I'll do it.'

Pippa stopped and took a deep breath. She realised she was shaking. She wasn't used to honesty, and she certainly wasn't used to laying her heart on the line for someone she barely knew and wasn't sure about. Nothing about this was normal, but at the same time, every word she spoke felt right. It felt true.

Danny stared at her. His silence was unnerving. She was waiting for him to tell her she wasn't worth it and that he was out of there.

'Do you know something, Pippa Craig,' he said slowly. 'You are amazing.'

Pippa stared back, wide-eyed. That was the last thing she'd expected him to say.

'I love this Pippa even more,' he said with a smile. 'Gutsy, direct and flat out honest. No bullshit. You are exactly what I need because I want changes in my life too. Since meeting you,

I've begun to see myself through other people's eyes, and I hate what I see. I know it sounds corny, but I want to be worthy of you. I want to be the perfect man for you and I know damn well that doesn't include drugs – either taking or dealing. It's over, Pippa.'

'Really?' she said, hardly able to breathe. 'You're not messing me around?'

He looked her directly in the eye. 'No, Pippa. That is the honest truth. The package we gave Missy was my last. I haven't bought any more and I've told my man that I won't be. I'm out, simple as that. You have my word, Pippa, that I'm going to change. My job pays more than enough to keep me afloat and there are a couple of promotions on the horizon that I could apply for. That's the right way to go. I stupidly thought I'd found a quick way to make it to the top by selling drugs.'

Danny reached over and stroked her face. 'I think we've had a fairly eventful start, but how about we try and turn over a new leaf together? There are no secrets between us now. That's a good thing, right?'

'I don't know if I'm able to take anything on board right now,' Pippa admitted. 'Lainey still doesn't know what she's facing and . . .'

'No pressure,' he said. 'We'll take it slowly and be patient with each other.'

'I can't afford to live the party girl lifestyle all the time.'

'I've had enough of that to last me quite a few years. So don't feel you'll be keeping me away from anything,' he pointed out. 'Maybe we can spend our weekends down here, helping out. Make money from other people's partying, in a whole new and legitimate way.'

Pippa smiled at him, feeling tears welling up in her eyes. She stepped forward and hugged him. As she rested her head against his chest, she closed her eyes and tried to steady her racing pulse. She'd never felt this way with any other guy.

Nobody had *ever* made her feel the way Danny did.

They kissed, and it was perfect.

Jodi

JODI HAD BEEN UP SINCE DAWN. THE SCRIPT SHE
was learning was compelling. She'd known since the first read-
through that this movie would be the next blockbuster.

She had less than two months to learn the remainder of her
lines before she began shooting. Normally, she'd be fretting about
how she'd keep her six-year-old son, Saul, at school until the
summer holidays. But her fiancé was a teacher at his school and
would mind him. Once school finished for the summer, they'd
follow her to LA. Saul was thrilled about being Harry's
tour-guide.

Jodi had never been happier. Her marriage to Darius Drew
actor and heartthrob extraordinaire, had ended amicably two years
ago. He was still an amazing father to Saul and they would always
be friends. Their marriage had been very public, very contrived
and very convenient. But both had reached a stage where they
needed to go separate ways.

Jodi first met Harry Matthews when he was teaching Saul in
junior infants. She'd been drawn to his incredible ability to make
his pupils happy. But as the school year had progressed, she'd
eventually responded to the sparking interest that he'd shown in
her. Back then, she'd assumed he was only interested in Jodi
Ludlum the movie star. As the months rolled by, she realised he
was actually interested in the real Jodi. The one who pitched up
at school dressed in sheepskin boots and trackie bottoms. The

one who wore no make-up and pulled her hair into a knot using an abandoned piece of twine. The one who was more interested in collecting conkers with her son than reading glossy magazines . . . it was a very new feeling.

Jodi treasured her new life in Ireland. She'd grown up in Dublin, the daughter of an addict on an estate that even the police wouldn't drive through. She'd worked tirelessly to better herself and had hit the jackpot as an actress. Adored the world over, she had carefully kept her deprived background and her arranged marriage to Darius under wraps.

One of the only people who knew the whole truth was Harry.

'None of that matters,' he'd said when she told him about her colourful and painful past. 'All I care about is the person you are today. The fact you've overcome so much and fought so hard to get where you are makes me love you even more.'

'You love me?' she'd said in astonishment.

'The entire world loves you, Jodi,' he grinned. 'But I love the *real* you.'

She'd learned from a young age to be on her guard. She knew that most of the people she met only wanted to use her for their own gain. Harry was different. He had no agenda. All he wanted was to be with her and Saul.

When he proposed last month after they'd been dating for a year and a half, he'd been awkwardly shy all of a sudden. The pretty diamond ring looked like a speck in comparison to the one Darius had given her eight years before.

'I know it's not much of a rock. You're used to bigger and better. But I'm hoping you'll find it in your heart to realise that there's more sentiment packed into this proposal than cash.'

She'd instantly begun to cry.

'Will you marry me, Jodi?'

The joyful tears and the emphatic nodding as she allowed him to slip the ring on her finger said it all. Realising she hadn't verbalised an answer, she kissed him and whispered *yes*, over and over again.

They both decided not to tell the press about the engagement. Jodi didn't want it to be splashed across every newspaper and magazine from here to kingdom come.

'It's our news and nobody else's,' she said emphatically.

'That's cool by me,' Harry said. 'I don't think your male fans are going to like me for taking you off the market and the ladies will think I'm a poor second to the delectable Darius.'

'Sod the lot of them,' Jodi said feistily. 'We'll keep it to ourselves for the moment. So we can savour this special time.'

Jodi was careful not to wear the ring during press calls and they'd decided to wait until nearer the wedding before telling Saul. Neither of them wanted their relationship to become a circus. Her village home would certainly be surrounded by paparazzi if she made the announcement.

Jodi knew Saul would be thrilled. Harry stayed for 'sleepovers', as Saul called them. And he loved when Harry played *Star Wars* Lego with him.

'We don't have to do a big wedding unless you'd particularly like it,' Jodi said.

'I couldn't think of anything worse,' Harry said. 'It'd turn into one of those crazy affairs with flashing cameras and crowds lining the streets.'

After the shopping trip the couple had chatted about Pippa and her home.

'I know of Huntersbrook,' Harry said. 'The Wicklow hunt used to start from there. It's meant to be magnificent. It'd be really private too.'

'I warmed to Pippa instantly too. She seems like a really cool girl, doesn't she?'

'It's definitely worth a look,' Harry agreed. 'It's only around the corner too. Couldn't be handier!'

Saul was going to a birthday party today, so it gave Jodi and Harry the perfect opportunity to sneak over and have a quick look at the venue. While she wanted to wear a pretty wedding dress and do a lot of traditional things, Jodi was certain she didn't want a massive celebrity blow-out. They needed a low-key, laidback venue that would allow them to do it their way.

Not wanting to create a bad impression, she changed out of her jeans and put on some of the lovely clothes she'd purchased the day she met Pippa. Putting on a light covering of make-up and brushing her hair, Jodi made a cup of herbal tea as she waited for Harry to arrive. She rummaged around for the car keys, not sure of where she'd thrown them. Harry was constantly teasing her about how disorganised she was.

'This place is like a pit,' he'd laughed. 'I thought someone like you would have a perfect house with everything perfectly organised.'

'I lived out of a suitcase in hotel rooms for years,' she reasoned. 'I can't boil an egg and I hang my clothes on the floor or a bedroom chair at best. Underneath all the Hollywood glamour I'm still a messy pup!'

Jodi wanted Saul to have as normal a childhood as possible. She'd seen the effects on her colleagues' children when they'd grown up with private tutors on film sets and no normal routine. She'd always longed to take him back to her birth-place and Wicklow, with its green rolling hills and pretty stone-clad villages, had appealed most. It was a quick drive from Dublin city and the airport, yet far enough away to afford her anonymity.

With Saul safely delivered to his friend's birthday party, she waited for Harry to arrive. In typical teacher fashion he pitched up exactly on the hour. She opened the door.

'I love the way you're so precise.'

'Someone needs to be in this relationship,' he grinned.

'Ready to rock'n'roll?' she asked as she kissed him.

'You look nice,' he said, 'is that dress new?'

'It's a skirt,' she said with a grin. 'You crack me up! Darius would know at ten paces what label I was wearing, let alone calling it the wrong thing!'

'Well sorry for not channelling my inner *haute couture* instincts.'

As she fired up her beloved red mini, Jodi turned the heating up.

❄

They turned into the wide entrance gates that announced the driveway leading to Huntersbrook. On the right-hand side stood a pretty gate lodge.

'The lodge isn't that different from your place,' Harry said. 'Makes it feel nicely familiar.'

On either side of the tree-lined avenue the view stretched away for miles, acres of grass that looked stiff in the November coldness. It was the last day of November and the chill promise of December was in the air.

'This is magnificent,' Jodi said with excitement. 'Imagine growing up here and looking out at this every day.'

'It really is spectacular,' Harry agreed.

The drive curved around, until a final bend brought the house into view. The pale stone of the grand house was off-set beautifully by the murky green of the fields. The light was slanting and it gave the windows a strange glow. As Jodi brought the car to a halt, she smiled at Harry.

'See what I mean?'

'Absolutely,' he said, slowly nodding his head.

❄

Pippa had spotted Jodi's car the second she drove through the gate. Matt had already left with Ely and was headed for the hospital to see Lainey, but everyone else was gathered about, drawn by the magnetism of Jodi Ludlum.

It had been a morning of hard slog, but the marquee was ready for inspection.

'I'm a little worried about the volume of balloons,' Holly said. 'They're terribly gaudy.'

'I think they're horrendous,' Paddy agreed. 'But we'll risk bursting them if we put them outside. I don't know about you, but I'm not too eager to spend a pile of money replacing them if something goes wrong.'

So the cough medicine pink and silver bunches remained. Luckily, the soothing cream tones of the tulle and matching seat covers made it all seem marginally less brash. Paddy had insisted on holding off on installing the pink spot lights until after Jodi's visit.

'Do you think you lot should make yourself scarce for a while?' Pippa asked nervously.

'Why don't we all say hello and then scarper,' Joey suggested. 'That way she can get the meet-and-greet stuff out of the way and hopefully relax and enjoy her visit.'

Pippa opened the door with shaking hands and stepped out with a wide smile.

'Hello, Jodi,' she said, hoping she didn't sound as terrified as she felt.

'Hi, Pippa,' she said, tucking her shades onto her head. 'You remember Harry?'

'Of course, hello, Harry, you're both really welcome to Huntersbrook.'

Pippa shook his hand as Jodi stepped forward to kiss her on the cheek.

'We can't get over this place,' Jodie said, smiling. 'It's stunning.'

'Thanks,' Pippa beamed. 'We love it, but seeing as we're the third generation to reside here, I guess we're a tad biased! We don't want to bombard you, but my family are all here getting things ready for Missy's party tonight. May I introduce you?'

'Sure,' Jodi said. 'I'd love to meet them.'

Pippa led them into the hallway, where Joey, Skye, Holly, Paddy and Sadie stood. She introduced them one by one and Jodi and Harry chatted easily, asking lots of questions about the house and their plans for it.

Pippa explained that the house was now available for rent, along with the bedrooms, and that the marquee would host up to two hundred seated guests.

'We've had these brochures made. They're hot off the press,' Joey grinned handing them one each.

'Depending on what type of event you're thinking of, we can adapt fairly easily to larger or smaller numbers,' Holly said.

Jodi tucked the brochure into her bag, making it clear she was more interested in seeing it all for herself.

The family excused themselves, saying they'd see her as she conducted her tour.

'Lovely to meet you all,' she said as Harry thanked them too.

Pippa started with the ground floor, showing them the kitchen, reception rooms and comfortable living room. New sofas had replaced the well-loved ones. While the space had maintained the cosy and welcoming atmosphere, it was now far more plush than shabby.

'This is gorgeous,' Jodi said with a gasp. 'Look at the intricate plasterwork on the ceiling. It's beautiful.'

Pippa forgot to feel nervous as Jodi and Harry made all the right noises in each room. They were equally as impressed by the bedrooms, pronouncing them 'divine'. Pippa made a mental note to tell Lainey later that Jodi Ludlum admired her taste!

'That bed makes me want to climb in,' Harry said. 'I'm a teacher and this time on a Saturday, I'm usually lazing in my bed,' he joked.

Spurred on by the positive feedback, Pippa took them out the kitchen door to view the marquee. The others were busy setting up the sound system they'd purchased.

'As I may have mentioned to you both, Missy Hassett, the girl who served you at the store,' Pippa said. 'She's having her birthday party tonight,' she explained.

'And she's going the whole hog with the balloons I see,' Jodi smiled.

'Eh yes,' Pippa hesitated.

'I think they're appalling,' Holly said as she walked by with a large vase.

'Mum!' Pippa said.

'Well I don't want Jodi thinking we go in for this kind of tat.'

Jodi burst out laughing.

'I can't say I'd want this many balloons,' Jodi admitted. 'But hey, that's just me. Maybe Harry likes the idea of the place looking like a fairground?'

'Not likely,' he said. 'Although it's almost Roald Dahl-esque. All you're missing are the Oompa-loompas!'

'Don't!' Pippa joked. 'If Missy heard that she may actually want them.'

Pippa couldn't help noticing Harry looked decidedly uncomfortable all of a sudden.

'Were you thinking we'd need a space this big?' he turned to Jodi.

There was a brief pause before she asked Pippa if they could go back toward the main house. Feeling really disappointed and sensing the couple weren't loving the set-up, she hoped her face didn't betray her emotions.

'Would you like to come to the living room and we can chat?' Pippa asked as they made their way through the kitchen. The couple nodded and they all sat down.

'Can I get tea or coffee?' Sadie asked popping her head in. 'I make a fine ham sandwich if I can tempt anyone?'

'Have you herbal tea by any chance?' Jodi asked.

'I have chamomile.'

'Perfect! Thank you.'

'I'd love coffee, if it's not too much trouble,' Harry said.

Pippa thanked her and explained to them that Sadie had been with them since before she was born. By the time Sadie arrived back with a tray of delicate sandwiches and some rich fudgy chocolate cake, Jodi and Harry were firing questions at Pippa.

They wanted to know the history of Huntersbrook and how long it had been since they'd lived here as a family. Pippa explained the situation and how they'd all united to keep Huntersbrook in the Craig name.

'I love the place. The sense of family and everything this place represents has stolen my heart,' Jodi said.

'Me too, except I want to live here all the time,' Harry admitted as he helped himself to a sandwich.

'Good man, I like a fella who eats his food,' Sadie said as she bustled from the room. 'You can come back anytime. I can't bear people who push food around the plate as if it's going to poison them.'

'Thanks, Sadie,' Pippa said with a grin. She added in a whisper. 'As long as you do what she says, Sadie's a pussy-cat!' She paused for a moment. 'Why don't I let you guys have a chat? I've to make a quick phone call and I'll be back to you shortly. Obviously you don't need to make any decisions today,' she stressed.

'Thanks, Pippa, that'd be super,' Harry said with a smile.

As she closed the door and walked to the kitchen, Pippa crossed her fingers and hoped Jodi and Harry liked the place enough to make a booking. Tiptoeing out to the marquee, she was instantly surrounded by her family.

'Well?' Holly asked. 'What's the story?'

'I've left them to have a private chat. They're having a sandwich and a bit of cake. I think they like it. Well, Harry wants to live here.'

'And Jodi?' Paddy asked.

'Yeah, I think she loves it all too. She loves the sense of family here. But I can't be sure they're going to take it for their event.'

Pippa left them for another few minutes and then went back into the room, not wanting them to feel abandoned either.

'We have a request,' Jodi said, looking excited. 'But we're not sure whether or not you and your family will be willing to accommodate us.'

'OK, hit me,' Pippa said, not sure what she was bracing herself for.

'Pippa, what I'm about to tell you is confidential,' Jodi said. 'My instincts are that I can trust you . . .'

'Oh you can,' Pippa assured her.

'Well, Harry and I are engaged.'

'Oh my goodness, that's brilliant,' Pippa's heart was thumping so loudly she feared Jodi would hear it.

'We want a really small and intimate wedding. No press, no fuss, just us.'

'Of course,' Pippa said, feeling slightly deflated. Bang went her image of a celeb-festooned champagne-athon!

'But here's the crunch. With Harry's job and my filming

schedule, the only time that would work for both of us in the near future is Christmas. What we're wondering is, whether we could have a Christmas wedding at Huntersbrook?'

Pippa meant to contain her excitement. But instead, she made a high-pitched squealing noise and leapt to her feet and clumsily clutched Jodi, then Harry to her. Poor Harry nearly choked on his sandwich in surprise.

'That sounds amazing,' she said. 'My mum is going to think she's died and gone to heaven. Christmas is her favourite time of the year and she will make this place look so magical!'

'Really?' Jodi said. 'Well my memories of Christmas as a child aren't great. That was another reason we'd like to put a new mark on that time of year.'

'You've come to the right place, let me assure you,' Pippa said, taking a deep breath and attempting to calm down.

'Obviously since Saul came along, Jodi has changed her mind about Christmas,' Harry was quick to point out. 'But this will make it *our* special time from now on. Draw a line under the past, you know?'

'That's such a lovely idea,' Pippa said, smiling at Harry. 'Oh my God, can I tell my family?'

'Well, I'd prefer if you'd ask them!' Jodi giggled. 'They might hate the thought of us barging in with our guests.'

'Roughly how many are you thinking of asking?' said Pippa.

'Well, I've only one brother, who lives in Australia with his wife and son. I want them to come home. Outside of that I have a maximum of ten people.' Jodi looked sheepish for a moment. 'I know more than ten people obviously, but I mean it when I say I want this to be intimate.'

'What about you, Harry?'

'I have one brother who's single and my folks live in the UK. Outside of that, I have two close friends I'd like to ask. But I'm with Jodi on the intimate approach. We're adamant we want this to be a cosy family occasion.'

Pippa chatted to them for a few moments longer as she sent a group text to her parents, Joey and Skye asking them to come over to the living room.

They appeared one by one and sat down.

'So, Jodi and Harry would like to have a Christmas wedding here at Huntersbrook,' Pippa announced.

Holly couldn't speak for excitement.

'You better fetch the smelling salts, Pippa,' Joey said with a snigger.

'Be quiet you,' Holly said, shushing him. 'Oh Jodi, I will turn this place into a winter wonderland for you! Minus the massive bunches of balloons,' she quickly assured her. 'I love making wreaths and my Christmas tree would win an award, if there was such a thing.'

Pippa went on to explain that the event was not for public knowledge.

'What we would happily do is have a professional photographer here on the day and, with your consent, release some pictures early in the New Year?' Jodi said.

'That would be amazing,' Joey said. 'If you were willing to show the world you got married here, it would obviously be such a boost for us.'

The details were ironed out very swiftly. Jodi confessed she wasn't crazy about the idea of using the marquee. She wanted to use the house alone.

'What about having the wedding on the twenty-third of December? That way we could be out of the Craigs' hair by Christmas Day,' Harry suggested.

'Perfect,' said Jodi. 'What do you all think?'

'Or, alternatively,' Holly said, 'you could have the wedding and stay with us and join our family for the most delicious dinner you'll find in Wicklow!'

Jodi teared up as she stared at Holly.

'Would you honestly invite us to share Christmas dinner with you guys?'

'No offence,' Pippa said dryly, 'but Mum would invite Jack the Ripper to Christmas dinner. The more the merrier as far as she's concerned. She's not happy unless there are far too many bodies shoe-horned around the table.'

'You're so kind to offer,' Jodi said. 'But we want to head away on honeymoon as soon as the wedding is over. But if the offer is still open next year, we'll be here.'

'Once you're invited once, you can take it you're invited going forward,' Holly said with a smile.

'I think this is serendipity,' Jodi said, smiling around at them. 'I don't know why, but that moment when I first met Pippa, it felt like meeting an old friend.'

Pippa's mouth fell open and before she could stop herself she said, 'My God, and I was in such a bad place then. I can't believe you saw through that to me.' Realising what she'd said, she stopped short, lost for words.

Holly was staring at her with concern, as was Joey.

'What do you mean –' Joey started.

'I need to talk to you about the floral decorations,' Jodi interrupted quickly. She talked on at speed for the next two minutes until she had drawn all attention in the room to herself. By the time she'd finished, she'd somehow bamboozled Pippa's family into forgetting about what she'd said. Pippa sat there and listened, but she still didn't know how Jodi managed it. But she was very grateful that she had because she couldn't have gotten away without giving some sort of explanation.

As they waved Jodi and Harry off at the front door, Pippa slipped outside and gave Jodi's hand a quick squeeze.

'Thanks,' she whispered.

'Any time,' Jodi whispered back. 'But you've intrigued me even more. You'll never get rid of me now!'

The two smiled at each other, then Jodi Ludlum stepped into her red Mini and was gone.

Lainey

LAINEY WAS THRILLED WHEN MATT AND ELY CAME
to visit. She was feeling a lot less groggy and nauseous. Two other
women had joined her in the ward, which was actually a relief.
The evenings had been so quiet and lonely, she was happy enough
to have people to chat to. One of the women was also awaiting
results on a biopsy, so it felt like someone else was in her sinking
boat with her, at least.

Chef Sally, as the family had taken to calling her, had phoned
Lainey earlier to say she was on the way to Huntersbrook and
hoped to reach there by four o'clock. The turkey and ham
were cooked and ready to be stored in the big free-standing
fridge Holly kept in one of the sheds. Some of the salads such
as the potato and coleslaw ones had been made and the ingredients for the last-minute ones would be left in the kitchen,
ready to be made up later on. Lainey thanked her and said to be
certain to call anytime, should she need anything.

When Matt arrived, Lainey couldn't hold back her tears at
the sight of Ely. He was so beautiful, it made her heart hurt. She
missed him even more during visits – it intensified the dreadful
ache she had inside because she was missing out on so much.
Lainey had experienced every emotion known to woman since
this whole sorry mess had begun.

She fussed over Ely, asking Matt to put him on the bed so
she could cuddle and kiss him. She whispered to him how much

she loved him and he grinned his lopsided grin at her. It was so easy with a baby – you just poured your heart and love out onto their heads, anointed them with it. So different from the minefields of adult relationships and affection.

Ely began to get restless, so Matt lifted him up and emptied some toys from his bag to keep him entertained. It was then it struck Lainey that Matt was unusually quiet. His pale faced looked pinched with worry and fatigue.

'How are you coping?' Lainey asked as he propped Ely on the end of the bed.

'Fine,' he said, rather too swiftly, 'but it's so strange at home without you.'

'It won't be for much longer,' Lainey said lightly. 'Once Dr Cumisky gives me the green light, I'll be out of here and back on my feet in no time.'

Neither of them wanted to verbalise what was going on in their heads. What if Lainey was really ill? What if she was headed for a long road of debilitating illness and ongoing treatment?

Pippa's call made for the perfect distraction. Lainey's phone lit up, and Matt smiled at her to take it. Not wanting to take over the ward, Lainey turned on the speakerphone but kept the volume down low and Matt bent his head against hers so they could both hear. Pippa filled them in on all the details of the day so far, and how the wedding was to be kept under wraps.

'I'll liaise with Jodi over the next couple of weeks so we can work out the details. But it looks like we're about to bear witness to the best advertising Wicklow has ever had, let alone Huntersbrook!'

'Aw, Pip, that's amazing,' Lainey said. 'Well done you! I'm so proud of you.'

'We just need you back here bossing us about and putting manners on us,' Pippa said. 'So hurry up and come home to us, you hear.'

'I hear,' Lainey said, holding back tears. 'Soon, I promise.'

'Love you,' Pippa said. 'Bye.'

They hung up, and she and Matt hugged each other in celebration.

'I feel really guilty,' Lainey said. 'I was getting totally browned off with Pippa lately. I actually thought she was slipping back into her old ways. She said she was working, but quite honestly I'd thought she was pulling a fast one.'

'Ah I don't blame you for thinking that,' Matt said mildly. 'Pippa can be a bit of a messer and she's never been particularly fond of hard labour! But she's certainly come up trumps with this one.'

Lainey lay back against the pillows. 'She was lovely to me when she came in here, though.'

'That's good to hear,' Matt said.

'I asked her to help out with Ely if I . . .'

'Now, there's none of that talk,' Matt said firmly. They sat in silence, watching Ely arranging his bricks with dogged determination.

'Can you imagine what Mum is going to be like?' Lainey said suddenly. 'Christmas *and* a wedding *and* a movie star! She's going to be buzzed!'

Visiting time ended and Ely was becoming fractious, so Matt decided to pack up the bag.

'Ely! It looks like a bomb went off in here,' he said grinning. 'Let's go and find Grandma and the grandpas.'

As soon as Ely realised he was being taken away from Lainey, he began to cry, holding his arms out to her. Not able to hold him, she asked Matt to tuck him in beside her for a moment. She cuddled him and stroked his head tenderly.

'Mummy will see you soon,' she crooned. 'You be a good boy, OK?'

Too young to understand anything other than the fact he was being taken away from his mummy, Ely sobbed and cried 'mama' repeatedly.

'Best go,' Matt said looking flushed and hassled. 'Sorry folks,' he said waving to the other patients.

Lainey smiled and tried not to cry along with her son. Not wanting to slip into depression mode, she lay back against the pillows once more, closed her eyes and tried to imagine what Jodi Ludlum was really like. She'd seen her in lots of movies over the years. Her trademark emerald green eyes and glossy black hair looked stunning on screen, but she was very interested in seeing her in the flesh.

Knowing this would be Jodi's second marriage, she wondered if she would go for a bridal look. According to Pippa she'd been very *normal* when they'd met at the department store. Apparently she'd chatted away to Pippa as if she were a long lost friend. But Lainey couldn't imagine how such a famous superstar could be anything but a diva.

Lainey was suddenly overcome with curiosity about her beau too. Who was this man she'd chosen instead of Darius Drew? Dialling Pippa's number, she willed her to pick up. When the phone went to voice mail, Lainey felt ridiculously disappointed and left out. Trying Huntersbrook, she prayed someone would answer. When it was Holly, Lainey briefly considered hanging up. She couldn't bring herself to do it.

'Hi Mum, it's me.'

'Lainey! How are you feeling, love? I was going to call you a bit later. I wasn't sure how long Matt would stay. I didn't want to interrupt your precious time together.'

'Yeah, he just left. Ely was bored and starting to make a noise so Matt took him away.'

'So you heard Jodi was here?' Holly asked.

'Yeah, Pip rang, but she didn't give much detail.'

'You should've seen her young man,' Holly said.

'I'm dying to know about him,' Lainey said, dropping her frosty tone.

'He's so . . . so normal,' Holly said. 'He's a school teacher and he was wearing chinos and one of those Abercrombie sweat shirts Joey likes.'

'What's the beef with him? What makes him different from any other bloke? In other words, how is he engaged to Jodi Ludlum?'

Holly launched into a full explanation of why she figured Jodi was with him.

'So you reckon he's the polar opposite of what she deals with in work?'

'Yes, I do. I think she adores her job but craves normality and that her biggest longing is the one thing money can't buy – love.'

'You could be right, Mum,' Lainey mused. 'So did you *like* her?'

'Instantly,' Holly admitted. 'She's a dote. Furthermore she loved our home and is so thrilled about getting married here.'

Lainey and Holly chatted for quite a while, going over the details for the party the following night, before Paddy's voice in the background interrupted them.

'I'd better let you go,' Lainey said, not wanting to end her connection to Huntersbrook. 'It was great to talk to you, Mum. Thanks for filling me in. I feel so useless lying in here when I should be there, helping.'

'We miss you terribly, Lainey. I know you're being incredibly brave and putting other people first and I admire you so much for that. I don't think I could. Your husband and son are very lucky to have you, the way you put them first all the time.'

Lainey was speechless. She couldn't believe her ears. Her mother was finally saying things in a soft voice with no irritation or reprisal.

'Wow, thanks, Mum, I don't really know what to say.'

'Darling, I know you don't want me there as you deal with all this, but I feel terribly for you and I . . . well, I do love you, Lainey.'

Silent tears began to course down Lainey's cheeks and she struggled to keep her voice even.

'Thank you so much for saying that,' she whispered. She cleared her throat. 'Good luck with all the last minute plans for tomorrow night. I'm so sorry to be missing the inaugural event.'

'I know you are. But tell you what – I'll text you during the night. Keep you posted on the happenings.'

'Thanks, Mum, I'd like that.'

When the nurse came to check on Lainey a few moments later, she understandably thought she was in pain or having a blue moment.

'Don't cry, love,' she said. 'It's perfectly normal to feel down post-surgery.'

'I'm actually really happy,' Lainey sniffed. 'I just had the best chat I've ever had with my mum. Normally we bite each other's heads off or spend our time being fractious. Maybe it's because we're apart, but I actually needed someone to talk to, and I can't imagine anyone who could've done a better job.'

'That's good, dear. Often, difficult circumstances like you're experiencing have a positive effect. Hospitals tend to put things in perspective for everyone.'

Lainey took her painkiller and allowed her mind to drift. Until her test results came back, she had no idea what lay ahead. But one thing was for certain. She was going to make a concerted effort to continue with this newfound relationship with Holly.

Skye

SKYE DIDN'T WANT TO COMPLAIN, ESPECIALLY IN light of Lainey's situation, but she was still feeling dreadful.

She desperately wanted to help out as much as she could but she was struggling.

'Poor you,' Holly sighed as she saw Skye stooping over. 'You're really suffering, aren't you? Did you go to the doctor at all?'

'I haven't had time. But I will,' Skye said as she forced a smile and tried to make out she was fine.

'I was on to Lainey a while ago,' Holly said. 'I think she's feeling very left out. Why don't you spin down and see her for an hour. I reckon everything is under control here. It'd be great to include her.'

Finding Joey and Matt up a ladder stringing white fairy lights around the roof of the marquee along with Missy's dreaded pink bulbs, she pitched Holly's suggestion.

'Good idea, love,' Joey said. 'We were only saying it was a shame for poor Lainey to be left out of the loop. You're still feeling crook, we all understand. You head on over to the hospital. Sadie had a flask of soup for Lainey, could you deliver that while you're at it?'

'I'll take a quick video on my phone to show her the look of the place too,' she said. She scanned around the marquee while chatting like a news reader. Pippa flew in the door and threw her arms up to block her eyes.

'Ugh those lights are hideous. It's like descending inside a Turkish delight in here.'

'Watch it. I'll swing over on these fairy lights and kick you,' Joey retorted. 'My arms are starting to ache. So less of the snide remarks thanks, Pippa.'

'Woo!' Pippa chimed. 'Who's being touchy up there!' Skye laughed behind the camera, delighted with the snap shot of insanity for Lainey.

'It's a wrap! See you guys in a while,' she said, moving off to the car.

Skye offered to take Ely along but he was having a snooze and they all felt he'd spent enough time at the hospital for one day.

'He's grand here with us,' Sadie said handing over the soup. 'She was fretting about who will babysit this evening, so please tell her I'll stay over at the farmhouse and mind Master Ely.'

'Oh brilliant plan,' Skye said. 'I'll be sure to let her know. That'll put her mind at ease.'

As Skye walked into the hospital ward a short time later she was genuinely shocked by how bad Lainey looked. Jules was parked beside the bed in a hard plastic chair.

'Hi Skye, how are you?' she asked standing to kiss her.

'Hi Jules. You're risking being admitted at this rate. Have you even been home? The others said you were here yesterday and the day before.'

'I've taken some time off work. I can't concentrate so it's better if I'm here. Lainz and I are sorting the problems of the world between us, aren't we, babes?'

Lainey nodded and smiled gratefully at her friend.

'Hi,' Skye said bending to kiss her cheek. 'How are you?'

'Judging from the look on your face, I'm not as good as I thought!' Lainey smiled.

'Sorry, I didn't expect you to look so washed out, which is completely ridiculous considering what you've been through.'

They chatted about the past few days and avoided the subject of what could possibly unfold.

'I'm disgusted with myself,' Lainey said as she grabbed a tissue from her bedside locker.

Skye took her hand gently and stroked it. 'Why?'

'I feel as if I've ruined Matt and Ely's life,' Lainey said diverting her eyes and taking a large gulping breath. 'I was terribly arrogant. I assumed we'd have one and possibly two more children,' she forced a smile. 'I guess we never know what's around the corner, right?'

Skye shook her head.

'We never know our destiny, that's for sure,' Jules agreed.

'This doesn't only affect me,' she said. 'What if he leaves me, Skye?'

'He's not going to do that,' she said softly. 'We're all going to be here for you.'

Lainey gritted her teeth and closed her eyes for a moment.

'Skye and Jules, can I ask you to consider something?'

They nodded.

'If this turns out to be cancer . . . If I don't make it . . . Would you promise to do the motherly things with Ely? I know Matt and Jacob will do all the man stuff. But he'll still need to be softened around the edges. Would you show him how to bake scones? Would you teach him that brown corduroys are only for old men? Would you let him know it's not cool to make girls cry?'

The girls nodded.

'Of course we will,' Jules said looking to Skye.

'Totally,' Skye added.

'I've asked Pippa to do the same and in fairness to her, she was brilliant. But Pippa is . . . Pippa. I think I've more hope of having you two around in Wicklow than my sister . . .'

'We'll all be there no matter what,' Skye assured her.

'I don't want to die, Skye. I don't feel ready. But I guess all cancer patients think that, don't they? But I mightn't have a choice. You know? I mightn't be able to fight.'

'But you're gonna try,' Jules said forcefully. 'And we're all going to help you. It's not always a death sentence nowadays. Medicine and treatments are advancing all the time. So many women battle and win. You could be one of those.'

'Pippa gets bored easily,' Lainey continued looking dazed. 'She'll probably only connect with Ely when he starts drinking. Don't let her buy him cigarettes or drugs, sure you won't?'

'I doubt if Pippa's into drugs,' Skye said reasonably. 'And I've never seen her smoking . . .'

'No. You're quite right. I'm totally wronging her. Sorry, Skye, you must think I'm a cow. I'm so panicked, that's all.'

'I understand. It's hard to be rational at times like these. But try to keep in the forefront of your mind that we're all here for you, OK?'

They group hugged and Skye sat back on the chair beside the bed.

'Hey, want to see a funny snippet of what's going on over at the marquee?'

Lainey and Jules leaned in and watched Pippa and Joey.

Giggling Lainey shook her head.

'My family are totally bats really. God, I don't know how you two are always so eager to hang out with us. And you're even willing to become one of us!' she said to Skye.

'Ah now listen. If there's a crazy family competition – mine wins hands down,' Skye said.

'Well I can't enter the family competition so can we make it a mad mother one instead?' Jules suggested.

'OK,' Skye giggled. 'You go first, Lainey.'

'Well I nominate my mother because she gets more excited than any toddler at Christmas time.'

'Yeah, not bad,' said Jules, looking unconvinced.

'Although, now we're on the subject. She's been quite amazing over the past few days. I was telling Jules earlier, Skye. Mum and I had the best conversation of our lives yesterday. It was relaxed and fun and I was totally on a high afterwards.'

'That's wonderful,' Skye said happily. 'So, I'm sorry. Holly is out of the running. We all love her and she's not a crazy lady . . .' They all laughed. 'But *my* mother on the other hand has crazy lady written all over her. She's stoned all the time, calls herself Heaven and has been known to knit sleeveless cardigans for hamsters.'

The girls pealed with laughter.

'Oh and I could be dead for ten years and she wouldn't notice or care.'

Before the mood could become maudlin again, Jules stepped in.

'Sorry, girls. But I am the hands-down winner. My mother blames my existence for her sad screwed up life. She told me last night that there is a man in the south of Ireland who performs rituals on people to "drive away the gay". She handed me a bill for the four pieces of bread I've eaten at home this week and concluded by saying she always wanted a son.'

Although the words were utterly shocking, Jules stood and bowed dramatically. Skye looked at Lainey and in spite of the awfulness, they burst out laughing.

'Oh Jesus, Jules,' Lainey said. 'I'm sorry for laughing, but your mother is a witch. You win. Gold medal. Large trophy. It's all yours.'

'Thank you!' she said bowing more and pretending to wave to the imaginary adoring crowd.

'I take it all back,' Skye said. 'My mother is amazing. I'm never complaining about her again.'

Skye remembered to tell Lainey that Sadie would stay at the farmhouse with Ely.

'She's so good,' Lainey said. 'Ely is lucky to have her influence. But she's getting old. He'll need the next generation of women to step up . . .'

Skye wanted to grab Lainey's shoulders and shake her and yell in her face that she wasn't going to die. That she wasn't allowed to die. That they all needed her and she was to stop acting as if she were on a countdown to the next life.

'What if this *is* terminal?'

'We're all terminal,' Skye said dryly. 'But you can't give up, Lainey. You've got to fight and fight hard.'

The ensuing silence let her know she'd said the wrong thing, Skye could feel the walls closing in. Her mouth began to fill with saliva as she had an overwhelming urge to stand up and run out. Jules was looking at the floor and the frivolous mood was all gone.

'I'm sorry, I'd better go now,' she managed. 'I love you and I'll call you tomorrow. I'll let you know how the party went.'

She pecked Lainey on the cheek and hugged Jules before hurrying out.

As Skye bolted through the main hospital doors the cold damp air was almost medicinal in comparison to the thick stale warmth inside. She'd begun to feel as if she were choking.

The image of Lainey in the hospital bed, looking as if she were waiting on death row caused deep heaving sobs to escape her lips. Skye found her car and drove back toward Huntersbrook as fast as she could manage. Knowing this was most certainly not a good time to have an accident, she slowed down and opened the window, hoping the country air would blow away the fug of sickness she felt was clawing at her clothes after the hospital.

Half way down the drive to Huntersbrook, she stopped the car and abandoned it. It was pitch dark out but Skye gained comfort from the smudgy evening air. Marching with her arms swinging purposefully she stopped at the side of a majestic oak tree. She slid to the ground and clunked her head against the trunk. She wasn't given to praying in public on the whole. But she had an unbending belief in God and Skye could sense the greater goodness that was in force in the world. She was certain that positivity was a palpable energy that pushed people in a better direction in life.

'If you're listening, please don't take Lainey away. Ely needs her. If she dies nothing will be the same again,' she said looking above. 'Huntersbrook will be steeped in sadness and regret. The corridors will sigh with sorrow. Mists of misery will roll off the land and this magnificent place will be drenched in tragedy for the next generation. Please don't let that happen. Don't ruin the magic.'

Skye stared at the ground and tried with all her might to will Lainey well.

Pippa

MISSY ARRIVED IN A FLURRY OF HAND GESTURES
and air-kisses. Pippa knew she needed to be on hand to disperse
any potential disasters. She had no doubt in her mind that Missy
was going to be totally off her face by two o'clock in the morning.
She'd already told Pippa that she was planning on keeping it all
above board until her parents and their friends vacated the
premises and then, 'all hell will break loose'.

It was obvious that Missy had her poor father wrapped around
her little finger. He looked at her adoringly as she spoke as if she
were the next Messiah. Pippa played hostess and introduced
Mr Hassett to her family while wishing them a pleasant evening.
As Joey took their bags to the room, he reiterated that they were
all there to help and all the Hassetts had to do was ask, should
they require anything.

'Mrs Hassett looks like a melted version of Missy, doesn't she?'
Pippa whispered to Skye as they disappeared after Joey. 'Her poor
skin has been pulled in so many directions by the surgeons, it's
hard to know whether she looks better or worse than another
woman her age.'

'Totally,' Skye agreed. 'But she only looks odd up close. From
a distance they could be the same age. I'm all for making the most
of yourself, but I can't help thinking her look is a little creepy.'

'Especially when Mr Hassett looks like both of their
grandfathers.'

'It might help matters if she weren't so horrible,' Skye said.

The guests were astonishingly prompt and extremely thirsty.

Joey and Matt looked very professional in their tuxedos as they poured champagne. Two of the hired barmen were mixing cocktails at a rate of knots in the corner of the hallway.

'I thought Joey had gone overboard with the supplies,' Skye admitted. 'I'd mollified myself by reckoning the drink would be used at some point over the next few months. But now I'm beginning to worry they're going to drink us dry.'

Holly, Pippa and Skye were less poker-faced and far less proficient than the men as they drank in the style, of which there was plenty.

Holly was wearing a dress belonging to Grandma that had been around for as long as Pippa could recall.

'You look great, Mum,' she said loyally.

'I'm hardly happening compared with Mrs Hassett.'

'Yes, but you're in genuine vintage gear and your face is your own and you're not a thundering bitch which can't be said for Mrs H!'

Pippa recognised a few of Missy's group from Fire and Rain. She did the air-kissing thing and nodded a lot as they told her how much they were loving the whole *Downton Abbey* vibe.

'It's such a current theme,' said Liddy. 'This is the type of countryside I like. No cow dung or dreadful big tin barns to blot the landscape.'

Pippa was finding it really difficult to be polite, but she did her best. As she turned to leave the group, she spotted Danny across the room, smiling at her. He looked gorgeous in his tux and was surrounded by stick-thin simpering women. It felt weird to be in the same room as him after all the emotion of their last talk, but she smiled and winked at him. As she was about to walk off, he made a bee-line for her.

'Hi,' he said kissing her. 'You look amazing.'

'In this?' she shrugged a shoulder. 'You don't look too bad yourself.'

Before he could answer, Missy shot over.

'There you are. I've been looking for you all over,' she said breathlessly to Danny.

'Well now you've found me. Happy birthday,' he said kissing her cheek.

'Yeah, thanks. Listen I've got quite a bit of Charlie, but some of my friends are looking for more. You see the group over there by the front door? Can you go sort them, please?'

'Ah sorry honey, but I've retired from crime,' Danny said evenly.

'Yeah, right,' Missy laughed. She turned on her heel to walk away, so Danny caught her wrist. 'I'm serious, Missy. I'm done with it all. So from here on in, you can't rely on me. Sorry. It's all too dodgy and I wanted out. I don't owe any money, I didn't get caught and I've had my fun. So that's it, I'm finished.'

'Holy shit, you're serious,' she said as her eyes darkened. 'Well if I'd known that, I wouldn't have bothered inviting you.'

'Missy!' Pippa said. 'That's so rude! I thought you said you like Danny?'

Missy looked Pippa up and down and smirked. 'Looks like both of you deserve one another. Pippa, you're a drag. You think you're the party queen but let me tell you, you suck. I have more fun with my mother.'

Pippa opened her mouth to retaliate and decided not to bother, instead leaving Missy to trot over to her group of minions.

'I'm definitely growing up,' she said to Danny. 'My usual response to an outpour of bull like that would be a savage attack. But it's Missy's party, she's a paying guest and, above all, she's a complete nightmare. So if I'm no longer on her partying list, that's cool by me.'

'Happily, I think she's burned both of our bridges,' Danny said with a smile. 'Here's to change,' he said as he sipped his champagne.

Pippa's heart fluttered in her chest.

'Now do you trust me, Pippa,' he said seriously. 'That I mean what I say about going a new direction with you?'

'I think maybe I do,' she said as she kissed him.

❄

The guests were very merry by the time the gong was sounded by Paddy to signify dinner was served.

'Your father is beside himself with that gong,' Holly said giggling. 'I'm sure he's hoping they don't go in on time so he can do it again.'

Joey grinned as he ushered the revellers toward the marquee.

Chef Sally looked as cool as a cucumber as the hungry hoards filled the room. Once the table plan was studied and people had found their seat, the Craigs began to guide set groups up toward the buffet. They devoured the extensive salads selection and meats. There was a surplus of desserts, and the four-tiered birthday cake was barely touched. 'This is more like a wedding than a birthday,' Skye said to Pippa. She had popped some painkillers and was determined to do her bit.

'Except little Miss Sunshine hasn't managed to find a man who can stick her for more than a couple of weeks.'

'She's a bit of a diva all right.'

'Eh, understatement of the *year!*'

After Missy's speech, which went on for fifteen minutes, leaving most of the guests looking glazed with frozen smiles on their faces, the band struck up.

Pippa knew from chatting to them earlier that they were being paid a small fortune for their appearance. They were big on the

Dublin scene and Missy was beaming as her guests were visibly impressed by their presence.

It was clearly meant to be a wonderful surprise and Mrs Hassett silenced the room by banging on a microphone with her hand.

'Sorry to interrupt proceedings folks. But I have a little pressie for Missy. Darling, you're more like my sister than my daughter,' she said, glancing around the room for applause. There was a soggy ripple followed by silence again. 'So without further ado, happy birthday darling!'

As Paddy pulled on a rope and Joey swivelled, two white spotlights one side of the marquee rose to reveal a brand new BMW jeep.

'Another bloody car!' Pippa said to Skye. 'Seriously?'

The applause began and as everyone focused on the windscreen Mrs Hassett screamed into the microphone before collapsing like an ancient rag doll, waving for the spot lights to be moved.

The booming laughter filled the air as three bare, hairy bottoms came into view inside the car.

'Holy shit!' Joey said to Matt. 'Mooners! I love it.'

Knowing he should move the spotlight instantly, he kept it there for a few more moments to give everyone a giggle.

'Ugh!' Missy yelled. 'I'm not driving that thing with bum juice on the windscreen!'

Joey thought he was going to fall off the ladder. His stomach ached from laughing as he flicked the lights off. The band struck up once more and the atmosphere was electric.

'Amazing,' said Pippa to Joey and Skye as the dance floor filled. 'All the technology and money they've thrown at the party and the highlight of the night is three bare derrieres!'

'We can safely say the night has bottomed out!' Joey grinned.

Pippa was busy clearing glasses when she spotted Danny coming her way. He really did look gorgeous in that tux.

'Hey, pretty Pippa. I think I'm going to head back to Dublin now. I have a lift that's leaving shortly. I think it might be best if I see you tomorrow or the next day? You said we ought to take it slow . . .'

Pippa longed to tell Danny to stay at the farmhouse with her. But she knew she needed to make him work for her acceptance. Even though they'd already slept together and hung out in Dublin. This was different. This was real, with no crazy edge to it.

'I think that's a good plan,' she lied. 'I need to be here for my family. What about you give me a call and we'll arrange to hook up during the week?'

'Like a date?' he grinned.

'Exactly like a date,' she said.

'OK, you got it,' he said. As he leaned in to kiss her, it took all her restraint to let him go.

Holly and Paddy lasted until two in the morning. Missy's parents had gone to bed and all of the older guests had dispersed. The lights went down and when they came up again, DJ Zoom from Fire and Rain was at the decks and the crowd went wild at the sight of him. The atmosphere changed as it was all taken up another notch.

'Jeez, this lot are insane,' Matt said with one finger in his ear. 'I know I'm hardly what one would describe as a raver, but this is lunacy!'

Luckily, Joey had had the foresight to hire young barmen, who were bopping around behind the bar, enjoying every second of the night. Skye went to bed over at the farmhouse, as did an equally shattered Matt, leaving Pippa and Joey to man the proceedings.

'We can't go to bed until the last person leaves,' he said. 'Which I've got a feeling won't be before dawn.'

'Ah ha!' Pippa said. 'The buses are arriving at four so the end is in sight!'

As the last person was encouraged onto the bus by Joey, Missy was spotted in a heap and needed to be supported up the stairs to her room.

Joey paid the exhausted barmen and thanked them for their work.

'Any time, this place is sick. That was one hell of a party,' one of them said.

Knowing Holly and Paddy were probably intending on rising early to clean up, Pippa and Joey decided to make a start. Grabbing a black sack each, they picked up the burst balloons, soiled paper napkins and abandoned beer bottles. Glancing at the jeep that was still parked in the parted fabric of the marquee, they burst out laughing.

It was almost six by the time they made their way next door to the farmhouse.

Ely and Matt were having breakfast.

'Morning, bleary-eyed-Daddy and full-of-beans-Ely,' Pippa said with a grin.

'How did it all pan out?' Matt asked.

They sat and had tea and toast with Matt and Pippa played with Ely until she couldn't stay awake a second longer.

Matt was going to the hospital to tell Lainey all about it, so they sent their love and went to bed.

As Pippa lay down her head buzzed after all the loud music. She'd heard so many people complimenting the venue and the house. She was certain they'd get at least one further booking from tonight. She was unbelievably proud of everything they'd achieved. She knew that Huntersbrook had not only survived the re-birthing, but it had been injected with a whole new lease of life.

As she drifted off into a much-needed sleep, all Pippa could think about was Danny. She had no intention of stringing him along for too long. But she was thoroughly enjoying making him wait until she was ready. Delighted to be off Missy's radar finally, Pippa felt more in control than she had for quite a while.

Lainey

ON MONDAY MORNING, LAINEY LAY IN HER hospital bed feeling a gnawing fear deep inside her. The nurses had tipped her off that Dr Cumisky was on his way with her test results.

Phoning Matt, she asked him to come and be there with her. When he arrived ten minutes later without Ely, Lainey had a mild panic.

'What have you done with Ely?'

'Ah I gave him a bar of chocolate and left him at home in front of the telly. I handed him the house phone and wrote my mobile number on a sheet of paper and told him to call if he needs me.'

'That's not even funny,' she said smiling distractedly.

'Your mother is minding him,' Matt said.

'But . . .'

'Lainey, she's been there all the time over the past few days. It's not easy for her, not being able to come in here, and I think it's a good way of letting her feel she's doing something pro-active.'

'I suppose . . .'

'Besides, Ely could have gotten lost whether you were there or not the other day, so there's no point in zoning in on one little mishap . . .'

'Whaaat?' Lainey shrieked. 'What the hell are you talking about?'

'Eh . . . Ah, it's nothing. Sorry, I'm so tired, I totally forgot you didn't know,' Matt said pulling his fingers through his hair in agitation. 'It was something and nothing . . . Ely ran from the marquee on Friday. We were all meant to be keeping an eye. But he'd been with Holly, so . . .'

'Where did he go?' Lainey demanded.

'Your folks found him out on the road. But he was totally fine. A lady had pulled over and waited with him. We all ran frantically looking for him, Lainey. But it was nobody's fault.'

Lainey felt her head thudding horribly. She felt as if she was going to vomit.

'He could've been killed . . .' She started to gulp and sob in panic. 'He could've been knocked down and killed. He's the only child we'll ever have and my mother could've allowed him to be fatally injured.'

'Lainey, please!' Matt said. 'It's not as awful as all that. Holly was devastated. She was shaking and so upset. Please don't hold it against her.'

'Don't hold it against her? Are you insane?' she said as tears soaked her cheeks.

'Listen, this isn't doing either of us any good,' Matt said firmly. 'I know it's shocking and upsetting to hear that Ely was missing. But he's fine. All's well that ends well. Dr Cumisky is about to come in here and deliver some news that could wipe the floor with us for the next while. So I suggest you go to the bathroom, splash cold water on your face and calm the hell down.'

'Oh . . . O-K,' Lainey said. She crawled out of bed and shuffled to the bathroom at the end of the ward. Matt had never spoken to her like that before. She was slightly shocked. She was only standing up for Ely. For their son . . . If he wanted to take her mother's side in all of this, then that was his prerogative.

No wonder Holly had been so damn nice on the phone. She was guilty as hell for almost killing Ely. It was obvious that Matt wasn't going to take her side in all of this. So she'd put on a brave face in front of him. That was fine. She could do that. But Lainey vowed she was never allowing her mother near Ely again once she got out of this damn hospital.

Skye had asked her to fight, should she get a cancer diagnosis. Well, Lainey was going to do just that. There was no chance in hell she was dying now. Not while other people were capable of letting her son run on a road by himself.

Lainey had just settled back in her bed when Dr Cumisky came into the ward, accompanied by two nurses.

'Good morning,' he said evenly. 'So let's cut to the chase. I have your test results back.'

Lainey felt lightheaded. This was it, the moment of truth. The next sentence would change her life, either way. If she had cancer, they'd be going down a whole new road. And if she didn't . . . Well, she wouldn't take another day for granted.

Matt took her hand and moved onto the bed.

'The tumours I removed were all benign,' he said. 'Thankfully, you won't require any further treatment at the moment. You've been very lucky. Often these things start off as fairly innocuous and can change and become sinister. So it was as well we did the surgery now.'

Lainey heard the words. They washed over her like lukewarm water, cleansing so much worry and fear and leaving her feeling instantly giddy with relief.

'Oh dear Lord, I'm so happy,' she said, bursting into tears. 'Thank you, Dr Cumisky.'

'I'm sorry you had to lose your uterus and fallopian tubes, but I stand by my decision. This is the best outcome we could have hoped for.'

Lainey was delighted to learn she could also go home.

'Provided you have some support with your little boy and that you promise to take things very easy, I think your own bed is the best place for you now.'

'I'll behave, I promise,' Lainey assured him.

As soon as the medical team left Matt began to shove all her belongings into a bag, delighted she was getting out. Lainey decided to put her coat on over her pyjamas and travel the short distance home like that.

❄

Holly was at the farmhouse when they walked in the back door.

'Lainey!' she said rushing to give her a gentle hug. Lainey didn't want to cause a scene in front of the others so she simply stood motionlessly until her mother eventually stood back. Ely looked up from his high-chair where he was busy pushing the crusts from his toast around his tray. His smile was the best medicine Lainey could have wished for.

Instinctively, she tried to pick him up. Realising she couldn't stoop or bear his weight, she sat on the chair beside him and wrapped her arms around him.

Jacob appeared, followed closely by Paddy, both having received a text from Matt.

'You're home, love!' Paddy said hugging her tightly.

'She certainly is,' Matt beamed. 'We've to mind her and let her recover. But her test results were all clear. There's no further treatment required and there's no cancer.'

Tears sprang to Holly's eyes as she took Lainey's hand.

'I'm so unbelievably relieved, love. You've no idea how worried I've been. We all have . . . Your little boy needs his mummy and we all need you here. It's been awful without you.'

'It has?'

'Ah Lainey, love, don't be silly,' Paddy said. 'We'd all be devastated if anything happened to you. Thank God we don't have to imagine that nightmare any longer.'

'At least Ely wasn't killed on the road the other day. So that's two things we can be thankful for,' she said, as she walked toward the stairs. 'Thanks for your help, Mum, but I'll be minding Ely from here on in.'

Skye had slipped upstairs and changed the bedclothes. Not only that, she'd bought brand new ones and laid out a matching set of pyjamas to boot. On the nightstand was a pretty bowl filled with fruit and a little heart shaped box of chocolates. There were two new novels and a gorgeous glass bottle of pink lemonade. She was putting the final clean pillowslip in place when Lainey found her.

'Men don't notice things like clean sheets. But you'll want to be as comfy as possible after that dreadful ordeal.'

'Thanks, Skye,' Lainey said. 'You've been so good . . . I can't believe you went and bought all this stuff. You're so generous.'

After a shower, Lainey managed to change her bandage and put on the fresh new pyjamas. As she slid gingerly into bed and lay back against the cool soft pillows, she finally relaxed. Home. It was the best feeling in the world.

Lainey, Joey & Pippa

AFTER A NIGHT IN HER OWN BED, LAINEY FELT like a different person. She'd always loved the farmhouse but she'd never been so grateful to be home.

She and Matt shared breakfast before he went to work. Jacob needed to go to Wicklow to look at fencing.

'The hen coop needs strengthening before the winter kicks in. I remember Cynthia lost a few birds due to a weakness in the side. The fox is a sly fellow and will be hungry with the biting cold. I'll take little Ely and we'll go to a café.'

'That'd be super,' Lainey said, relieved she didn't need to argue with Holly about minding him. 'Take your time.'

'I was half thinking of bringing him to the indoor play centre. A few of the men who I meet at the community centre have said it's great. There's tea and coffee there and plenty of grandparents go seeing as they're the minders.'

'Well I know Ely would prefer that to a café,' Lainey said. 'If you think you can cope with the noise, go for it!'

By the time she'd waved them all off, Lainey was tired again. She made her way back up the stairs. She was settled in bed ready to read one of the books Skye had chosen when she heard voices down stairs.

'Only us!' Joey called up. 'Coffee or tea? We've robbed some of Sadie's coffee cake.'

Lainey grinned. 'Coffee in that case,' she answered.

Moments later he and Pippa appeared at the top of the stairs.

'Hey you two,' she said pleasantly surprised. 'I thought you'd both be at work.'

'I suggested we come visit,' Pippa said. 'It's only a quickie and we'll both head back to Dublin.'

'Well, thank you,' Lainey said. 'I'm touched.'

Joey could barely get the words out as he recounted the moment when Missy's new jeep was revealed.

'You're still snorting about it,' Pippa giggled. 'It was so funny though, Lainey. And poor Mrs H nearly died. She couldn't look shocked due to her plastic surgery, but her legs went from under her.'

'It'll go down in history as a bummer of a party,' Joey added. 'Speaking of parties, I've got this Christmas ball coming up. It's a massive deal at the firm and I need you gals to give Skye a dig out.'

'Oh really?' Lainey said looking over. 'In what way?'

'Well,' Joey pulled his fingers through his hair. 'Janet, Clive's wife is running the show and she's high-end.'

'High maintenance more like it,' Pippa scoffed. 'From what I've heard about her, she's a total rip.'

'Who told you that?' Joey asked defensively.

'She shops at the store,' Pippa said. 'She's obnoxiously rude to the staff and short of spitting on us, thinks we're all beneath her.'

'Well they are very wealthy and influential,' Joey said.

'Joey!' Lainey scolded. 'Don't tell me you're taken in by that nonsense. Shame on you! You know better than to kow-tow to that kind of bullshit.'

He scratched his head and splayed his hands.

'This isn't let's-all-attack-Joey hour,' he said. 'All I wanted was for you two to help Skye. She's going to be way off the mark with her usual gear. So would you girls talk her into a bit of a make-over session?'

They both burst out laughing.

'What? It's not a joke. I need her to look the part.'

'Why don't you bring a blow-up doll instead?' Lainey said grinning. 'You could dress it in a nice slinky black number. Make it one of those thigh-high slits and it could do an Angelina Jolie with its leg stuck out!'

'Now you're being ridiculous,' he scoffed. 'Pippa, will you help Skye?'

'Bog off, Joey,' she spat. 'Skye is a grown woman with her own sense of style. She would drop-kick us if we tried to barge in and make her do what you're suggesting. And she'd be dead right. You're the one who fell in love with the girl and asked her to marry you. You didn't fall for her because she looks like a clone of all the other men's wives.'

'True,' he said guardedly. 'But when it comes to these corporate events, there's a certain level of expectation. I'm a partner now. I need to act accordingly and sad as you two clearly think it is, that also entails having a potential wife who fits the bill.'

'Huh, good luck with that, brother dearest,' Pippa said. 'None of the women in your life are silly saps. So you ought to know by now that we don't do sad-submissive little wifey crap.'

Joey looked utterly perplexed, but the girls weren't giving in. Knowing he should drop it, he figured it would all work out in the long run. He'd buy Skye a nice voucher for the beauty salon and tell her to treat herself. Say that it was to cheer her up and make her feel better with this ulcer business making her feel awful. Satisfied he'd made yet another good executive decision, he congratulated himself.

'So what's the beef with you and Mum?' Pippa asked Lainey.

'In what way?' Now it was Lainey's turn to act defensively.

'She's really cut up about the incident with Ely. Dad says she hasn't slept properly since. She's waking up sweating and crying.

And the fact you're not speaking to her much isn't helping. She totally blames herself.'

'So she bloody well should,' Lainey shouted. 'Pippa, in case you've forgotten I've just had all my baby-making bits chopped out. My only child could've been killed and it was on *her* watch.'

'Lainey, we all know why you're so upset. It's a terrible thing to have happened,' Joey reasoned. 'But Mum wasn't the only one there that day. You can't lay the blame solely at her feet. That's unreasonable. It really is.'

Lainey folded her arms and pouted.

'She's never been on my side. Everything I do is sub-standard as far as she's concerned,' Lainey said.

'That's not true,' said Pippa. 'She adores us all. She'd walk over hot coals for each one of us. And as for Ely . . . We all pale into insignificance when he's around. He's the apple of her eye. You're really killing her by shutting her out, Lainey.'

'I did have a really lovely chat with her on the phone while I was in hospital,' Lainey admitted. 'She said she loved me.'

'Of course she loves you, you bloody goon,' Joey said. 'She loves all of us and she doesn't deserve to be given the cold shoulder. Why don't you try and put your worry and hurt over the attempted murder on your son aside and try again.'

'Jeez, Joey!' Pippa laughed. 'It was hardly an attempted murder.'

'OK,' Lainey conceded. 'Point taken. But if we're all having a grilling here, spill about Danny-boy, Pippa! What's the suss there?'

'Yeah, Pippa!' Joey chimed in.

'Ah it's a work in progress,' she said coyly. 'He's a great guy and we're taking it as it comes.'

'Does he make good money?' Joey asked.

'What the hell has that got to do with anything?' Pippa asked. 'Joey, you're turning into a real corporate bore, do you know that? I'm not sure this being made partner situation is good for you. Back off and stop acting as if you're Bill Gates all of a sudden. It's kind of nasty.'

'Whatever,' he said rolling his eyes.

'So you really like Danny,' Lainey said lying back against the pillows. 'I'm glad you're being level-headed about it though. Good for you, Pippa.'

Lainey yawned and the other two took the hint.

'We'll leave you to rest. Take it easy, sis,' Joey said kissing her.

'See you soon,' Pippa promised.

'Don't be strangers,' she begged. 'And thanks for coming. You've both been great. I'm so lucky to have such an amazing family. Between yourselves and Jules I really know I'm loved. I couldn't have gotten through without you.'

If Lainey noticed the uneasy glance between Pippa and Joey, she didn't comment.

Joey

JOEY WAS STANDING IN THE FOYER OF THE IMPERIAL hotel. Above him a crystal chandelier was elegantly decorated with candles and mistletoe. The place looked beautiful – he'd actually taken some photos to give Holly inspiration for Jodi's wedding décor. If they could do something as good as this, Jodi would be singing their praises.

He looked at his watch for the umpteenth time and looked anxiously about the foyer and towards the entrance doors. He'd told Skye how important this night was to him and yet here he was, waiting for her and she was late. He called her mobile for what must be the tenth time in half an hour. Clive and Janet wouldn't stop going on about Skye helping out and it was making him decidedly nervous.

'No sign of your lady friend yet, I take it?' Janet asked walking across to him. She wasn't his type, but he had to admit she looked stunning tonight in a floor-sweeping black gown with diamonds studded in her ears and around her neck.

'She's stuck in traffic. She'll be along any second,' Joey lied. He sincerely hoped Skye was on her way and had forgotten her mobile. He was about to call her again when she raced through the revolving hotel door in a flurry.

'Sorry, were you waiting for me?' she asked.

'You're really late,' he whispered through gritted teeth. 'I've had Janet asking repeatedly where you are. She needs someone to put up balloon bunches and I said you could do it.'

Skye looked crestfallen. She also looked a bit of a mess, Joey noticed. She removed her waxy rain jacket and woolly hat to reveal a static mass of unruly curls.

'I thought you were going to the salon,' he said impatiently. 'That voucher is for three-hundred euros.'

'I told you . . . I don't feel like going at the moment. Besides, when I've gone in the past, which isn't often let's face it, they always seem to feel I'd be better off with poker-straight hair and make-up that resembles pancake batter. It makes me feel quashed. I'd only be uncomfortable all night.'

'It's black-tie, Skye,' he said looking down at her. 'Why didn't you borrow something from Lainey or Pippa?'

She stared down at her dress and smoothed her hand over the skirt in dismay.

'I always wear this. It was really expensive when I bought it. I didn't think there was anything wrong with . . .'

'It's brown.' He threw his hands up in the air and strode off toward the function room.

Not sure what she was meant to do, Skye followed him. She was wearing some semi-high shoes, which she'd thought would add a touch of glamour. She'd also added diamanté earrings, which she'd felt were pretty when she'd scanned her reflection at home.

As she entered the massive bedecked room that dripped from roof to ceiling with black and silver themed decorations, her jaw dropped. Skye thought it was horribly tacky.

'Ah,' Janet said as she walked toward Skye. 'So you're here. Joey did tell you this is black tie didn't he, sweetie?'

'I told her,' Joey said snidely. Skye felt as if she'd been slapped.

Wanting to turn and run out of the room, she stood feeling vulnerable and let down as her cheeks burned.

'You won't have a massive amount of time to change and get your hair and make-up done. You'll be cutting it quite fine actually,' Janet said. 'But anyhow . . . Let's press on. Can you take the stepladder from over there and tie the remainder of the balloons around the pillars? Maria and I are wearing Valentino and Westwood respectively, so obviously we're not chancing climbing ladders.'

Janet swatted Skye's arm and did a false laugh. She pointed a long shiny painted claw-like finger in the direction of the stepladder. When Skye didn't walk toward it immediately she stopped, put her hand on her hip and stared at her.

'Well? Come on. Chop-chop, get to it. Nothing is going to get done by standing and gawping. Maria and I have to finish putting goodie bags on the chairs. We're all pitching in here, Sly.'

'It's Skye,' she said.

'Yes of course, dear,' Janet said. 'Listen,' she moved in close and talked out the corner of her mouth. 'It's not my fault if you have such a funny nickname. But you're not the first. Petra McGuinness's real name is Petunia, Lord help us all. So I've no doubt you were called some God-awful name by a narrow-minded mother and have longed to change it since. I *get* it.'

She strode off, leaving Skye standing dumbfounded. Terrified she'd be yelled at, she scanned the room to find Joey. He was over near the stage at the other end of the room with his head bowed as another man was clearly briefing him.

She made her way to his side and waited for him to talk to her. She coughed gently and he moved his hand to touch her, but didn't actually address her or even turn to face her.

'Eh can we help you?' said the man.

'Yeah, Clive, meet Skye, my fiancée,' Joey said.

'You're joking?' Clive guffawed rudely.

Skye turned and walked as fast as she could without running. She bore down on her tongue in an effort to stop the tears from falling. She didn't care what Joey said to her, she wasn't staying in that room.

'Skye!' he called. She kept walking. She'd almost reached the end of the room when he grabbed her.

'What's going on?' he said. 'I need your support here. Of all the times to choose to go off in a strop, this isn't a good one. Clive is a bit of a messer. Don't take his comments to heart. He was only joking. Please just do the balloons and then we can have a few drinks.'

'I'm not getting up on the ladder,' she said.

'Skye, for fuck's sake,' Joey said, throwing his hands up. 'You turn up late dressed as if you're going to a druids' day out and you're rude to my boss *and* his wife. Thanks a bunch.'

She stood and squeezed her eyes shut. She could hear him hyperventilating. She knew he was fuming . . . Absolutely boiling with anger. She knew it was now or never.

'I'm not getting on the ladder, Joey, because I'm pregnant,' she said. 'I'm dressed this way because that's the way I feel comfortable. I've never been any different and until recently that was OK by you.'

He stood wide-eyed as his hand shot to his mouth.

'I'm leaving now. You can make up whatever excuse you like. I don't belong here and quite clearly I don't belong in your new world. I love you, Joey, but I'm not prepared to spend the rest of my life being made a mockery of.' Her hands were hot and swollen, but Skye managed to twist the engagement ring off her finger. Carefully she took his hand and folded it into his palm.

'Please don't lose it. Holly deserves to have it back safely.'

Joey didn't protest or even speak, so she turned and walked

out. The hailstones were falling in hard, face-stinging fistfuls as she negotiated the slippery footpath.

The past few weeks had been awful. She'd found out about the pregnancy the day Lainey had come out of hospital. But Skye hadn't wanted to tell anyone. For a start Joey was so caught up in his work, she hadn't even had an opportunity. But secondly she couldn't bring herself to make such a heartless announcement in light of Lainey's surgery.

The look on Joey's face just now had said it all. He was completely stumped when she said she was pregnant. Not for one second had he shown any sign of delight or excitement. In her dreams he'd picked her up and spun her around and told her he was ecstatic at the thought of becoming a father.

But she'd known deep down that it wasn't about to happen any time soon. Joey had changed. He was moving up the ladder in work and he was certain to be a massive success.

Skye was sadly aware that he would need a more cosmopolitan girl by his side. Someone who would be in a position to fit in with Janet and her crew . . . Someone who would add to his CV by being pretty, bright, funny and a social butterfly . . . Not a bog standard brown moth like her.

❄

By the time she reached their apartment, Skye was feeling truly awful. Her tummy ached and her head pounded. When she'd found out she was pregnant she'd been so relieved. At least she wasn't sick.

But now that Skye knew she'd be doing this on her own, the full realisation of what was happening hit her.

She made her way into their bedroom, removed her dress and shoes and curled into bed.

All her dreams of spending Christmases and summers at

Huntersbrook faded before her. She'd miss Holly and Paddy dreadfully. She adored them. They had always made her feel welcome and worthy. But she wasn't meant to be marrying them. If Joey didn't love and respect her, nothing they said or did would change that.

Pippa was a sparky, wonderful girl and she'd miss her too. Lainey had become such a close friend. They were like sisters. The thought of not seeing her and watching little Ely grow up tore at her heart. Perhaps, over time, they'd all find some sort of footing. She was going to be mother to their grandchild and niece or nephew so Skye hoped they'd all want some kind of contact. But it wasn't going to be the same. She wasn't going to be Joey's wife. She'd give him a year at the outside before he replaced her with a more cosmopolitan and streetwise girl.

Skye cried until she felt she might die of a broken heart. Eventually, exhausted and utterly miserable she fell into a restless sleep.

❅

The ball had gotten underway and Joey was doing his best to clamber back into favour with Clive and Janet.

'I'm so sorry Skye had to leave. She started vomiting and I knew I had to get her out of here, pronto.'

'She didn't even have time to change into her gown, poor love,' Janet said.

'Well that's the way it goes sometimes,' Joey said. He was so torn between telling Janet to go and swing and wanting to shake Skye for making a scene. Every time he thought of his grandma's ring zipped into the inside pocket of his tuxedo jacket, he placed his hand there to ensure it was still there.

How could Skye have lied? She was pregnant and hadn't told him. What else had she been concealing? Suddenly, he didn't know this woman any more. How had they reached this point? He thought they had it all sorted. That they could tell one another anything . . .

Feeling guilty and angry in equal measure, Joey couldn't ignore the horrible voice in his head that taunted him and told him that he'd dropped the ball. He'd been so intent on making his mark at work and getting Huntersbrook up and running, he'd taken Skye for granted.

The evening turned out to be a dreadful chore. He had to run from Billy to Jack looking after clients and balancing tray after tray of drinks as he plamaused the customers.

Once the band struck up and most of the couples were on the dance floor, he slipped to the bar and ordered a double whiskey. He downed it in two large gulps. It burned the hell out of his insides, but the horrible sensation fit his mood. He pulled his Grandma's ring from his pocket and examined it in the light. It was stunning. All at once memories of Grandma came flooding back. What would she think if she saw him now, he wondered.

He thought of his parents and sisters. They'd all have rather a lot to say about him and Skye breaking up. He looked around at the other women. Each was more polished than the next. They were huddled in groups guzzling champagne and admiring one another. Their easy laughter and obvious enjoyment of the event made him scowl. He loved Skye. But she'd never be able to do what these women were doing right now.

If he stayed with her, he'd have a lifetime of either going to functions alone or having her there looking like a fish out of water . . .

He'd been so happy until this evening. His five-year plan had been working out so well . . . He was managing to juggle all this workload with project Huntersbrook and he'd thought he had it all sussed.

Emma Hannigan

The thought of becoming a father made him want to vomit. How was he supposed to do it all? He wasn't ready, was he? The only answer was to order another drink. He decided on a brandy and port. He had some vague recollection of it being a medicinal cure-all type thing . . .

Lainey

PIPPA WAS MAKING A MASSIVE EFFORT TO HELP OUT and spend time with her family. Even though there were tons of Christmas drinks parties on the go in Dublin, she was intent on helping at Huntersbrook.

Things were ticking along nicely with Danny and she'd asked him to come and join them this evening, but for now she wanted to help prepare the house for Jodi's wedding.

'Have you had some sort of epiphany?' Holly asked.

'Why do you ask?' Pippa said.

'Well it's Saturday. It's December and you're here helping and correct me if I'm mistaken but you don't even have a hangover. Have you and Danny split?'

'No, actually we're getting on really well. I've kind of burnt myself out with that clubbing scene in Dublin. Danny's going to come down later if that's cool?'

'Of course,' Holly said smiling. 'We'd be delighted to see him.'

'I'm starting my cookery course after Christmas,' Lainey said. 'Dr Cumisky says I'll be well enough by then.'

'Good for you,' Holly said.

'It'll give me something positive to focus on, seeing as my life is pretty much in the toilet right now,' she said.

'Ooh, it's Jodi!' Pippa said as her mobile rang and she ran from the room.

'Perhaps we can nail down some details now,' said Holly. 'We need to know where she wants the ceremony to take place so I can decorate accordingly.'

'Where have those men gotten to?' Sadie said. 'They went to get the Christmas tree nearly two hours ago.'

'I asked them to get a few bags of holly as well,' said Holly. 'No doubt they'll be back soon. If they're not, believe me I'll be up that back field in a jeep to hunt them down!'

'Ouch, my arm is literally going to fall off,' Lainey complained. 'Will you come and give this pudding mix a final stir, Sadie?'

'Mama out!' Ely said throwing himself at the back door. 'Cows?' he added with his eyebrows raised in hope.

'Ah bless him,' Holly said. 'Why don't I take him out for a bit of air? He must be fed up in here. Come on pet, Grandma will bring you out.'

'No you won't,' Lainey said.

'Why ever not?' Holly said in exasperation. 'Lainey, he's . . .'

'I don't need you tell me about my own son, thank you.'

'Lainey . . .'

'So!' Pippa burst through the door oblivious to the tension. 'It's decided. Jodi will have the ceremony in the hallway. Then we'll clear that while they do drinks in the living room and move on into the dining room . . . What?' She looked from Holly to Lainey and down to Ely who was trying to pull on his own tiny wellingtons.

'I want to take Ely out for a bit of air but it seems that's against the law according to Lainey.'

'How can you be so flippant?' Lainey said as her voice rose to a yell. 'You could've killed Ely and you wonder why I'm not delighted about letting you off with him? Get a grip, Mum.'

'Lainey, I've told you a thousand times I'm sorry for letting Ely out of my sight when you were at hospital. Nobody feels worse about it than I do.'

'That's not true,' Lainey said. 'Believe me, Mum, it keeps me awake at night thinking that I could've lost my only child.'

'Lainey, I know you're hurting. I understand this is a really hard time in your life. But you can't punish everyone else. Let me help, please.'

Holly almost toppled backwards as Lainey stood up with force and her hand on her hips.

'You have no idea how I feel,' she yelled. 'Nobody does. Everything I'd dreamed of has been ripped away. I was in the process of organising a builder to make new bedrooms for our babies. I had everything to look forward to. Now we have nothing.'

'Ah now girls,' Sadie said. 'Let's try and sit down and have a calm chat here.'

'There's no calm chat required,' Lainey spat. 'I'll hand my son over to people who know how to mind him. End of. It's hardly rocket science.'

'OK Lainey, this needs to stop right now,' Holly said. 'Don't you think I'm punishing myself enough for what's happened? I still don't sleep. I would curl up and die if anything happened to Ely.'

'Amazing seeing as he's *my* child. I could understand if he were Pippa or Joey's child. But not anything belonging to me.'

'That's not fair.'

'Isn't it?'

'Lainey, we've chatted about our differences. I thought we'd agreed to try and be civil?'

'That's all fine and well, but I can't just wipe the fact that you've made me feel less loved than the others for my entire life. It's not a secret that you resent me. I don't know what I ever did to deserve that, but it's a fact.'

'Maybe it's because I wasn't well. We missed some key time when you were a child . . .'

'Or maybe, Mum it's because you blame me for the fact that you had postnatal depression?'

A horrible silence filled the air. Holly didn't answer.

'Wow,' Lainey said. 'That was your opportunity to tell me I'm wrong. To say that you love me and it couldn't possibly be my fault. Well now we all know the truth. God, you're a sad, selfish woman, do you know that? Stay away from me and stay away from Ely, you hear?' She marched toward the door.

'Go, if that's what you want. But not before I say what needs saying.' She took a deep breath. 'You've always been the same, Lainey. You've tried to blame me for everything that goes wrong in your life. No matter what you have it's never enough. You spend your time looking on the dark side of life. You can't blame *that* on me or my postnatal depression. That's simply *your* personality and you have to be aware of and work against it.'

'That's not true,' she shouted.

'Isn't it? Look at Matt . . . He's terrified to say anything to you. We're all walking on eggshells when you're around. Nobody is allowed to say or do anything that might set you off. Well it needs to end here and now, Lainey. What's happened is awful. But we all feel the loss too. It didn't just happen to you. It involves Matt too and he's struggling right now. He's no idea what to do to make this better. Be careful, my girl. You could drive him away and believe me I wouldn't blame him if he ran for the hills.'

Holly glanced over at Ely who was cowering in the corner looking terrified.

'Now look at your son,' she said through her teeth. 'He's totally confused and shocked. It's not just up to you whether I see him or not. He's Matt's child too and furthermore Ely loves me. I'm his grandma. The day he got lost will be branded in my memory forever. I still wake at night crying over it. I will never forgive myself for letting him out of my sight. But it was an accident . . . A mistake . . . If you want to punish me for the rest of my life for it, I can't stop you. But never forget that I love you and Ely.'

Holly walked over to little Ely and bent down.

'You're going home with Mum now, lovie,' she said. 'But I'll see you soon, OK?'

Ely looked from Holly to Lainey in utter confusion. 'It's OK, Ely,' Lainey said scooping him up. 'Let's go now.'

As they walked back toward the farmhouse Holly sobbed as if her heart were breaking. She hated conflict and certainly hadn't wanted to say the words she'd just spoken.

She had no idea what Lainey would do now. But she sincerely hoped her daughter would take stock and perhaps try to fix things.

Joey

MATT AND JOEY PUT THE FINISHING TOUCHES
to the outdoor lights. They'd done a lot of work today. Holly
seemed pleased with the tree and was busy decorating it inside.
Joey had asked Pippa why their mother had red eyes and she'd
shook her head mouthing that there'd been a row with Lainey
– again.

He and Matt had made the executive decision to stay outside
doing the lights. But as the temperature dropped and the light
began to fade, Joey felt a sudden need to get away from the house.
It felt oddly empty without Skye waiting for him inside.

'I don't suppose you'd like to go for a sneaky pint, would
you?' he asked Matt.

'I'd love it,' he said.

They asked Paddy and Jacob if they'd like to join them, but
they were happy sitting in front of the fire reading the papers.
They walked to the farmhouse to square it up with Lainey.

'Hey sis,' Joey said. 'I'm looking to snatch your hubby away
for an hour. Is that OK with you?'

'Yup,' she said curtly.

'I won't go if you need me here,' Matt said looking at Joey.

'It was only a thought,' said Joey. 'We can stay.'

'I said it's fine,' Lainey spat. 'We're only having spaghetti
bolognaise for dinner, so it can be ready at any time. Go.'

'What's up?' Matt asked.

'Not a single thing,' Lainey said, bashing a pot down on the cooker.

Matt turned and strode from the house and Joey decided to follow. They didn't talk much during the fifteen-minute walk to the local pub. But it was bitingly cold and didn't exactly promote chat.

'We should have a hot whiskey,' Joey joked.

'Good plan,' Matt said and ordered them. The barman said he'd bring them over as soon as they were ready, so they found a table in the corner.

Joey was lost in his own thoughts when Matt shifted in his seat and dragged his hand wearily across his face.

'Joey, do you mind if I say something?' Matt began. 'I don't know what to do. I'm getting to a stage where I can't deal with Lainey. She's so bitter and angry all the time. She won't let your mother near Ely and she's acting as if she's got the worst life. I'm at a loss.'

Joey didn't answer for a second.

'Sorry,' Matt said. 'I shouldn't dump on you. You can't really say much, being her brother.'

'Ah it's not that at all,' Joey said. 'It's more that it's all a bit close to home. Skye and I are actually on a break . . .'

'What?' Now it was Matt's turn to look shocked.

'At least Lainey is shouting at you. Skye won't even talk to me. I've been staying at a hotel.'

'No way,' Matt said. 'I'd no idea.'

Joey explained what had happened last weekend and how he'd upset Skye and was now in turmoil trying to figure out what he wanted.

'And she's pregnant,' Matt said. 'Wow.'

'I'm sorry, Matt. I know that's probably the last thing you need to hear right now in light of Lainey's surgery and all that . . .'

'Hey, I'm delighted for you guys. That's not the issue. I'm more worried that you get things back on track. With a baby on the way, it's a real shame that you're fighting.'

'Tell me about it,' Joey said. 'I've tried every day to get Skye to talk to me, but she's not interested. She says she needs to take stock of the situation. She's adamant she's not bringing a child into a situation where things are fraught.'

'Well I can understand that,' Matt said. 'But you've got to try and work it out, Joey. Being a dad is the best job in the world. Nothing comes close to it, man . . . Ely is just the most incredible thing that's ever happened to us. That's why Lainey is hurting so much right now. She wanted half a dozen Ely's . . .'

'I know,' Joey said.

'More than that,' Matt said sadly. 'She wanted Ely to have a little brother or sister so he'd have someone to play with. Just imagine how cool it'd be if your little fella or lady were here instead?'

'My world is different from yours though, Matt. With all due respect, I'm up in Dublin in a high-powered position and I'm still climbing up that ladder of success. Babies were nowhere on my horizon if I'm honest.'

'You're just not getting this,' Matt said. 'I'm not trying to insult you here. But none of that shit you're talking about makes any sense if you're alone. What are you planning on doing? Having a big flat with gold leaf wallpaper where you can sit every evening and count your money like Silas Marner?'

'No . . . But . . .' Joey was suddenly at a loss.

'I'm all for ambition, Joey. Don't get me wrong here. It's great to do well. Money helps a lot of situations, but it doesn't even compare to holding your own flesh and blood in your arms. To hearing a little gremlin-like voice say "dada" for the first time.'

Joey nodded.

'We had that hideous period of time where we wondered if Lainey was going to live or die. I sat and thought about how I'd cope. How I'd manage to carry on. I even thought of whether or not I ought to remarry so Ely would have a mother. I couldn't bear to bring that thought to a conclusion. Nothing and nobody could replace Lainey. If our family means three people, that's a damn sight better than two.'

'And Skye isn't sick, nor is she asking for anything other than love,' Joey concluded. 'I'm a fucking asshole . . .'

'I won't answer that,' Matt said with a grin. 'But I will buy us both a pint.'

Pippa

AFTER THE TERRIBLE ROW WITH LAINEY, PIPPA was feeling torn. She'd driven back to Huntersbrook from Dublin for the weekend and intended trying to help build bridges. She was feeling a little bit like Bob the builder in fact, as she had a little building of her own to do too.

The doorbell rang and she ran through the black and white chequered hallway to answer it.

'Good morning, Sir!' she said kissing Danny and inviting him in. 'Come this way please.' She took his hand and led him to the dining room where she'd laid the table with a crisp white cloth and her mother's good china service.

'Wow, this is fancy!'

'Breakfast fit for a king,' she joked.

'I'd prefer if it were morning-after-the-night-before brekkie where I've worked up a serious appetite with you,' Danny said nuzzling her neck.

'All in good time,' she said winking. Pippa was thoroughly enjoying wooing Danny. He was playing a blinder, too. He'd sent her flowers at work with a hand written note, telling her he loved her. This was her love-volley to keep him going. She was longing to give in and jump between the sheets with him, but she knew this was the best way to take things.

As they finished their coffee her mobile phone rang.

'Hey Jodi,' she said cheerfully. 'No, it's a good time to chat.

How are things?' They had a quick chat and Pippa agreed to call to Jodi's house the next day and go through the final details for the wedding. As she hung up Danny was laughing.

'Ooh look at you with your A list friends!'

'She's so bloody cool. I want to *be* her,' Pippa said. They decided to clear the breakfast things and go for a stroll up the fields.

As they walked back into the kitchen Holly was on the phone. From the conversation Pippa deciphered it was Mrs Hogan from the mini supermarket in the village.

It seemed her son was returning from five years in Australia with his Aussie wife and two-year-old son.

Holly hung up and explained that Mrs Hogan asked if there was any chance she might be able to do a little welcome home party for them in two days' time.

'Owen will be dying to introduce us all to his wife Cindy and their son Scott. Mrs Hogan wants to know if I could do a mulled wine and mince pie reception here at Huntersbrook.'

Holly had made a management decision to accommodate Mrs Hogan come what may.

'If nothing else it will give me something to do for the next two days. I'll need some extra back up so I'll call Chef Sally too.'

'Sounds great, Mum. Well done.'

Quite out of the blue, Holly burst into sobs. Pippa made eyes at Danny to go. He excused himself and went back to the dining room.

'Mum, what is it?'

'I can't bear another minute of this awful situation with Lainey. It's killing me. I miss Ely so badly it hurts and I wish to God we could resolve all this. It's nearly Christmas and for the first time ever – I'm dreading it.'

'Oh Mum,' Pippa said hugging her. 'Why don't I have a word with Lainey. Or even better, let's call Jules? She'll listen to Jules . . .'

'No love,' Holly said sighing as if from her toes. 'I need to sort this myself. I'm calling over to Lainey now. I need to be the mother here. We're both adults, but she's still my daughter.'

Pulling on her wellies and a coat, Holly pulled the back door open and walked out. Pippa sat at the kitchen table unsure of what she should do. This really wasn't any of her business. She could listen to both sides, but it wasn't her problem to fix. She crossed her fingers and hoped that her mother and sister could find common ground.

❄

Her heart lurched when Lainey saw Holly tramping across the path to her kitchen door. For a fleeting moment she considered going upstairs and pretending to be out. But anger took over and she marched to the door, flung it open and confronted her.

'What can I do for you?' she asked nostrils flaring. 'I thought I made myself clear.'

'May I come in?' Holly's voice was calm and without accusation or conflict.

Lainey considered telling her to bog off, but the look of sheer desolation in her mother's eyes stopped her. She stood to the side silently and allowed her to walk past.

'I can't continue like this,' Holly said. 'I'm lost without you and Ely. I feel as if my heart has been ripped out.'

Lainey sighed. She wasn't enjoying the bust-up either. Much as her mother irritated her and made her feel small at times, she missed her.

'I don't like it either,' Lainey eventually conceded.

'You were right,' Holly said. She looked up at Lainey. 'You were right when you said I hated you for giving me postnatal depression. I don't think I even realised it. I certainly never thought about it that way . . . But when you were little, all I could see when I looked at you was my own pain. You were like Mummy's little shadow. You turned to her with your tears but most of all your smiles were all for her too.'

'Mum, I . . .'

'Wait, please. Let me say this and then it's your turn. Is that fair?'

Lainey nodded.

'Instead of trying to build a relationship with you once I was better, I was cowardly and let you slip further away. When Joey came along I had medication to balance my chemicals and it was so much easier. I held onto him like he was my life raft. That pushed you further away again.'

Lainey began to cry.

'I'm sorry I've been a terrible mother to you, Lainey. All the good parts of you are from your father and Grandma. The grabbing, unhappy and discontented parts are from me. The most ironic part of all this is that you're probably the most like me of all my children. When I look at you, I see myself.'

'May I speak now?'

She nodded.

'I've been a nightmare. You said what needed saying. I *am* pushing Matt away. I'm taking my pain out on all of you. All you've done is try to help and I've been a cow. Thank you for saying that you blamed me. I understand that you never meant to. But the truth is very freeing. At least I know I wasn't imagining it all.'

'So where do we go from here?' Holly asked.

'We go onwards and upwards, Mum. I learned some really good things from you too, you know? I'm a good mother. I know I am. You showed me how to do that. Maybe it was more with Joey and Pip, but I learned from you all the same.'

'I think I'm quite good at being a grandma – when I don't lose him that is.'

'That wasn't your fault, Mum,' Lainey sighed. 'I know it wasn't. I needed an excuse to punish you and it was a bloody brilliant one.'

'I'll say,' Holly rolled her eyes.

'Can we draw a line in the sand? It's not too late to build a relationship. My childhood is in the past. But there's so much of my life left, and all of Ely's. Can we go from here – together?'

'Darling, I could think of nothing I'd like more.'

Holly held out her arms and Lainey went to her. They embraced and it felt wonderful.

Pippa

THE FOLLOWING MORNING PIPPA WAS UP AND dressed with plenty of time to spare. She couldn't believe she was actually going to Jodi Ludlum's house.

Not wanting to arrive too early, she forced herself to wait until the agreed time. As she pulled up outside, Jodi's cottage was not at all what she'd expected. In fact, she'd shot past it the first time, ending up at a dead-end and what appeared to be a wild meadow with a river running through it. She clunked the car into reverse and pulled up at this small, rather plain-looking gate lodge. Situated at the entrance to a long driveway it wasn't unlike the gate lodge her parents had moved into, only this place was a lot older. Jodi had joked on the phone that it was a blink-and-you'll-miss-it property, but Pippa had assumed she was playing it down. As she turned the car engine off, a red Mini pulled up and Jodi jumped out waving furiously. She was leaning into the car holding the seat forward with her hand, so her son and his friend could climb out.

Pippa got out and walked over to her smiling.

'As you can see, my sense of direction is dreadful. I was practically in the river before I realised I'd missed you!'

'I told you it was easy to pass,' Jodi said. 'You probably thought I was kidding and really lived in a mansion,' she giggled. 'We were down in the village getting milk. Come on in!'

As they walked into the house Pippa chatted to Saul and his

friend. She remembered her mother's words and tried not to crane her neck or look around corners. The cottage was very pretty, but quite tiny. It looked as if a couple of smaller rooms had been knocked into one open-planned space with a kitchen, dining and living room all in one. There was a corridor with wooden doors and latched handles, which she guessed were the bedrooms. The two boys shot off into one of the rooms and the door was slammed shut.

'Tea or coffee?' Jodi asked.

'Coffee, please,' Pippa said, sitting at the kitchen table. Jodi pulled a cup from a mug tree and banged the milk carton on the table. Rooting in a cupboard she paused and pulled her fingers through her hair. 'It looks like I've no sugar,' she said. 'Sorry, can you bear your coffee without it?'

'I'll gladly drink it black,' Pippa said waving a hand.

'I'm the least domesticated person you'll ever meet,' Jodi said. 'I know how to pick clothes off a hotel floor and sit in a catering truck and have food handed to me on set. Outside of that, I'm utterly useless!'

'How does your little boy manage?' Pippa grinned.

'Saul is probably a better cook than I am,' she said, nodding toward the corridor where he'd gone with his friend. 'Harry is improving all the time, but we tend to eat quite a lot of prepared meals, you know the high end ones from the supermarket?'

Pippa put the menu folder Lainey had carefully prepared onto the table, wondering if her sister ought to have bothered putting so much time into the details.

'Don't look so crestfallen,' Jodi laughed. 'I love eating when it's made for me and I definitely know what I like!'

'Sure,' Pippa smiled as she thought – note to self, don't betray your emotions, especially to an actress.

As she showed Lainey's menu, with the goat's cheese, beetroot and toasted hazelnut salad, followed by lobster bisque and a main course of roast goose with potato and apple stuffing, pickled red cabbage and roast potatoes, Jodi looked thrilled.

'That sounds divine,' she said. 'So sumptuous yet nothing that will be unrecognisable or weird. My brother Tommy has to be one of the fussiest eaters I've ever come across. I reckon it's because we ate such appalling food as kids. It was either deep fried from the local chipper or a sandwich.'

Pippa accepted the coffee Jodi had made and took a sip. Not sure whether or not she should comment, she decided to remain silent and let Jodi do the talking.

'I grew up in one of the most dodgy places in Dublin,' Jodi explained. 'Your version of estate and mine are two different worlds. Yours has trees and fields, mine had burnt-out cars and drug pushers.'

'But you're a million miles from all of that now,' Pippa said. 'You're amazing. Everyone admires you.'

'Ah thanks, doll,' Jodi said.

They chatted about the timings for the wedding. Pippa said she didn't want to give too much away but that her family, particularly her mother, were putting everything into the décor and personal touches for the wedding.

'My first wedding was insane,' Jodi mused. 'My agent organised the entire thing. I didn't even choose my dress. It was sent to my hotel room by a courier. I literally took it out of the plastic, put it on and walked into the cathedral.'

'Wow,' Pippa said. 'I know lots of people would think that's wildly glam and so rock and roll, but I think I'd like to have a bit of fun trying stuff on . . .'

'I didn't really care,' Jodi said. 'I was like a puppet and my people decided what I did next.'

'But you loved Darius, right?'

'Darius is my best friend. He always will be. But we were both very young and naïve.'

'And Harry?' Pippa held her head to the side, wondering where he fit in. If Darius was still Jodi's best friend, what was Harry?

'Harry is different,' she said hugging herself and sighing happily. 'I found him all on my own. Nobody told me he was "suitable". There was nothing to link us apart from the fact he taught Saul for a year. He's real. He's not connected to my career nor does he think of me as anything other than Saul's mum, his girlfriend and of course a dreadful cook!'

Pippa laughed. She'd always assumed the fame thing was a blessing. Sure, she understood that it must be a pain trying to buy the newspaper in Spar if people were staring and accidentally walking into displays in shock. But Pippa had always dreamt of being the person who went to a store after hours and pointed at the things she liked . . . Or going to salubrious restaurants whenever she wished . . .

She'd settle for someone to do her ironing and change the bed linen once a week. But as Jodi chatted more and more openly, Pippa began to understand that being famous wasn't all sunshine and roses.

'At least I have the next few weeks off,' Jodi said. 'I can get ready for my wedding and enjoy our honeymoon in peace, before I have to start filming again. I'm having a hell of a time learning my next script. But it'll all come together in the end. I hope . . .'

'Where are you going on honeymoon?'

'Well, Harry and Saul think we're going to LA. Which we are, but not until we've spent a week in the Caribbean. A friend of a friend owns an island and I've hired the house there as a special surprise. If we go anywhere with other people in situ, it'll be a nightmare. Whatever about Saul, who is well used to people swarming both me and his father, Harry is still getting accustomed to having all the eyes in the room on us everywhere we go.'

'Are people generally nice to you?'

'Oh yes, I can count on one hand the times I've had oddballs being obnoxious. In general the fans are simply trying to say hello and have a picture taken or a body part signed.'

'Body part?'

'I went through a spate of having bare bums exposed to me while an indelible marker was poked up.'

'Was that after your famous beach scene?'

'You got it! And I wouldn't mind but that infamous tattoo they did the close-up on wasn't even real! But as a result I had more butt cheeks shoved at me than you'd believe!'

'Now that's gross,' Pippa giggled. She tasted her coffee and wasn't quick enough to hide the gagging face she pulled.

'I told you! I'm the world's worst cook. I can't even make coffee!'

Jodi's mobile rang and she looked suddenly anxious. Excusing herself she answered it.

'Hello? I see. Well I can't be there on Monday I'm afraid . . . I see . . .' She looked at her watch and exhaled. 'I might have to bring my son . . . OK, that's kind of you . . . Yes . . . I understand.'

She hung up and apologised profusely to Pippa, saying she had to take the call because it was the wedding dress shop. Her dress was being custom-made by a well-known eccentric couture designer.

'It's a gorgeous bodice with antique lace skirting and I have to get to them now for a fitting or they can't guarantee it'll be done in time for the wedding. I'm not around tomorrow, which is their cut-off point.'

'I could mind Saul and his mate if you want to shoot off,' Pippa offered. 'I could even bring them around to Huntersbrook. Mum is there. She knows what to do with kids, so you'd be guaranteed he wouldn't be poisoned or maimed?'

'Would your mother mind?' Jodi asked. 'Because if she would, I'd love you to come with me to the fitting. Nobody has seen the dress bar Darius. But that was only the mock-up version made from cheap lining. I'd love another female opinion.'

Pippa thought she was going to expire. Her hands shook as she dialled Holly's mobile number.

Needless to say, her mother was slightly astonished but very happy to oblige. She explained that she was up at the kitchen in Huntersbrook baking and she'd be thrilled to have the boys' company. So they put the children in the car and Pippa folded herself into the passenger seat of Jodi's Mini. Trying not to yelp with the thrill of it all, Pippa made idle conversation until they arrived at the door of Huntersbrook. Holly came out to the door.

'Hello boys,' Holly said. 'Maybe you two would like to help? I'm making special decorations as well as mince pies.'

'I love baking,' said Saul. 'Do we get to taste any of the pies?'

'Of course,' Holly laughed.

'Thanks dude,' Jodi said to Saul. 'I promise I won't be long. But I know you'd be so bored at the dress shop.'

'That sounds totally girly, doesn't it?' Holly said wrinkling her nose. The boys laughed.

'Thank you so much,' Jodi said sincerely. 'You're being amazing. I don't think I'll want to leave after the wedding. If you decide you'd like rent-an-extended-family, we'll gladly apply!'

Holly laughed and reiterated she was delighted to help any time.

'Oh by the way,' Jodi said as she and Pippa walked back to the Mini. 'I love the menu, Holly. I give the green light for every part. It sounds divine. As Pippa will tell you, I can't even boil water. So I know it's going to be perfect.'

Holly looked exhausted but a lot happier as Pippa waved as she sat back into the car. As they zoomed down the drive and out towards Dublin, Pippa couldn't help asking a few questions.

'Did you always know you were going to be a household name?'

'No!' Jodi laughed. 'I'm still waiting for a great hand to come from the sky as I'm tapped on the shoulder and told I'm living someone else's life.'

'That'll never happen,' Pippa said. 'You're far too beautiful and talented. You were born to shine, Jodi. The entire world can see that.'

'Aw thanks for saying that, Pippa, but believe me it took me until very recent times to have any real belief or pride in who *I* am. I knew a long time ago that I'd gained respect as an actress, but there were a lot of things going on in my head that needed addressing.'

'It's crazy,' Pippa mused. 'But I assumed your life is perfect. That money, fame and a cool job meant you didn't have the usual hang-ups us ordinary people are plagued with.'

'Uh, if only,' Jodi grinned.

They drove on in silence for a moment as both women tried to digest the fact that the grass isn't greener on the other side.

'I've never done this,' Jodi said sounding suddenly shy. 'I've never gone somewhere with a friend. The only other women I know are parents of Saul's friends. But we're kind of thrown together because of the kids.'

'It must be hard to trust people,' Pippa mused. ''Cause everybody wants a piece of you, right?'

Jodi nodded. 'As I said, there's usually an angle.'

'I hope you feel comfortable with me. You know I have an

angle! I want you to come and support Huntersbrook. So that's all out in the open!'

Jodi drove on and glanced across at Pippa.

'I felt a connection with you the second we met. You were slightly different though. Obviously I didn't know you. But you were noticeably edgy.'

'That may have had something to do with the fact I was meeting Jodi Ludlum,' she said.

Jodi grinned and drove on.

'That's a lie actually,' Pippa rubbed her face. 'Can you keep a secret?'

'I'm the queen of secrets, believe me, Pippa. I don't tell anybody anything. Most things I say are splashed across the covers of magazines. That probably sounds totally rock'n'roll to you, but it can be wearing. My world is a stage 24/7.'

Pippa proceeded to tell Jodi about Missy and the pressure she'd been under to take coke and keep her happy.

'That's horrible,' she sympathised. 'Now I understand why you said that thing about being in a bad place. To be honest, I know how it feels. I had a boyfriend years ago, Mac, and he used me too. It was more my money he abused. He did try his best to get me into the drug scene, but he was fighting a losing battle with that. My childhood was destroyed by drink and drugs, so neither ever held any appeal for me. Not even Mac could convince me of anything different.'

'How did you break the cycle?' Pippa asked agog.

'I had to release myself from him. He was my addiction, Pippa. No matter what he did or how badly he behaved, I still thought I loved him.'

'And now?'

'Now, I look back and I feel such hurt and sadness in my heart. I honestly thought he loved me as much as I loved him.

He was the first person to take an interest in me as my star was rising. We were both Irish and trying to make it abroad.'

'So there *was* a connection. You didn't dream that part.'

'Mac loved me at first. I know he fell for me hook, line and sinker. But he couldn't handle it when I hit the big time. I tried to take him with me, Pippa. I would've given anything for him to support me and stay by my side and be my *person*.'

'But he was too caught up with the dodgy stuff?'

'Yup.'

'Where is he now?'

'Still knocking around London. I see him the odd time. He's one of those guys who manages to get invited to wrap parties and other stuff. It used to leave me traumatised when we bumped into one another. But Darius, and now Harry have shown me that I deserve better. More than that, I can see Mac for what he really is. He's not the boy I fell in love with. He's selfish to the core. He doesn't even care about himself, let alone anyone else. He's his own worst enemy. He's turned into a bitter and sad person who feels the world has dealt him a raw deal.'

'That's heavy,' Pippa said. 'I'm still a little dubious of Danny,' she admitted. 'I can't talk to my sister or my mum about this. They'd be horrified if they knew what he was up to when I met him. I feel as if I'm lying to them all the time. They've taken him under their wing. Dad and Joey think he's a great guy.'

Having explained the situation and how he'd made such an effort to change his lifestyle, Pippa was relieved by Jodi's reaction.

'Pippa, he's doing what I longed for Mac to do. He's changing. He's turning his life around. He has a job and now he's attempting to become healthier. He wants to be with you and why wouldn't he?'

Pippa grinned. They'd arrived at the design studio, so Jodi led the way.

'Hi, this is my friend Pippa,' Jodi said.

The three designers were huddled together, eyes shining as they looked from Jodi to Pippa. Feeling like a bit of an imposter, Pippa tried to look as if she'd been hanging out with Jodi Ludlum all her life.

'We have your skirt and bodice in the fitting room down the end of the shop if you'd like to try it on.'

Jodi tugged Pippa's hand so she followed and stood dumb-founded when she saw the outfit.

'Oh wow,' Pippa said, forgetting totally about the onlookers. 'Jodi, it's magnificent.'

Afraid to actually touch anything, Pippa gravitated toward it and stared.

'You're going to be like a fairy princess. It's the most beautiful thing I've ever seen. I'll wait out here,' she said as she pulled the thick velvet curtain across to give Jodi some privacy.

Jodi slipped it on and shuffled out clutching the front of the bodice and asked Pippa to close it up.

'I can see why this is called couture. The finish is outstanding. If this fabric was sent to a high street designer, they'd make four dresses out of it.'

Expertly, Pippa criss-crossed the ribbon at the back and pulled the bodice together, ensuring it was sitting correctly at the front.

'Can you breathe?'

'Just about,' Jodi giggled.

The ladies led her to a podium where she could stand in front of a three-way mirror.

'What do you think?' one of the designers asked tentatively.

'I love it,' Jodi said. 'It's exactly what I had in mind. Thank you all for everything!'

'We need to put the finishing touches to the hem,' said one of the ladies.

'There's a tiny bit of edging to be finished just here also,' Pippa said, examining it.

'Ah you see, I told you I needed your expert eye,' Jodi said winking at Pippa.

By the time they got the two-piece back onto the hanger, Jodi was beginning to panic about Saul. Pippa called Huntersbrook and spoke to her mum. It seemed they were all baking and Saul had a surprise for Jodi, which had only just gone into the oven.

As they drove back toward Wicklow, Pippa quizzed Jodi about the rest of her wedding outfit. It turned out she hadn't organised shoes or any clothing for the honeymoon for that matter.

Pippa offered to pick some things out and bring them over to the house next time Jodi was at home.

'Would you do that for me?' Jodi asked.

'Of course. I know the exact pair of shoes you need, too. I can't afford them and clearly you can. So it'll get that out of my system!'

Pippa instructed her to drive around to the back of the house and the kitchen door. The boys were very surprised when they landed in the back door.

'Glad to see you're using the family entrance,' Holly said with an easy smile. 'Wait until you see what these fabulous boys have made!'

Saul and his friend looked so incredibly pleased with themselves, it brought a tear to Jodi's eye.

'Thank you,' she whispered to Holly as she hugged her. Saul had made a very oddly shaped mound out of scraps of pastry with jam oozing out.

'It's a baked brain!' he said giggling. 'It was Holly's idea.'

'Guilty as charged,' she said. 'I used to do them with Joey way back when. He didn't think it was macho to be baking, so I'd invent things that sounded disgusting and he'd go for it every time! Somewhere along the way he left home able to cook basic food.'

Jodi hugged Saul and promised to eat some of the baked brains later at home. They chatted for another while before Jodi reluctantly told the boys they'd better get going.

'Don't be a stranger,' Holly said. 'There's always someone around if Saul wants to come and play. He's such a great boy.' She turned to Saul. 'If you and your mummy are our friends, which you are, that means you have a free pass here any time. Besides you need to learn how to make eyeballs in swamp mud.'

'Ew!' Saul and his friend giggled.

'They're dumplings in beef stew but we prefer to call them eyeballs in swamp mud.'

'Really can I come back?' Saul said. 'Mum, it's so much fun here. Wait until you see the Christmas tree too. Would it be all right if I show her?' Saul asked.

'Sure,' Holly laughed. They all went to the living room and Holly rushed to flick on the fairy lights. 'I don't leave them lit all the time or the tree would dry out too much.'

Jodi floated toward it utterly entranced. 'It's magical. I can't believe I'll be having my wedding here.' She turned around. 'I'm so lucky to have found you all. I just know you're going to make this the most amazing day of my life.'

Pippa walked her out to the car and said she'd let her know about the shoes and clothes. The spring and summer ranges were beginning to come in, but none of it was out on shelves yet. Brianna would be ecstatic to hear that Pippa was already selling stuff directly from the stock room. Pippa of six months ago would've been in the staff room with her phone, showing people photos of Jodi's house, car and the star herself. But Pippa knew Jodi trusted her. She knew the conversation they'd shared today was special. Unbelievable as it seemed, Pippa had a feeling she and Jodi were going to remain good friends long after this wedding was over.

'Thanks for listening to me earlier,' Pippa said shyly. 'I feel so much better about Danny. I was nervous I was making a really stupid judgement. I'm sick of messing up and being the errant toddler of the family. I suppose I need to learn to trust my instincts too. The other messing in the beginning was a step too far and I think it's left me feeling scared.'

Jodi let the boys climb into the back of the Mini as she leaned on the car door.

'If you weren't a good judge of character and you didn't give a toss, you'd be sprawled on some random sofa right now, hung over and wondering how you were gonna drag your sorry ass out clubbing again tonight. You dipped your toe in the water. You realised that stuff was a one-way ticket to nowhere-land and you retreated. You're a smart girl, Pippa. You like your thrills and that's OK. But you're nobody's fool.'

'Thanks, Jodi,' she said hugging her. 'I really enjoyed today. I'll be in touch.'

'I had the best time,' Jodi said sincerely. 'See you during the week with the shoes and stuff. Thanks for being there for me today, Pippa. I really appreciate it.'

As she drove away, Pippa ran back inside. Sleet had begun to fall and she knew exactly where she was headed. Operation mince pie and pomander was done and dusted and Holly was pouring tea as Pippa joined her.

'Tell me everything,' Holly said.

Pippa perched on the Aga and accepted a mug of tea.

'She's such a surprise, in the nicest possible way,' Pippa said. 'She's so down to earth. No bullshit. No diva strops. I can't believe she's stayed so sane.'

'Her life must be unimaginable really,' Holly said. 'Yet she has done a fine job of raising that boy. He's a dote.'

'She is quite simply the coolest person I've ever met,' Pippa said. And best of all, the coolest person she'd ever met had given Danny her stamp of approval.

Joey

JOEY EMERGED FROM HIS ROOM AND ARRIVED down to the kitchen looking like he'd crawled out from under a rock.

His chat with Matt in the pub the night before had been just the ticket. By their fourth hot whiskey, both men had made a pact that they were going to assume their roles as real men.

Come hell or high water, Joey was going to try and win Skye back.

He said his goodbyes to the family and drove at top speed to Dublin.

As he approached their apartment, Joey's mouth was dry. What if Skye hated him now? What if she wanted to go and live with her crazy mother and he'd never see his baby?

He fumbled with his key in the lock and eventually got inside the apartment.

'Joey,' she said emerging from the bedroom. 'You scared the life out of me.'

They made their way into the living room and he took her hands and sat her down on the sofa.

'I've been such an idiot, Skye,' he said.

'Joey,' she said. 'We've gone past the point where this is anyone's fault. I'm not willing to spend the rest of my life trying to compete with your job.'

'Please!' he said silencing her. 'I've had time to think. Time to really see what I want. I've never had such clarity in my life. I need *you*, Skye. You make me complete. I've been focusing on all the wrong stuff. I'm sorry I was such an ass at the black-tie ball. I should've told snobby Janet to sod off. I should've stuck up for you.'

Skye began to cry.

'I'm so ashamed at how much of a pig I've been that none of my family bar Matt even know we're not talking. I couldn't bear to tell them.'

'Really?' she said looking brighter. 'I was wondering why none of them have even called me . . .'

'They'd have my head on a stick if they knew. They all adore you, Skye. You're one of us. All that's missing is the piece of paper to make it all official.'

'I'm never going to be a lady-who-lunches,' she said firmly.

'And I don't want you to be,' he reiterated. 'I want my beautiful, sensitive and real Skye. I love you the way you are. Will you marry me again, Skye?' he asked as he pulled the ring out of his pocket.

She nodded as her beautiful smile lit up his heart.

'Did Holly know I gave Maggie's ring back?' she asked looking nervous.

'Nobody except Matt knows a thing. And believe me he's not about to tell anyone.'

Agreeing they'd go down to Huntersbrook the following day, the couple settled down to a quiet day in the apartment grateful to be back in each other's arms.

❄

At the farmhouse, Lainey was in the kitchen making a cup of tea. Matt asked Jacob to give them a bit of privacy so he had taken Ely to visit Holly and Paddy. The house was quiet.

'Hey,' he said walking over to her. 'We need to talk, Lainey.'

'I know,' she said looking to the floor.

'I feel as if we're drowning . . . You're shutting me out and I don't know how to reach you any more. Anytime I try to say something you take it the wrong way or storm off. I'm on your side, Lainey. I swear.'

'I know you are,' she said as tears seeped down her cheeks. 'Mum came over last night.'

'Really?'

'Yeah, while you were at the pub. We had a really tough but good chat. I think we're going to be able to find a new common ground. She admitted she had been blaming me for her postnatal depression.'

'Really?'

'She didn't do it on purpose,' Lainey added. 'But it's taken us both until now to admit that we've both behaved dreadfully toward one another. We have to let old hurts heal and try to move forward.'

'Wow. I'm delighted,' Matt said. 'But you and I have something weird going on too. What are you thinking? Do you still love me?'

'Oh Matt,' she said raising her hand to touch his face. 'I've never loved you more. But I was going to ask you the same question. I'm afraid . . .'

'Of what exactly?'

'That you've been left with a barren wife who can't give you any more children. This isn't what you signed up for. I'm not what you signed up for. What if you feel hard done by?'

'Jesus, Lainey, what kind of man do you think I am?'

'I . . .' She didn't quite know how to answer.

'Lainey, all I want is you and Ely. I can't believe you think I don't love you.'

'I don't . . . Oh God . . . this is really silly, isn't it? I've been totally mad lately.'

'Can we say it's all down to the shock and surgery?' he grinned. 'Can we kiss and make up?'

'You bet,' she said happily.

Skye

PIPPA WOKE EARLY AND PHONED DANNY.

'How are you?' she asked.

'OK,' he said edgily. 'I miss you. I wish I could come and see you.'

'So do I,' she said with a smile.

'You do? But you saw me yesterday, you weirdo!'

'I know, but I've been dithering. I think I'm a bit afraid of what I feel and I'm scared of messing up.'

She put the phone down and laughed. Danny said he was already getting into his car and would be with her in record time. Knowing he wasn't in possession of the Bat mobile, Pippa looked up in surprise as the back door opened.

'Morning all,' Joey boomed as they came in.

'Hey Pippa,' Skye said.

'Hi you two,' Pippa said. 'I've just put the phone down to Danny. He's on his way and I knew it couldn't be him already! How are you both this fine day?'

'You're in a good mood,' Joey grinned. 'And we're here to add to the jovial atmosphere. We've just been with Mum and Dad . . .'

'Yeah?' Pippa raised an eyebrow.

'Skye and I are having a baby!'

'No way!' Pippa shouted.

'Yes way,' Skye said. 'I'm nearly five months pregnant.'

'What?' Pippa said. 'You've been keeping that a secret for a long time.'

'We'll explain later, but it was all a bit of a shock and we were having a rough time so we decided to keep it to ourselves for a bit. In light of Lainey's surgery, it didn't seem like the right time to mention anything . . .'

'Oh I'm sure Lainey will be so happy for you, Skye,' Pippa insisted as she hugged and kissed and congratulated them.

'I'm going to pop over to Lainey on my own,' Skye said. 'I'm hoping she'll take it well, but I think it'd be fairer if she hears our news quietly. I really don't want to upset her.'

'Fair enough,' Pippa said.

Joey kissed Skye and she let herself out the back door.

She was incredibly nervous as she made her way across the well-worn path to the farmhouse.

She could see Lainey through the window in the kitchen with Ely and Matt. Knocking on the door, Skye felt butterflies in her tummy. What if Lainey yelled at her and told her to get out?

'Skye!' Lainey said hugging her. 'How are you? Gosh, I feel like I haven't seen you for ages. I'm sorry I haven't been in touch. There's been a lot going on,' Lainey rambled. 'Come in and sit down. Tea?'

'Ah no thanks,' she said, as her voice cracked with nerves.

'Ooh, you look pale, love. What's up?'

Matt looked over and winked and Skye remembered Joey had told him the news.

'I might go over to Huntersbrook with Ely. Holly rang to say there's a wine and mince pie thing on tonight for Mrs Hogan's son. We need to sort a few bits. Joey and I are moving a couple of round tables into the hallway for Holly.'

'OK,' Lainey said looking mildly perplexed. Matt passed Skye and hugged her briefly.

'Congratulations. I'm so happy for you,' he whispered. She squeezed his hand gratefully.

As soon as he left, taking a babbling Ely with him, the kitchen seemed suddenly quiet.

'Lainey, I'm really nervous,' Skye confessed. 'I need to tell you something but the last thing I want is to upset you.'

'OK,' Lainey said cagily.

'The thing is . . .' Skye hesitated. 'I'm pregnant.'

There was silence for a moment as Lainey computed what Skye had said. Rushing forward, she hugged her.

'Oh Skye,' she cried. 'I'm not upset,' she said. 'Gosh, I've been such a tyrant lately, everyone seems to think I've no good will left in me.'

'Nobody thinks that,' Skye said. 'But I was so scared that you'd hate me. It's hardly the best timing for me to appear with a bump.'

'Yes it is,' Lainey said firmly. 'This little person will be the most amazing thing. He or she will be Ely's little cousin and my niece or nephew. It's wonderful news, Skye!'

'Thank you for understanding,' Skye said sobbing with relief. 'Ooh I'm so emotional all the time,' she grinned. 'It's a crazy feeling, isn't it?'

'Yes, but it's wonderful,' Lainey said. 'Now will you have tea?' Skye nodded.

Over the next hour the two girls chatted ninety to the dozen.

'Oh I've missed our chats,' Skye said as she relaxed. 'I've been so scared and lonely over the past while. I'd nobody to turn to and I was really beginning to convince myself that I'd be raising this child alone.'

Skye filled Lainey in on all the awful arguments.

'I can certainly relate,' Lainey said with a sigh. 'I've been falling out with everyone it feels like. I've patched up with Matt, now, and Mum and I are going to work really hard at finding a new "us".'

Skye laid her hand over Lainey's. 'I don't know what went on in the past, Lainey, but to me it's plain that right now, today, Holly loves you to bits. You might drive her scatty at times,' she said, smiling, 'but she's devoted to her three children.'

'Skye, you're too nice,' Lainey said, shaking her head. 'You're going to be the most amazing mum.'

❄

Pippa met Danny out the front of the house and climbed into his car.

'What's happening?' asked looking puzzled.

'The fecking house is crawling with people. Drive. Up the back field to the wooded part. We need to get this car rattling and rolling!'

Danny didn't wait to be told twice as they shot off in the direction of the love zone.

❄

As the daylight eventually faded, Holly went about turning on fairy lights and grouping large red pillar styled candles. Once lit, along with the roaring fires, the place took on the most magical and festive aura.

'Do you think I've overdone it with the pomanders out here?' she asked Paddy, sniffing the air loudly.

'It does smell a little bit like marmalade now that you mention it,' he said seriously. Holly spun around and caught him smirking.

'You're not teasing me are you, Paddy?' she laughed.

'Darling, would I dare?'

A knock on the door sent her flurrying forwards waving her arms.

'Jeez, she's off,' Joey said appearing down the stairs.

One by one the local orchestra members filed in and made for the bottom of the stairs where they proceeded to set up.

'I didn't know you'd organised music,' Joey said with his hands on his hips.

'Ah Mrs Hogan has looked after everyone over the years. I mentioned tonight to a few people and hey presto, we've a couple of surprises for her.'

The orchestra had agreed to be paid in pies. Lainey had half a dozen wrapped for each of them in cellophane tied with festive red ribbons.

This was turning out to be a real community event. Mrs Hogan had been there for all of the local inhabitants at different times over the years. She'd never bat an eyelid at anyone knocking on the door of her flat above the shop looking for eggs or milk late at night. Any time they were stuck for an ingredient, she'd oblige. She gave so much of her time to others over the years. She always supplied the biscuits at the community centre without so much as a whisper for anything in return. She'd hand out home grown shamrock on safety pins at St Patrick's Day and tiny chocolate eggs to the children at Easter. Every year without fail she raffled a hamper that sat on the counter for Christmas, giving the proceeds of the ticket sales to a worthy recipient.

The whole village knew she was heartbroken when her only child, Owen, had been forced to take a job in Australia. The sole hint that she wasn't happy were her red-rimmed eyes and the defeated expression she sometimes couldn't manage to hide. She never complained and certainly didn't create an atmosphere where folk were loath to go into her shop for fear she'd moan.

As the weeks had turned to months she seemed to accept Owen wasn't coming home. Three years ago she'd proudly showed photos of Owen's wedding to anyone who asked after him. When the pictures of the baby scan came up on her Facebook page, she beamed with delight.

'I know it's only a scan, but I think it looks like Owen.' Her laptop was kept behind the single cash desk in her mini market and she'd check it constantly to see who had 'liked' the latest photo of Scott. She mastered Facebook and moved seamlessly onto Skype, where she'd chat to Owen as if he were in the chair beside her.

'Wouldn't you go to Australia?' Holly asked her once.

'How could I leave the shop, Holly? Besides I don't have the money or the energy to get there and back alone. It's not London or America. If my Michael is looking down on me, as I suspect he is, he'll send our son back to me some day.'

Holly also believed that good things came to those who wait and nobody was more delighted than she was when Owen finally announced that the plastics manufacturing firm he worked for were opening a branch back home in Ireland. Although they wouldn't be living in Wicklow, the new motorways meant they'd only be a two-hour drive from Mrs Hogan's door.

Owen was what the girls of the village deemed 'a catch'. Clever in school and witty as Oscar Wilde, his biggest asset, in Pippa's opinion, had always been his eyes.

'There was more to him than bedroom eyes,' Lainey giggled.

'Not where I was standing,' Pippa said. 'God he was gorgeous. He has one of those faces that would look amazing whether he was male or female.'

As Mrs Hogan, Owen, his wife Cindy and baby Scott arrived in the door of Huntersbrook that evening, a lively version of *Mary's Boy Child* struck up.

'God dang it he looks even better than I remember,' Pippa hissed to Lainey. 'Look at that face and tell me he's not divine.'

'He's pretty dishy,' Lainey agreed.

'You two are a disgrace,' Joey said poking his head in between his sisters. 'You're like two vultures waiting to pounce on your prey.'

'Go on out of that, Joey,' Lainey scoffed. 'I'm married, Pippa is half way there. We're only doing a live version of Google.'

'Ogle more like it,' Joey smiled. 'Still it was awfully considerate of him to bring such a fox of a wife for us boys to look at.'

The girls followed Joey's gaze to the tall bronzed woman with full wavy blonde hair who was cheerfully shaking hands with people. In her arms baby Scott was calmly looking about seeming perfectly at ease with all the new faces.

'Beautiful child too,' Pippa commented. 'They're *the* beautiful people sent to give the village a lift!'

The hallway was filled to the brim so guests spilled into the living room where the tree and decorations were complimented non-stop.

'We all help,' Holly said proudly. 'The men get the tree and our Joey hung the huge baubles and bells in the hall. The girls do the more intricate work. We love it.'

They were thrilled to see the mince pies disappearing as people munched happily. Lainey had told Holly that there was no need to get chef Sally involved and capably made a couple of trays using a recipe she'd tweaked herself. She'd added orange rind to the mix, thinking it might go with the mince-meat.

'How on earth did you make that pastry, Lainey?' Sandra from the village asked. 'No matter what I do, mine looks and tastes like leather.'

'It's easy when you know how,' Lainey insisted. 'I'm about to do a cookery course actually. I've always loved cooking and I'm hoping to take over the catering here at Huntersbrook.'

'Well I wish you'd teach me some time.'

'Um, me too,' said another lady. 'You wouldn't consider doing a few classes in the New Year, would you?'

'Ah no,' Lainey laughed. 'I'm only starting out. I'm hardly in a position to teach!'

'I'd beg to disagree,' the woman argued. 'I think you're gifted at baking.'

Lainey thanked them and walked over to Matt, who was ladling mulled wine into paper cups.

'OK, love?'

'Yeah,' she said. 'Some of the ladies have given me an idea.' She explained what they'd asked for and Matt nodded, immediately agreeing.

'We could easily set up some classes. Either in the kitchen or out in the marquee. There's a gas hob in the shed that would be perfect for demonstrating on.'

'Let's wait and see how it all goes,' Lainey said. 'I'll have to be pretty on the ball and take it all in on my course or it won't work.'

'I've no doubt you'll manage if I know you,' Matt said. Lainey grinned, thrilled at how project Huntersbrook was constantly evolving.

After a while Lainey got chatting with Owen and Cindy and they turned out to be a really fun and friendly couple. There was a matter of weeks between Scott and Ely, so they arranged to hook up over the next few days.

'I'm delighted to meet another Mum,' Cindy said. 'I've left my sister behind in Australia. We're really close and I don't know how I'll survive without her.' She took a deep breath and tried to steady herself. 'Still, this is a new venture for us all and I'm excited about our life together in Ireland.'

Lainey thanked her lucky stars that her own family was in such close proximity. She couldn't bear the thought of having to leave her family. Lainey couldn't imagine being without Pippa.

Mrs Hogan made her way over to the base of the staircase and spoke with the musical director. The music ceased as she waved happily and appealed for silence.

'Sorry to interrupt, folks,' she said. 'I'll only speak for a moment. Thank you all for coming this evening. This is a moment I've prayed for and longed for, ever since Owen got on that plane five years ago. Not only has he returned but he's brought Cindy and Scott too. I hope you will all make them welcome and let them know how thrilled we are that they've agreed to join our community.'

Paddy took to the microphone next.

'Before we ask the band to resume with some more delightful Christmas music, Jacob and I would like to invite you all to step outside for a few moments.'

Holly looked at Lainey, Matt, Pippa, Skye and Joey in confusion.

'Don't ask me,' Joey said holding his hands up.

The crowd filed out the side door in the kitchen to see what was awaiting them.

The once clutter-filled shed was dimly lit with white outdoor fairy lights. Inside was the most attractive live crib imaginable.

'The only fake parts are the people,' Jacob said. 'But as you can see, we've modelled them as best we could.'

Mary, Joseph and the baby Jesus were fashioned from straw, just like Jacob's scarecrows. But his attention to detail was jaw-dropping.

'Mary's cloak looks familiar,' Holly laughed as she spotted the pale blue duvet cover she couldn't find the week before. The donkey, sheep and cows all seemed perfectly delighted with their new home as they chewed on straw while lazily gazing at the delighted onlookers.

'The crib will be open every afternoon between now and Christmas,' Jacob announced. 'All donations will be gratefully received, with the money raised going to Wicklow's under-privileged children's fund. We'll buy toys which we'll distribute on Christmas Eve.'

Instantly the guests began to toss coins and notes into the bucket Paddy and Jacob had attached to the front of the shed.

The biting cold wind sent people back into the house, where they all huddled around fires and enjoyed the music as the band struck up with a medley of well-known Christmas tunes.

'I've been thinking,' Paddy said to Holly. 'We might be wise to have a couple of kegs installed. One of Guinness and one of lager.'

'I see,' Holly smirked. 'It could become Paddy's bar, open for business three hundred and sixty-five days a year eh?'

'Why not?' he grinned.

'You're a good man, Paddy,' she said wrapping her arms around his waist. 'That's a lovely thing you and Jacob did out there. I'm sure there'll be a decent amount raised for the kids too.'

'It's nice to be nice,' he said. 'It was a good bonding session for Jacob and me too. He's been ever so good to our Lainey and I didn't want him thinking that goes unnoticed.'

The party went on until the wee hours of the morning as the locals reminisced on the many happy evenings they'd spent at Huntersbrook over the years. Between events and hunts, they all had happy memories of the Craigs' hospitality.

Holly was delighted to take several bookings for a whole range of events, from a sixtieth birthday to a christening as well as a spring wedding.

Even though they were mostly local bookings, all the people had expressed an interest in renting the house in its entirety.

'I'm a curious old beggar,' said Mr Lukas. 'If I'm having my daughter's wedding here, I'll take the opportunity to see what it feels like to wake up in this magnificent home. I'm dying to see the bedrooms.'

Holly and Paddy laughed, adoring his honesty.

'I'd do the very same if I were you,' Holly said. 'I'm one of those people who loves to see into other people's lives. I used to love that programme *Through the Keyhole* on the television years ago.'

As the last person left, Holly and Paddy pulled on their coats, linked arms and made their way down the drive to the gate lodge.

'I'm so looking forward to Christmas now,' Holly said. 'I've finally stopped feeling hollow in my heart about Huntersbrook. We're very fortunate and it'll serve me well to remember that.'

'Good for you, love. You and Lainey seemed to be getting on fine.'

'It was a bit awkward when she arrived over at first but I honestly think the worst is behind us. She's a great girl.'

Holly was always wide-awake after hosting a party. Paddy went on into bed and she began to add to the decorations she'd begun to hang in the gate lodge. It was all on a much smaller scale to Huntersbrook, but that didn't mean the pleasure was any less.

The new and modern feel to the place gave her a different canvas on which to work. She'd gone for colours that would be alien to the main house, such as raspberry pinks and bright clean turquoise. The non-traditional colours lifted the look of the gate lodge, making it seem almost trendy.

The big shopping centre in Wicklow had a discount store where she'd picked up a huge selection of baubles and swags for next to nothing. Her wreath wasn't finished, so she figured it would be just the thing to help her unwind. The base was done, so she picked up the green fuzzy circle and found the bag of glitzy treasures she'd bought to decorate it. Instead of the usual berries and tartan ribbon, she attached fairies and frosted fruits in bold colours. By the time it looked good enough to hang, Holly's eyes were heavy and peppery. Knowing it would only take Paddy a few minutes to hang it the following day, she laid it carefully on the kitchen table and stood back to admire her work. Huntersbrook had always dictated similar and very traditional pieces. Holly was enjoying embracing this new and alternative slice of life she and Paddy had been given.

For the first time, Holly could understand why her mother, Maggie, had absconded for a year in the winter of her life. It had been her widowed mother's job to keep the estate running at a profitable pace for so many decades. The news of her cancer had clearly prompted her to see things in a different light. She'd suddenly wanted to taste different foods, wines and inhale another type of air.

Holly hadn't seen past her own hurt and disappointment when her mother had skipped off into the Australian sunset. For a full year, Holly had actively encouraged the family to shun Maggie. Nobody bar Sadie had even kept in touch with her.

Regret and shame washed over Holly in a fresh wave of clarity. How ridiculously selfish she'd been. Not for the first time, she wished she could have that year over again.

'Now I understand, Mum,' she whispered into her reflection as she cleansed her skin and brushed her teeth.

As she remembered the good and the bad times with Maggie, she knew how fortunate she was to have another chance with Lainey. Holly climbed into bed, spooned her body around Paddy's and drifted into a calmer sleep than she'd had for quite some time.

Lainey

THE NEXT MORNING LAINEY WOKE TO FIND MATT sitting up in bed staring at her.

'Good morning,' she said with a smile.

'Hey,' he said as he pulled her into his arms.

'I'm lucky to be alive,' she said. 'I'm even luckier I don't have cancer. I know all of that and believe me I remember it each and every day, but every now and then it creeps up behind me and bites me. It's like a horrible nightmare that still scares me even though it's over.'

'I know, honey.' He sat around and faced her. 'I don't want to put any pressure on you here,' he began. 'But I've been doing a little research.'

'You have.'

Matt took a folder out from the chest of drawers. Lainey had noticed it when she was putting his T-shirts away, but hadn't thought much nor had she opened it. She trusted Matt and figured it was either work or something that didn't concern her.

As Lainey read the documents Matt looked incredibly nervous.

'It's about surrogacy,' she said in astonishment.

'Neither of us ever wanted Ely to be an only child. So I figured there was no harm in finding out the facts.'

'Wow,' she said. 'This place is in America and we can purchase a donor egg and use a surrogate mother.'

He nodded and filled her in on the details. Being an accountant, he'd worked out the cost right down to the price of the flights over. He'd need to go and donate sperm and then the IVF cycle would be conducted.

'We'd go back over when the baby or babies are due.'

Lainey looked at him in awe. 'I can't believe you've done all this groundwork.'

'I was worried you might be upset with me,' he said. 'It's literally just an option that we can keep in the back of our minds. Adoption can take years and years, while this would be so much quicker. When you said you felt like you'd cheated me, it tore my heart apart. I'm not suggesting this because I think you've done me out of more kids,' he said. 'But I think we'd be crazy not to look at our options before it's too late, that's all.'

'And if we opted for surrogacy, you would be the baby's biological father,' Lainey finished. 'So the baby would be Ely's brother or sister.'

Lainey sat and stared into space. This was such a massive thing to take on board, but instantly she felt something sparking in her heart . . . Hope.

'Obviously we need to talk about this lots more,' Lainey said. 'But I love this idea.'

'You do?' Matt looked so incredibly relived Lainey had to grab his ears and kiss him on the lips.

'Matt, imagine if we could have a brother or sister for Ely after all!'

'It could even be twins,' he said. 'If we opt to have more than one embryo implanted, we could have two babies.'

'Oh my God.'

Matt went on to explain that he'd been in contact with the clinic and should they wish to go ahead, they could travel to America at the end of January to get started.

'That soon?' Lainey said, eyes shining.

'I know that may feel dreadfully rushed,' Matt was quick to point out. 'But I figured if we decide to go down this road – and that's a big if . . . What's the point in waiting around? We were chatting about trying for another baby when you got sick. So if a natural pregnancy had happened, that's where we'd be right now.'

Deciding they would keep it to themselves for the moment, the couple hugged as if their lives depended on it.

'I have such an amazing feeling about this,' she said. 'I might have to tell Jules though,' she said. 'I can't tell nobody . . .'

He kissed her and got up to begin his day. As she walked down into the kitchen, Lainey flicked on the radio. She thought the music sounded more cheerful, the decorations they'd started to put up for Christmas were brighter and the atmosphere was electric. As Christmas drew ever closer, Lainey felt sure that she and Matt were headed for a lot of excitement in the coming year. From here on in, Lainey intended making each and every Christmas count. Now she was more determined than ever to make this one extra special for Ely. After all it could be his last one alone before he became a big brother.

Instinctively she grabbed the phone and called Jules.

'No way!' Jules said squealing with delight. 'Oh that is just the most inspired idea, Lainz. Matt is so clever. Good for him for going off and being proactive.'

'I know,' she said. 'He's such a good man, isn't he? I was being such a bitch and he says he really wanted to try and fix it all. We've agreed to think about it, but I honestly feel it's the most brilliant idea ever!'

'Oh I agree,' said Jules.

'So it's top secret for now,' Lainey reiterated. 'We're not telling the family until we're certain.'

'I hear ya. Mum's the word!'

Feeling the day simply couldn't get any better, Lainey was surprised when the landline rang the second she put it down.

'Hello?'

'Lainey, it's Mum.'

'Hi, how are you?'

'I'm well. Can you come over to Huntersbrook, please?'

Intrigued, Lainey pulled on a coat and made her way across. Jacob had taken Ely to his new favourite haunt – the indoor play area. It had been a resounding success the week before and Jacob had thoroughly enjoyed the other grandparents' company. So Lainey had the morning off.

As she walked into the kitchen at Huntersbrook, she was met with a glassy-eyed Holly.

'What the?'

'Look,' Holly said eagerly. 'It's us. You and me. We did have a relationship when you were a baby. See!'

Lainey pulled off her coat and began to sift through the albums and photographs her mother had unearthed. There were dozens of them. Some had Lainey gazing up at Holly and so many showed Holly kissing her baby's head and face.

'These are lovely,' Lainey said, stroking one showing her, Holly and Grandma. 'Mum, thank you for doing this.'

'It was for me just as much as you,' Holly admitted. 'I needed to know that I'd been some sort of a mother to you. I hated myself for thinking I'd never even tried. What scares me, Lainey, is that I don't remember much of this time. It all seemed like a big foggy mess.'

'I'm guessing it was.'

'You know, when I look at these it brings me back to that time. I remember standing in your room one morning. You couldn't have been more than a month old. You were crying with your arms flailing and you wanted to be fed. It was as if my feet were glued to the carpet. I longed to rush and pick you up. I knew that it would stop your tears. But I couldn't do it. Mummy barged past at high speed and grabbed you.'

'Did she make you feel bad for not being able to do it?'

'Oddly enough, no. She simply got on with it and allowed me to be in that no-man's-land. She did what she thought was best. But it was soul-destroying. I felt like I'd been wrapped in a thick coating of Clingfilm. I was in a horrible, lonely bubble where feelings couldn't penetrate.'

'I can't imagine how you must've struggled.'

'I wanted to feel something . . . Anything . . . Pain or pleasure. I wasn't actually fussy which one. But it was all . . . beige.'

'And when you had Joey it was different?'

'Only after two weeks. I went to the doctor and got medication. Slowly the fog cleared and I began to feel emotions once more.'

'And by then Grandma and I were a little twosome?'

'Yes. I had Joey and your father. Mummy had you. They were the teams and it seemed fair. Lainey, you've got to believe me. There was no malice in any of it. I did my best.'

Lainey suddenly thought of how she'd been feeling these past weeks. She'd been a dragon. She'd thundered about acting whatever way she saw fit.

'We're not that different, Mum,' she admitted. 'I'm not great at controlling my emotions. I need to learn some emotional manners actually.'

'You and me both, love . . . Let's not waste this second chance. Because that's what we've been given, you know?'

'I know, Mum.'

'I have so many regrets about Mummy. The year she went to

Australia . . . When she was battling cancer. I poisoned you all against her. I led the movement that dictated her punishment. Sadie was the only one who remained loyal.'

'Did I hear you taking my name in vain?' Sadie asked as she bustled through the door.

'Hello Sadie,' Holly said. 'I was just saying you stood by Mummy when we all turned our backs on her.'

Sadie looked at the photos and smiled.

'I had a very good reason for that,' she said matter-of-factly. 'Lainey knows. I told her while she was in hospital. But Maggie was my saviour once upon a time.'

'Why, because she employed you?' Holly asked.

'Not only that. She helped me when I returned from the mother and baby home after the nuns took my daughter.'

'What?' Holly's face drained of colour. 'Sadie, I had no idea.'

'No, pet. Nor did I want you to. It was better that way. Or so I thought. In those days talking wasn't allowed. We were to brush all our problems under the carpet and never speak of them again. It's not healthy. It doesn't work and it only compacts the damage.'

They talked about Sadie's situation and how she'd suffered for years. How she'd never stopped thinking of Elizabeth and how Maggie had minded her.

'Why didn't you tell us Mummy was sick?' Holly asked.

'She asked me not to,' Sadie said. 'I asked her not to tell people about Elizabeth and she didn't. I owed her.'

'We need to learn from this, Lainey,' Holly said firmly. 'No more secrets and no more lies. We have to be open with one another from here on in. We need to make sure that we don't find ourselves on our death beds with regrets.'

'Maggie would be so proud of you both,' Sadie said. 'You're

doing the strong, brave and positive thing here. It's easier to bury things and never go back. Trying again is hard, but I've no doubt you'll both come out of this feeling even happier than you do now.'

Holly

Holly

THE DAY OF JODI'S WEDDING DAWNED. THE BUZZ about the house was fabulous and Holly couldn't wait to see the star in her gown. By all accounts it was utterly breathtaking. She and Pippa seemed to have formed a genuine friendship that was doing her youngest daughter the world of good. Needless to say, it was a marvellous thrill for her to have a famous friend, but Holly was pleasantly surprised. When Pippa oozed 'Jodi says this' or 'Jodi thinks that', it was always incredibly sound advice.

'For a young Hollywood star that girl has a sensible head on her shoulders,' Paddy commented. 'She's the best influence our Pippa could have.'

'I agree,' Holly said. 'It seems being ambitious and not acting the maggot has suddenly been made cool by Ms Ludlum! Who'd have thought it?'

Holly was delighted as Joey and Lainey helped her roll out her special red carpet.

'Mum, it's amazing,' Lainey giggled. 'I can't say I loved the idea in the beginning, but it's so festive and pretty, I don't see how Jodi and Harry won't love it.'

'I like to think it's a little bit of Hollywood right here in Wicklow!'

Paddy set out the chairs for the ceremony and Holly hung the large pomanders, made from grapefruits, on the side of each one.

'The smell from those is divine,' Lainey said. 'Nice touch with adding a tiny silk holly leaf to match the red carpet.'

'It's cute, isn't it?' Holly said standing back to admire her work.

The sound of voices coming from the staircase made Holly look up. Jodi's younger brother Tommy had arrived the day before with his wife and child. He and Harry seemed to bond instantly and Jodi had taken a management decision to stay at her own cottage the night before the wedding.

'You boys go to Huntersbrook and I'll see you when I walk down the aisle.'

Tommy was giving Jodi away but she was insisting on arriving in her Mini.

Darius and his agent were checking in today along with Jodi's agent and a small group of friends.

'Morning, folks,' Tommy said. 'We had a great sleep thank goodness. I was terrified we'd be like zombies at the wedding today.'

'Must be the country air,' Holly said. 'Come on into the kitchen and Sadie will look after you. Can I interest you all in a full Irish?'

Tommy looked at his wife Maisy and she nodded eagerly. Sadie was thrilled to have people to fuss over. Tommy's three-year-old boy Liam was a little character too.

'Dad says it's always cold here at Christmas time,' he said squinting up at Holly. 'Is that true?'

'Sure is,' she said. 'Where you live it's summer now, isn't it?'

'Yeah, and we go to the beach instead of wearing coats.'

'I hope you'll enjoy your Irish Christmas. We love it in this house and Santa loves stopping here.'

'Ah good on ya,' he said, making Holly laugh.

Ely was very pleased to see another little person and tagged after Liam like a lost puppy.

'I hope you don't mind Ely being your friend,' Lainey said as she stooped to talk to Liam. 'You're a big boy so he's very excited to see you.'

'I love making friends, don't I, Dad.'

'Liam is Mr Outgoing,' Tommy confirmed.

'He chats to everyone he meets,' Maisy said with a grin. 'Come on Ely, mate, why don't you have brekkie with us?'

Much to Lainey's delight, Ely took her hand and sat at the table.

'I'll keep an eye,' Sadie said.

Holly and Lainey went back to finish the last minute bits and pieces in the hall before moving to the dining room.

'I think I'll wait a while before lighting the scented candles,' Holly said over her shoulder as Lainey laid an ornate Christmas cracker at each side plate.

'Good plan,' Lainey said. 'Mum, could I ask your advice on something?'

'Of course,' Holly said, pausing and expecting her to ask about a garnish or something menial.

Nothing would have prepared her for what Lainey actually came out with. As she explained about the egg donation and the surrogacy, Holly was astonished.

'And it's really as easy as that? You go to America and it's all organised?'

'So it seems,' Lainey said. 'Matt and I have talked about nothing else since last week. Obviously the baby or babies if there are twins, will have no biological link to me. But Matt will be their dad.'

'And you don't have a problem with that?' Holly asked.

'Well the only other option would be adoption and obviously I'd have no biological link to that child either.'

'Being devil's advocate here. Would it be easier if you adopted and neither of you had any claim on the baby? It might even out the playing field more?'

'I can't imagine not loving any baby I'm given,' Lainey said as her eyes became glassy with tears. 'But if Matt is the father and I'm going to be the mum, literally from the day it's born, how could I go wrong? I don't want Ely to be on his own. If we have the opportunity to do this, I know I'd regret it for the rest of my life if I don't grasp it with both hands.'

'How will you afford it?'

'That's the thing,' she said. 'Jacob has money tucked away. It was meant to be for Matt's wedding.'

'But we had it here and your father wouldn't let him pay for so much as a bread roll,' Holly finished.

'Precisely. Jacob told Matt about the money and brought it up again while I was in hospital. He says it's there for us should we need it. Would it be wrong to accept his money, Mum?'

Holly walked over and tucked Lainey's hair behind her ear. 'Dad and I would go to the ends of the earth for all of you. Matt is Jacob's only son, so I would imagine he would lay down on a railway track for him. If we had the money we'd give it to you in a heartbeat too and we'd hope you'd accept it.'

The sound of Ely calling sent Lainey running. Holly straightened the table and looked at the room one last time. It looked incredibly festive with the crackers and poinsettia plants crowded onto the sideboard. Holly couldn't wait to hear the room filled with laughter. Once the wedding was over, they'd set it all up afresh for Christmas Day.

The idea of Lainey and Matt doing this surrogacy thing was a little shocking. Holly wished she didn't find it jarring, but she did. She'd get used to it though. Just like emails, smart phones, internet shopping and turning her childhood home into a venue. Holly would get it all set in her head and learn to accept it with time.

The thought of more babies joining their family was wonderful. Huntersbrook was only as sound as the family that inhabited her. She knew only too well how difficult it was growing up without siblings. In her heart of hearts, Holly would prefer if that didn't happen to little Ely.

Humming as she walked, Holly felt wonderfully privileged that Lainey had chosen to speak to her first. Pippa and Joey had always come to her with things over the years. But this was Lainey's first time and, boy, had she chosen a massive thing to discuss! Holly put her own reservations on the subject aside and focused on the positive side. She came to the conclusion that if it meant Matt and Lainey could extend their family, then it must be a marvellous thing.

❄

Skye was sitting in the living room being entertained by Ely and Liam. The little Australian boy was hilarious. He was telling Skye all sorts of things she honestly didn't need to know.

'Then my Daddy goes about the house with no shorts on and my Mum tells him he's going to have his winky bitten off by a crock.'

'Let's talk about Santa,' Skye suggested as she stifled a giggle.

'Santa!' Ely said clapping.

'Why are you fat in your belly?' Liam asked staring at her bump.

'Because there's a baby in there,' she explained.

'How will it get out?' Liam asked looking really dubious.

'I'll go to the hospital and they'll help me take it out,' she said.

'Will they use a tin opener?'

'I don't think so, but it'll be very exciting.'

'Is it a boy baby or a girl baby?'

'We don't know, Liam. We were going to ask the doctor to tell us but the baby was lying in a funny way so they couldn't see.'

'Did the doctor look down your mouth and see the baby?'

Lainey followed the giggles. Ely was sitting with his thumb in his mouth listening to all the chatter.

'Ely's having the best time,' Skye said. 'The two of them are so cute. Liam chats away and Ely gazes at him in such awe, he'd have you believe he's related to Spiderman.'

'It'll be lovely for him when your little one appears,' Lainey said easily. 'They'll keep one another company.'

❄

Pippa was dressed and ready for Jodi's wedding. Although the family had said they'd join her for a drink afterwards, they were all very much in work mode for the day. Just as she was closing her Swarovski crystal choker around her neck, Danny appeared. They were staying the night at the farmhouse.

'You look . . . like my pretty Pippa,' said Danny as he staggered over to give her a hug.

'Ugh, you stink. Where on earth were you walking, you're covered in some sort of black stuff.'

'I went for miles up the back of the top fields. It was gorgeous.'

'Well you look like you went for a roll in a cow pat,' she laughed. 'Get your ass into the shower and smarten yourself up or you can't come next, nigh or near Jodi's wedding.'

'Ay, ay captain,' he grinned as he made his way into the shower at the farmhouse. 'I never thought I'd swap the artificially induced buzz for natural adrenaline. I feel so much better these days. I can see why your family wanted to keep this place. If I'd grown up here, I wouldn't have stepped foot outside the land.'

'I'm only beginning to appreciate it properly now,' Pippa admitted.

'Sometimes we need to go away and experience another way

of doing things to really be thankful for what we've got,' Danny said.

Pippa shooed him into the shower and stepped into her shoes, topped up her lip-gloss and decided she'd do. She hoped Jodi enjoyed every minute of her special day.

The more she got to know Jodi, the clearer it all became. Successful, rich and enviable people got to be that way via sheer hard work. Nothing fell out of the sky and landed on people's laps. There had to be a certain amount of luck involved with life, but Pippa now understood that she was in charge of her own destiny. She wanted to do well. She wanted to travel the world and make something of herself. That was on the horizon now thanks to Jodi's offer.

But Pippa was also acutely aware that when push came to shove, the place she wanted to come back to, to rest her head, recharge her batteries and feel loved was right here, at home.

'Everything is ready to go next door, so I think I'm going to pop over to Jodi and make sure she's OK.'

Pippa shuddered as she turned up the heat in her car. It was one of those sharp frosty winter days. Everything was so crisply clear that it looked as if it had been magically enhanced by God's HD web designer from above. The sky was a decidedly odd shade, making her suspect snow.

❄

As she pulled up at Jodi's house, Pippa spotted Darius in the living room. Suddenly feeling she shouldn't have come, she was about to drive away when Jodi peeped out and waved. She looked so thrilled that Pippa sighed with relief and got out.

'Hello!' Jodi said pulling the door open. 'What a lovely surprise. Wow, you look amazing.'

'You are utterly divine in navy,' Darius said. 'So chic.'

Suddenly star struck and lost for words, Pippa stared. Darius was wearing a deep plum coloured velvet suit. On anyone else it would probably look a fright, but he was so gorgeous it blew her away.

'Ugh, I know,' Jodi said. 'He's disturbingly good-looking when he's dressed up. Give it an hour and you'll get used to him.'

They all laughed as Pippa had to force herself not to gawk. He really was like a Greek god.

Harry was a lovely guy and Pippa was very fond of him, but she honestly had no idea why Jodi was marrying him in place of Darius. She knew that was a dreadfully fickle thought, but she couldn't help it.

'I won't stay long, but I was worried you were on your own. I had visions of you contorting to close your bodice and arriving hassled and upset!'

'You're so sweet,' Jodi said as she opened her bathrobe to reveal the dress. 'I had the makeup artist help me. But that wasn't up to Darius's standards, so I've been laced up twice,' she grinned.

'I'm going to go on over to Huntersbrook,' Darius said. 'You sure you're all set, babes?'

'Totally,' Jodi said, kissing his cheek. 'See you shortly.'

'Good luck, darling girl,' he said hugging her tightly. Pippa had never felt more awkward.

'I should go too . . .'

'Oh no, Pippa, please stay,' Jodi begged. 'I'm so grateful you called over. I could do with someone to keep me sane. I can do massive movie sets, but walking down that hallway to Harry is just about one of the scariest things I'll ever have to do.'

Darius left and Jodi turned to look at Pippa clearly feeling she ought to say something significant. Hesitating she took Pippa's hand.

'Today isn't the right day. But sometime I'll explain the full story about Darius and I. I can almost read your mind. You're thinking why am I marrying Harry when I had him, right?'

Pippa nodded.

'It's complicated, Pippa. Really complicated. As I said, I'll tell you some time. But for now, I'm ready to get going. Harry is my *one*. He's what I've always waited for. Trust me.'

'I'm glad,' Pippa said. 'You deserve the very best, Jodi.'

'Ah,' she flapped her hands in front of her face. 'I don't want to cry. Will you lead the way?'

Pippa wished her well and promised she'd be there all day, should Jodi need her.

'I'm so glad we're friends,' she said.

'Me too, Jodi,' she laughed. 'I still feel like I'm living in a bubble any time I say your name. You'll have to bear with me. I don't have many cool super star friends.'

'That makes two of us,' Jodi jibed.

❄

As Pippa drove up the main drive of Huntersbrook the little tea-lights in jam jars were all flickering prettily. Pippa looked in the rear view mirror at Jodi, who was beaming in delight. They parked slightly to the side, so Jodi could go in the kitchen entrance. Tommy emerged and opened the car door, handing her the bouquet of red roses Holly had created.

A single photographer took pictures discreetly as Jodi manoeuvred out of her car. The ribbon matched the pomanders and the colours mirrored the carpet and décor. Pippa wished her well and adjusted the back of her skirt before sending her in through the kitchen.

'You were supposed to come down the stairs, so you can walk the aisle to the front door this way.'

The string quartet, assembled by Holly from the local orchestra once more, struck up as all the guests stood to gasp at how beautiful Jodi looked. In a vision of antique lace her dark curls and exquisite green eyes made it obvious to everyone there how she'd become a star. As Tommy took her arm proudly and walked her slowly toward the front door, the surrounding windows gave enough of a glimpse to the outside to allow the guests to see the snow that was softly falling.

Pippa found it hard to hold back her tears as Harry turned to kiss her. The ceremony was simple yet meaningful as the couple exchanged vows they'd written personally.

Paddy led the group into the living room as Matt, Joey and Jacob stacked the chairs and set them aside. By the time everyone had a glass in hand, the hallway was free for them to mingle once more.

'I know it'll be freezing, but could we have one photo on the front steps with the snow falling?' the photographer asked.

Delighted with the idea, Jodi and Harry went out the front as the guests peered out the front room window.

'Ugh, Steve McQueen couldn't come up with a better setting,' Darius said as he bit his knuckle. 'Stunning.'

The aromas from the kitchen were delicious as darkness fell. Holly lit the candelabras in the dining room and turned on the strings of fairy lights.

'Now that looks magical,' Paddy said happily. 'Fit for a movie star!'

The meal was perfect. Holly, Pippa and Lainey served the food guided by Sadie's careful direction. She was supposed to be in charge of Ely, but old habits die hard and she was enjoying being part of the occasion. Matt and Joey served drinks and cleared plates.

Skye sat at the kitchen table helping Sally with garnishes and making the plates look pretty.

'I feel so useless,' she said. 'I'm like a beach ball. It's not conducive to work I can tell you.'

'All the more reason to have four or five,' Lainey joked. 'That way Joey will have to mind you.'

Once the cake was cut and the speeches were finished, Jodi came into the kitchen and begged the family to come and join them.

'You've all been amazing,' Jodi said. 'I'm going to do an exclusive interview with *Society* magazine where I'll show-case Huntersbrook.'

'Seriously?' Lainey said.

'I'm in two minds about it though,' Jodi said. 'If I tell everyone about here, it'll probably be booked out next time I want to come!'

'You can come anytime you wish,' Paddy said. 'Even if you're not getting married! You're pretty much family at this point.'

The evening was so relaxed as the children played skidding on their knees in the hallway. Saul had two of his school friends and little Ely and Liam shadowed them in awe.

Skye discreetly went off to bed and Lainey took Ely at midnight. Matt and Jacob decided to go too, leaving the others to finish off. Holly and Paddy went home as soon as Jodi and Harry said they were off to bed.

'What time is brekkie in the morning?' Tommy asked.

'Whatever time you want to eat it,' Pippa said. 'It's up to you. You guys rule the roost.'

Joey didn't even try to wake Skye as he joined her in the room. She was out for the count and looked so angelic.

They were the only non-guests staying at Huntersbrook, so Joey would be on duty in the morning. He left the bedroom door open a crack so he could hear if any of the guests needed anything during the night.

Sadie was coming in to do breakfast and the wedding party

were all departing in the afternoon. Jodi had also announced that she was taking Tommy, Maisy and Liam on honeymoon with them.

'I haven't seen him for so long. I couldn't bear the thought of him being here while I was gone.'

Harry seemed perfectly happy with the scenario, saying he'd never been to the Caribbean and he didn't mind who accompanied them.

❄

As she climbed into bed Jodi couldn't have been happier. She'd enjoyed every second of her wedding day. It was light years away from her first wedding to Darius, when the world's press had been there clambering to get the most up-close and personal photo of the happy couple.

She couldn't fault any part of today. It was exactly as she'd dreamt it should be. Surrounded by the people she truly cared about, Jodi vowed this was how her life was going to be from here on in.

Gone was the girl who felt she had to prove herself. Gone were the lies that had shrouded her life for so long. Harry would keep her feet on the ground. He was funny, self-effacing and the most genuine guy she'd ever met.

The added extra was the friendship she'd struck up with Pippa. She was everything Jodi would've wanted to be as a child. Fair enough, she was now a world famous star and the envy of many. But to Jodi, Pippa was the one who had it all. Pippa came from a loving home with happy parents, supportive siblings and more togetherness than she'd ever known possible. This family weren't perfect by any stretch but Jodi could see that they'd gladly walk over hot coals to help one another.

Pippa had a wild streak that Jodi loved. She was nobody's fool and there would probably always be something happening in her life that called for arm waving and mild panic. But she had a heart of gold and Jodi knew she was totally trustworthy. The day she'd passed her that note with her mobile number scribbled on it, Jodi had hoped she'd be dependable. But she'd never have guessed quite how lovely Pippa Craig really was.

She was looking forward to having her on tour when her next movie opened. She already knew they'd giggle until their stomachs ached and that Pippa would do her utmost to make Jodi feel confident about walking out in front of the endless red carpets lined with flash bulbs.

Not only would she have someone with an eye for fashion, but that person would also be her friend. To Jodi, that was price-less. At long last she had a circle of real and trustworthy people to call her own.

Jules

SHE'D LITERALLY JUST MOVED BACK TO HER FLAT after the refurbishment, but Jules wasn't able to appreciate the time, effort and enormous amount of money she'd put into it. She hadn't intended on spending any time here alone. She was supposed to stay at her mother's before heading to Huntersbrook for dinner with Lainey and her family on Christmas Day. Her mother always spent the day with the couple next door, whose idea of fun was a ready-meal in front of the TV with gallons of cheap wine.

Lainey had come back from doing some last-minute shopping when her mother had let rip.

'No presents for your boyfriend in there, I'm guessing?' She'd put her finger to her lips and pondered. 'Oh nō, you don't have boyfriends, do you? You're still insisting on this ridiculous notion that you want to be shacked up with another woman.'

'Mum, please . . .'

'Don't look at me as if I'm soft in the head. I'm not the one who's in the wrong here. Do you know what it's like to be me? Do you? First of all you come crashing into my life when I didn't *need* a baby. Then your useless bastard of a father decides he's had enough. I scrimp and struggle for over three decades and put my life on hold for you . . . You stole the life I was supposed to have, Julia. And for what? Nothing, that's what . . . I'm ashamed of you.'

Jules didn't wait to hear another word. She took a roll of black plastic bin liners and filled them with all her belongings.

'Oh fabulous,' her mother sneered. 'So you're leaving me on my own at Christmas! Well that just proves my point. You're good-for-nothing, Julia. *Nothing.*'

'For the record, Mum, you've never shown me anything but contempt. Crazy as it might sound to you, I didn't ask to be born. I never intentionally set out to ruin your life. You did that all by yourself. You've nobody else to blame. At the end of the day when you look in the mirror, that reflection shows the only person who can tell you how you feel. The bitterness and negativity that you ooze is all your own doing. I won't spend another minute with you if you're going to treat me so badly. You're the only family I've got and it tears me up inside when you speak to me that way. I want to love you, Mum, but you make it so damn hard . . .'

'You can't choose your family, Julia, and God help me I was saddled with you,' she said refusing to hear a single word Jules was saying.

Moments later, Jules was driving down the motorway with her car stacked to the roof with bulging black bags. She didn't cry until she finished moving all the stuff back into her flat. The smell of fresh paint and new carpets should've lifted her spirits, but instead it made her feel even more alone. The idea had been to go to the January sales with Lainey and buy some accessories and personal touches to brighten the otherwise neutral palette she'd chosen. She'd bought the flat two years previously and hadn't a spare cent to do anything with it. So until now, it had been a mish-mash of donated and unwanted pieces all of which clashed with the orange walls.

'In fairness,' said Lainey diplomatically. 'Not much actually *goes* with that shade of Orangutan.'

The Heart of Winter

She could go to Lainey's house now. She knew her friend would welcome her with open arms, crack open a bottle of wine, wrap her in a blanket and tell her that her mother was Satan's sister. But Jules couldn't even face Lainey right now. She needed to take stock. She needed to figure out where her life was going.

She was making good money at the County Council offices. It was a dependable and pensionable job and she knew there were further promotions to be gained. But it hardly set her world alight. Since Lainey had left she had nobody to bounce things off or to share an eye-rolling glance with when the boss went off on a tangent with those little pools of spittle at either side of his mouth.

Jules needed a sense of purpose. She needed to know that there was a valid reason why she absolutely needed to be part of the population. She didn't want to kill herself. She'd no desire to harm herself. But she knew one thing – she felt empty. She poured a large glass of red wine and lit the fire. It was one of the swanky new gas ones that jumped to life instantly and looked pretty darn real. She dimmed the lights and put on the radio. She couldn't stomach Christmassy TV and felt the music might help lift her spirits.

It had been an odd year. She'd thought Sylvia was the love of her life. They'd clicked instantly and had so much in common. The relationship wasn't forced or frenzied in any way. It just seemed to roll smoothly. She'd been genuinely gutted when Sylvia had strode into the bar and stood at the table, clutching the strap of her handbag and announced that she was no longer a lesbian and she was going out with her flatmate, Mike.

In relationships past, Jules would've run after her sobbing and begging her to change her mind. She'd have called her at two o'clock in the morning, drunk and desperate. Not this time. Although she was hurting more than she ever had before, she knew there was no point in throwing herself on the railway track when the train had already left the station.

Her head throbbed as her mother's cruel words resonated through her head like a woodpecker slowly boring a hole in a tree. She'd finished the first glass of wine and poured the second when the idea came to her.

'You can't choose your family, Julia . . .'

The idea was inspired! She sat back and took a large gulp. The more she thought about it, the better it seemed. Grabbing her phone, she dialled Lainey's number.

'Jules?' She answered on the second ring.

'Oh thank God you're still awake. Can you talk for a minute?'

'Yeah. I'm just home. We had Jodi Ludlum's wedding at Huntersbrook today.'

'Of course you did,' she said. 'I forgot for a minute. How was it?'

'Amazing, Jules. She's such an awesome girl. I think she really enjoyed it all too. But forget that, what's up? You sound . . . Odd . . .'

'Yeah, it's been an odd evening. I'm back at the flat. Mum had the queen of all meltdowns earlier so I stuffed all my things into black sacks and came to the flat.'

'Aw Jules, come down here, sweetie. Don't stay there on your own. I'd say it's depressing.'

'It's not too bad. The fire is deadly. Mixed with the wine, it's all the accessorising I need for the moment.'

Lainey laughed.

'Was it really bad earlier with your mum?'

'Yeah,' Jules said honestly. 'She's never going to accept me, Lainz. The main problem with her is that she hates herself. She's toxic and I can't actually help her any more. It's exhausting, quite frankly.'

'I honestly don't know how she managed to produce you,' Lainey said. 'You don't deserve to be stuck with her.'

'I think I used her as my example of what *not* to do and how *not* to behave. The thing is. I've got this huge void in my life, Lainey. I was sitting here feeling kind of numb. I hadn't even reached the sobbing stage. It was the stare-at-my-own-shoe for half an hour phase . . .'

'Yeah, I get you.'

'When the answer came to me.'

'You're going on a world cruise?' Lainey guessed.

'No, I would like to be your surrogate mother. I'm offering my womb and eggs to grow a human for you and Matt.'

There was silence on the other end of the phone. Jules bit her lip.

'Lainz?'

'I . . . I don't know what to say . . . I . . . Jules, would you really consider doing that for us?'

'It fits, Lainz. You want another baby. Your lady parts are no longer available whereas mine are in full health with absolutely no potential for use. It's the perfect solution. It feels right, doesn't it?'

Jules heard Lainey's sobbing down the line as she tried to take stock of what was being offered.

'I know it's going to need major discussion, with Matt and your family. But wouldn't it be amazing? I'd be Auntie Jules, which I am anyway. But this way we'd all be a family.'

'I'm blown away . . .'

'I wouldn't be there morning, noon and night telling you what to do either. Nor would I go around thinking it's my baby. I don't actually feel ready to be a full-on mother, but I'd love to be a special Auntie.'

They chatted for another hour as Lainey slowly came to terms with the fact that Jules meant every word she was saying. As usual, their conversation became louder and louder until Matt appeared.

'Ooh ooh, Matt has just come downstairs to see who I'm talking to,' Lainey said. 'Will I put him on?'

'Go for it,' Jules said. She chatted to him and explained her offer, saying that she could think of nothing she'd love more. 'Obviously we'd have to do all the legal stuff and it's going to have to be done medically. You're an attractive man, but it would be wrong on every level to try and . . .'

'What, have a swingers night or invest in a turkey baster?'

'Precisely,' Jules said smiling.

They decided to sleep on it and talk again in the morning. But all three agreed that although the idea was embryonic, it had the potential to become something much bigger – like a baby.

Tired, but decidedly elated, Jules made up her bed with fresh sheets from the tiny airing cupboard and climbed in. She thought of her mother and how she'd react if this plan came to fruition. Once she started giggling, Jules couldn't stop.

❄

Early the following morning Lainey called.

'Before you even say hello, this is me calling to let you know that you have a get-out clause. If you were pissed drunk last night and feeling emotionally charged after your mother's attack and were purely looking for a way of getting back at her, you can back out now.'

'I don't want to back out. Do you?'

'Noooooo,' Lainey said screeching happily. 'Jules, I was awake for most of the night thinking. Matt and I have just had a really great talk and we both think your offer is the kindest, most self-less and amazing gift imaginable. There'll be lots of things to iron out and I'm sure it's going to be a difficult process, but we'd love to accept.'

'Oh Lainz, this is incredible! Can I come down now?'

'I'll put the kettle on.'

'Will you bake scones? With glacé cherries in them?'

'Oh Jesus, you're going to be a diva, aren't you?' she giggled. 'I'm already weighing up flour. Get your ass down here! This is the best Christmas present ever! See you soon.'

Jules jumped out of bed and grabbed the things she needed, remembering to take her outfit for tomorrow. Christmas Day at Huntersbrook was always amazing. Jules felt happier than she could ever remember feeling. A wonderful notion came to her. By proxy, she would now be part of the Craig family. Well, the baby would. But as the special Auntie, she would have a legitimate connection to this marvellous family. They had always made her feel welcome and she was ecstatic that she could now give them something that would add to their lineage.

One of the aspects of being gay that had always made Jules feel sad was the thought that it was highly unlikely that she'd ever have a child. This would tick that box. The idea needed to sit with them all and time would have to pass before the details were ironed out. But Jules knew in her heart of hearts that it was absolutely the right thing to do.

'Happy Christmas, Auntie Jules,' she said out loud and did a happy dance.

Jodi

HOLLY WAS AT THE BOTTOM OF THE STAIRS IN Huntersbrook sweeping up the last of the debris from the night before, when Jodi and Harry appeared.

'Oh, hold it there for one second!' Holly said as she rushed to find her digital camera.

'It's a family tradition! There's a photo of my mother, then me and most recently Lainey a couple of years ago making this very descent.'

Jodi gazed at the intricately decorated banisters.

'Your attention to detail is incredible,' Jodi said, as she and Harry stood and posed. 'Holly by name and holly by nature.'

'I was well named, wasn't I?' she grinned.

As she reached the bottom of the stairs, Holly held her arms out to Jodi.

'Well done, lovie. I'm sure your mother is looking down on you ever so proudly today. You're a super girl, a fantastic Mum, and I hope you'll be very happy.'

Jodi hugged Holly and didn't say a word. As she stood back, she hesitated before speaking.

'. . . I never had a relationship with my mother. She was poisoned by drink and drugs. Sadly I was nothing but an inconvenience in her life. If I could've been born as one of your daughters, God only knows where I might have ended up,' she said sadly. 'For you to take my photo with the view of including me in your family album means more than you will ever know. I should've been sad yesterday, getting married without either of my parents by my side. But I had my Tommy and all of you to keep me smiling.'

'Eh what about me?' Harry said dryly nudging her.

'We all know you're my knight in shining armour,' she grinned and kissed him. 'I used to dread Christmas. As a small child it was the most lonely and awful time. Ma would go on three day-long benders and I'd be left on my own for hours on end.'

'You poor child,' Holly said shaking her head sadly.

'Things improved when I had Saul. Darius and I cherish and adore him. But the demons were still in the shadows whispering and taunting me.' She put her hand out and touched the mossy-based swag that Holly had carefully entwined around the staircase.

'I lifted myself out of the life I was born into. I know the cycle has been stopped too. Our Tommy is happy as a pup with two tails. I've carved a whole new niche in this world. The name Ludlum will hopefully be associated with the little actress from the Emerald Isle rather than the drunk from Dublin city.' She shuddered and forced a brave smile. 'Thank you for helping me to put the final piece of the jigsaw puzzle in place.'

'You're more than welcome, darling girl,' Holly said as she hugged her. 'Now, let's seal the deal and send you on your way with one of Sadie's hot breakfasts.'

By midday the members of the wedding party had all said grateful goodbyes as the Craigs waved them off. The snow hadn't stuck but it was still extremely cold.

'It's very pretty when the place is covered in a blanket of white, but it plays havoc with the roads,' Holly said. 'At least you know your flights won't be delayed.'

Jodi and her family were going straight to the airport to catch their flight. They'd arrive on the island in time for dinner on Christmas night.

'I know a lot of people wouldn't like to fly on Christmas Eve,' she said. 'But we wanted to make the most of Harry's holiday time.'

'The door is always open, Jodi. Don't be a stranger,' Paddy said loudly.

Pippa hugged her and wished her well.

'Don't worry about us either. We'll wrap up warmly. I'm sure if we wear ski gear we won't end up with chilblains on our fingers and toes.'

Jodi laughed.

What none of them knew was that Jodi had already conducted an over-the-phone interview giving excusive details of her private wedding to *Society* magazine. They'd already confirmed Jodi for their front cover. She'd insisted they use the image of her and Harry on the front steps of Huntersbrook House. It was her tiny way of thanking the Craigs for the incredible kindness they'd shown her.

❄

One by one the Craig family arrived into the kitchen where they sat around the table and congratulated one another on a fantastic event. The atmosphere was one of relaxed cheer.

They'd all cleaned as they went the day before, but there were still chairs to be moved back out to the marquee and Holly wanted to put up the family stockings on the mantelpiece.

'I didn't want the guests to feel we were only biding our time before they went away,' Holly said. 'There's a fine line between being made to feel welcome and thinking you're intruding on someone's home.'

Holly always boiled the ham on Christmas Eve, so she fetched the huge pot that had rested in the larder for two generations and stood it on the Aga. Pulling the ham out of the large fridge in the shed, she hoofed it into the great pot and scored the skin with a sharp knife. She found it incredibly therapeutic as she studded each diamond shape with a clove. The warm, pungent, spicy scent filled the air. Roughly chopping several onions, she tossed them in too. Maggie's favourite way of cooking it was by glugging cola over the top, which she duly did. It brought back another flood of memories as she'd stood on a chair and watched in awe as a little girl.

'It'll give the meat a lovely sweet flavour,' Maggie used to say.

They rarely had fizzy drinks in the house and for many years Holly only associated cola with the Christmas ham.

Paddy and Jacob took it upon themselves to stack logs and briquettes as well as a bucket of coal by each of the fires in the hall, living room and dining room.

Lainey put the custard layer on top of her homemade trifle.

'That looks delicious,' Sadie said with interest. 'What did you make the jelly from?'

'It's our own rhubarb that I'd boiled in sugar, strained and frozen.'

'I'm impressed,' Sadie said nodding with approval. A couple of years previously, Sadie would've done the lion's share of the cooking. That responsibility had been removed from her shoulders organically as Lainey gravitated toward the kitchen. Lainey was very aware that she was being passed the baton and made certain to ask Sadie for her precious advice regularly.

'Would you have used any special flavouring in the custard?' she asked.

'No, the vanilla pods are my favourite, too. Maggie was a dreadful woman for lashing brandy into things. But the taste isn't appealing to the little ones.'

'I think Ely is a little young for being sozzled,' Lainey agreed.

Skye's cousin Echo's arrival from Dublin was the signal that it was officially Christmas.

'Nicely timed,' Joey said clapping him on the back. 'We've just finished all the cleaning up!'

'Aw shucks, and you know how much I love vacuuming.'

When Jules arrived, everyone stood to greet her as usual and they all grinned as she and Lainey hugged as if her life depended on it.

'Is everything OK?' Holly asked suspiciously.

'Yeah,' Jules said. 'I'd a bust-up with Mum last night. I'm back in the flat and she's pretty much cut me off. But it's probably for the best.'

'Well I don't like to speak out of turn about others,' Paddy said gruffly. 'But that woman needs her head examined. If she's too caught up in her own doings to realise what a super girl you are, it's her loss and our gain. We're honoured to have you as part of our family.'

They were all mildly surprised when both Lainey and Jules burst into tears and hugged one another again.

The rest of the afternoon was spent playing Scrabble. Skye slept in the big armchair and wasn't even roused by the loud yells as Paddy tried relentlessly to cheat.

'Dad,' Pippa laughed. 'We've told you a million times that you can't invent words, even if you have a very convincing meaning made up!'

'I think I'm on to something,' he said. 'I might go and manufacture my own *mousecream*. I think it'd be a hit. Cats apparently love mice and they drink milk. What's the problem?'

'For a start, you can't put the tiles there as it's interfering with the letters above and that word still doesn't exist!'

'*And* you're sitting on two "x's" and a "z",' Holly said, swiping at him with a cushion.

'But it's such a cute word,' Jules said. 'I think it should be allowed.'

'Thank you, Jules,' Paddy said winking across at her.

The roads were icy and slightly sludgy from the wintry showers all afternoon, so Paddy got his way when he suggested travelling to Christmas Eve mass on the tractor with the trailer.

Skye looked very doubtful however.

'I don't think I'd survive being bumped about.'

'You'd be fine, my girl,' Paddy said, not wanting anything to jeopardise his drive in the hay-loaded vehicle.

'We don't need her falling off or going into early labour while you trundle down the road oblivious,' Holly said.

Paddy looked so crestfallen that Joey, Jacob, Lainey, Matt and Jules said they'd pile in with Ely and Echo. Pippa wanted to drive, which was met with a chorus of negative comments.

'I'm not that bad,' she said, pretending to be hurt.

'Pippa, you drive like a maniac while putting on make-up and talking on your phone,' Joey said. 'You are not going on a road, even if it's a private one through our own land, with innocent lives at stake.'

Each year Paddy parked at their back gate, which was only a stone's throw from the village church.

'I'll come down in the car with Skye. I think we'll use the public thoroughfare and avoid large potholes, deep rivets and other potentially dangerous obstacles,' Holly said. 'We can take the food from the chippers back with us too. It'll work out nicely.'

Each year the Craigs went to the family mass. It was wonderful to see all the eager and excited little ones who were almost bursting with anticipation. The carols, readings and poems were always organised by the school, so it was poignant and heartwarming and the most lovely way of celebrating Christmas Eve. Afterwards they collected food from the takeaway, which they brought home to eat out of the packets in front of a roaring fire. This was traditionally washed down with either wine or beer from paper cups.

'It's illegal to do washing up on Christmas Eve,' Paddy always said.

The live crib along with the small children always proved to be as touching as it was entertaining. This year one of the goats helped herself to a pile of missalettes which she proceeded to chew noisily as the final prayer was being said.

'Were there actually goats in the manger way back when?' Pippa whispered to Joey.

'I can't be certain, sis, cause I wasn't there myself. But I don't think I've ever seen a pretend manger with a goat included.'

'It belongs to Mr O'Malley,' Holly said authoritatively. 'He donates the straw every year. Apparently he got a present of the goat from a niece soon after his Nuala passed away. He's very attached to it and lets it into the kitchen to sleep in front of the Aga with the dog. He asked if it could be included in the crib and Father Tom hadn't the heart to say no.'

The mass ended just as the goat was attempting to gnaw its way out of the crib.

The chipper was crammed with like-minded hungry folks, but Paddy managed to get served fairly swiftly. Mario handed over the enormous bulging bag of food and wished them all a happy Christmas. Matt ushered them all back onto the trailer and drove home. The loud screeching rendition of Rudolf the red-nosed reindeer was more of an exercise in spleen-venting than melodious singing as they pulled up at the front door.

Paddy and Holly had brought their bedclothes and moved back into their old room for the few days.

'It's lovely to be back here as a family once more,' Holly said. 'I love our gate lodge now. It feels like home when we're there, but nowhere will ever replace Huntersbrook at Christmas time.'

Paddy pulled out the bellows and blew air onto the freshly stoked fire, getting a blaze going.

'I vote we start with a bottle of bubbly,' he said. 'After the year we've had, I reckon we deserve it.'

Matt found some paper cups, knowing that no matter what happened they couldn't break the golden rule and create a pile of washing-up. Even Skye said she'd have a mouthful.

Jacob, Lainey, Matt and Ely were staying Christmas Eve and Christmas night at Huntersbrook, too, so they decided to head off to bed. Pippa and Jules were sharing a twin room and Echo was sleeping on a fold-out bed in the front room and said he was ready to turn in for the night too. Joey offered Skye a piggy-back, which she declined.

'I can't see my bump fitting on your back, Joey!'

'Oh yeah! I forgot that,' he grinned.

'I'll follow you in a minute,' Lainey said. 'Matt, don't wake Ely. He was out for the count earlier. We don't need him waking in a strange room and deciding two hours is enough sleep to last him until morning!'

He was still a tiny bit young to understand the ins and outs of Christmas, so Lainey had managed to get him to sleep without too many problems when they'd finished eating.

'I'll give you a quick hand with the stockings,' Lainey said to Holly.

'Indeed you will not,' she said indignantly. 'Santa Claus won't come if you're still up. No matter how old you are, if you don't believe . . .'

'You won't receive . . .' Lainey finished with a grin.

'I just need to do Ely's stocking,' she said, rummaging in the cardboard box she'd brought from next door. 'I hope he'll like his things.'

'We'll get more joy out of watching him open his presents than anything else,' Holly said excitedly. 'Children are what it's all about at this time of year. Family and being together, that's what counts. Ely will probably prefer the box to his train set, but that's par for the course. Things can be as stressful as you like every other day of the year. But on December twenty-fifth, none of it matters one jot as long as we have each other.'

Lainey stuffed the stocking she'd bought at the local Christmas fete a few weeks ago. Satisfied it looked just right, she hugged her parents and left them to do their Santa duty.

'These are the moments I treasure most,' Holly said to Paddy. 'I save these priceless times in my memory banks. When I'm having a bad day, I close my eyes and take a deep breath and cast my mind to a time just like now.'

'That's lovely, pet.'

'We're blessed, Paddy. This has been a good year in the end. I miss my mother all the time. But I feel she's with me. I've mended a lot of bridges with Lainey. I know that was Mum.'

'It's great to see you two chatting more.'

'I've never been closer to Joey. He's a fine young man. He and Skye are going to make a wonderful little family, please God.'

'He's a good lad all right.'

'Pippa's an odd one,' she smiled and shook her head. 'I thought she was headed off the rails in a hang-glider earlier in the year. But she's come full circle. I like her fellow Danny too.'

'Pippa will always keep us guessing,' Paddy said. 'She has the mischievous gene in abundance. But I reckon she'll be OK now.'

As she filled each stocking, Holly said a little silent prayer of thanks.

By the time they climbed the stairs to bed, she was exhausted.

'It's actually odd being back here, isn't it?' Holly said as she lay down in their old room.

'Ah well, it's different from when we were here. Those swanky curtains and the matching bedspread and lamp shade business . . . It's nice and all that, but it's like a hotel.'

'That's the general idea,' Holly said with a smile.

'It's not exactly homely, though. It's not the way we had it, at least. I almost prefer the gate lodge at this point.'

Holly smiled in the dark as Paddy put his arms around her.

'I do too, love,' she said. 'We have the best of both worlds though, don't we?'

Within minutes the house was silent. As Christmas Day rolled in, Huntersbrook protected the Craig family majestically as they slept soundly in their beds.

Epilogue

NEXT MORNING PIPPA AND JULES WERE THE FIRST out of bed as usual. Grabbing Paddy's gong, they stood at the foot of the stairs and bashed it until everyone appeared.

'Bloody hell, Pippa,' Joey said. 'Are you trying to wake the dead?'

'It's Christmas and we can't waste another minute of it!' she said cheerfully, oblivious to Joey's grumping. As the family gathered around the tree, Ely was the star of the show. They'd all assumed he'd be far too small to understand much, but he was utterly ecstatic.

'Choo-choo!' he shouted pointing at the train while jumping up and down. Once all the bought gifts were opened, Pippa stood on the coffee table and cleared her throat, announcing she had a bit of news.

'This is a gift that can't be opened as such,' she said smugly. 'But I've sold my website and I'm using the money to buy equipment for a new gym to add to the facilities here at Huntersbrook.'

'No way,' Joey said. 'That's an amazing idea.'

The others all oohed and ahhed as Pippa showed them brochures of what she was thinking of ordering.

'Well if we're sharing presents that can't be opened,' Skye said looking up at Joey, who nodded. 'We have a bit of news about the baby.'

'It's not *a* baby,' said Joey grimly.

'I beg your pardon,' said Paddy in alarm.

'It's bab*ies*,' said Skye in delight. 'We had a scan and it seems we're having twins! That's why I was so ill and it also explains why I look like I've swallowed a house!'

'That's incredible news,' said Lainey, with tears in her eyes. Before anyone could even ask if they were sad tears she continued the trend. 'Well Matt and I have yet another gift that cannot be opened!'

'Oh dear Lord, I think I'm going to have a heart attack,' said Paddy dramatically as he laughed. 'Go on, love. What is it?'

'You say it,' she urged Matt.

'Well, Lainey and I have made the decision to go for surrogacy. We don't want Ely to be on his own. He needs someone to fight with and this is the best option for us. We hope you'll all come around to the idea.'

'I think it's marvellous,' Holly said, hugging Lainey.

'You knew about this?' Paddy said with a slow grin.

'Yes, Lainey asked my opinion, didn't you love?'

'Sure did.'

Just as they were hugging and working themselves into an excited frenzy, Jules stood on the coffee table.

'I'm copying Pippa because I like the stage setting,' she said dramatically. 'We need to talk about this more,' she held her hands out and Lainey grasped one, with Matt taking the other. 'But I've offered to be the surrogate mum.'

'And we think it's the most amazingly wonderful and priceless gift imaginable,' Lainey finished.

'I'd be proper Auntie Jules then. I'm not going to be in the position to have a child of my own. So why not put my baby-making bits to good use?'

There was a moment of silence as they all tried to digest the information.

'We'll need to iron out all the details and see if it'll work, but why not try?' Jules said.

'You're the kindest and best friend in the world,' Lainey said, hugging her again.

'I'll vouch for that,' said Joey as he opened his arms to her. Jules hugged him and Joey whispered to her, 'Thanks for the kick in the butt. I needed it. You rock.' He kissed her head and smiled.

'I think we all need a strong cup of coffee,' Paddy said standing up to make his way to the kitchen.

'Before we all disperse, I have another gift that can't be opened,' Sadie said. They stopped and stared at her.

'Mine is a little different from all the others . . . I'm dying.' She took a deep breath as Holly gasped and Paddy rushed to hug her. Instantly, the room was filled with sorrow as each of them tried to take it all in.

'How . . . how is that a gift, Sadie, love?' Holly managed.

'I'll tell you now, if you can bear with me,' she said. 'I have about four months, so the doctors tell me. So I'm going to plan it all. I'll know what music I want at my funeral, what food and who's to come.'

'Oh Sadie,' Lainey said sobbing.

'Don't cry, love,' she said taking Lainey's hand. 'I made a deal, too. With your man up there,' she said pointing to the sky. 'I said that I'd be happy to go, if he let you stay.'

'No!' Lainey said crying openly.

'Oh yes, pet,' she said firmly. 'I've lived my life. I've done my time and I've no more "i's" to dot or "t's" to cross.' She turned to the others and bravely told them about Elizabeth.

'I've found her. I traced my baby to a place in the north of England and we're meeting up next week. We've conversed via email for a few days and she knows my situation.'

'Well I'll be damned,' Paddy said in awe. 'You're a dark horse, Sadie.'

She winked at Paddy. 'But my gift to you all is this: a reminder that you must never forget what really matters. Family and love are the be all and end all of life. Everything else is just padding. Added to fill in the hours. I intend using the time I have left to do all the things I love.'

'Are you going travelling?' Pippa asked through tears.

'No lovie, I'm staying right here. I'll eat all my favourite things, walk my favourite fields, wear my favourite clothes and talk to my favourite people. I'll get to meet Elizabeth next week. I'll hold her in my arms and know that she is safe. Then, when my time comes, I'll head on up to see Maggie. I know she'll be there waiting.'

'Oh Sadie,' Joey said rushing to scoop her into his arms. 'We'll be here with you every step of the way. We'll do all we can to ensure you see your days out with love and dignity.'

'So there's no time to waste,' she said clapping her hands gently. 'It's Christmas. There's a turkey to be stuffed. That fire needs stoking, Paddy, and we could all do with a glass of bubbles. It's a celebration, you know . . . Life is a celebration!'

They made quite a scene several moments later as they raised their champagne flutes while wearing red and green glittery disco-boppers and crazy Christmas-themed Hawaiian shorts over their clothes.

'Why do we have to look quite so ridiculous?' Pippa asked in a whisper.

'Because I don't want any of you to forget my last Christmas,' Sadie said with a smile.

❄

What a year it had been. As they bustled around and prepared for their Christmas feast, each of the guests at Huntersbrook was acutely aware of what really mattered. This year would mark the end of an era. Next year at least one person would be missing, but as Sadie seemed keen to remind them, they could possibly be too busy to fret. With one set of twins already on the way, medical science could possibly have another set waiting in the wings.

Lainey didn't want to sound trite, so she kept it to herself. But that woman who'd read her tealeaves and predicted twins in the family may indeed have possessed the direct link with the angels that she advertised on her sandwich board at the fete. If she was there again next summer, Lainey was going to pay her another visit!

Acknowledgements

AS ALWAYS I AM HUMBLED BY THE CONTINUED support I receive from every avenue of my life. Without the people who matter the most to me, I wouldn't be able to carry on.

Thanks to my friend, cheerleader and agent Sheila the Great, AKA Sheila Crowley of Curtis Brown UK. Along with her able assistant Becky Ritchie, they keep all the balls in the air.

Work is always a pleasure. When I am writing I am at peace. I know I'm lucky to be surrounded by the marvellous team at Hachette Ireland. My fabulous editor Ciara Doorley along with Breda, Jim, Ruth, Siobhan, Joanna and Bernard make my books appear as if by magic! Thanks also to Susie Cronin of Plunkett PR for all your hard work.

This time I've been privileged to have additional help and editorial guidance from the one and only Mari Evans of Headline UK. All I can say is that Mari's ability to edit is second only to her skill at applying a perfect flick of black liquid eyeliner. I know I am truly blessed to have both you and Ciara on my side.

Thanks also to Rachel Pierce for her razor sharp and astute copy edits. What an amazing team you all are and I am curtsying in awe at the fabulous job you've done for me.

Thank you to all the UK team at Headline who have welcomed me with open arms and embraced me in their warmth. In spite of residing in an imposingly swanky glass London building, you make me feel at home.

My hubby Cian and children Sacha and Kim are always there to keep me on my toes! I love you with all my heart and soul. Thanks also to my favourite neighbours, Mum and Dad. You are my backbone and my strength. That song – You're nobody 'til somebody loves you – rings true for me. With all of you in my life I know I am somebody . . .

Thanks to my extended family and friends who bend over backwards to help support me and most of all make me laugh.

I have recently finished treatment for my ninth cancer diagnosis. Quite literally, I owe my life to the astonishingly dedicated people who keep me alive. Professor John Armstrong, Dr David Fennelly and all the staff of St Vincent's Private Hospital and Blackrock Clinic, there are no words to convey how grateful I am that you all chose to save lives. Not a day passes that I don't thank my lucky stars that I know you all. I appreciate each day I spend on this earth and I know I'm here as a result of your care and dedication. Thank you from the bottom of my heart. I am feeling stronger with each passing day and I will do my best to refrain from darkening your doors, but I can't promise anything!

Thanks to Mark Bourke (info@slapbangwallop.com) for re-designing my website and being so astute at adding new bits and keeping it all up to date.

I'm so grateful to all my fabulous readers. The emails and letters, tweets and Facebook messages make me smile on a daily basis. It's always wonderful to hear from you all. Your messages help me through the bad times and make my days that little bit brighter.

The Heart of Winter revisits Huntersbrook house where we first met the Craig family in *Driving Home for Christmas*. Don't worry if you haven't read *Driving Home for Christmas*, I promise you won't be lost! I had so many letters from readers asking to hear more from this family, so how could I refuse? I sincerely hope you enjoy *The Heart of Winter* and that you find it as comforting to read as I did to write.

Please continue to stay in touch on Twitter @MsEmmaHannigan, on Facebook (AuthorEmmaHannigan) or contact me via my website info@emmahannigan.com

Love and light
Emma x

Emma Hannigan

The Heart of Winter

Bonus Material

My Perfect Christmas ...

Writing both *Driving Home for Christmas* and *The Heart of Winter* provided me with a wonderful feeling of indulgence. Why? Both books centre on my favourite time of the year. I have always loved Christmas and I know it's due to the magical and special days I shared with my family as a child. That magic has continued since my own children came along. Now both teenagers, they too have had a love of all things Christmassy instilled in them. Well, let's face it; they hadn't much choice with me as their mother!

Our family has grown but the traditions all remain the same. There's a gorgeous sense of familiarity in the annual rituals that never grows old. My husband and I built a house in my parents' garden, so we are only a stone's throw away. We always have Christmas dinner there with some of my many cousins, aunts and uncles. My parents' house is Georgian and was built to be decorated with holly and towering pine trees. They have a separate dining room where Mum and I, now helped by my daughter, transform the place into a twinkling area with entwined holly, ivy, seasonal flowers and tiny lights that any fairy or elf would be proud of. The table is set and the crackers we've deliberated over and chosen with great fanfare are given pride of place at each plate.

I trained as a chef when I left school, so I love nothing more than rolling my sleeves up and helping Mum with preparations. The cake and pudding are usually made in October, so they're plated and made to look pretty with holly leaves. We usually prep as much as possible the day before. So turkey stuffing, carrot and parsnip puree, pâté for starters, and the now customary meringue roulade, are prepared. The meringue came about when my son decided he doesn't like Christmas pudding – I'm still working on him! How could anyone *not* love pudding?

We start Christmas Day in the wee hours of the morning when someone eager wakes the house. Santa Claus still comes to us all, filling stockings for the humans and furry people – yes, Tom the cat and Herbie the dog have stockings too! Once the flurry of unwrapping ends, we have enough time to dress and venture to the country where my in-laws live. There we share breakfast and exchange gifts. By midday we're back in my hometown of Bray and I immediately slip in the back door of Mum and Dad's house and don an apron. We feed a minimum of eighteen people, but some years it's more. A roast turkey aroma is already filling the air as last minute jobs are tended to. I slice and plate up the pâté for the starter, and take the home-baked bread from the freezer – I cheat by slicing it before I freeze it so it can all go into a basket and thaw by the time we eat! I am a staunch supporter of sprouts and, although my husband insists they are created by the devil, I lovingly peel them and enjoy their waxy texture alongside the rich meat. As well as turkey and ham we always have spiced beef. Bring on the meat sweats! We buy ours from a local butcher and his recipe has been passed down through the generations. I parboil the potatoes and roll them in goose fat for the ultimate crispy on the outside, fluffy on the inside roast spud. Bread sauce, cranberry sauce and gravy ensure the flavours are all maximised.

My Dad is a wine buff and plans the vintages and specific choices weeks in advance. We all eagerly help him drink it. Aren't we kind? Once things are ready to go, we all congregate in the living room and our guests arrive. More gift exchanges happen, this time accompanied by champagne! Are you beginning to see why I love Christmas so much?

We always sit down to eat at five. This gives us enough time to savour each course. Everyone *must* wear his or her paper hat and all cracker jokes must be read out. Yes, this is a militant rule. Each year we also pass around an added extra for each person to wear. Last year the men got Christmas jumpers and the ladies got flashing earrings. Classy, right?

The volume rises and laughter prevails as we chat about times gone by, and our plans and hopes for the year ahead. When the children were younger they would dip in and out of the dining room, preferring to play with their visiting cousins while us adults digested slowly. Now they're of the age where they enjoy sitting and joining in more, which is fabulous. How else would us adults know that most of the things we say are wrong – coupled with the fact we're utterly embarrassing?

My brother is chief pudding-setter-on-firer and does this with great fanfare each year. I've often thought he's confusing the ritual with bonfire night, but it wouldn't be wise to interfere . . . It's nothing short of a miracle that the ceiling hasn't been charred!

Cheese and port follows dessert before we settle in for a calm and serene game of Trivial Pursuit. Ok, that's a complete lie. Trivial Pursuit on Christmas night has been known to verge on violent chez nous. We split into teams and the cheating is appalling. All the children in our family have been set the most dreadful example when it comes to board games, and I know we've created another generation of chancers. By the time we haul our full bellies across the garden to our own home I am always like a bewitched fool. My smile is unstoppable as I begin the countdown to the following year.

Christmas is my ideal day. It's everything dreams are made of as I'm surrounded by the people I love. Each year without fail, I am appreciative of the gifts I've been given. By that, I don't just mean the ones I've unwrapped – but the ones that have been bestowed upon me as I cherish each passing year.

No matter how you spend your Christmas, I hope you spend it with the people who matter to you the most.

Merry Christmas one and all!

Emma x

Melting Snowman Cookies

These divine shortbread biscuits make wonderful edible gifts. They are incredibly cute and always turn out looking the way I hope. Adults, teenagers and children all adore them and they make perfect gifts. You can of course use shop-bought cookies for the base, but they won't taste the same. I give the old-fashioned ounce measurement also as it makes it so easy to recall!

Ingredients for the cookies:

2 oz (50g) caster sugar
4 oz (110g) butter (at room temperature)
6 oz (170g) plain white flour
Grated rind of ½ an orange, lemon, lime or grapefruit

Method:

* Simply place all the ingredients in a food processor and blend until it forms a soft dough. (This can be done by hand but that requires considerable elbow grease!)
* Chill in the fridge for at least an hour
* Roll to ¼ inch thick and use a round cutter or upturned tumbler to make your shapes

445

* Bake at 180°C/350°F/Gas Mark 4 until the cookies are a pale, golden colour
* When they come out of the oven the biscuits will be slightly floppy and very delicate, so transfer them to a wire rack at once using a fish slice so that they'll crisp up and cool
* If you need to make the biscuits a couple of days in advance, store them in an airtight plastic container

Top tip: Don't add any liquid to the mixture – it will combine eventually, I promise!

Ingredients for the melted snowmen:

1 bag of large white marshmallows
1 bag of royal icing (to be made with water according to the instructions on the packet)
1 packet of writing icing tubes (these can be found in most supermarkets in the baking aisle)

Method:

* Mix the white royal icing in accordance with the instructions on the packet, taking care to ensure the icing isn't too runny
* Place your cookies on a sheet of tin foil on an even surface
* Add approximately 1 tablespoon of royal icing to the centre of the cookie, and coax it with the back of the spoon so it covers most of the surface (and looks like melting snow)
* Working swiftly, snip the large marshmallows in half width ways, and put each half on the top edge of an iced cookie
* Allow to set for at least 30 minutes

446

* Using your writing icing, draw eyes, a nose and a mouth onto the front of the marshmallow
* To create the illusion of buttons, draw dots in a line from the marshmallow toward the opposite edge of the cookie
* For added effect, draw two stick arms on either side of the buttons
* Leave to set overnight before placing in single layers on paper plates, covering with florist crystal wrap and tying with a ribbon

I am yet to meet a single person
who hasn't smiled at receiving these!

Ten things I love about Christmas . . .

* Togetherness – catching up with loved ones
* Christmas trees – the more the merrier
* Decorations – everywhere from the banister to the bathroom
* Baking – what could be more therapeutic?
* Buying gifts – it's a shopaholic's favourite time of year!
* Finding that perfect Christmas outfit
* Finding the shoes to match that perfect outfit
* Planning surprises and picking up stocking fillers
* Selection boxes – it wouldn't be Christmas without one
* The joy on my children's faces on Christmas morning

My darling, my beautiful, my daughter,

You are ten days old and we don't have long left together. Panic is a terrible thing. It takes away all rationale. But my love for you has spurred me on and helped me find a way to leave you a part of myself.

Beside me on the bed sit twenty-nine cards, to be sent to you each year on your birthday. I want you to know that I am thinking of you always. You must have so many questions about me and the circumstances of your birth. The most important thing you need to know is this: I love you as only a mother can.

What I want more than anything else is to stay, to watch you grow up, learn to walk and talk. To see you find happiness. To know you've found love.

The truth is, I am dying. A large part of me wants to scream and throw things violently at the walls and let all the anger out at the injustice of it all. But I cannot waste the energy I have left. I want to cherish each and every moment I have left with you, my darling girl.

Being pregnant with you, feeling those tiny flutters in the beginning as you grew, then bringing you into this world, holding you, feeding you – this has been the perfect finale before I go. All my life I have been weakened by my illness. So knowing that I defied the odds and you are here has made it all worthwhile.

Being your mother has given me the greatest sense of achievement and happiness. I will never tire of stroking your cheek and watching your solemn eyes gazing purposefully back at me. Having you has made sense of everything. I now know my main purpose in life was to bring you into the world. And I know you were brought here to carry on where I've had to leave off. Live for us both and seize every moment. For me and, most of all, for you, my little miracle, just as I have been doing for these past nine months. Enjoy the scent of every flower, dance to every song, laugh until you cry, walk barefoot by the sea, but no matter what, let your passions soar.

I will watch over you always and I know we will meet again some day. There is nothing more I can say except that I love you. I love you. I love you. I love you, my darling girl, my perfect gift.

Mam

Chapter 1

Róisín stifled a yawn as she stretched up her arms and rose to the tips of her toes to engage the pole with the shutter in order to close her shop for the night. Well, Nourriture – Food For The Soul might be just a shop to the passing gaze of a tourist, but it was Róisín's entire world.

Clicking the sturdy padlock in place, she grinned at her own suspiciousness. The sleepy fishing village of Ballyshore was hardly up there with the crime hotspots of the world. As she turned and inhaled the damp saltiness of the early evening air, she closed her eyes momentarily. Her time away from her home village had made her appreciate the rugged West of Ireland beauty that surrounded her all the more.

A spatter of fat raindrops plopping onto her cheeks dragged her from her reverie. Stooping to grab the bottle and the box of Sushi she'd swiped from her well-stocked food emporium, she slung her battered soft leather fringed bag over her shoulder. She knew all too well that the heavens could open and drench her with a chilly late spring shower. The cottage she shared with her oldest and best friend Jill was a ten-minute walk at a brisk pace. Róisín had grown up at the other side of the bay, a short drive away, but she preferred living near the hub of the village.

Despite the low temperature the air was unmistakably soft. Róisín could almost hear the kinks forming in her dark, glossy hair as the salty air worked its magic. Glad of the sturdy comfort of her scuffed Dr. Martens black boots, she wished she'd brought a downy puffa coat instead of the leather biker jacket she'd paired with her pale pink tulle skirt today. The watered-down lemony sunshine this morning had lulled her into a false sense of summer.

Balancing the shopping bag containing the wine bottle and sushi in the crook of her arm, she wrestled with the jacket zip. The cross-over cardigan with flimsy tank top underneath was adequate while she ran from the kitchen to the counter and back up to her office in Nourriture during the busy working day, but it was no match for the now squalling rain.

At a trot she passed the sharply curving stone wall that separated the narrow country road from the sea. Darting across to the other side, she hoped the overhanging trees might offer more shelter. In another few weeks the tiny buds that dotted the hedgerows would flourish and ripen into juice-laden blackberries. She licked her lips, longing to taste the rich jam she'd make from her pickings.

Róisín sighed in grateful relief as she rounded the corner and saw the small white-washed cottage shining like a beacon through the rain. Bellows of grey smoke belched from the chimney and Róisín trotted happily towards the door.

'Hi honey, I'm home!' she called out, then started coughing. The open-plan kitchen-cum-living room was filled with smoke and her friend was nowhere to be seen.

'Jill?'

Setting her bag and wine on the kitchen table, she rushed to the potbellied stove and snatched up the poker. Shoving the single log and pyramid of peat briquettes into the back of the grate, she secured the door shut. She was too cold to open the windows and doors, so instead Róisín escaped into her bedroom. The room was too small to host a double bed as well as the wardrobe and dressing-table, so she'd opted for an iron-framed single bed.

'It's not as if I'm entertaining queues of hot lovers,' she had joked with Jill. 'For the moment, a single bed with a feather duvet and a pile of pillows will do me nicely.'

Jill, on the other hand, had said she'd rather hang her clothes on the floor than pass up her double bed.

'I mightn't have a steady boyfriend yet,' she'd said, hands on hips, as they'd moved in together three years ago, 'but I've every intention of interviewing for the post.'

A teacher in the local primary school, Jill was vivacious and enthusiastic. From the time they'd held hands in the Montessori room in Ballyshore National aged three, she and Róisín had been inseparable.

'That you, Ro?' Jill called out now.

'No, I'm a masked murderer.'

'Stop it!' Jill said, bursting into the bedroom and flinging herself onto the end of Róisín's bed with her hair turbaned in a towel. 'How's it going? Good day at the office?'

'Yeah, it was really busy. That burst of sunshine this morning brought the tourists and locals out in force.'

'So aren't you going to ask me how I got on last night?' Jill said, eyes shining.

'I heard how you got on,' Róisín grinned. 'You weren't exactly keeping it to yourself last night.'

'I know! And on a school night, too. I'm such a rebel.' She sighed. 'I was a bit hung-over this morning. Dreadful idea when there are twenty-five pairs of eyes squinting suspiciously at yours for six hours.'

'I don't know how you work as a teacher, but doing it with a hangover and very little sleep seems like self-inflicted torture to me.'

'Gordon was worth it,' she said dreamily.

'Gordon? With a name like that he hardly sounds too rock 'n' roll.'

'He didn't seem it either when we first met. He was at the

enrolment for the summer evening classes. He's not actually taking part, he was simply there to set up the computer for one of the lecturers. I enrolled for bird-watching.'

'Bird-watching? You? Don't you need to be quiet and still for that?'

'Yeah,' she sighed and rolled onto her back while rubbing her damp hair with the towel. 'I'll call and say I've changed my mind. I really wanted to do Italian. But the woman enrolling that course was like an ancient little shrivelled person who'd been exhumed after the disaster in Pompeii.' Róisín laughed and shook her head. Jill was incorrigible, but she adored her.

'I brought Sushi for you to try,' Róisín said. 'And some delicious white wine. It's a Riesling. A really special Spätlese to be precise.'

'A who?'

'Spätlese, or sweet wine from the Rhone valley. It's usually served with desserts, but I think it'll work magically with the fish and rice along with the pickled ginger.'

'You're not selling this to me, Róisín,' Jill said, looking mildly disgusted. 'I'm hankering after a bowl of creamy pasta or a bag of chipper chips.'

'Trust me, you'll love this. I'll get it sorted while you get dressed.'

She padded into the kitchen and waved her hand to try and clear the settling smoke. Róisín prepared a platter with the sushi, hoping the pretty array of pinks and white would entice Jill. She popped the cork on the wine just as Jill appeared in a rabbit onesie and snuggled into the sofa.

'Let's eat in here, by the stove,' she said. 'The chairs are too hard and upright for my poor body.'

Róisín brought the platter to the coffee table and instructed Jill to remove the pile of corrections she'd flung there.

With the encouragement of the glass of wine and Róisín's earnest nods, Jill popped a piece of Sushi into her mouth. Grimacing, she held it there without chewing.

'For crying out loud, you're acting as if I'm feeding you slugs! Eat it, you goon!'

As she chewed, Jill's eyes popped open in surprise. 'Wow,' she said swallowing. 'That's really tasty.'

'I know,' Róisín said in mild exasperation.

'Wine is divine too,' she said, drinking greedily. 'Looks like that time in France wasn't a total waste after all. You know your gargle, my friend,' she said, helping herself to another piece of Sushi.

Róisín smiled, because that was what Jill expected. But whenever France was mentioned, and specifically her time spent there, it was as if Róisín had been punched in the gut. She had learned far more than wine appreciation in her time there. Over the two-year period she'd spent near Bordeaux, she'd probably experienced every emotion known. But she knew the best policy was to keep France and all the events that had unfolded there at the back of her mind.

'Looking forward to your party tomorrow?' Jill asked, with a fresh look of glee in her eyes. 'Do you feel old? I can't believe you're leaving your twenties behind and heading for your thirties,' she teased.

'Jill, I'm two months older than you. Enough of the old talk,' she said. She tried to keep her tone light-hearted, but Róisín was actually dreading hitting the big 3-0. She glanced at Jill, who was horsing into the Sushi and making appreciative noises. She wished she shared her friend's carefree attitude to life.

'Touchy, touchy,' Jill said. 'So answer my question. Are you looking forward to the party or not?'

'So-so,' Róisín said honestly. 'Actually, I'm dreading it. I feel like a total wipe-out. What have I got to show for myself at thirty? Look at Liv. She's younger than me and she's married with two children. I thought I'd be settled and happy too by now.'

'Oh bloody hell, Ro, let's tune the violin. Seriously? Are you really saying you'd be happier if you were surrounded by nappies and whinging?'

'Well, when you put it like that ...'

'Take it from me. I'm with small children day in, day out. They're gorgeous and funny and full of life, but completely head-wrecking. Thirty is young, for God's sake. It's only the beginning. We have years ahead for worrying about body clocks or wiping noses all day. There are places to see, wine to drink, men to shag and a whole host of nonsense we need to get involved with. So enough of your depressing talk. Tomorrow is the beginning of the next decade. Grab it by the balls and live your life, my friend!'

In spite of her inward gloom, Róisín couldn't help laughing at Jill. Her *joie de vivre* was infectious. Jill filled their glasses and raised hers up high. 'To you,' she said. 'May your thirties be flirty and fabulous!'

Róisín stood up, clinked her glass against Jill's and smiled.

The perfect magical read from Emma Hannigan . . .

Christmas at Huntersbrook House has always been a family tradition – log fires, long walks through the snowy fields and evenings spent in the local pub. And this year the three grown-up Craig children are looking forward to the holidays more than ever. Pippa to escape her partying lifestyle and mounting debts in Dublin; Joey the demands of his gorgeous girlfriend who seems intent on coming between him and his family; and Lainey to forget about her controlling ex and his recent engagement to another woman.

But with the family livery yard in financial trouble, this Christmas could be the Craig family's last at Huntersbrook as they face the prospect of selling the ancestral house.

As the holiday season gets underway, the family need to come up with a way to save their home, and face the problems they've been running away from in Dublin. And what better place to figure things out than around the fire at Huntersbrook House?

THE BESTSELLING AUTHOR

Emma
Hannigan

The Secrets
We Share

'A writer who understands
exactly how women think'
CATHY KELLY

**Don't miss this beautiful moving story of
heart and home . . .**

Devastated after a tragedy, Nathalie Conway finds
herself on a plane to Ireland. She is on her way to stay
with her grandmother Clara. The woman who
up until now Nathalie had no idea existed . . .

As Clara awaits her granddaughter's arrival, she is filled
with a new sense of hope. She has spent the last twenty
years praying her son Max would come back into her life.
Perhaps now he can find a way to forgive her for the past.
And her granddaughter may be the thread to stitch the
pieces of her beloved family back together.

THE BESTSELLING AUTHOR
Emma
Hannigan
The Summer
Guest

'A glorious read –
wonderfully uplifting'
CATHY KELLY

'A truly touching tale'
IRISH INDEPENDENT

Uncover the secrets of Caracove in Emma Hannigan's enchanting novel.

A little magic is about to come to sleepy Caracove Bay . . .

Lexie and her husband Sam have spent years lovingly restoring No. 3 Cashel Square to its former glory. So imagine Lexie's delight when a stranger knocks on the door, asking to see the house she was born in over sixty years ago.

Kathleen is visiting from America, longing to see her childhood home . . . and longing for distraction from the grief of losing her husband.

And as Lexie and Sam battle over whether or not to have a baby and Kathleen struggles with her loss, the two women realise their unexpected friendship will touch them in ways neither could have imagined.

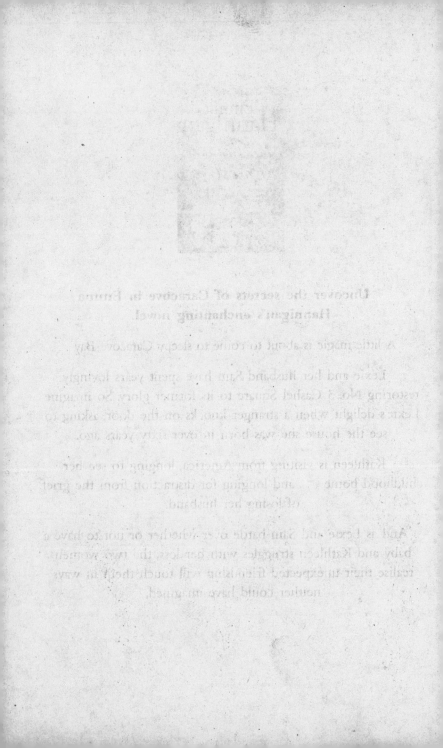